OUR TWISTED LOVE AFFAIR

ALI PARKER

BRIXBAXTER PUBLISHING

Our Twisted Love Affair

Copyright © 2019 by Ali Parker

The novel is a work of fiction. Names, characters, places and plot are all either products of the author's imagination or used fictitiously. Any resemblance to actual events, locales, or persons – living or dead – is purely coincidental.

First Edition.

Editor: Laura LaTulipe
Cover Designer: Ryn Katryn Digital Art

FIND ALI PARKER

CHAPTER 1

JACK

I strolled through the lobby of Bancroft Estates, nodding and smiling to the many employees milling about the ground floor of the high-rise building of the company headquarters. I rode the elevator up, going through the process of acknowledging the people who worked on our floor. I approached my office, with JACK BANCROFT VICE PRESIDENT OF OPERATIONS emblazoned across the door.

I stepped inside my office, set my briefcase down, and took a seat behind the desk. My secretary strolled in a minute later, bringing me a cup of coffee and a stack of papers.

"Good morning," she said in a cheery voice.

"Hi, Danielle," I said, then smiled.

"Grayson wants to see you when you get a minute," she announced.

"He's already in?" I asked in surprise, checking my watch to make sure I hadn't somehow lost an hour.

She smiled. "He is. He said he was up, so he may as well go to work."

I laughed, thinking about my sleep-deprived brother. Little Leah Bancroft was putting her daddy through his paces. Like a trooper, he

1

was hanging tough. Hannah refused to hire a nanny and Grayson, not wanting to irritate his wife, went along with it.

"I'll head over there in a minute. Coffee first. Anything exciting today?" I asked, making small talk with her.

We had been friends for years and I enjoyed the friendly relationship we had. She was one of the only women I had a purely platonic relationship with.

"Nothing too exciting. Do you have any plans for the weekend?"

I smiled. "I have a hot date tonight," I said, waggling my eyebrows.

She laughed, seeing right through me. "Mama Bancroft?"

"How'd you know?"

"You Bancroft boys are mama's boys and I know you would never tell me you had a hot date. You'd say something like you were going out for a bit or having drinks with some girl."

I sighed. "You're right. Yes, dinner with Mom, and the rest of the weekend … I don't know. No plans."

"Be nice to your brother. I'm glad I haven't had to turn the hose on the two of you in a good long while, don't ruin your streak."

I stood up, buttoned my suit jacket again, and grabbed my coffee. "Those days are behind us. We've turned over a new leaf."

"Good. I like you two being nice to each other. It certainly makes for a much better work environment."

"I'll keep that in mind the next time I want to kick his ass," I quipped, carrying my coffee out of my office and heading toward Grayson's office.

I was grateful we had managed to repair our relationship—it had only taken thirty-four years, I mused. Now that Grayson was convinced I wasn't interested in being the head of the company. Grayson, out of the six of us, was the only one truly interested in running the company. For whatever crazy reason, he'd gotten it in his head that we all wanted the company, most especially me. He couldn't be more wrong. I liked being the spare. I didn't have all the stress and pressure he had to be great. I could just be me and date who I wanted —almost.

I smiled at the woman waiting on one of the couches in front of

Grayson's office. She smiled at me and made eyes. I smiled back, not encouraging her. I wasn't interested. I had eyes for only one woman.

"I see you have an admirer," Grayson's deep voice came out from behind me.

I turned, shrugged a shoulder, and followed him into his office. "You rang?"

He nodded. "Are you going to Mom's?"

"Yep. Why?"

He shrugged. "I was just wondering. Wanted to make sure someone was visiting her this weekend. I was supposed to, but I think Hannah and I are going to stay in for the night."

I nodded. "Ah, I see."

He was a happily married man and a new father. I couldn't begrudge him of that. I was happy for him. I only wished I could find that same happiness. I was a tiny bit jealous, but him being happy made my life easier. I hoped Natasha Levy and I could one day have a relationship, but deep down, I had to accept it would cost me a great deal. I wasn't sure I was ready to pay the price.

"How is Leah?" I asked.

His face lit up at the sound of his daughter's name. "She's great. Growing like crazy."

I smiled. "Good. I saw the report for the makeup line. Things are going very well."

He nodded. "They are. Hannah is already working on something new."

We chatted a bit more before I left to get back to my own office. The day stretched on and before I knew it, I found myself in the back seat of the town car, my driver taking me out to Mom's for dinner. I was looking forward to a little time alone with her. With a big family it was a little tough to get our only surviving parent to ourselves.

"Hi, Mom," I said and greeted her with a kiss on the cheek.

"Good evening, Jack," she said, kissing my cheek in return.

"I'm sorry I'm late," I apologized.

"It's fine. We won't have time for drinks before dinner. The cook is already holding it," she said in a tight voice.

I knew she was irritated by my tardiness. She did not appreciate anyone running late. We were seated immediately with dinner served within minutes of sitting down.

"How've you been?" she asked.

I knew what she was really asking. "I'm fine, Mom."

"I only want you to be happy. You aren't getting any younger. It's time to think about finding a woman you can spend your life with."

I let out a long sigh. I couldn't very well tell her I already had a woman in mind. She wouldn't approve. Hell, she'd forbid it and try to ground me. For now, Natasha was my secret.

"I'm looking for the right woman. I haven't found her yet," I lied.

She smiled. "You've always been a loner. Even around here. You and Grayson should have been close, but instead, you both kind of separated yourselves from everyone else."

"You're a loner. I get it from you. You know I prefer to keep a close circle," I said, shrugging a shoulder.

She chuckled. "I'm not a loner. I don't know that I've been alone in thirty-five years."

"We don't count," I pointed out.

"You boys do count. You are my life. I don't regret it for a minute."

I watched her closely. I didn't detect sadness or regret. "Were you really happy, Mom? You rarely went out with friends. You were always at our games or going to one of Dad's charity events. I mean, you never went to the movies or shopping with girlfriends."

She nodded. "I was very happy. You may not understand it, but my joy came from doing things with all of you. To be honest, I had a couple girlfriends, but the more successful your father became, the less I could trust them."

I nodded. I knew exactly what she was talking about. My dad was an attractive man and extremely wealthy. Women—married, single, young, or old—were always throwing themselves at him.

"Are you happy now?" I asked in a soft voice.

She smiled. "I am. I miss your father, but I'm not going to dwell on the sadness. He was a good man, my partner, and my everything. I'm not interested in finding another husband. I had my one true love. I want to focus on my family."

"Mom, I don't think any of us would be upset with you if you wanted to date. You deserve to be happy," I insisted.

She waved a hand through the air. "I'm not interested. I'm not saying I never will be, but right now, I have too much to be happy about. I've got one of my sons married off and I have a beautiful granddaughter and a daughter-in-law I absolutely adore. I'm looking forward to the future with lots of grandchildren and more daughters-in-law."

I laughed. "You're that confident, are you?"

"My boys are handsome, well-spoken, and most of you are charming. What woman wouldn't want to marry a Bancroft man?" she said nonchalantly.

I had at least one name, but I would keep it to myself.

"I think it will happen in time, Mom. This isn't something you can rush," I told her.

She cleared her throat and looked a little uncomfortable. "Jack, there's something I need to tell you."

That didn't sound good. "What's wrong?"

"It isn't that anything is wrong," she started.

"Then?"

"Mason is coming home for a while," she said on a long breath.

I stiffened. "What?"

She nodded. "He called a couple days ago to let me know he was coming home for a while."

I groaned. "Is he running from the law? The mob? Is his face on a wanted poster somewhere?"

"Stop. I doubt it's like that," she scolded.

"I bet it's exactly like that. When is he coming?" I asked, not excited to see him.

She shrugged. "He didn't give me an exact time. I expect soon."

I nodded. "Then I should probably get going. I'm not interested in seeing him."

"Jack, I will not put up with another fight between brothers. I will make you hug him and sit in the same room with each other until you both get this worked out," she said in that familiar, firm tone.

I rolled my eyes. "I'm not hugging Mason."

She took a drink from her wineglass. "We'll see about that."

I knew there would be no seeing anything. Mason was my brother, but he and I had never been close. Hell, Mason had never been close to anyone, not even our parents. He was a free spirit and the ultimate black sheep. He loved his image and played it up. I didn't know how many tattoos the guy had anymore.

"I should get going," I murmured, trying to think of a good excuse.

She smiled and nodded. "Please don't let Mason keep you away. It's a big house. There's room for everyone."

"I know, Mom. I'll call you in a couple days," I said, rising from the table.

I knew it was a little rude to get up and leave immediately after dinner, but I did not want to risk running into Mason. I walked out and got in the car to be driven home to my town house. Grayson's new life had gotten me thinking. I was only a year younger than him. I had never set out to be a bachelor. The problem was, the only woman I wanted couldn't be with me.

I should move on. I knew that. I could find another woman. Unfortunately, every time I tried to date or even hook up with a woman for a mindless one-night-stand, it was Natasha's face I saw. It was her I wanted. There would never be a replacement for her. I could probably find a woman who would warm my bed, give me children, and even be a good friend, but I seriously doubted I would ever truly love a woman with my whole heart.

I hated keeping the relationship from my mother, but I didn't want to hurt or anger her. Natasha and I had spent eight wonderful months together before she'd gone away. I hadn't seen her in two years. She'd left and never looked back. I should have done the same. I should have been able to move on. She didn't want me. That had been made very clear.

There was also the small problem of Elijah Levy, my best friend in the world and Natasha's big brother. He would kick my ass all over the place if he knew about Natasha and me. Everything about Natasha and I being together was wrong. It was wrong, but I couldn't seem to forget about her. I had it bad. No matter how many times I tried to block the image of her, all I could see was that long black hair, those killer blue eyes, and that petite, little body of hers that made me hard just thinking about her.

CHAPTER 2

NATASHA

I sat my seat forward, looking out the window of the Levy private jet, staring at the clouds below and around us. My reflection in the window had me using my hands to push back the stray black hairs that were falling around my face. I couldn't see anything, but I knew we were close to the city. Soon, I'd spot that familiar skyline, dotted with some of the world's tallest buildings and the American flag. I had been gone too long. I missed home. I missed my family, friends, and the city I had grown up in.

New York was one of those places you loved or hated. There didn't seem to be an in between. During my travels around the world over the past two years, I had talked to hundreds of people. Each of them had strong feelings one way or the other about New York City. I loved to hear the horror stories as well as the stories about finding adventure three blocks away from your apartment. I was definitely in the love category, even if I hadn't stepped foot in the place for two long years.

I was going to be jet lagged. The journey from Australia had been long and I was ready to get out, smell some fresh air, and really stretch my legs. The jet made the journey far more comfortable than a commercial flight, but it was still boring after several hours.

"I cannot wait to have pizza. A real New York pie," Ashley Cooper said from across the aisle.

I laughed. "We've had pizza countless times since we've been gone. You had pizza in Italy!"

She shook her head. "You know nothing beats Roscoe's pepperoni pizza. When I die, I'm not going to heaven unless there is a written agreement in place that I will have pizza," she said firmly.

I laughed. "After the last two years of shenanigans, do you really think you're headed to heaven?" I asked, one eyebrow raised.

She winked. "Hell doesn't want me. I'll take over."

I rolled my eyes. "You have to be a good girl now. Daddy will be watching over your shoulder."

She shook her head. "He'll be too busy jetting around the world himself, trying to find the next best place to build a destination resort."

"My parents will have the limo waiting for us at the airport. Are you going to come over for a while?"

She shrugged. "It isn't like I will have a welcoming party, but I don't want to crash a family thing."

I laughed. "Please, you're like one of the family, Ash."

"We'll see. I'm kind of anxious to get home now that I know we're close. When we left Sydney, I was a little bummed for our grand adventure to be over, but now I'm so looking forward to getting home to my own apartment and sleeping in my own bed," she said on a long sigh.

I smiled with a quick nod. "I agree."

"Will Elijah be there?" she asked, pretending it was an offhand question when I knew damn well it was anything but.

Ashely had been crushing on my brother since we were in junior high. He was an attractive guy, but he was my brother. I looked at her natural blond hair, with fresh streaks of lighter tones from the Australian sun and sea. Her deep tan made her green eyes stand out even more. She was a beautiful woman and I knew Elijah had definitely noticed her before.

"I'm sure he will be there," I said with a knowing smile.

She nodded and leaned her head against the seat. I smiled and turned my attention back to the window, seeing the first signs of the city come into view. I felt a little flutter of butterflies in my stomach, knowing I was going to be in the same city as Jack Bancroft once again.

Once we landed, it was a rush of activity, our bags were loaded into the waiting limo and we were off again to my parents' estate outside the city. It felt like forever since I'd been home. I could see the changes in the new storefronts, some of the other ones long gone.

When we pulled through the heavy gate, I smiled. "I actually missed this place." I sighed.

"How could you not?" She laughed.

My family's wealth was well known all around the world. My dad had built this mansion shortly after I was born, and it seemed it was constantly being renovated with new amenities added. Really, it was a compound. I knew my parents would ask me to move back home. It was the same conversation we always had. They were worried about me living in the city, despite the security in my building. I was not moving home. I loved the city and did not want to be under the same roof as them. I was thirty years old and too damn old to be living at home.

My mom and dad were both standing out front when the limo came to a halt. My dad opened the back door and quickly wrapped me in his arms in a bear hug.

My mom had tears shimmering in her eyes when I moved to hug her. "Hi, Mom," I greeted.

"You can never stay gone that long again."

I laughed. "I saw you not all that long ago," I reminded her.

"That doesn't count."

"You saw me for Christmas!"

"But it wasn't home. I'm going to lock you in your room and throw away the key," she threatened.

"Sherryl, stop. She'll never come home if you threaten her. Come on inside, girls, we had the cook make all your favorites," my dad said, wrapping his arm around my shoulders and squeezing me close as he ushered us inside.

We walked into the large living room where there was a spread of snacks arranged on various tables.

"Wow!" Ashley exclaimed when she saw all the food and the glasses of champagne already poured.

"Champagne?" I asked.

"We're celebrating your return!" my mom exclaimed.

"The prodigal daughter returns." I heard my brother's deep baritone voice coming in behind us.

I spun around and ran to him, wrapping my arms around him in a serious bear hug. "Elijah!" I squealed.

"How've you been, sis?" he asked, squeezing me back.

"Good! I've missed you—a little," I teased, looking into the eyes that were so much like my own. People said I was a mini, feminine version of my big brother. We both inherited my dad's coloring, but I inherited my mom's petite stature while Elijah took after my father.

He laughed and together we walked back to where my mom was chatting with Ashley. I saw the look she gave Elijah when his attention was on the spread of food. I smiled at her before grabbing a plate and loading up. I hadn't realized I was hungry until the feast was spread before us.

I sat down on the couch, Elijah sitting next to me with Ashley sitting in one of the chairs. My mom and dad sat down and we all chatted about the latest news around the city and in our social circle. I had kept up with a lot of the gossip, but my mom always had more to share.

"I have a job ready for you after you've got your bearings," my dad, Wayne Levy, said.

I shook my head. "Dad, I told you, I don't want to work for the company. I want to start my own."

He waved a hand. "Why do that? It's a lot of work and a lot of capital to get a company off the ground and there's no guarantee it'll succeed. I can save you the trouble and give you a job within the family business."

"I want to do this on my own. I want to go through the hard work and the stress of building something great. Look how proud you are with your own company. You did that with your own two hands. I want to do that too," I insisted.

"You've always been stubborn, just like your mother."

"Hey!" My mom laughed, swatting at his arm.

"I think Nat will do great," Elijah chimed in.

"Thank you. I know it's going to be hard, but I want to do this. Please, can I have your support?" I asked my stern father.

He hesitated before throwing his hands up. "You're going to do it regardless of what I say."

I grinned. "Thanks, Dad."

"I hope you know what you're doing."

I laughed. "Not really, but I know you'll give me excellent advice."

One of the housemaids stepped into the living room. "Mr. Levy, you have a call on the office line."

My dad stood and excused himself, heading out of the living room and down the long hall to his home office.

"I should get going," Ashley said, wiping her hands on a napkin and leaving.

I stood with her. "I'll walk you out."

My mom gave her a quick hug and Elijah nodded. We parted ways with the promise to call each other in a day or two once we had settled in. When I returned to the living room, it was only Elijah.

"Where's Mom?"

"More champagne," he said, shaking his empty glass.

I sat down beside him. "How are things? I didn't hear a lot from you while I was away."

He nodded, his black hair falling forward onto his forehead. "Busy. Dad's getting ready to retire."

My eyes bulged. "What? He never said anything to me!"

"It's not going to be right away, but we're getting ready for the transition."

"Are you going to do it?" I asked softly.

He shrugged. "I can't say no. This was what I was born to do."

"But is it what you want to do? Do you want to be the CEO and take over for Dad?"

"I know I always said I didn't want anything to do with the family business, but it's not so bad. I can see myself at the head of the table. I was young and immature back then. I'm ready now. My friends are all settling down and it's time I did as well."

His use of the word "friends" had my attention. Was Jack settling down? I wanted to ask him about Jack, but I couldn't. I couldn't even say his name. It would open up a can of worms I wasn't prepared to deal with. My curiosity would have to remain unanswered.

"I'm happy for you, if that's what you want."

"It is. It'll be good. Dad deserves some time off to see the world and enjoy the billions of dollars he's earned with all the hard work he's put in over the years."

I laughed. "Yes, he does. I have a feeling you're going to have a hard time getting him to actually leave."

"Mom will make him."

I smiled thinking of my petite mom forcing my big dad to do anything. She was small, but a fierce woman to deal with. My dad didn't stand a chance. My mom walked back into the room with a bottle of champagne.

"Lookie what I found," she cooed, as if she didn't know exactly where a new bottle would be.

"One more glass, then I have to go home, Mom," I told her.

She smiled. "Of course, dear. Oh, I'm sorry, I forgot to mention, you no longer have an apartment."

My mouth dropped open. "What? Where's all my stuff?" I shrieked.

"In storage for now. That flooding nonsense last year, your building was affected. We didn't want to spoil your trip. When you're ready, we'll help you find a new place."

I couldn't believe I was homeless. No wonder they had put on such a big spread. They were trying to soften the blow.

"Mom, you know I love you, but I need my own place."

She nodded. "I know. We've done a little renovating," she started.

Elijah and I both knew what that meant. "A little?"

"I had them create an apartment of sorts. You have your own living room and bedroom," she said with a smile.

"Oh, uh, thanks. But, Mom, this is only temporary," I told her.

I knew she had missed me and I didn't want to hurt her feelings. Crashing at the mansion a few weeks wouldn't be the end of the world. I hadn't meant to stay gone for so long, but it was hard to come back. I was trying to exorcise Jack Bancroft from my heart and soul. I was pretty sure I had failed miserably.

CHAPTER 3

JACK

I was meeting Elijah at the club we were both members of. It was a place for the wealthy. I hated the whole idea of the elite upper crust, but I really did enjoy the perks of having a place to go for a quiet drink without everyone looking and watching. I wasn't a celebrity, but I was a Bancroft boy, never mind the fact we were all grown men. Our reputations during some of our misspent youths had earned us the nickname by others in our social circle. When my parents would show up with six boys in tow, it tended to cause a scene.

The Bancroft boys were all very different, but there was no hiding our heritage. We all resembled my father; a fact I was rather proud of. Unfortunately, our rowdy ways evolved, and our reputations were greatly exaggerated. Now, if one of us went to a club or party, we drew unwanted attention. Some of it wasn't so bad, but sometimes, it was nice to just kick back and blend in with the crowd.

"Good evening, Mr. Bancroft," the hostess greeted, escorting me to the table I had reserved earlier.

Drinks and dinner on a Saturday night felt very old, but I wasn't exactly a twentysomething anymore. I had given up the partying years ago. Mostly, because all I wanted to do was spend time with Natasha.

"Hey, you beat me here. That has to be a record," Elijah said, walking in almost right behind me.

I chuckled. "Barely, but I made it."

We ordered drinks and dinner, not bothering to look at our menus. The chef on staff at the club didn't offer many options, which was fine, whatever the man made was amazing.

"Are you doing anything later?" he asked casually, sipping the scotch.

I laughed again. "Me, my TV remote, and a pair of comfy sweats have a hot date."

"Damn, when did we get old," he grumbled.

"You too?" I asked.

He shook his head. "No, I almost wish those were my plans. I'm going out."

"Really? Hot date?"

He shook his head and grinned. "No. I wish. Nat's home."

"Oh," I said, every one of my senses going on high alert, hanging on every word he would say.

He nodded. "Yep, got in yesterday. They spent the last month in Australia. She and Ashley look like they could use a week of sleep."

I laughed. "I'm sure two years of partying would wear anyone down."

"Ashely has a deep tan, but poor Nat just went from transparent to ghost white," he teased.

I smiled, thinking about her contrasting features. Her hair was black as coal and her skin was pale. She was a modern-day Snow White and the most beautiful woman in the world. I was glad she was still pale. I loved her milky skin that always gave her a bit of a porcelain-doll look.

"I'm glad they enjoyed themselves. I think when I retire I'll do something similar," I mused aloud.

He shrugged a shoulder. "Honestly, I've never been bitten by the travel bug. I like where I am. I mean, I like a tropical vacation now and again, but I cannot imagine being gone for months or years at a time."

"Ah, you're a homebody. A woman will appreciate that one of these days I'm sure," I teased.

"Ha. Ha. My parents are treating her return like she's risen from the dead. They're throwing her a welcome home party tonight at Evolution. It's going to be huge."

I raised an eyebrow. "Your parents are going to Evolution? I would think it would be more of a swanky event held at one of the hotels in the city," I asked with surprise.

"Ha! As if my mother would ever step foot through a sweaty night-club door. No, they rented out the place and it will be all our friends. They'll probably throw her another party for their friends. You have to come," he added.

I shook my head. "I shouldn't. I don't want to crash the party."

"Come on. I don't want to be the only thirtysomething there. Besides, you're one of her friends."

"Nat's thirty. Most of her friends are in their thirties. Besides, your dad," I reminded him.

He wrinkled his nose. "Really? I always view them as teenagers. I guess we're all getting old and my dad isn't going to be there. Come on, you have to go. She'll be hurt if you don't."

I laughed again. "The age thing happens, concurrently, too, if you can imagine and I don't think she'll even notice if I'm there."

He shrugged a shoulder. "They still look and act much younger. Nat will want to see you, even if it's only for a minute."

"You act like you're thirty-four going on seventy," I quipped, ignoring the invitation as best I could.

He sipped his drink. "Probably. You're still coming. Don't think I don't know you're trying to change the subject."

"How is Nat? Did she enjoy her trip? She was gone, what two years?" I asked, feigning ignorance when in fact, I knew exactly to the day how long she'd been gone.

He nodded. "Two years. She's good. She seems to have enjoyed herself, but how couldn't you have fun when your only job is to get out of bed and have fun. She's been on vacation for two years. That has to be relaxing."

"If I remember right, your parents encouraged you to take one of those around-the-world trips as well. They wanted you to sow your wild oats before you started work at your father's company," I reminded him.

He laughed. "They wanted to get me out of the country because I was driving them batshit crazy. They were worried I was going to do something that really landed me in trouble with you by my side. It was their subtle way of telling me to grow up."

We both laughed at the memories that made up most of our misspent youth in high school and college. We had managed to find plenty of trouble. Some of it borderline serious, but most of it was all in good fun. When we had met in school and figured out who each other was, we naturally became friends, just to piss off our families. We discovered we had a lot in common and had gotten along really well.

"Is she going to start work with you now?" I asked, wanting to know everything, but not sound like I was asking too many questions.

Elijah was my best friend and there was a code that said best friends couldn't hook up with little sisters. I thought it was a stupid code, but it was there, and I had to follow it. There was also the minor inconvenience of our parents being archenemies.

He smiled and slowly shook his head. "Not yet. She's got some grand plans about starting her own company. My dad is humoring her, but I think we all know she'll be back at Levy Industries within five years. We'll let her have her fun—again."

I knew Elijah loved his little sister. They were a close-knit family and Natasha was treated like a royal princess. She still had to work for things she wanted, but they were always there to support her whimsical ideas.

"That sounds interesting," I mused.

"You have to come tonight. You can't leave me alone," he insisted.

"You'll be anything but alone."

"Come on. It's going to be people you know. People you haven't seen in a long time. Let's go and dance, drink, and act like we're twenty-five again," he said, waggling his bushy black eyebrows.

I sighed, knowing I was playing with fire, but the temptation to see her was too much. "Fine, but I'm going to go home and change. I don't want to show up wearing a stuffy business suit. They'll call me dad and shit like that."

He laughed. "I agree. I was planning on changing myself."

"Should we talk about what we're going to wear?" I laughed.

"No."

We ate our steaks and enjoyed one more drink, not wanting to overdo it before we got to the club. I for one knew I needed to keep my wits about me if I was going to be around Natasha. I couldn't let my guard down and risk letting Elijah or any of our other inner-circle members know about our feelings for each other. It was a fine line acting as if I cared for her like a good friend, but not caring too much.

We finished eating and both headed to our own places with the promise to meet up later.

"Don't you dare stand me up," he warned.

I smiled. "I won't. I'll be there by ten," I promised.

He nodded. "Good. I'll see you then."

By the time I got home, I actually felt nervous, excited, and very much like a teenage boy getting ready for the big school dance. Would she dance with me? Would she pretend she didn't know me? I scoured my closet, looking for something casual and hip. I didn't go out a lot. I wasn't all that up to date on all the latest fashions. I considered calling my youngest brother to ask him what all the cool kids were wearing these days but held off. He'd give me shit and want to know why I cared about what I wore.

I finally settled on black slacks and a V-neck shirt. I had debated jeans, but it wasn't my thing. I was more comfortable in my casual attire rather than something I would wear if I were going to a basketball game. Besides, I wasn't there to impress anyone but Natasha. For all I knew, she could have met some hunky, young Italian and be absolutely in love.

I should have asked Elijah if she was with anyone.

"No, you shouldn't have," I said to my reflection as I slicked back my black hair.

19

That would have been too obvious. I debated shaving but scrapped the idea. I liked the scruff and years ago, Nat had liked it too. I took one last look in the mirror and decided it was as good as it was going to get, then walked out of my large three-bedroom apartment. It wasn't a penthouse like Grayson's, but it wasn't a shack.

I strolled through the lobby of my building, smiling to my neighbors coming and going. I knew I was probably making a huge mistake by going to the party, but I had to see her. It had been too long, and I was desperate to lay eyes on her. I wanted to see if she'd changed at all. I wanted to see if she felt anything for me. I hadn't been able to stop thinking about her for two long years. Had she forgotten all about me?

CHAPTER 4

NATASHA

I heard the doorbell and knew it would be Ashley. We were getting ready at my place for the big party at the club. The stuff I had sent back home had been neatly unpacked, steamed, and hung in the huge closet my mother had put in during the renovation. I really liked the closet. My mom had an eye for the little details that could make a space a hundred times better, like a closet the size of a standard bedroom.

All of my new stuff was on one side, with the clothes I had left behind on the other. That side would be going to auction for our family's charity. The items were outdated and there were only a few pieces I could see myself ever wearing again. They were all high-end garments that would pull in a great deal of money. Some of the dresses had never been worn, but I just couldn't see myself wearing them now. My style had evolved over the last two years, picking up different fashions from every country I visited and creating a look I felt was unique to me.

There were also the gifts from designers hoping I would wear their clothes for some free advertisement. It always blew my mind to see how much free stuff I got. I could buy anything, but I was given almost everything. It was a very unique way things worked, but I was not going to complain.

Ashley came through the double doors of my room, her mouth dropping when she saw the massive apartment I had been given.

"Seriously?" She gasped, taking in the gorgeous dark-blue settee facing a flat-screen television that practically took up the entire wall. There were signs of wealth and opulence dripping from every corner, but it somehow managed to stay just on the right side of pretty, brushing up against gregarious in certain areas.

"I know. My mom really went all out in here," I said, looking around the space once again.

"It's gorgeous. I love it. I love that there isn't a drop of pink in here." She giggled.

I shook my head. "That would have been a deal breaker. As she calls it, this is my big girl room."

Ashley burst into laughter. "It does look like something you would expect to see in Buckingham Palace. It's very nice. I wonder if she would do my apartment."

I shrugged a shoulder. "You know she would. She's always wanted to be an interior designer."

"Why didn't she do it? Seriously, she has an amazing eye."

"Because she's married to my dad and that is a full-time job in itself. She has to run his household and keep up with all the social stuff while he works. She gets her kicks by renovating the mansion every couple of years," I explained.

Ashley smiled. "This explains why the furniture and decor changes all the time."

"You ready to pick out our outfits?" I asked, nodding at her arm.

She was carrying a garment bag draped over her arm with the dresses she was considering for the night. We were both slender, but she was several inches taller than I. She had the build of a model with a lithe body, while I was a little curvier. We could swap some things, but most dresses were out of the question. That meant sharing clothes was almost impossible.

"Where's your closet?" she asked. "And your bed?"

I laughed. "You know my mom doesn't do anything half-assed. Come and look at the closet," I said, grabbing her hand and leading her through the door.

"Holy shit. I thought this was your bedroom."

I laughed. "Nope, my bedroom is on the other side and my bathroom is through another door."

"I'm in love. Your bedroom is the size of my apartment."

I laughed. "That isn't even remotely true," I replied.

Ashley lived in a big, airy condo in Manhattan. It was luxurious and perfect for a single woman. I envied her. I needed to find a new place to live, but I had to admit the apartment my mom created for me in the west wing of the mansion was pretty spectacular. I could handle staying in the room for a little longer.

"Did we really buy all that?" she asked on a giggle, staring at the rows of dresses, tops, and pants. There was a tall shelf lined with heels, sandals, and slip-ons in every style and color.

I nodded. "We did."

She raised an eyebrow. "Where are your boots?" she asked, worry on her face.

I grinned. "Watch."

I pushed a button and the racks of clothing rolled back and my extensive collection of boots in every shade, height, and style appeared.

"Holy Mother of God. This is amazing. First, holy shit, I didn't realize how many pairs of boots you had, and second, just wow. I could spend all day in here playing dress-up."

"It is awesome," I said, looking back at all my clothes.

"What's your first choice?" she asked.

I reached for the sparkly black dress that was a little risqué with its incredibly short hemline and open back. "This with those new thigh-highs I picked up in London."

Her eyes went wide. "You will look hot."

"What about you?"

There was a knock on my bedroom door. I walked into the living area, opened it, and was handed a bottle of champagne and two glasses by our butler. "Courtesy of Mrs. Levy," he said with a smile.

"Thank you, George. Please tell Mom I said thanks as well."

He nodded and left. I headed into the closet and poured us each a glass of champagne. It was like being back in one of the high-end shops in Paris, drinking champagne while trying out tons of clothing. The only thing missing was the cheese.

"Okay, now you have to help me decide," she said, finishing the first glass of champagne.

She pulled out several choices. We both settled on black dresses for the night. It was our first time getting to wear the dresses we had picked up and it felt wonderful to know I looked good. We did our makeup, me perfecting the smoky eye and doing Ashley's as well. When it was time to go, I suddenly got a case of cold feet. I stepped in front of the mirror and wondered if it was too much. What if Elijah invited Jack. I prayed he didn't. I couldn't see him and contain my joy at laying eyes on him again.

No matter how hard I tried to forget him, it was always his face I saw when I flirted. It was always him I wanted to talk to when I arrived at a new place and took in the sights and sounds of a new country. My two years away had done nothing to relax my feelings for him. If anything, I think the absence definitely made my heart grow fonder.

"Are you okay?" Ashley asked, standing beside me in the mirror.

I smiled. "I am. Was just having second thoughts on the outfit."

She shook her head. "No way. You look amazing. You're the star of the party. You have to look good."

I smiled and nodded. "Thank you. Well, we better get going."

We walked downstairs, finding my parents in their private sitting room. My dad reading the paper and Mom curled up on the couch with a book. My mom looked up when she saw me, her jaw dropped.

"Nat! You look gorgeous!" she exclaimed.

My father put his newspaper down, his eyes bulging when he saw my outfit. "Are you going to wear a jacket?" he asked in a gruff voice.

The three of us women all laughed. "No, Dad."

"I hope there's a lot of tape or something on that thing. I don't need your body splattered all over the front of the tabloids in some wardrobe malfunction scandal."

I waved a hand. "Nobody has wardrobe malfunctions anymore, Dad. That's very last year," I assured him.

"Sherryl, that room is absolutely gorgeous. I'm so jealous! You have to come and do my apartment," Ashley said.

My mom's face lit up. "I would love to give you a hand. You just let me know when," she said, beaming with pride.

My dad stood up and hugged me. My mom gave me a quick kiss on the cheek. "Have fun."

We waved and headed out for the waiting limo. We enjoyed another glass of champagne on the ride over. Both of us bubbling with excitement at the thought of seeing all our friends. It had been a long time.

When we arrived, there was a red carpet rolled out. "Oh, my mom," I said, not getting out of the limo.

Ashley laughed. "Come on, it's going to be a blast."

I was a little embarrassed by all the attention, but I strolled toward the door of the club with my head held high and a smile on my face.

We were escorted to a seating area that had been reserved for myself and my closest friends. The place was already packed with people I hadn't seen since high school as well as friends of friends. The security was tight, which I knew was all my dad's doing. I would be back under his protection now that I was home. He was always worried I would be kidnapped and held for ransom. I tried to tell him I wasn't that interesting, but it was no use. When he got something in his head, it was staying for good.

"Can I buy you a drink?" a man who looked vaguely familiar said, coming up to me the moment we walked in.

I shrugged. "Sure, thank you. A martini is fine."

He winked and strolled away. Ashley was already out on the dance floor, leaving me alone to greet the people who had come to celebrate our return. No matter how much I tried not to look, I found myself

25

constantly scanning the room in search of Jack. Maybe he hadn't come. That was good. He shouldn't.

The mystery man returned with my drink and I politely chatted with him until the next admirer came along. The dress was doing wonders for my social life, I thought with a smile. The drinks were flowing freely. I had to pace myself, asking for club soda in between to avoid getting completely trashed.

"Hey!" Ashley said out of breath as she bounced up beside me and stood against the rail looking down at the dance floor.

"Hey you! You look like you are having fun." I grinned.

She nodded. "I am. I know we have been to some of the best clubs in the world, but seriously, nothing beats being home."

I smiled. "I think you're right."

"You're not dancing much," she pointed out.

I rolled my eyes. "Every time I turn around there is someone new wanting to chat and buy me a drink."

She threw her head back and laughed. "Oh no, such problems."

"I'm having fun. I love watching everyone else have fun as well."

"Come dance with me." She cajoled.

I shrugged a shoulder. "All right."

She grabbed my hand and we made our way down the stairs to the dance floor. Everything was perfect. I was surrounded by people I cared about and even quite a few people I had never met. I liked meeting new people. In the back of my mind I couldn't help but think about Jack. Where was he at? Had he moved on? I imagined him at home in his apartment, sitting on the tired, old brown leather sofa he loved so much with a woman snuggled against him. The twinge of jealousy I felt was wrong, but I couldn't stop it.

I pushed the thought away and lost myself in the music and the good buzz I had going. I had too much to be happy for to dwell on the one thing in life I couldn't have.

CHAPTER 5

JACK

It was like riding a bike I mused. Some things truly never changed. I mean, the music changed a little, the fashion tended to get a little skimpier and there was always a new trendy drink, but beyond that, it was all the same. I walked into the club with Elijah, and it was as if I had never left. The music was thumping, the smell of cloying perfumes and colognes was in the air mingling with the sweet scent of liquor. It was a recipe for sex. The bumping bodies on the floor was testament to the number of people who were going to go home with someone they picked up at the club.

I sighed, remembering how easy it had been to have mindless sex with women I'd met an hour or two before. Those days were gone. I'd been unable to get one woman off my mind. The thought of picking up one of the women currently checking me out almost made me curl my lip in revulsion. Instead, I smiled, not wanting to offend the ladies who were trying to catch my eye. They were all very attractive, but they weren't her.

"Hey," I said in protest as Elijah was swallowed by the crowd, a woman dragging him onto the dance floor, her breasts pressed against his chest as she grinded her body against him.

I smirked watching Elijah as he openly groped the woman who

seemed very pleased to have his attention. I scanned the dance floor, knowing she was somewhere in the crowd. My eyes were thirstily searching. One small glimpse. That's all I needed to satisfy my craving for her. It didn't take long.

Like a magnet, my eyes were immediately drawn to the sexy woman in the tiny dress. Her long black hair flowing down her bare back. She was laughing and swaying with the music, her arms high in the air as she spun around, her ass shaking in perfect rhythm to the music. I felt that familiar twinge of excitement that sparked a pool of heat in my stomach as I watched her body do a dance of pure unadulterated sex.

I couldn't believe I was actually watching her after two long years. I was so close and yet, I had to stay so far away. Or did I? She was dancing and shaking that tight ass of hers, making me think of all kinds of dirty things I wanted to do to her body. I had to school my features. I couldn't let anyone know what was running through my mind in that moment. If her brother caught a glimpse of my expression as I watched his sister, I was likely going to end up in the emergency room.

"Hey there," a woman said, sidling up to me, her fake tits nearly falling out of the low-cut top she was wearing.

"Hi," I said, turning my eyes back to Natasha.

"I'm thirsty. I'll let you buy me a drink and then, if you play your cards right, I might let you do other things," she cooed.

I looked at her, doing my best to appear friendly and interested … and failing miserably. "Actually, I see my friend over there. Maybe another time."

She pouted and walked off. I moved away, doing my best to blend in with the crowd so I could watch Nat without anyone noticing. I couldn't take my eyes off her. She was the most beautiful woman in the place. Sure, she was dolled up and had very little on, but she managed to make it look classy and sexy at the same time. I thought back to the last time I saw her.

We had agreed to stop seeing each other after eight months of dating. It was one of the worst days of my life. Well, maybe that was being a little dramatic, but it still sucked. I hated it, but I knew her leaving was the right thing for us both. We had agreed it was the best way for us to move on. Neither of us was interested in starting a war with our families. I closed my eyes, willing myself to look elsewhere. There were plenty of other women I could ogle. She was the only one off-limits. She was the forbidden fruit. That had to be the draw. I wanted what I couldn't have and that's what was driving me right into her arms.

I headed for the bar. I desperately needed a stiff drink. I ordered a scotch and before I even could think twice about what I was doing, I ordered her favorite martini. It was stupid, and I knew better. There were about a million voices going off in my head demanding I stop what I was doing. Those voices were quickly pushed way down. I gave the bartender a healthy tip and left with both drinks in hand, I climbed the stairs to the VIP section. I nodded to the security team and was allowed to enter. I was a Bancroft after all. I spotted her immediately. Natasha had made her way up the stairs and was sitting on one of the couches, chatting with her girlfriend.

When she looked up at me, I smiled. Her eyes widened before she turned back to her friend. I watched as she leaned forward and said something to the blonde next to her. I walked toward Natasha, staring into her beautiful eyes and feeling my breath catch in my throat. She was breathtaking.

"Jack Bancroft," she said with a smile, taking the drink I presented.

"Natasha Levy," I greeted in a smooth voice.

"It's a been a long time," she said in a voice just loud enough to be heard over the music.

"Too long," I said.

She sipped the drink and turned to talk to her friend Ashley, giving me a glimpse of her naked back.

I knew what she was doing. She was doing her best not to start rumors. I should follow her lead and go about my own business. I should go find a woman to dance with. All of those were things I should do—none of them were things I wanted to do.

Fuck it.

"Ladies," I said in my most charming voice.

Natasha turned to look at me. I smiled in return.

"Thanks for coming, Jack. I didn't think this was your scene," she said in a sarcastic tone.

"When the loveliest ladies in the world are all in one place, I can make it my scene," I replied easily.

Ashley giggled. "Oh, Jack. There's that Bancroft charm."

"You look like you've spent some time in the sun," I said to Ashley.

She nodded and winked. "And no tan lines."

I raised one eyebrow at her blatant flirting. "Interesting."

Ashley looked from me to Natasha before making up an excuse to leave the area. Nat turned to look at me, sipping her martini. I reached out and took the glass from her hand.

"Dance with me," I said, putting the glasses down on a table.

"Jack," she said in a warning tone.

"I want to dance with you and I don't care who's watching. We're dancing."

. I grabbed her hand and led her down the stairs, cutting through the crowd and taking her straight into the middle of the dance floor. I grabbed her hips with both hands, bringing her body close. I wanted her to feel me. I heard her sharp intake of breath and I knew she was feeling the same lust, the stirring of old feelings being reignited.

"We shouldn't do this," she whispered close to my ear.

I leaned close to her. "I don't care. I need you."

"We're playing with fire. People will know," she hissed.

I pushed her body away from mine, demanding she dance. I watched her slowly gyrate, going low, spreading her legs before coming back up to stand against me. It was akin to a striptease. It was an exotic dance meant to tease and turn on. It was working. If I wasn't careful I was going to be sporting a giant hard-on there on the dance floor.

"Your body is amazing," I said, growling in her ear, moving my hips against her.

"We can't do this." She gasped.

My hands gripped her hips, holding them in place while I let her feel the erection stirring to life. Her eyes dropped closed and I could hear her moan softly.

I pushed her away once again, letting her dance like the other women in the club, bouncing and moving her arms in a mesmerizing motion. I watched her for as long as I could, doing my best to appear as if I were part of the dance. My eyes glanced around the room. Everyone around us was involved in what could only be described as a mating ritual. The heated looks, the bodies blending together, and the scent of sexual arousal pungent in the air was too much to ignore.

"Nat, let's get out of here. No one is paying attention," I said, bending down to rub my lips over her ear as I talked.

She pushed against my chest with her hand. "Jack, stop. You know we can't."

I grabbed her, pulling her close to me. She grinned, her arms going around my neck as she swayed against me. Her pelvis rubbing against me, her breasts pressed against my chest, letting me feel exactly how turned on she was.

"You're teasing me." I snarled.

She smiled. "I'm not teasing. You know we can't. It's too risky."

"I don't care. You're playing with fire. I can feel the burning in you. You want to get burned?"

Her features softened. "You do care. We both do. We've talked about this before. There is too much at stake. Neither one of us wants to hurt our families."

I shook my head. "No one has to know. We can keep it between us, like before."

"Jack," she said my name on a plea, both of us wanting the same thing. Both of us knowing we couldn't have it.

Her eyes dropped to my mouth and I knew she was feeling the same thing I was. It was bullshit that we had to deny ourselves. It wasn't fair. Why were we forced to pay for the sins of our fathers? Or father. Their baggage was their own. I was a grown man and could decide who I liked and didn't like. I was long past the days of my parents deciding who I could and couldn't hang out with.

"We're leaving." I growled, grabbing her hand and pulling her several feet as I practically dragged her off the dance floor.

"Jack, we can't," she said, pulling her hand away.

I turned and looked at her, letting her see the heat in my eyes before I stalked back toward her, lifted her into my arms, my hands under her ass as she squealed against me.

"We can, and we damn well are!"

"Jack!"

I moved off the dance floor, her legs wrapping around me as I walked. Nothing was going to get in my way. I kept moving, doing my best to shield her bare back, holding her close to me as I kept my gaze focused on the door. Nothing was going to get in my way.

She sighed against me. There was little she could do to deny me. I knew she liked it when I took charge. It was really all I knew how to do.

CHAPTER 6

NATASHA

O utside the club, Jack slid me down his body, my heels hitting
the sidewalk. I leaned close to him and kissed him. I had to
have a taste.

"My place?" he asked, even though I already knew it was more of a
statement. No, it was a demand and one that I knew I should ignore
but was helpless to the pull that always brought us together.

"We shouldn't," I said the words in weak protest.

He walked to the edge of the sidewalk and raised his arm, hailing a
cab. I grimaced. It had been a long time since I'd taken a cab. I knew it
would have been for him as well. We were both a little spoiled and
used to having drivers with clean, comfortable cars. A cab was better.
There was little chance anyone would recognize us.

"Get in," he ordered when a cab pulled alongside the sidewalk, at
the same time Ashley appeared and threw my purse at me, shaking
her head at me.

I looked up at him, knowing I should tell him no, and climbed in
the back anyway. Jack was right behind me, pulling me against him as
he barked out his address. I could feel the tension in his coiled
muscles. I was already imagining what he would do to me the

moment we were at his place. Thinking about him touching me, fucking me, and making me shout his name was making me wet. I gasped as a little wave of excitement snaked down my spine.

"We'll be there soon," he whispered near my ear.

His hot breath caressed my skin, making me squirm in my seat. His hand went to my knee, before slowly traveling up my bare leg, exposed by the short dress I was wearing.

"Jack," I said his name on a breath. It sounded like an invitation. It was. I knew we were in the back of a cab, but two years apart had left me wanton.

"Open your knees, just a little," he instructed.

I looked into his eyes before glancing at the cab driver, then I opened my legs. His hand traveled higher. I could feel my breath coming faster.

I moaned when his fingertips brushed over the thin fabric shielding my core.

"Shh," he whispered, sending more shivers down my spine.

I heard myself moan again. It snapped me back to reality. I pushed his hand down and out from under my dress. "We can't."

"We are."

I shook my head. "Not here."

"We're going to the minute I get you home."

"Jack, maybe I should just go back to the club."

He leaned forward, kissing me in an aggressive, mind-blowing way that made me forget all about what I was saying. A low growl in his throat made him sound dangerously feral. I could feel his need pouring through every pore in his body. The man was horny and determined to have me. I could admit I wasn't really putting up a fight. I wanted him too much to tell him to stop.

"Twenty-two fifty," the cabbie said, stopping the car and our kiss in one fell swoop.

Jack reached into his wallet, handed the man a fifty, and threw open the door, practically dragging me out of the back seat. Then, with breakneck speed, he hauled me through the lobby and into the elevator where he pounced on me once again. My legs felt like jelly by the time the elevator doors slid open on his floor. I was so hot and wet I could have dropped to my knees right there and let him take me in the hallway.

The second the door to his apartment opened, his hands were on my dress, yanking it up around my waist, his thumbs hooking on my thong and dragging my panties down. The boots were a problem. He solved it by tearing my thong off, leaving me exposed for his touch.

"I can't wait. I'm sorry," he muttered, flicking open the fly of his pants, freeing his erection that was already beaded with moisture.

I shook my head. I didn't want to hear about it. I just wanted him to push inside me. I slapped at his shoulders, pulling him close with mindless need.

He lifted me, my back pressed against the wall before I managed to find what I wanted. With one hard, long push, he was deep inside me. My body erupted around him, the orgasm hot and fierce, with no warning at all.

"Fuck me, you were ready." He grunted, pushing into me higher as he nailed me against the wall.

My body had been desperate for him. I had been desperate for him, unable to deny myself the pleasure of his touch for another second. The release barely scratched the surface.

"More," I demanded, my fingernails digging into his shoulders.

"Baby, I'm going to need a minute." He gasped a second before I felt him tense, his body exploding deep inside mine.

I rode him as he worked through an orgasm that was nearly as fast as mine. When he slowed his movements, he dropped my feet to the ground. "My room, now," he ordered.

"Do you need a minute?" I half teased.

"No. Now."

I smoothed the bottom of my dress back down and let him lead me toward his master suite. I walked inside, looked around, and noticed nothing had changed. It was the same as I remembered. He stalked toward me, his mouth slamming into mine as he kissed me. I could feel the need still possessing him. His desire fueled my own. His hands reached around and slid under the top of my dress, quickly trying to remove my backless bra before he stepped back.

"Take it off," he ordered.

I carefully pulled my arms through my dress and removed my bra.

"Damn, I've missed you," he muttered, his mouth closing over one breast and then the other. He suckled and squeezed as if he were a starving man.

His hands moved to my dress, pushing it the rest of the way down my hips. He stepped back and looked at me as I stood in front of him in nothing more than my thigh-high boots. His hazel eyes were heavy lidded as he stared at me.

With quick, jerky movements he stripped, standing before me with nothing on. I let my eyes roam over his body, drinking in the sight of him. I had spent many nights over the past two years thinking about his body. He was physically strong, and it was very clear he had stayed in shape. His six-pack abs were tanned, telling me he'd been enjoying some time in the sun. The smattering of hair in the center of his chest, which connected to the happiest trail I'd ever laid eyes on, had me stepping forward, cupping him in my hand, feeling the weight of his growing erection.

I looked at him and smiled. "Already?"

"I've got a lot to make up for." He growled.

His hands went to my upper arms, walking me backward until my legs hit the bed. I stood, still holding him in my hand, slowly stroking and bringing him back to all his glory.

"Sit," he ordered.

I did as I was told. His fingers reached for the zipper on my boot and slowly slid it down before pulling it off and moving to the next. When both boots were off, and I was completely naked, he stepped back and stared at me.

"Lie down, I want to look at you. I've thought about you and that beautiful body every night for two years."

I slid back on the bed, moving to prop myself up on his pillows, giving him the view he wanted. His eyes roamed my body, pausing at my apex where I had been recently waxed.

"Fuck me." He growled, climbing on the bed beside me.

"I want you to fuck me," I replied coolly.

He looked at me and arched an eyebrow. "Oh, I'm going to. I'm just trying to think of which way I want to take you first."

The way he said it was enough to make me squirm. I loved the way he was looking at me like I were a feast to be devoured. His hand stretched out, going to my breast where he pinched one of my erect nipples.

I automatically arched my back, begging for more. I was ready. I needed him again. I was nowhere near satisfied.

"Jack, please, I need to feel you inside me again," I whispered.

His mouth closed over one nipple while his hand went between my legs, one finger sliding inside my slick passage. "Here?" he asked.

I gasped as he pushed deeper. "No."

I reached for him, encircling his swollen length in my hand and squeezing. "This. I need this."

"You need my dick, is that what you're saying?" he asked, pushing a second finger inside me.

I nodded, spreading my legs a little wider, silently begging him to mount me. My demand was answered. He moved over me, his mouth gliding to mine and kissing me slowly. I could feel him probing my entrance, and I opened my legs wider until he pushed inside in an excruciatingly slow move.

I held my breath, holding onto every tiny inch as he moved inside me.

"Breathe," he ordered.

I gasped for air as he finally filled me completely. He didn't move. My body was still spasming from the first orgasm. Each little ripple squeezed him, contracting and releasing, sending me into a spiral of white-hot desire.

"Oh God." I moaned when I realized I was about to climax for the second time with almost no effort from him.

All he had to do was get near me with that gorgeous dick and I turned into a hot pile of quivering goo.

"Damn, girl, I think you've missed me," he said, his body hovering just above mine as he stared into my eyes.

When his lips closed over mine in a sweet, passionate kiss, it was all I could take. My body exploded around his. He let me slow my breathing before he began to move, sliding in and out of me, his length scraping across the sensitive flesh below, sending aftershocks coursing through my body one after another after another until I felt my third orgasm stirring to life.

"Jack, more," I begged.

"You're going to get more. I'm not stopping." He grunted, picking up the pace as his body drilled into mine in a furious push-and-pull action.

I heard him shout, his arms going stiff as he held himself off me, his hips arching and pushing deeper inside my body. I spread my legs wider, giving him all I could. My body convulsed under his as I watched him release the passion he held for me.

His body dropped on mine, pressing me into the mattress. I could feel his heart pounding in his chest. He moved to rest his forehead against mine, his dick still buried inside me. My arms went around him as I hugged him impossibly closer to me.

"Give me a minute," he said through gasps.

I laughed. "You're not going to be ready in a minute."

He jerked his hips and I felt his cock growing inside me once again. My eyes went wide.

"No way."

He chuckled before getting very serious. "Two years is a long time, Nat. A really, really long time. This has been building for two fucking years. Trust me when I say it'll be a minute."

I nodded. "Okay," I whispered, more than eager to accommodate him.

He rolled to the side and ran his fingertips between my breast and over my navel, staring into my eyes the entire time.

"I missed you," he said, and I knew he meant it.

"I missed you," I replied.

He leaned forward and kissed me. It started off as a leisurely exploration of each other's mouths, but it slowly turned into fiery passion. In one quick move, he was on his knees and rolling me to my stomach. I had never been so happy in all my life. I turned to look over my shoulder and watched his jaw clench as he prepared to mount me from behind.

CHAPTER 7

JACK

It was a weird way to wake up and it took my brain a few minutes to catch up to what was happening. There was a shock of hair tickling my nose and warm breath brushing across my bare chest. The last time I had woke with a woman draped across my naked body in my bed was two years ago. Two fucking years was a long time. It was no wonder my brain seemed to struggle to put it all together.

My eyes opened, and I looked down to make sure I wasn't imagining things. I smiled when I saw silky black hair. Nat was back, and she was in my bed where she belonged. I rubbed the tips of my fingers down her spine, moving hair away from her face, as I stared at her. She had grown more beautiful while she was away. I wanted to hold her in my arms all day. Well, I wanted to do a lot more than snuggle. We had two years to make up for. I had thought I had slaked my lust for her last night, but it was back. I listened to her breathing, stroking her back and then her upper arm, thinking about how much I had missed her.

She stirred and looked up at me. "Hey," she said with a grin, kissing me before moving to the side. I rolled to my side to face her.

"Good morning," I said, staring into her beautiful blue eyes that showed no sign of sleepiness.

She giggled softly. "I think it is."

I smiled again. She was always so chipper when she woke up. I wouldn't say she was a morning or a night person. Natasha was a happy person and always found a reason to giggle. I leaned forward and kissed the tip of her nose.

"Want to make it an even better morning?" I asked, waggling my eyebrows.

She burst into a fit of laughter. "Smooth, buddy, real smooth."

"Is there a better way to ask for a little morning delight?"

She studied my face. "I missed you," she said in a soft voice.

"I missed you."

"Did you think of me?"

"All the time."

"Are you seeing anyone? Should I be worried about a girlfriend trying to kick my ass for sleeping with her man?" she teased, but I knew she was serious.

I gently shook my head. "No girlfriend. What about you? Did you leave a long list of boyfriends all around the world?"

"Nope. None."

I knew I didn't have the right to ask, but I'd been focused on the matter for two years. The thought of her kissing another man or sharing her beautiful body with someone else was extremely difficult for me to think about.

I let out a long sigh. "I want you."

"I'm right here."

I shook my head again. "You know what I mean. We're good together."

"We can't be together, Jack."

"Bullshit."

She giggled. "I like to think of us as a modern-day Romeo and Juliet. Our houses would surely crumble if our families knew about our torrid love affair."

"Don't you think it should all be in the past? My dad is dead. I don't know why our fathers hated each other so much, but with my dad gone, the animosity should be gone," I reasoned.

"You would think, but it is one of those things. It's like the Hatfields and McCoys. Our families are not the only two to have this weird hate."

"Why do they hate one another so much?" I asked the question we'd talked about more than once.

"Business deal gone bad is my best guess. They were friends when they were first starting out. I think we can assume one of them screwed the other over and neither is willing to apologize or forgive," she said.

"Bullshit," I muttered again.

She reached one hand up and touched my cheek. "It is bullshit and I'm sorry it is this way."

"My mom is far more reasonable than my dad. Maybe I can talk to her and ask her to give us her blessing to be together," I offered.

Her thumb brushed over one of my brows. "Even if she were to be okay with it, my father never would be, and my mom does whatever he says."

She moved her hand back and we stared at each other for a long while. "It's never going to work is it?" I asked, my voice rough.

A soft smile rested on her lips. "I don't think so. As much as I hate it, I think we both know it's never going to change. There is too much water under the bridge. It's been forty years and they haven't been able to forgive one another. They raised all of us to hate one another. I remember family dinners and some of the dinner parties we had. Your family was a subject of contention. My dad and your dad shared some of the same friends. It was an unspoken rule that your dad's name was never mentioned."

I chuckled low in my throat. "It was the same at our house."

"We shouldn't keep doing this to ourselves," she whispered.

"No."

"It'll never work. We're fooling ourselves. We can never be happy together," she insisted.

I knew her words were true. It hurt. "You're right. What do we do?"

"Move on?" she suggested.

"I'll never find someone I want to be with more than you."

"I agree."

"I don't want you to be alone the rest of your life. We both need to try and find someone we can at least be with to avoid being alone," I said, hating the way the words tasted on my tongue.

She wrinkled her nose. "I don't want to think of you with another woman. It's going to be hard not to be jealous. Maybe all this will fade, and we will find someone we can love with all our hearts."

I chuckled. "It didn't fade after two years of not seeing or speaking to each other. Do you really believe it's going to go away?"

Her long sigh was the answer. "I don't know if I can date or do other stuff with someone else."

That gave me some satisfaction, but I truly didn't want her to be miserable her entire life. It wasn't fair to her. She should be able to have a family and grow old with someone. The ridiculous feud between our families was going to ruin our lives.

"We're giving it too much power," I blurted out.

"What?"

I reached out and grabbed her shoulder. "This feud. We're giving it too much power. Why do we have to follow the rules?"

"Because we love our families."

I took a deep breath. "Let's make a pact."

"A pact? That sounds naughty." She giggled.

I rolled my eyes. "Get your mind out of the gutter. If neither of us finds someone to be with by the time I'm thirty-five, I say we get married and screw the stupid feud. I don't want to waste my life keeping up a feud I don't believe in."

"You're crazy." She laughed.

I shook my head. "I'm serious. If we're both still single and miserable, we get married and deal with the consequences. I don't want to sound morbid, but our parents aren't going to live forever. I would like to think we will outlive them."

"Which is why we should be careful. I don't want my dad to disown me before he dies. You're thirty-four. One year isn't all that much time."

The thought was not a pleasant one. I didn't want to alienate my mother by doing something she would hate. I felt torn between my own happiness and my mother's. I was fiercely loyal to her and I would never willingly betray her. Hooking up with a Levy would almost certainly be seen as a betrayal. I needed coffee. The morning had started out so well and now it was taking a turn for the worse.

"I'm going to make some coffee," I said, giving her a quick kiss before throwing the blanket off and getting out of bed.

I grabbed some clean underwear from the dresser and stepped into them. I turned back to find her staring at me. I grinned.

"I really missed you," she said.

I debated crawling back into bed, but knew it was time to step back into the real world. I had to get her home before her family started looking for her. It had been her big night and dragging her out like I did left her no time to let anyone know where she was going.

"I missed you, more than you could possibly know," I muttered and headed to the kitchen to start some coffee.

She walked out about ten minutes later, wearing the same dress she had on last night. Seeing it in the light of day gave me a whole new appreciation for her body. The dress was tiny, tight, and sexy as hell.

"Here you go," I said, pushing the coffee toward her.

"Thanks," she said, sipping from the cup.

"I can take you home when you're ready," I told her, feeling the mood change.

She was anxious, and I knew it was because the stark light of day made things real. Sneaking away from the club to be together was different from spending the day together. Once again, I was reminded of how much I hated the constraints being put on me when I was a grown adult, capable of making my own decisions.

"I'll call Ashley. It's probably not a good idea for me to be seen getting out of your car," she said.

I nodded. "You're right. Can I make you some breakfast?"

"I'm fine, thanks."

She walked into the foyer where she had dropped her purse on the floor. She fished out her cell phone. I watched as she sent a text before coming back toward me. We stared at each other, feeling the weight of the world on our shoulders. I hated this part of our time together. The part where she had to leave, and I couldn't make a promise to call her later or arrange to see her again.

"I don't want you to go. Stay. We can spend the day together," I blurted out.

She let out a long sigh, slowly shaking her head. "You know we can't. My parents have a luncheon planned. My mom will kill me if I didn't show."

"Okay. Can I see you again?"

"Jack," she said my name. The single word said more than my name itself.

She was shooting me down. It was always the same. We'd spend a glorious night together and then part ways as strangers. Despite our commitments not to see each other, I knew we would drift back together. We always did. We couldn't be on the same continent and not want to be together.

I nodded. "Will you think about what I said earlier?"

"What you said?"

"The pact. That gives us a full year to find someone. We're not getting any younger. I want to have a family one day and if that is going to happen, it needs to happen sooner rather than later."

"Jack, I thought you were joking. I can't make a pact like that. I told you I don't want to alienate my father. No matter what I feel for you, I love my family. I'm loyal to them. I have to be," she said, her voice soft.

"Think about it."

She smiled. "I'm going to head out. Thank you for a fun night. I won't forget it or you."

We kissed one last time before she walked out the door. I stood there staring at the door, unable to stop myself from wondering if that was the last time I would kiss her or see her in my apartment. The thought was too much to deal with.

CHAPTER 8

NATASHA

It was slightly embarrassing to wait in the lobby of Jack's building wearing the rather sexy getup I'd worn to the club last night. It was evident to anyone who looked I was doing a walk of shame. I hoped Ashley hurried up. I tried my best to look inconspicuous, sitting in the corner and trying to look like I was interested in the *New York Times*.

My eyes kept drifting out the window. When I saw her little Beemer pull up, I tossed the paper on the table and made my way out. I jumped in her car, refusing to look at her. I already knew what she would say.

"You look like you had a good night," she quipped.

I wished like hell I had my sunglasses but when I had left to go out last night, I had not planned on being out in the morning sun.

"I did."

"You were home for what a day before you jumped back in his bed?"

I rolled my eyes. "You know it isn't like that."

"It is exactly like that," she quipped pulling into traffic.

"I didn't know he'd be there last night," I retorted.

"But you were hoping he would be. That outfit pretty much guaranteed he wouldn't be able to ignore you. I guess the whole two-year break was ineffective," she said on a laugh.

I slapped a palm to my forehead. "I tried. He tried. We did. We know it's so wrong, but it's impossible to deny what we have."

She was sympathetic to my plight. "You did try, and I think that has to be worth something."

I leaned my head back and closed my eyes, the sun reminding me of every drink I had consumed the night before. I let her drive me back to the mansion, mentally preparing myself for a day with my family. I loved them and missed them, but I always felt so much guilt when I had to pretend nothing had happened with Jack and me. I kept expecting them to smell him on me or just know.

Ashely parked in the driveway. I climbed out of the car and steeled myself for the lecture about coming home in the same thing I had left in. This was one of the moments that reminded me why I needed my own place.

Elijah happened to be walking out of the den when we came through the front door. He smirked and shook his head.

"Oh, sister dear, the walk of shame doesn't look good on anybody. You better get your ass upstairs before Mom or Dad sees you."

I glowered at him. "Like you've never done it."

He shrugged. "Somehow me crawling home after a night of debauchery in a pair of slacks and a shirt doesn't look nearly as shameful as that getup you've got on."

I ignored his teasing. "I'm going to shower."

That made him burst into laughter. "Feeling a little dirty?"

"Shut up. I was with Ashley," I lied.

Elijah grinned. "No, you weren't."

"You don't know that," I shot back, testing to see just how much he did know.

"I danced with Ashley and you were nowhere to be seen. You sneaked out of your own party pretty early. I don't want to know with who," he said, making a disgusted face.

I was relieved he didn't seem to know about Jack. When Jack had carried me out of the club, I had been convinced everyone would know. Ashley had. She had seen what happened and brought my purse to me. I was so grateful for her friendship and her ability to keep a secret.

"Bye, Elijah," I said, heading for the staircase.

Ashley was right beside me as we headed for my room. Thankfully, my parents were occupied and hadn't witnessed my return home. I knew my mother would have lectured me about being a proper lady and sullying the family name.

"That was close," Ashley muttered, closing the door behind her.

"No kidding."

"Do you think Elijah would be mad if he knew? I mean he and Jack are best friends. He has to know Jack is a good guy and not his father."

I sat down on the blue settee and unzipped my boots, pulling them off and tossing them to the side. "I don't know, but I don't want to take that risk. Elijah has always been a little overprotective. It was hard enough to date in high school with him trying to scare all the boys away."

"True, he does take his big brother job pretty serious."

"I can't be with him. We both know it."

Ashley sat beside me. "You both know it, but you've known it for years and it hasn't stopped you."

"Why him? Why does it have to be him I want? There are literally millions of other men out there, but it's him I want. It's him I crave. I can't imagine ever being with anyone else. Am I crazy?" I asked, wanting a cure for my romance problems.

"Your heart doesn't care about some family feud. You two have always had chemistry. Did you guys talk at all?" she asked.

I shrugged a shoulder. "A little. We both know it will never work."

Her arm reached out and rubbed my back. "I'm sorry."

"When I saw him, it was like no time had passed at all. I had hoped it would cool things down or I would look at him and realize the memories were built up and not based on reality. That was not the case at all."

"You still care about him."

I felt my heart squeeze. "I do. In fact, I feel like the feelings are stronger. When I saw him last night I didn't have a chance. I didn't even resist. I mean, I did, but it was weak. I wanted him. If he hadn't gone all caveman, I probably would have been the one to club him over the head and drag him into the nearest dark corner."

Ashley burst into laughter. "I believe you. I saw the way you two looked at each other. It was intense."

"What do you think? Should I defy my parents and be with him?"

She shook her head. "I can't answer that for you. This is your decision. Only you know what is in your heart. I do think your parents love you, unconditionally. They might be angry, and they might even throw you out, but I think they would eventually come around."

That gave me a glimmer of hope, but I couldn't help but think about Jack's dad. "His dad died unexpectedly. None of them could have been prepared. When he died, it was a slap in the face. The reality of it all is life is short. We never know what the future holds. What if my being with Jack gives my dad a heart attack? I would never be able to live with myself if my decision to ignore their wishes caused him serious pain."

"Sweetie, you can't think like that. Accidents happen all the time. You deserve to be happy."

"But the chance is there and it's not a chance I'm willing to take."

She was silent for a moment. "It's your happiness or your misery. The choice is yours. You know I've got your back no matter what you decide to do."

"Thank you for sticking by me. I know I've been a big whiner the last two years."

"We had a blast. I don't regret it for a minute. I'm only sorry the time away wasn't enough to cure you of what ails you," she teased.

"I need a vaccine. A Jack Bancroft vaccine," I muttered.

That made her giggle in earnest. "That would be too easy. You don't do anything the easy way. You're the type who loves to bleed and sweat."

I sighed. "True, but in this one thing, I would love easy."

"Go shower. You'll feel better once you get cleaned up and some food in you."

I nodded and headed for my bathroom. I couldn't afford to be moody and sullen. My parents would want to know what was wrong. They didn't need me moping around. I would have to push Jack to the back of my mind. Two years had done nothing to lessen what I felt for him. I doubted there was anything that would ever make my heart give up on Jack. I thought about his offer and grinned. How archaic. No one made marriage pacts.

I couldn't agree to the pact. I knew if there was even the slightest chance I could be with him I would never truly try and find true love and happiness with someone else. I'd always have the idea of the pact holding me back.

My dad's face floated into my mind. He'd been so happy when I came home. To say I was a daddy's girl was an understatement. My dad and I had always gotten along well. Like many teenage girls, I had clashed with my mom, but my dad was always my hero. He used to tell everyone I was his little angel. In many ways, I felt like my mom had been a little jealous of the relationship between father and daughter.

Two years away and it was my dad who I had missed the most. Well, Jack and my dad. When I had returned home, I had seen nothing but love and adoration on his face. I didn't think I could live with him looking at me as if I had betrayed him. I knew he'd be disgusted and hurt. I couldn't do that to him. As much as I wanted to be with Jack, I really didn't want to lose my dad's love.

By the time I got out of the shower, I had reached a new level of sadness.

Ashley was sitting in my new living space in my room, her phone in hand. She looked up at me and shook her head.

"I knew that would happen."

"What would happen?" I asked.

She patted the seat next to her. "You'd get all bummed. You're tired. You'll feel better after a good night's sleep. You're probably still jet lagged and need some downtime."

"You're right. I better get dressed. Mom will not be happy if we're late for lunch."

She walked with me to the massive closet and helped me pick out an outfit. It was a casual lunch, but casual for my mother meant something different entirely. I settled on a pretty pink dress with a wide white belt.

"You look cute. I feel like you've been shopping in Duchess Kate's closet," Ashley commented.

I turned to look at myself in the mirror. "I did pick this up in London."

"You ready for this?" she asked.

"I am, but I think I'll skip the champagne."

She threw her head back and laughed. "Me too. That hair of the dog nonsense will kill a girl."

I nodded in agreement. Together we headed downstairs and into the large formal area where my mother typically entertained. I spent the next several hours kissing cheeks and having my cheeks kissed. I felt a lot like the belle of the ball. More than one of the ladies volunteered information about their handsome, single sons.

I knew I had been given a two-year reprieve, but now that I was back, people, especially my parents, would be watching closely to see what my next move was. What eligible bachelor would catch my eye. It was not a game I was looking forward to. My heart had already been snared by another bachelor. I knew deep down no other man would ever measure up to him. I was ruined. If I couldn't have Jack, I didn't want anyone. I'd die a spinster. A spinster with her father's love and respect.

CHAPTER 9

JACK

I wasn't a workaholic like my big brother Grayson, but I did tend to get caught up with work and forget I was supposed to be living a life now and again. The last few weeks had been very busy at the company and it was time to take a little time off. If I were being honest with myself, I would admit seeing Natasha had set my world on fire. For two years, I had worked and done little else, trying my best to put her and our relationship behind me. Then she showed up, looking hot as hell, and I was unable to think of anything else but her.

When I woke up that morning, she had been on my mind. I hadn't talked to her since she left my apartment. In the back of my mind, I was a little worried about her. Our exit from the club wasn't subtle. If her brother had noticed or someone had told him, Nat would be paying the price for my impulsiveness. So, today, I was treating myself to a little golf. I had nothing on my schedule for the day and had decided to cut out early. Elijah was more than happy to meet me at the club for eighteen holes. When I strolled into the clubhouse, Elijah was already there, flirting with the pretty blonde behind the bar.

"Are we going to golf or you going to stand around and flirt?" I said, slapping him on the shoulder.

It had been a dangerous move to step close to him. If he knew about my night with his little sister, he'd lay me out on the floor.

He looked over his shoulder and grinned. "Unlike you, I can do more than one thing at a time."

Relief flooded my body. He didn't know. If he did, I knew there was no way he'd be cool about it.

"Let's do this," I said, anxious to get on the fairway. I wanted fresh air, some exercise, and to hit something really hard. I needed to relieve my frustration over my dilemma with not being able to have the woman I wanted.

We headed out the door with our clubs already loaded in a cart. Golf was one of those things that helped center me. I didn't have to think much about it. I wasn't exactly playing for the PGA and didn't plan on it anytime soon. I could swing, hit, and throw a man tantrum —and get away with it—when I was on the course. It was the one time I didn't have to be the polite spare to the Bancroft throne.

"You disappeared the other night," he said as I teed off, nearly causing me to slice the ball.

I shrugged a shoulder. "I did," I said, not admitting anything.

"Who'd you leave with?" he pressed.

I grinned. "A beautiful woman."

He chuckled low in his throat. "I told you it would be a good time. You've got to learn to listen to me. I got your back. I didn't expect you to hook up with someone so early, though. I looked around for you and figured you'd already found your mark for the night and ditched me, not cool by the way. You could have let me know you were leaving."

I shrugged a shoulder, not revealing it was his sister who'd been my mark. "I had a great time. I'm glad you made me go, and I didn't want to try and find you. It was a strike while the iron was hot kind of thing."

That made him laugh. "So, who was it? Anyone I know?"

I shook my head. "I don't think so."

"Was she hot?"

I gave him a look that said that had been a stupid question. "Seriously? What kind of question is that? Of course, she was hot. I told you, she was the best-looking girl there."

"Did you take her to your place or get a hotel?" he asked, clearly not ready to drop the subject.

I cleared my throat. "We went to my place."

"Aha! Then you knew her!"

I scowled. "Why do you say that?"

"Because you never take the ones you pick up at the bar back to your place. That means you've hooked up with her before," he said, grinning like an idiot.

I sighed and shrugged a shoulder. "Yes, we've hooked up before."

Elijah was practically crowing. "Who? Come on, you've got to give me some details."

"You don't know her and I'm not giving you details. We're not seventeen and we're not in a locker room."

He laughed. "Whatever. You know you want to tell me. I can tell by the way you're not telling me anything that this one is different. Are you going to see her again? Is this a potential Mrs. Bancroft?"

I shook my head. "I don't think so."

"You know you have to settle down."

"What about you?" I snapped.

He shrugged. "I've got some time. My dad has a list of women he has approved for marriage that is about as long as my arm. I plan on working my way down the list."

I rolled my eyes. "Whoever is best in bed wins?"

He grinned. "Something like that."

I wondered if Wayne had a list of suitable husbands for Natasha as well. Who was I kidding? I knew he did. She'd be set out and paraded in front of the approved eligible men. Wayne would only allow the best of the best from families he approved.

"What about you? Are you going to start shopping around? The lady from the other night, does she have potential to be something serious?" he asked.

I wished like hell I could tell him it was very serious. I wanted to tell him I was crazy for the girl. I shared a lot with Elijah, but this one little part of my life I couldn't tell him. I had played out how that conversation would go several times and it never ended well. Elijah was my best friend and it sucked I couldn't share the joy I felt when I was with Natasha.

"What about you? How'd your night go?" I asked, turning the tables on him.

"Probably not as great as yours, but I didn't go home alone," he said with a cocky grin on his face.

I raised an eyebrow. "Hotel or home?"

It was one of the things we had both agreed on long ago after experiencing some stalker-type situations. Renting a room for the night was worth it to keep a one-night-stand out of our apartments. With our names, it wasn't hard to find women to take to bed. It was hard to find women who wanted us for us or wanted the no-strings attached hookup. A lot of the women knew our names and our net worth. While they were gorgeous women, they weren't the kind of women we could ever take home to our mothers.

"Hotel."

I nodded in understanding. "There was a big turnout. I only recognized about half those people."

"Apparently someone tweeted it and then it kind of spun out of control."

"Did Nat have a good time?" I asked, carefully broaching the subject.

Elijah chuckled. "I didn't see her at the club, but she was doing the walk of shame the following morning. I would say she had a good night."

I took my swing and turned back to glance at him. "She looked amazing. Her sabbatical agreed with her."

Elijah stopped what he was doing and turned to glare me dead in the eye. "Don't even think about it."

"What?" I asked innocently.

I had wanted to test the waters, see if there was any chance he would be okay with me dating his sister. Clearly that wasn't going to happen.

"Don't touch her. Don't ask her out. Don't you dare put your famous Jack moves on my little sister. I'll kill you if you try. That's assuming I got to you first. If my dad gets to you before I do, he'll tear you limb from limb. Stay away from her, Jack. I'm serious," he said, his voice deadly calm.

I stared back at him. I wanted to rage and tell him it was none of his damn business, but I kept my cool. "Relax. I said she looked good. I'm sure you realize your sister is a gorgeous woman."

His eyebrows shot up. "You've never said anything before."

I shrugged a shoulder. "I did now."

I was being cocky. I knew it, but I hated the idea of Elijah and Wayne Levy telling me how to live my life. It plucked a nerve.

"Listen, I don't want you causing drama in my family and it will definitely stir up some shit. You might be my best friend, but there is no way you're ever going to be allowed to date my sister," he said, his voice and facial expression telling me how serious he was.

I cleared my throat. I wanted to argue, but I couldn't do anything that would disrupt Natasha's life. "Relax."

Elijah wasn't ready to drop it. "I'm serious man. I know you and I are friends, but I don't care for your family. You're different."

That pissed me off. "Tell me something, why don't you care for my family? Is that a blanket statement in general or did each and every one of my brothers, along with my mom and dad, do something to earn your dislike?"

I knew I was playing with fire, but I was sick of the family feuding. Natasha had no idea what the feud was over. I doubted Elijah did either. Elijah was loyal to his family, even if he rebelled against them at every turn.

He shrugged one shoulder before selecting his six iron. "Your dad screwed my dad over."

"How? I'm asking because I don't know, and I would love to know what happened."

"I don't know the specifics, but I do know my dad warned me not to trust the Bancrofts. Anytime the Bancroft name is mentioned, his head turns into a giant tomato. Whatever it was, I believe it was serious and not something he will ever forgive. He'll never trust you or anyone else from your family," he said.

I rolled my eyes. "But you trust me."

"Yes, but I would also beat the shit out of you if you gave me a reason not to trust you."

I smirked. "You could certainly try."

That seemed to lighten the mood a little. Elijah took his turn and we fell back into our easy way of things. I didn't press the issue of the family feud. I knew Elijah had always been very protective of his sister. He didn't like most of the men she had dated throughout her high school years. I helped him on more than one occasion scare guys off, letting them know there would be hell to pay if the guy went out with Nat again.

Back then, I had done it because it was fun to scare the shit out of some of the losers who were always chasing after her. With the passing years, I enjoyed chasing off her boyfriends for an entirely different reason. I didn't want her to see anyone else. I had developed a crush on her years ago. It wasn't until I started to notice her looking at me that I made a move on that crush. It had been dangerous, and we had both been a little drunk at a party. From there, things heated up and we ended up where we were today. In a hot mess of lies and deceit and a lot of misery.

"Hello?" Elijah snapped his fingers in front of my face.

"What?"

"Are you going to hit the ball or stare at it all day?"

I nodded, bringing my attention back to the game. I was no longer interested in golf. I wanted to go home and call Nat. It was definitely going to have to remain our secret. I had thought I could say screw our family's opinions and do what we wanted, but I was wrong. I couldn't do it to her and I didn't want to hurt my mom either.

CHAPTER 10

NATASHA

I pulled my hair into a loose bun on top of my head before sliding my feet into a pair of ballet flats. It was breakfast with my dad this morning. My mom got me all to herself on Sunday and my dad had requested I join him for breakfast today. He was working from home that morning. He told me he had the cook preparing my favorite strawberry crepes. Breakfast in the Levy mansion was far more decadent than the Four Seasons. It was always a posh affair.

I jogged down the stairs, smiling at the housekeeper as I made my way to the formal dining room. I could smell the fresh flowers that had been placed on the table in the hall. When I walked into the dining room, there were several arrangements of gorgeous lilies on the table and the sideboard. My mother insisted on fresh flower deliveries every morning. It always left the house smelling like a garden. The flowers did have a way of freshening up a room.

I smiled when I saw my dad was already at the table, a newspaper held in front of his face with a champagne flute filled with fresh-squeezed orange juice in front of him. The table was already set with the fine china and the expensive cutlery my father insisted on using.

"Hi, Dad!" I greeted him.

He put the paper down and set it to the side before standing to give me a hug and a quick kiss on the cheek. "You look well rested this morning. I see you're finally getting ahead of that jet lag."

I smiled. "I am. Too many time zones in too short a period of time."

"I'm glad you enjoyed yourself. When I was younger, I had always dreamed of traveling the world."

I took my seat to his right and sipped the orange juice already waiting for me. "Why didn't you?"

He grinned. "You."

"Me?"

"When I was your age, I was married and in the beginning years of my company. It wasn't easy. I had enemies nipping at my heels constantly. I couldn't afford to take a week off, let alone a month or more. I knew I wanted my children to have something big. I wanted to have the best and I was not about to let anyone get in my way of achieving my dreams."

I nodded, seeing his line of conversation as a good way to broach the Bancroft subject. "Was Art Bancroft one of those enemies?" I asked, hoping I sounded nonchalant.

His face twisted in anger. "Art Bancroft was the worst out of all of them. He wanted everything I had. The man thought he was better than everyone else. He's a snake and I'm not sorry he's dead."

I was a little surprised by his vehemence. It was unlike my father to ever speak that way about anyone in front of me. I'd heard plenty of the shouting matches between him and Elijah, but he always spoke with an even tone around me. He never let me see that other side of him I knew existed. He truly treated me with kid gloves.

"Did he try to steal your ideas?" I asked, hoping to get to the heart of the feud.

"He'd steal anything he could get his hands on. Men like that have no honor. He bred a bunch of little monsters. The apple never falls far from the tree. His brats are no better than he is." He seethed.

I knew the Bancrofts by reputation mostly, but Jack was not a dishonorable man by any means.

"I've met Jack, he doesn't seem like a bad guy," I said, unable to sit back and let him group Jack into sins he had nothing to do with.

My dad's eyes narrowed at me. "I don't care if Elijah thinks that punk is worth his friendship, that man will never step foot in my house. I don't want you to have anything do with those vermin. When you lie with dogs, you get fleas, and those Bancroft brats are dogs. They're always sniffing around where they shouldn't. They think money makes them respectable—it doesn't. I don't want to ever hear their name spoken in my house again. Is that understood?"

"Dad, you're being a little extreme. The Bancroft sons cannot be held responsible for whatever it is their father did."

"Natasha, I'm serious about this. Stay away from the Bancroft trash," he said, his voice firm and leaving no room for argument.

I nodded, not willing to push the subject anymore. I could see how upset he was getting as we talked about the Bancroft family. Whatever happened was big. I didn't want to give him a heart attack by bringing it all up again.

Our breakfast was served, giving us something new to focus on.

"These are amazing," I said, then moaned as the strawberries and sweet cream burst in my mouth.

He nodded, shoveling the delicious crepes into his mouth. "So good."

Thankfully, the topic of the Bancrofts was easily brushed to the side and we spent some time catching up and talking about his plans for the company.

"I should probably head into the office. I have a few things I need to deal with," he said, putting his napkin on the table.

A housekeeper quickly stepped in to remove both our plates before scurrying from the room. My father had built an empire and loved to show off his wealth by surrounding himself with the nicest things money could buy. I glanced around the dining room with the three massive chandeliers hanging from the ceiling that were perfectly aligned over the long cherry wood table, which could easily seat twenty people or more.

"Thanks for having breakfast with me," I said, standing and giving him a hug.

"Thank you. Take the rest of the week to relax before you start planning your next adventure," he said.

I laughed. "I'm staying put for a while."

"Good. It's nice to have you home. I hope you'll stick around."

I knew he wanted me in the house, but I was still going to look for my own place. "I'll see you for dinner."

We both walked out of the dining room, him heading toward the grand foyer to leave and me heading back up to my room. I had nothing planned for the day. Normally, that would make me crazy, but I was a little tired of constantly being on the go. I was looking forward to a little downtime.

When I got into my room, I closed my door and grabbed my cell, preparing to do something I knew I shouldn't. It was stupid, but I was going to do it anyway.

"Hi," I said when he answered the phone.

"Hey you," Jack replied.

"Got a minute?" I asked.

"Give me a sec," he said, and I could hear him say something to whoever he was with. A few seconds later he came back on the line. "What's up?"

I laid my head on one arm of the settee with my feet propped up on the other side. "Nothing really. I just wanted to hear your voice."

"Did you now?" he said, and I could hear the sexy tone in his voice.

"I did. What are you up to today?"

"Meetings. You?"

I sighed. "I just had a late breakfast with Dad."

"How was that?"

"I tried to ask him what it was that caused the feud between our two families."

He laughed. "You're a brave woman. Did he give you an answer?"

"Nope. More of the same nonsense about not trusting you guys and stuff like that."

"I'm sorry. I wish I knew how to fix it. It's a little tough to fix something if you don't know what's broken."

"I've missed you," I blurted out.

"I've missed you. I wanted to call, but I don't want to pressure you into anything."

Hearing his voice was making me wish I wasn't a Levy. "I know I shouldn't, but I can't stop wanting you. You're not pressuring me. It's me pressuring me. It's like I have no control over my feelings."

"I know what you mean. I feel the same way. I can't stop thinking about you. The more I tell myself not to think about you, the more I do. I keep thinking about Saturday night and how I wish like hell it could have lasted longer."

Hearing him mention the night of passion we had spent together stirred up my own feelings. I could feel the familiar flutter of excitement in my stomach. Every time I was near him, my nerves felt raw. Every little touch was more intense. I closed my eyes thinking about how good he made my body feel.

"I do too. I think I am truly addicted to your body," I confessed.

"Baby, your body is all I think about." His voice was low and husky and sent shivers of excitement over my body.

I glanced around the room, making sure no one had sneaked in while I wasn't looking.

"I think about yours and what it feels like to have you deep inside me," I whispered.

I heard him groan. "I want to kiss you. I want to run my tongue over every inch of your body. I want to taste your very core. I love to hear you come and I love to taste you."

I felt heat between my legs, my eyes closed as I thought about him doing exactly that. "I love your tongue."

"We had so little time Saturday. I want to take you again. I want to take you in the shower, in my bed, on my kitchen table. I dream about your body writhing under mine. I woke up this morning with you on my mind," he said, every one of the words he spoke made me feel as if he were right there, his breath washing over me.

"Were you hard?" I asked, wanting to tease him a bit.

"Damn straight I was hard. Fuck, I'm hard right now just listening to you talk." He groaned.

I giggled softly. "I hope you're alone."

"I am. Are you wet?"

"Maybe a little."

"Damn it, Nat, I want you so bad. Can you meet?" he asked, desperation in his voice.

"I can't. You know we can't."

His growl of frustration made me feel guilty. I shouldn't have teased him. "I'm sorry. I am. I want you, I really do, but we've been over this so many times."

He let out a sigh. "Fine, but we can still have phone sex. I'll call you tonight when I'm in bed. I want to give you the next best thing."

My breath hitched at the thought of something so naughty. "Okay," I said, breathlessly.

"It's a date. Wear something sexy and be prepared to describe it in detail."

"I could send a picture," I quickly volunteered.

"No! That's too dangerous. I don't want to risk getting caught. No texts, emails, or anything that could get you in trouble," he said firmly.

I pouted a little but knew he was looking out for my best interests. "Fine. What time?"

"Ten."

"I'll be waiting, and I'll give you a hint. I'll be wearing something black and very tiny," I told him in a sultry voice.

"Goddamn it, Nat. You're fucking killing me here. I can't face anyone with the raging hard-on you're giving me," he complained.

"Bye, babe," I said and hung up the phone, laughing at his growling tone.

I loved having the power to make him so crazy with lust. He always drove me crazy with insane lust for him. If I couldn't have him, I could have this little part of him. It was all I had to keep me going.

CHAPTER 11

JACK

I pulled in the driveway of our family home and parked my car. My mom had invited me for dinner and I wasn't going to turn her down. Each of us boys had agreed to try and have dinner with her at least one night a week. We knew she was lonely and after her accident, we all realized how much we loved her. I liked checking in on her now and again.

"*Mooom*, I'm home," I called out as I strolled through the front door.

I knew she wouldn't be able to hear me. She was probably on the second floor or in her private sitting room where she loved to read or sew. If she wasn't in there, she was probably bingeing on some Netflix show. The broken hip had given her plenty of time to get addicted to television. I had caught her on more than one occasion curled up with a bowl of popcorn and zoned out on some mindless reality show.

She popped her head out of the kitchen. "You're early! Grab a drink. I'm just finishing up."

"You're cooking?" I asked with surprise.

She scowled at me. "Yes, I'm cooking. I know how to cook. I'll have you know I cooked most of the meals around here for a good twenty years."

I held up my hands in surrender. "I'm sorry. You're right. Carry on."

I headed for the den to pour myself a small glass of scotch. I loved her cooking, but with just her in the house and my youngest brother, James, rarely around, she hardly ever cooked anymore. We had insisted she hire a cook, which she had—reluctantly.

I took a seat in one of the chairs and put my feet up. It had been a long day and a home-cooked meal was exactly what I needed. I heard footsteps coming down the hall and assumed it was my mom. When Mason appeared in the doorway, I groaned.

"What are you doing here?" I asked, not exactly thrilled to see number three in the Bancroft order of kids.

"Shut up. Mom asked me to come by for dinner," he shot back, heading for the bar to pour himself a drink.

"I didn't realize anyone else was coming."

He sat down and put his black boots on the table. "Now you know. Leave if you want."

"I'm not going to leave," I snapped.

Mason's black sheep status was one he had cultivated and worked very hard to maintain. He could pretend he was indifferent to us and our parents, but I knew better. He cared a great deal for the family, even if he didn't show it.

"What?" He growled when he caught me staring at his arm.

I nodded. "New tat?"

He looked at the area I had been focused on. "Not new."

I wasn't sure how he could tell. One arm was nearly a full sleeve. He started getting tattoos when he was sixteen, and it seemed like they were spreading.

"Why?" I asked.

"Why what?"

"Why another tattoo? Does it have some significance?"

"They all do."

I nodded. "I thought it was just a way for you to rebel against Mom and Dad."

He chuckled. "That was your mistake. You all thought I was doing this to piss them off. The truth is, I like the tats. I did it because I liked it."

"Got it."

He sipped his drink before looking at me. "I heard Natasha Levy was back in town."

I didn't let him see how hearing her name affected me. Mason was the only one in the family who knew about our torrid love affair. We had thought we were being sneaky and went to some dive bar a couple years ago, only to be caught by Mason. I should have known it would be the type of place he would hang out at. He'd kept my secret, which earned my respect.

"She is."

He grinned. "You've seen her."

I didn't admit to anything. "She had a welcome home party at a club over the weekend."

Mason nodded. "Still hung up on her?"

I considered lying but knew it would be pointless. Out of all my brothers, Mason was the one I knew could keep a dark secret. I was sure he had plenty of his own.

"Yes."

"Gonna do something about it this time or let some old bullshit stand in your way?" he asked bluntly.

I smirked. "It isn't that easy. I can't invite her over for dinner and vice versa."

"Yes, it is. That's the difference between me and the rest of you. You all follow the rules, even if the rules are stupid and make no sense. Why? If you are happy with her—and she very clearly is happy with you—why are you letting our parents dictate your future?" he asked as if it were the most ridiculous thing he'd ever heard.

I shook my head. "It isn't so easy."

"Bullshit. You just do it. Fuck the consequences. If this is what you want, then you have to do it."

"Like your tats or leaving home?" I growled.

He shrugged a shoulder. "Basically, yes. Dad wanted us all to be good little Bancroft soldiers. I couldn't do that. I tried, but it made me miserable. I'm not going to live a lie or ignore what makes me happy just to please everyone else. My life, my rules."

That was Mason. He didn't care what others thought. I admired him for his ability to go against everyone and do his own thing, but it wasn't always best for everyone else. Mason tended to leave a trail of destruction in his wake. He steamrolled through life, without caring about consequences. He had enough money to buy his way out of trouble most of the time. I had a feeling that was one of the reasons he and my dad were never close. Mason didn't jump when my father demanded. He didn't need the family money. An inheritance had left him extremely wealthy in his own right.

I thought about adopting Mason's way of life but couldn't do it. "I can't do that. It isn't just me I have to think about. She has a stake in all this too. I am not going to force her to do something that will cost her everything she holds dear."

"Like her money?"

"No! She isn't like that. She truly loves her dad. They are very close, and I don't want to ruin that relationship. That would be selfish on my part."

Mason grinned. "Wayne Levy would shit his pants if he knew you were sleeping with his precious daughter."

I laughed. "Yes, he would. Do you know why he hates us so much? Nat doesn't know. Elijah doesn't know. All we know is he hates all Bancrofts and thinks we're the scum of the earth."

"I don't know. I'm sure it has something to do with money. It's always about money with guys like that," he quipped.

I wasn't so sure about that. "Dad was never all about money. I mean yeah, he had a lot, but he wasn't flaunting it like Wayne does. Wayne goes out of his way to make sure everyone knows he is one of the richest men in the country."

Mason shook his head. "Look at the house we're in. You don't think that's an expression of wealth?"

"Yes, but he was wealthy. This house is what Mom wanted and dreamed of. He was making his wife happy," I defended.

My dark-haired brother sat back in his chair, chugging the scotch as if it were water. "I think Wayne was jealous of Dad."

"Obviously, but why?"

"Something big went down and there are only two things that will make men want to kill each other."

"What?" I asked, interested to hear his wisdom.

"Money and women."

"Interesting," I said, wondering about the latter.

I had always assumed it was money, but maybe there was a woman involved. My mom hated Wayne just as much as my dad had. I couldn't imagine she would be at the center of the feud. I thought about Nat's mom and immediately dismissed that idea. I could never picture my dad wanting her. She was the exact opposite of my mother.

"Regardless of the reasons for the feud, you better figure out what you're going to do. You either go all in with this girl or back the fuck out. If you go all in, I've got your back, but you have to know Wayne Levy plays dirty," Mason warned.

"How do you know?"

Mason got very serious, leaning forward to look me directly in the eye. "I know people, and I know those who have gone up against Wayne. They didn't come out on the winning side of things."

I shook my head, dismissing his insinuations. "He's not the head of some mob. He's a wealthy man who throws tantrums. What could he possibly do to me?"

Mason raised an eyebrow. "I think the fact you are keeping your little relationship with the Levy princess on the down low proves you know damn well he is capable of some dirty shit. You don't want to get your hands dirty and are making sure to keep it a secret."

His words rang true. I wasn't sure if I was worried about what Wayne would do because of the rumors I had heard and my father's own hatred for the man, or if it was because of Natasha's genuine fear of what would happen. In either scenario, Mason was right. Wayne Levy was not a man to be toyed with. I wasn't all that sure of what he was capable of. I didn't think he was the type of man to order a hit on me, but one never really knew.

"I'm keeping it a secret because I don't want to hurt Mom, and she doesn't want to lose her relationship with her father."

Mason started laughing. "Pick a side, Jack."

"What do you mean?"

Mason stood, his tight black T-shirt stretching across his heavily muscled chest, revealing his dedication to the gym.

"You're either, Jack, the spare who does no wrong or you're Jack, the bad boy who rebels against his parents. I have to say, I'm pretty sure I've got the market cornered on the bad seed, but I'm sure we could share the spot if you want," he said with a toothy grin.

I stared up at him, wondering at what point in his life he decided to buck tradition and be whoever the hell he chose to be. We were all a little wild, but Mason—he was the kind of guy you saw riding a motorcycle without a helmet and a cigarette hanging out his mouth.

"I'll figure it out," I murmured.

"Ah, I see you two boys found each other," my mom said coming into the room.

"We did. I wasn't aware it was a family dinner," I replied.

She smiled and touched my shoulder. "My boys are always welcome to my dinner table. The more the merrier. Dinner is ready."

She turned and walked out of the room. I set my glass down and followed behind her, Mason on my heels.

"You better not tell Mom, not until you know what you're doing. I won't let you stress her out if you're not serious about this girl," Mason hissed.

I turned and looked back at him. "Relax, big boy. I know what I'm doing."

He scoffed. "No, you don't, or you would have already done it."

I ignored his comment and walked into the dining room. My mother sat at the head of the table with Mason and me flanking her. I looked at her and was happy to see her color was back and she looked like the vibrant woman I remembered her to be before the accident. Mason was right about one thing. I didn't want to hurt Mom. I couldn't risk hurting her or distressing her if the thing between Natasha and I wasn't ever going to amount to anything.

CHAPTER 12

NATASHA

I was taking my relaxing very serious this week. I couldn't ever remember a time when I had been quite so lazy. It seemed like my lazy approach to life this week was contagious. It was my dad earlier and now Elijah had decided to take a personal day off as well. The weather was gorgeous, which always made it hard to adult.

I leaned back in my lawn chair, adjusting my bikini top to make sure I didn't have one of those wardrobe malfunctions my dad was always so worried about. I had decided a day by the pool was the perfect way to spend a Friday afternoon. I was used to exotic, tropical beaches and as much as I loved them, there was something about the comfort of being able to lounge poolside with supreme privacy. I didn't have to worry about anyone trying to catch me in a weird, unflattering pose or worry about guys hitting on me. The only guy around was my brother.

Elijah was sprawled out next to me, his dark sunglasses on as we both lounged by the pool. He was bare chested, wearing only his swim shorts. I noticed his tan had faded quite a bit and gave him hell for it. Neither one of us tanned well at all, but he had managed to look less ghostly than I had.

I let out a long sigh, totally content in my chair, my sunglasses on, and the sun beating down on me. There was no music to ruin the moment. It was complete serenity. It was moments like this that made me happy to be who I was. The life of a wealthy, privileged woman certainly had its perks.

"I'm thirsty," Elijah mumbled after we'd been by the pool for about an hour.

"Me too," I said, not moving from my chair.

"Don't be pissed, but I'm going to do it," he said.

"Elijah, no. I'll get up," I replied, knowing exactly what he was going to do and not approving in the slightest.

"Don't get up," he replied and before I knew it, he waved his hand in the air, summoning Marla the housekeeper who was nearby on the patio.

"Yes, Mr. Levy," she asked in a pleasant voice, walking toward us.

"Can you bring us a couple mimosas, please?" he asked, flashing that charming smile of his.

Marla laughed. "I'll be right back. I'm surprised you waited so long."

When she walked away, I reached over and swatted his arm. "You're obnoxious," I hissed, hating that he was so comfortable ordering people about.

"I am not. She's paid to do that. You never ask the help for anything and it's offensive," he lectured.

"You're so full of it."

The mimosas were delivered a few minutes later. As much as I hated being treated like a spoiled princess, it was nice. I took the first sip and smiled.

"She makes a mean mimosa," I said.

"See. And she likes to do it," he retorted.

"Oh, I'm sure she told you that."

He shrugged. "Maybe she has. I convinced Mom to let Marla throw a big birthday party here for her son. Mom supplied all the food and drinks. Marla is a good lady. I like her, and she likes all of us."

"That's cool. I'm glad Mom did that."

"Hey, it was my idea," he said defensively.

I rolled my eyes. "Good job, Elijah. This is me patting your back," I said, miming the motion.

I enjoyed hanging out with my brother. It had been a long time since it was just the two of us. We had always been close, and this was the first time we had been together since I'd been home.

"Enjoying your week of leisure?" he asked.

"I am actually. What about you? I heard you went golfing the other day."

"How'd you hear that?" he asked, and I realized my mistake.

"Dad told me," I quickly covered.

"Oh, it was good," he replied.

"How's Jack?" I asked conversationally.

He didn't immediately reply. "Fine, I suppose."

"Do you ever wish you could go back?" I mused aloud.

"Go back where?"

"To the time when we were in school. I used to love tagging along with you and Jack, even if you did tease me way too much. I miss just being kids."

He laughed. "You and I have very different memories from those times. I was in trouble a lot."

"Because you and Jack were always doing stuff. I never even knew half of what you did, I just remember Dad was always mad at you for one reason or another," I said with a small smile.

"I blame Jack. He was usually the one who came up with the bad ideas," he said, laughter in his voice that told me he was lying through his teeth.

"Why don't I believe that? You were always thinking of ways to rebel when you were young. I remember you coming up with so many plans that always involved me doing the actual deed. If I got caught, you could claim innocence and you wouldn't get in trouble."

He was laughing again. "That's because Dad would never yell at his princess."

"But Mom would."

He shrugged a shoulder. "Mom was never the one we had to worry about."

"True. She always told Dad and he was the one who would yell, scream, and threaten to take away our toys or cars," I remembered.

"Empty threats for you—not so much for me."

I lowered my sunglasses and looked at him. "That's because you were always so naughty."

"I'm telling you, it was Jack," he insisted.

"Liar. Remember, I used to tag along quite a bit. You were the one who wanted to steal the principal's desk that year," I reminded him.

That made him shake his head. "That did not end well. For me or Jack," he said, his face grimaced at the memory.

"Dad was pissed. I do remember that. He blamed Jack for putting you up to no good," I reminded him.

Elijah shrugged his shoulder. "Jack had some pretty wild ideas. He was not the innocent guy you're making him out to be. Remember when I crashed Dad's golf cart? That was Jack's idea. He said we couldn't drink and drive, but we were out of beer, so he said we could take the golf cart because it wasn't really driving."

I smirked, thinking of the logic behind his reasoning. "I think the idea had merit. Were you driving?"

"Yes, right into the damn pond." He snarled.

I almost choked on the drink I had taken. I loved imagining Jack and Elijah in their youth. "That was the second golf cart you ruined, if I remember right."

"Yes, but the first one was really an accident. I was on the course and didn't know where the brakes were. I drove into a pond that time too," he said as if he was just realizing the similarities between the two.

"Note to self, never ride with you when there is water nearby."

"Ha. Ha. We couldn't all be the perfect princess like you," he teased.

I laughed. "You made me look perfect because you were such a terror. Let's see, who blew up the toilet at the private school? That wasn't me. Or, wait, who was it that egged the teacher's house after said teacher took away his iPod? Again, not me."

"I was a crusader for justice. In all those cases I was unfairly prosecuted," he defended in a haughty tone.

"I think your memory is a bit skewed. You and Jack are still legends at that school. I sneaked into the boy's bathroom just so I could see the patch job in the wall after you had destroyed it with your little toilet bomb."

"It was a prank. No one was at school. No one got hurt or was at risk of getting hurt. You would have thought we blew up a building with the way everyone reacted," he grumbled.

"I love you," I told him.

"I love you too," he said, reaching out and slugging my arm.

I sighed, leaning back against my chair. "I hope I have a wild kid one day."

"Are you out of your mind. Why would you actually wish for that?" he asked in horror.

In my mind, I was picturing a little Jack running around, being precocious in the cutest way. I'd scold him for dumping out the flour canister or pulling all the flowers out of the garden to make me a bouquet and then turn around and laugh.

"Because, the naughtiness makes for some good stories later on," I said, sounding a little wistful.

"I don't think Mom and Dad would agree. I know I gave Mom gray hair and damn near made Dad go bald."

"It's life. You were so full of life. I loved when you and Jack would show up at the park or the mall and just be so carefree."

He sighed. "Those were some good days. I did have a lot of fun with him back then. He was always my partner in crime. He wasn't always willing, but somehow I always managed to convince him to go along with whatever I planned."

"Speaking of Jack, I saw him at my birthday party," I said, easing into the topic.

He nodded. "I had to practically drag him out. He's gotten old. He never goes out and he never wants to get up to no good anymore."

"Well, he looked good, that's for sure," I said before I even thought about it.

The second the words crossed my lips I knew I had made a dangerous misstep. Elijah sat forward and turned to face me in his chair. I gulped down the lump in my throat and turned my head, hoping to feign nonchalance.

"Nat, listen to me and I'm dead serious," he started.

"What, Elijah?" I snapped, irritated I was thirty years old and being lectured by my big brother.

"Stay away from him, do you hear me?"

I sat up, pulled my sunglasses down, and glared at him. "Seriously? He's been your best friend forever and you're going to tell me to stay away from him?"

He nodded. "It's different. Don't you dare mess with him, Nat. I forbid it."

"Shut. Up. You can't forbid me to do anything. You're my brother, not my father."

He looked me in the eye. "I'm telling you not to do it because of your father. He will be livid, Nat. He will never allow you to date Jack. I don't know what it is with the two of you, but you both better back off."

I grabbed my drink and stomped away from the pool. I was not a child. I was not going to listen to it from my brother of all people. I wasn't sure what he meant by the two of us, but I had a feeling Jack may have slipped up. We were treading in very dangerous territory. If we weren't careful, we were going to screw up and the world of shit we would stir up was not something I was ready to deal with.

I headed upstairs to call Jack and let him know about my conversation with Elijah. I needed him to lie. I needed him to assure my brother there was nothing between us. I couldn't have my brother sniffing around and finding out who I went home with on Saturday. I didn't think he would tell my dad, but he would try and kill Jack.

I did not want to have to choose between my big brother and the man I had fallen for.

CHAPTER 13

JACK

Boredom is a tool of the devil, my mother used to say. She was right. If I stayed busy, I only thought about Natasha once every fifteen minutes. When I was sitting at home alone, I thought about her constantly. Like now. I had woken up with her on my mind and she wasn't going to disappear. That was the problem with not working on weekends. I thought about going to the gym or going for a run, but that wasn't what I wanted. I wanted her.

I had been pacing my apartment with my phone in my hand. I couldn't call her. I couldn't risk her being with her parents or Elijah. If they managed to hear my voice over the phone, or if Elijah saw my number come up on the screen, it would ruin our cover. I couldn't do it. I was desperate to hear her voice.

"Do anything else. Don't risk it," I told myself, walking into the kitchen to make myself a smoothie.

I pushed the button on the Vitamix and tried to focus on the drink rather than the woman who was dominating my every thought. I stared at the smoothie dancing around in the blender, completely lost in thought.

"Fuck it." I groaned, turning off the mixer and grabbing my phone. *Can you talk?*

I sent the text and held my breath. I hoped she was alone or had her phone shielded from view. I put the phone on the counter and waited. There was no response.

"Shit."

I grabbed a glass and poured the smoothie in it. My eyes kept drifting to the phone. I had just turned away when I heard it chime. I spun around, then grabbed the phone from the counter to read the message.

Yes.

With my smoothie forgotten, I pushed the call button.

"Hi," she said in a sultry voice.

"Hi. What are you up to?" I asked.

"I just got out of the shower."

My dick jumped to attention. "Are you naked?"

"I have on my satin robe," she said in a husky voice.

"You're naked underneath?" I asked, needing clarification for the fantasy I was conjuring up in my mind.

She giggled softly. "I am."

I groaned and imagined her with nothing else on, the robe hanging open in the front and exposing plenty of cleavage. The satin would brush over her silky smooth skin.

"You're teasing me." I groaned, my body responding just like it always did when she was near.

"Ah, that's not my intention. I'm more than happy to follow through with whatever," she teased.

"Good. Get dressed, we're going out for lunch," I ordered, my mind made up.

"Jack," she said my name on a weak protest.

"I'll be there in forty-five minutes."

There was a brief pause. "I'll meet you at the end of the driveway."

I hung up the phone, making another quick call before heading for my room to quickly change. All week I had been telling myself I couldn't see her again. After my talk with Mason, I realized it was a huge risk. I knew there was no gray area. What we were doing was too dangerous.

I sat on the bed and tied my shoes with quick, jerky movements. The excitement to see her was making me act like a silly teenager. With keys, phone, and wallet in hand, I left my apartment and headed straight for the massive Levy estate. The long driveway shrouded by huge trees and the tall concrete wall was going to work out in my favor today. No one at the house would see who was picking her up.

When I pulled in front of the house, she wasn't there. I checked the time and realized I was about five minutes early. I didn't even let myself think she would stand me up. No way. I knew she wanted to see me as much as I wanted to see her.

I hit the button for the door lock when I saw her coming out of the gate. I watched her in the rearview mirror and sucked in air through my teeth.

"Damn," I whispered.

She was wearing a pair of skinny jeans, knee-high boots, and a flirty, long-sleeved shirt with shoulder cutouts. I was glad to see she was carrying a jacket; it would be chilly where we were going. Her outfit was casual and sexy as hell. The woman was always at the height of fashion without even trying. She was classy, sexy, and elegant all at the same time. The moment she opened the door I could smell her perfume. It instantly stirred up memories of her body next to mine. I sharply inhaled, letting the sweet smell of fruit and what smelled like vanilla wash over me.

"Hi," she said, closing the door of my black Mercedes.

"I better get out of here," I mumbled, leaning over to give her a quick kiss before putting my car into gear and driving away. I didn't want to risk being seen by the security team I knew her father had regularly patrolling the perimeter.

When we stopped at the end of the road, a good safe distance from her family's estate, I leaned over and kissed her again. I leisurely explored her mouth with my tongue, sucking on her bottom lip, my hand at the back of her head holding her steady for my exploration. I wanted to take so much more, but managed to remember we were in a car, in the middle of the day, in the middle of the street.

"Now that's a kiss," she said with a smile, leaning her head back against the leather seat.

"You look beautiful," I said, kissing her again.

"Thank you. So, where are we going? You didn't give me a hint about what to wear, so I had to make an executive decision," she teased.

I chuckled, letting my eyes roam over her body. "I love the boots. You and boots make me crazy."

She burst into a fit of giggles. "Almost all girls wear boots. Is this a fetish for you?" she asked, rubbing her hand over the black leather boots.

"They weren't before, but when they are on you, it makes me insane with need for you."

I pulled away from the stop sign and started driving.

"Where are we going?" she asked again.

I winked. "It's a surprise."

She clapped her hands together. "I like surprises."

"Good, this will be a good one, I promise."

I headed for the marina, a place I hadn't visited in a long time. I wanted to be with Natasha outside the walls of my apartment. It had gotten a little old the last time we had tried to have a relationship. We were both recognizable because of our parents' wealth, which meant it was next to impossible for us to go out to dinner in the city or anywhere else. Our families' feuding was something that was well known. It was one of those things that was talked about at parties and social gatherings when no one thought we were listening.

"Where are you taking me?" she asked when I took the exit off the freeway heading toward the water.

"I told you it's a surprise."

She grinned and focused her gaze out the window. I headed down the road a little farther and pulled into the parking lot of the exclusive marina.

"Did you buy a boat?" she asked.

"No, I did not buy a boat."

"Then we're looking at boats?" she asked, confusion in her voice.

I parked the car and killed the engine, looking over at her and shaking my head. "You have zero patience."

"No, I don't!"

"Come on, I'll show you."

I locked up the car, took her hand, and we walked down toward the dock. There was a man waiting for me.

"Mr. Bancroft, it's good to see you." The man greeted us.

"Luke, thanks for meeting on such short notice," I said, shaking his hand.

"Everything is ready for you," he said, unlocking the gate and allowing us onto the dock where some rather large, expensive boats were docked.

"Thank you, I really appreciate it."

He nodded and waved as we continued down the dock.

"Jack, what's going on?" she asked.

"We're taking a little ride," I told her.

She looked around her. "I think this is more than a little ride."

I chuckled low in my throat. "You're right, this is our ride."

I held my arm out, pointing to the yacht I had rented. It was a friend's yacht and for a small chunk of change, he was letting me borrow it and the full staff to go along with it.

"Seriously?"

I nodded. "Seriously. It's staffed and loaded with food and whatever we want. We can't go out, but we can be together here. Here we are in our own private little world. No one is going to say anything."

"Wow." She gasped, her hand going to her mouth.

"Come on, let's go."

I grabbed her hand and took her on board. The staff greeted us with mimosas. With her hand in mine, I led her to the top deck. It wasn't long before I heard the engines start and the yacht slowly pulled away from the dock.

I wrapped my arm around her waist, pulling her close to me. She looked up at me with a sparkle in her eyes.

"Amazing. It is the best idea. We can be us. We don't have to hide or look over our shoulders. Thank you for this," she said, leaning up on her toes to kiss me.

"I'm happy to do it. I want to enjoy the day. I'm hoping you'll stay the night," I said.

Her eyes were full of excitement. "Let me make a call before we get too far out."

She took her phone and moved away a few feet. I could hear her soft voice and knew she was probably talking to her mom or dad. When she was done, she moved back to me, sipping from her glass.

"All good?" I asked.

"All good. Come on. Take me on a tour," she said, giddiness in her voice.

I laughed and gave her a quick kiss. "It'll be an adventure for us both. I think the last time I was on here was two years ago, and I'll admit I had a little too much to drink."

"Even better," she said, taking the lead as we meandered around the top deck before moving downstairs to check out the cabin.

"Damn," I muttered as we walked into the stateroom.

The man had spared no expense. Wealth was dripping from every inch of the room.

"Your friend likes expensive things, doesn't he?"

I nodded. "I had no idea. We don't exactly hang out a lot."

She stopped moving and spun around to look at me. "Does he know Elijah?"

I shook my head. "No. I mean he might know of him, but I don't think their friends."

She visibly relaxed. "Let's go back up on deck. I wish I would have brought my bikini."

"You could sunbathe naked," I suggested.

She raised an eyebrow. "We're not alone."

"They won't say anything. I paid them a lot for their silence."

"I think I'll stick to what I have on, naughty boy," she said, giving me a quick kiss.

I hadn't felt so carefree in months, years really. It was freeing to be away from all the rules and restrictions our names put on us when we were on land. On the yacht, it was me and her and no one else mattered. None of the bullshit between our parents mattered.

We both sat in comfortable lounge chairs and drifted away together. The warm sun combated with the cool breeze coming off the water. We didn't have to talk or do much more than occasionally reach out and brush a hand over the other's arm. We were both perfectly content to just be together without fear of judgment.

I was strongly considering buying a yacht and setting sail with her. It was one way to solve our problems, I mused.

CHAPTER 14

NATASHA

I loved being on the water. It was one of the few things in life my dad didn't own. I never knew why. Maybe because he was too busy to enjoy a boat or a yacht. I decided once I got my company built up, I was definitely going to buy me one. The fresh air washed over me, reminding me how good life was. It was easy to get caught up in the hustle and bustle and focus on the things that weren't going right in my life, but out here, it was all good.

Being with Jack was amazing. I reached out and grabbed his hand. I had a feeling he had dozed off in the chair next to mine. His sunglasses blocked my view of his eyes, but I could see the slow, steady movement of his chest that told me he was asleep or very relaxed.

He turned to look at me and smiled. "Hungry?"

"I could be."

"Let me tell the cook that we're ready for lunch," he said, sitting up, kissing me, and walking away.

He had thought of everything. We were truly on our own little floating island. There were no weird stares or disapproving glances. It was only he and I. I didn't think I had stopped smiling since we boarded the yacht. I wanted to tell Ashley, but, for now, that night had to remain our secret. Besides, I doubted I had any cell coverage where we were, which was fine by me. I liked being out of reach and out of touch from the real world.

Jack returned a few minutes later and handed me a glass of white wine. "Lunch will be served in about fifteen minutes."

I sipped the wine and nodded. "Thank you. This is amazing. I still cannot believe we're out here."

"It's good, huh? Just you and me."

"Maybe we should set sail and never go back," I suggested.

"Works for me."

I sighed, wishing it were that easy. "Maybe one day."

"Did your dad give you any hint about the fight? I keep thinking maybe there's a way to solve it, make it better. If my dad did something that cost your dad money, I'll write a check right now and put an end to this whole thing."

I shook my head. "No. I have heard nothing. My dad just gets furious if I try to bring it up."

"Elijah doesn't know what happened either. My brother Mason thinks it has to be over money or a woman, which makes sense, but seriously, if it was money, both of them have plenty of it. If it was a woman, they were both happily married. It seems like they could have buried the hatchet a long time ago," he said, his voice full of sadness.

"I know. I agree. Whatever it was, the cut runs deep, and it's too late for your dad to make amends. You can't fix what you don't know is broken."

He shook his head. "It's such a waste. I mean, we could be happy together. It is such a waste for them to hold onto something that is so far in the past it can't possibly matter."

"Hey," I said, reaching out and grabbing his hand. "Let's focus on the present. We're here and this is amazing."

He kissed me. "You're right. No more talk about the feud."

"Good. What's for lunch?"

He chuckled. "I think I heard something about crab cakes, but beyond that, I have no idea."

"Sir, would you like your lunch served here or in the dining room?" one of the waiters asked.

He looked at me. "Here is great," I said enthusiastically.

It wasn't long before there was a table set up, complete with a white tablecloth and a lunch that looked like it came out of a five-star restaurant. Looking at the food I suddenly felt ravenous.

"Damn," he muttered, taking a bite of one of the crab cakes.

I followed suit, anxious to know if it all tasted as good as it looked. It did. I heard myself moaning in pleasure, shaking my head in disbelief.

"Amazing," I said around a mouthful.

We dug into our meals. The food was too good to be ignored.

"Do they think you're out with Ashley?" he asked once we had slaked our hunger and were able to actually have a conversation without blowing crumbs all over the table.

I sipped my wine and nodded. "Yes. She'll cover for me."

"Elijah will kill me if he finds out I took you out here," he commented.

I grimaced, not able to assure him it would be okay. "He would. I know he would. I'm sorry. I know how much of a risk this is for you as well."

"Don't worry about me. I can handle Elijah."

The gravity of the situation slammed into me. "If he finds out, you know we're only extending the feud for another generation."

"What do you mean?"

"He'll hate you. He'll want to kill you, and I have a feeling you won't walk away. You two will end up hating each other because of me. The feud between our families will be kept fresh and alive for another generation," I explained.

He nodded. "You're right, but are you willing to walk away from this?"

I felt my stomach twist in knots. "I should say yes. I know I should, and I know I have said I would walk away on more than one occasion, but I'm always drawn back to you."

"Me too."

"We're playing with fire, Jack. One or both of us is going to get burned. It isn't a matter of if, but when."

"Nat, I will walk away if you want me to. I won't call you again or try to see you if that's what you really want. I don't want to cause you any trouble. I don't want you to get hurt by all this. I would never do anything to hurt you," he said in a low voice.

I felt tears in my eyes and quickly blinked them away. I wasn't going to spoil our little piece of paradise by talking about how it would all end.

"We're going to have to stop one day, but that isn't today. We can worry about it later," I said, taking a long drink from my wine, wanting to dull the pain I could feel coming at what I knew was the inevitable outcome to our relationship.

The waiter came out and quickly cleared the table, leaving the bottle of wine before scurrying away.

"Did you think about the pact?" he asked, surprising me with the question.

I scoffed. "No! I thought you were joking."

He slowly shook his head, his hazel eyes holding mine. "I wasn't joking."

"Jack, we can't do that and besides, that is not how I want the beginning of my marriage to be. I don't want to get married because of a pact. I want to have the happily ever after, the ring, the wedding, and most importantly, a real proposal."

He shrugged a shoulder. "We could have all that."

"Not if we're getting married by default. That is not romantic," I said in a haughty tone, pulling a laugh from him.

"I can make it romantic."

"I'm sure you can, but when I get married, I want my dad to give me away. I want to listen to my mom freak out because it's the wrong shade of blue on the tablecloths. I want your family to be there. I want your brothers to be your groomsmen," I said wistfully.

He nodded. "I want that, too, but what about us and our happiness?"

"What about our families and their happiness?" I shot back.

"You're killing me here," he said with a grin.

I smiled, happy he could keep the tone light. "I'm sorry. You know how sorry I am. This whole thing is horrible. I want to be with you, and I will admit, I often think about my life if you and I were to be together. I imagine not having my family in my life. Dealing with the guilt they would make sure I felt and not being able to share holidays with them. It nearly cuts me in two when I think about it," I said, feeling the tears in my eyes again.

"Don't," he whispered, reaching out to take my hand in his. "It's okay. We're going to figure something out. For now—for today—we're together. That's what we focus on."

I nodded, dragging in a deep breath. "You know what's bullshit?" I asked.

He raised an eyebrow at my use of the word. I didn't care if it wasn't ladylike. I was angry. "What is *bullshit?*" he asked, a smile playing on his lips as he said the word.

"I'm thirty years old and I still can't make decisions about my life. Mommy and Daddy are right there dictating what I can and can't do." I pouted.

He shrugged a shoulder. "I don't think it is the fact they are telling you what you can't do, but the fact that you are a good daughter who loves and respects her parents very much and you are making a choice not to hurt them or disappoint them. I don't think that is a terrible thing at all, even if I hate it."

"It makes me feel like a little kid wanting dessert and being told no." I groaned.

"Am I the dessert?" he said, his eyes glistening with that naughtiness I loved so much.

"You are." I smiled.

"I think there's a saying about that."

I shook my head. "About me wanting my dessert?" I asked with confusion.

"About you wanting your cake and the icing too," he said with a smile.

I slapped my hand on the table, not terribly hard, but hard enough to shake the vase full of fresh flowers that was still sitting in the center. "I do want my cake and the icing and ice cream on the side. I'm an adult and I should be able to make these decisions."

He shrugged. "You can, and you have," he said solemnly.

His words stung a little. I knew it was ultimately up to me, and I had made my decision to ignore my feelings for him and remain the dutiful daughter. I stared at him, wondering how that made him feel. I knew it was wrong and I shouldn't keep dragging him on, but I couldn't bring myself to walk away from him for good … not yet.

"Should we take a walk?" I suggested.

He laughed. "I hope you're not asking me to take a long walk off a short pier."

I rolled my eyes. "How long have you been waiting to say that?"

He burst into laughter. "A long time. Come on, let's walk. I caught a glimpse of dinner when I was in the galley and we need to walk off this lunch, trust me."

I groaned. "I'm going to gain twenty pounds overnight."

"And I will love every pound," he said, running his open hand over my ass.

I giggled and leaned into him as we strolled alongside the railing, staring off into the endless sea. "The sunset!" I gasped.

"What about it?"

"I cannot wait to watch the sunset out here! It's going to be gorgeous!"

He kissed the top of my head, his arm still around my shoulders and pulling me into his warm body. "It is. We can have dinner up here again if you'd like."

"I'd like. Most definitely. I love it up here. Maybe we could sleep on the deck?" I suggested.

He stopped walking. "That may be a little uncomfortable and cold."

"I'll have you to keep me warm."

"Damn straight you will," he said, and we continued our leisurely stroll around the deck.

"I never want to go home." I sighed when we decided to head downstairs for a bit.

"I know, babe. I know," he murmured against my neck as we snuggled together on the couch.

CHAPTER 15

JACK

The smells coming from the kitchen were making us both very hungry. We had spent some time downstairs, watching TV and snuggling with each other before moving back to the top deck for some more fresh air. I saw her shiver and knew the evening chill was getting to her.

"I'll be right back," I told her, giving her a quick kiss and heading back to the stateroom to grab a blanket.

As I was headed upstairs, one of the staff was coming down. "Are you cold?" he asked.

"She is," I said, not wanting to say her name.

I still felt the need to protect her from the scandal our being together would create. I wanted to provide her with as much anonymity as possible.

"I'll get the heaters going if you'd like?"

"Heaters?"

The young man smiled and nodded. "There are a couple patio heaters we can put out to take off the chill. It doesn't do a lot of good unless you're seated near them, but it helps."

I grinned. "That would be great, thank you."

I headed up and let Natasha know she was soon going to be warm and cozy. We watched as the young man dragged the tall heaters out of a closet and then fired them up. Soon enough, the area where we were seated was toasty warm.

"This is the best," she murmured, snuggling against me on the lounge chair we were sharing.

"The sunset is already starting," I told her, pointing at the orange streaks in the sky.

We watched the sun go down, the canopy of stars brighter than I had ever seen them before without the light pollution from the city lights. It was a spectacular view. I suddenly had a new appreciation for those folks who liked sleeping under the stars. There was something about it that made you feel alive and closer to the universe.

"I'm going to get us a couple glasses of wine. Something this beautiful should be enjoyed with a good wine," I told her, disentangling our bodies and then striding toward the cart that had been set up with wine and a cheese tray.

I brought the cheese and two glasses of wine back to the chair we were sharing, then crawled under the blanket with her once again.

"Snack?" I asked, holding out the tray.

She giggled. "I'm afraid to eat anything. I can smell dinner from up here and it smells divine. I'm sure I'm going to totally gorge myself."

I laughed. "You only live once. Gorge yourself. You'll work it off later," I promised in a husky voice.

She leaned over and kissed me, slowly savoring my mouth. It was nice being able to take our time. Usually, we were always rushed or so frantic to be with each other we never really got to take our time and simply enjoy the moment. We were now.

"I'm going to," she mumbled, popping a square of cheese in her mouth.

We enjoyed our wine and cheese until it was announced dinner was ready.

"We'll eat up here again, please," I said.

Once the table was set, I dismissed the staff and told them to enjoy the rest of the night off—downstairs. I wanted to be well and truly alone with Nat.

"So, tell me, Jack Bancroft, exactly *how* did you pass the time while I was gone?" she asked in a playful tone.

I knew what she was asking, but I was going to tease her a bit. "Oh, man, where do I begin. It has been two years of debauchery."

"Jack!"

I grinned. "I don't remember a lot about those first few months. I know there was a lot of alcohol and women."

The look on her face was a combination of fury and sadness. "Oh," she said, her voice so soft I could barely hear her.

I reached out and grabbed her hand. "Only half that statement is true," I told her, gazing in the liquid pools of blue staring back at me with unshed tears.

"What part?"

"The part about the women. I've not touched another woman since you, Nat. I swear on everything that I love. I'm not going to lie. I did date and there were some attempts at kissing, but I couldn't do it. You've had my heart from the moment we met, even if you were illegal for many of those years."

"Really? You haven't been to bed with another woman?"

I shook my head. "I haven't. I understand if you can't say the same, but for me, it was too much."

She looked down at her plate and I knew I shouldn't be jealous, but I was. I wanted to rage and beat the hell out of the man or men who had touched her intimately and knew her body like I did. I couldn't. We had parted ways with no intention of ever being together again. I knew I should have moved on and I had tried, but I always felt like I was betraying her when I danced with another woman or took a woman out to dinner. I was always looking over my shoulder, hoping she didn't catch me cheating—even if there was no way it could ever be called cheating.

"Jack, I haven't been with another man. I've not kissed a man ... nothing. I have done a lot of dancing and there was a lot of flirting, but it wasn't on my part. I wasn't interested. I cannot tell you how many times Ashley had to stop me from calling you or jumping on a plane and coming home to you. I wanted to, but I remembered our last night together and our vow to move on, to never look back," she said, emotion filling her voice and reflecting in her eyes.

"Damn, girl, you have no idea how happy that makes me."

She grinned. "Me too. I thought I was going to have to slap a bitch."

My eyes widened. "You sound like you just walked out of a cellblock."

She shrugged a shoulder. "You pick things up when you travel the world."

"I hope you didn't pick up how to make a shiv," I quipped.

She threw her head back and laughed. I loved hearing her laugh and couldn't stop smiling.

"Other than not sleeping around, what else have you been up to?"

I shrugged a shoulder. "I worked. I beat the shit out of Grayson and then I watched him marry the woman of his dreams. He has a baby girl; did I tell you that?"

"I did hear he got married and had a baby. That's surprising."

I nodded. "Yes, it sure is," I said and quickly filled her in on the story.

"I can't believe you two actually got into a fistfight. You two were always at each other's throats."

I shook my head, holding up my fork. "No, no. He was always at my throat. I was always trying to stay out of his way. Enough about me. How was your trip?"

She sighed. "It was a lot of fun and I will always cherish the memories of the places I visited. Ashley and I skipped a lot of the touristy stuff and made an effort to really see the places we were at through the eyes of the locals."

"That sounds fun."

"It was."

"Nat, I'm going to say something, and I know it is probably not the right time, but I have to say it, okay?"

She wrinkled her nose. "With that kind of a lead-in, I think I might strongly consider jumping overboard."

"Baby, you know I love you more than anything else in this world, and it is because I love you so much that I'm going to make sure we never see each other again—unless you are ready to take that plunge. I can't keep hurting you and putting you through this pain. I know it kills you to lie to your parents and to do stuff behind their backs. I wanted to bring you out here to give us one last night together. I'm here and I always will be if you ever change your mind, but everything else has to stop," I told her.

I knew it was the right thing to do and one of us had to be strong enough to do it.

"Jack, please don't say that. I'm still working through it."

"I know you are. I don't want to pressure you. We could agree to the pact I mentioned earlier?" I suggested, hoping she would reconsider.

She took a long drink from her wineglass before setting it down and looking me in the eye. "I can't, but I can be here with you, right now, in this moment and not think about tomorrow."

I nodded. I could do that, and I was going to make the night one she would look back on and seriously reconsider my pact idea. I wanted her hot and wet every time she thought about our last night together.

"Good, because I'm going to leave you wrung out and unable to walk normal by the time I'm done with you," I promised.

Her eyes sparkled. "You sure about that? Maybe it will be *you* who won't be walking right."

I shrugged. "Possibly, but you're going to scream my name to the heavens. I'm going to have your body quivering and dripping with need."

"Jack." She gasped.

"Nat," I replied.

She looked down at her food and took another bite before taking a long drink from her glass. I casually refilled it for her.

"Are you trying to get me drunk?" she said, a naughty smile on her lips.

I shrugged. "I don't think I need to get you drunk, do I, Nat? You'll take me. I bet you're wet right now. I bet you're thinking about me inside you. I can practically feel your nails scouring my back as I fuck you hard and dirty, just the way you like it."

Her mouth fell open and her cheeks stained red. She used the napkin to wipe her mouth, taking another drink from her glass, her eyes on mine the whole time.

"Well?" I asked.

"Well what?"

"Are you wet? Should I check for myself? I want to slide my fingers over you, inside you."

Her lips formed a small O and I knew she was ready. I loved bringing her to the brink of an orgasm without ever having to touch her. The last week had been many conversations, just like this, as we both lay in bed at night, talking on the phone.

"Jack, I think I'm finished with my dinner," she mumbled.

I tossed my napkin on the table and jumped from my chair so fast I nearly knocked it over. I was standing in front of her, my hands on her hips as I yanked her pelvis against mine. I was already hard. I knew she was wet, I could feel the heat coming off her.

My mouth slammed over hers and despite my earlier desire to take things slow and savor every moment, I wanted her with a fierce passion I couldn't control. It was always the same when I was with her. I couldn't get enough of her.

Her arms went around my neck as she leaned her body into mine. I heard her soft whimper and knew she was begging for more. I wanted to give her everything she needed, but I had to drag it out, just a little more.

Her hands went to the button on my slacks. "No," I said more forcefully than I intended.

"Jack," she demanded.

"Slow down, baby, we've got time," I whispered against her lips.

"I need you." She groaned, grinding her hips against mine.

"You have me."

CHAPTER 16

NATASHA

He was taking his sweet time and making me shake with need. His mouth moved over my neck, sucking and nibbling on the sensitive skin as he held our bodies close together. When I felt a cool breeze wash over my bare skin, I gasped. I hadn't even felt him stripping me. Hands were yanking and tugging with fierceness now, leaving me standing in my boots, red panties, and matching bra.

He took a step back to admire the underwear I had picked up in Paris. "I think my new favorite color is red." He growled.

I ran a hand over the sheer lace on my bra. "I feel dangerous."

"You are dangerous."

He was on me once again, dropping to his knees in front of me, his face buried in my stomach as his hands massaged my breasts. It was like he was worshiping me. His hands slid down my rib cage and over my hips to quickly unzip my boots before pulling them off one at a time.

I glanced around the deck, feeling extremely exposed. "Should we go downstairs?"

"No. I want you here, under the stars with the spray of the ocean washing over us. We have privacy. It's only you and me, no one else," he assured me. "I'm not going to wait. I have to have you now."

I gasped at the fierce demand in his voice, which was quickly followed by his mouth slamming over mine once again, his hands roaming my body with exquisite pressure. He lifted me up and carried me to the circular sofa, which wrapped around one end of the deck, before depositing me on it. It was much darker at the end with none of the lights around us.

He stood, looking down at me, his heated gaze making me feel warm inside. I watched as he stripped off his pants, then yanked his shirt over his head, his wide chest looking bigger in the muted light from the moon. I reached up, touching the six-pack abs and tracing my finger over the dark line of hair that disappeared under his briefs. I cupped his balls, smiling when I felt his hard dick jump.

I could feel him watching me, I used my fingers to hook on the elastic band and slowly pulled his underwear down, coming eye to eye with his thickness. My mouth opened and before I knew what I was doing, I leaned forward and closed my mouth over the head, moaning low in my throat as I slid my lips down his hard length.

"Fuck," he said, groaning, then pushed my shoulders back.

"Hey." I pouted.

He shook his head. "Lie down, stretch out," he ordered.

I wanted to finish what I had started, but I did as he asked. His body lay next to mine, cocooning me between the back of the couch and his warm body. One big, warm hand caressed my skin, starting at my knees and working up.

"I want these off," his husky voice washed over me, and I could feel him tugging on my panties.

I lifted my hips and with his help, shimmied out of the red thong. His hand cupped between my legs, sending heat spiraling through my body. My back arched, pressing myself against the heel of his palm a little harder. He pushed back, the pressure making me quiver with need. I ground my hips, needing more from him.

"Jack, please." I moaned.

Without warning, his index finger slid over my slit and pushed inside. I cried out at the glorious invasion, my body bucking upward. With us both squeezed onto the couch, I couldn't spread my legs very wide. I was trapped in the best way possible. The inability to open myself wider made his finger feel much bigger as he rubbed past my slick folds before pushing once again.

I moaned softly as he continued his slow ministrations. He answered my moan with a searing kiss. I could feel the orgasm coming. He seemed to be in no hurry as he lazily kissed me, stroking his finger in and out, swirling it around my clit and spiraling me higher and higher. I could feel his erection pressed against my leg. The cool night air was a welcome addition and helped cool my over-heated body.

"Jack." I groaned, just before my legs stiffened, my toes pointed, and my body exploded into a beautiful orgasm.

"That's it, baby, that's it," he encouraged stroking and rubbing his finger over my clit, sending shockwaves through my body.

He rolled off the couch, staring down at me before yanking me up to join him. His mouth was on mine as he spun around and sat on the couch, pulling me down with him. His magic fingers unhooked my bra, releasing my breasts as he tossed it to the side. I sat down on his lap, my knees on either side of his hips as I took over the depth of our kiss. I plunged my tongue in, dueled with his tongue before sucking his bottom lip into my mouth.

"Fuck me, Nat," he said, panting when I finally freed his mouth from mine.

I grinned, rising onto my knees, using my hand to find his hard shaft, and lining it up so I could slide down. I loved fucking him. I loved how he filled me so completely. His jaw was clenched and his eyes closed as I slid down him. I took it slow, giving my body time to adjust as I finally rested on his lap, his dick buried high and deep inside my body.

I couldn't move. Wild sensations of white-hot lightning were rocketing through my body, my nerves felt like they were short-circuiting. I gasped as one blinding sensation of ecstasy zipped through my body, quickly followed by another and then another.

"Fuck me!" he ordered, his fingertips digging into the flesh on my hips.

I moaned and moved forward, doing as he demanded. My body didn't want to cooperate. I was shaking with uncontrollable need, another orgasm leaving me in a paralytic grip.

"Jack," I cried out, begging for him to take and give at the same time.

He growled and moved my body over his, sliding me back and forth as my hands dug into his shoulders. I began to move in time to the rhythm he was setting, throwing my head back and letting my hair brush across his thighs, my breasts thrust up into the cool night air. I could feel my nipples pucker as a cool breeze washed over us. The stark cold was in direct contrast to the heat we were producing, creating new sensations that were erotic and feeding our passion.

When he slapped my ass, my body erupted into a pool of liquid heat. I cried out, riding him faster as the orgasm spun me higher and higher. He jolted up, standing with me still connected to his body. He walked to the railing, dropped me to my feet, and spun me around. My hands gripped the railing, my body still quivering with the orgasm.

"Hold on tight, baby. Look at the moon while I fuck you under the stars." He growled near my ear as his hand moved up and down my spine before grabbing my ass and squeezing hard.

His body moved against mine, his slick head found my opening and pushed inside my body with one easy thrust. I pushed back against him, taking him a little deeper and pulling a groan from his lips.

"More," I demanded, holding onto the railing for dear life.

"I'm going to give you more," he shot back.

He thrust hard, my feet sliding over the smooth deck before his hands gripped my hips and pulled me back to my original spot.

"More," I cried out.

He muttered something incoherent and thrust hard and deep, repeating the action several time until I found myself pressed against the railing once again with nowhere to go. His body pummeled mine, as I stared out over the water. I couldn't believe we were fucking on the deck of a yacht with a full staff below.

I looked up at the stars and smiled, letting myself get lost in the moment. One hand reached around and grabbed my breast. I pushed back, bending over, creating a new angle that tickled new nerves deep inside my passage.

"Fuck me." He growled, his tempo picking up as he drove in and out.

"Yes, yes, yes!"

The stars erupted before me as he took my body to new heights. A soft spray of mist washed over me as my body arched and bucked. I heard him shout his release, his arm snaking around my waist and holding me in place as he jerked and spasmed inside me. I was gasping for air, smiling as his breathing began to slow.

"Holy shit," he muttered, kissing the side of my throat before brushing my hair to the side and kissing the back of my neck.

"That was amazing." I breathed out.

He stepped away from me before spinning me around to face him. His mouth was gentle as he gave me the sweetest post orgasmic kiss.

"You're amazing," he whispered.

He took my hand, leading me across the deck and picking up our scattered clothing as we went. We both dressed, stopping to kiss every few seconds.

"I can't believe we just did that up here," I said as we moved back to the couch.

He crouched in front of me, grabbed one foot and slid my boot on, carefully zipping it up. He put on the other one before sitting beside me on the couch, his arm wrapping around my shoulders and pulling me close.

"I should tell the captain to start heading back," he said in a soft voice.

"Do we have to?" I pouted.

He kissed the top of my head. "Unfortunately, we do. Come on, let's get you back to the heaters and I'll go let them know it's time to head in."

I sighed, sad to have our night over. I flopped in one of the chairs, the patio heater sending out heat and warming my chilled skin. I was determined to stay right where I was until I had to leave the little slice of heaven we had carved out for ourselves. He returned to the deck a few minutes later and quickly tucked the blanket around me before curling up in the chair next to me. We held each other close, watching the scenery change from the sweet serenity of the open water to the busy city skyline.

"Thank you for tonight. Everything was absolutely amazing," I said as we pulled into the marina.

"You're welcome. It was one of the best nights of my life, and I'm glad I got to spend it with you."

He walked me down the dock to his waiting car. "I should call a car for you," he said.

"Ride home with me?" I asked.

He grimaced. "I don't know. That could be risky."

I shook my head. "I don't want the night to end. No one is going to see us."

He kissed me again. "I could never say no to you."

We climbed into his car, and I tried to snuggle against him. We shared a few sweet kisses on the ride home. I wished it would take hours. I didn't want to leave the warmth and safety of his arms. I sighed with resignation when he passed the gates of the estate before coming to a stop.

"I'll miss you," he whispered against my lips.

"I'll miss you," I said before getting out of the car and making my way up to the gate.

As I looked up at the sprawling mansion awash in soft lighting with the glorious moon hanging in the sky above it, I couldn't help but feel like I was walking into a gilded cage. I had a real under-standing for all those fairy-tale princesses who were locked in a tower unable to enjoy life. The mansion was beautiful and despite its vast size, it had always felt warm and welcoming. Not now. All I could think about was the fact that the moment I stepped onto the property, I was a prisoner behind the luxurious walls. I couldn't be with the man I loved.

CHAPTER 17

JACK

This time, I had stuck to my guns. I hadn't called her or texted her since I dropped her off in the early morning hours after our night together on the yacht. I had kept my promise to myself. When she had texted me, I had tried to make myself ignore her—I couldn't.

The idea of the pact was still stuck in my head. As far as I was concerned, if we both agreed to wait one year before we made a move, it would give us both time to really clear our heads. We could each work on our families and try to find out what the feud was about. I wanted to test the waters and find out what was the worst that could happen should Nat and I choose to get married.

I knew it would have a serious ripple effect, which was why the one-year time period would give us a chance to smooth things out. It would prove to our families we tried. We tried to make them happy, but ultimately, we wanted to be together. I knew it meant we would both need to date other people to see if we could move on from each other. It was going to be extremely difficult, but I was willing to sacrifice if it meant there was a chance to be with her. If it was meant to be it, it would be. If she or I happened to meet someone else and fall madly in love, we would have to accept the fact our love wasn't real.

"Bullshit," I muttered. It was real. There was no doubt in my mind about that.

I shoved the last of my toiletries in my overnight bag, grabbed my phone charger, and stuffed it in the pocket before I headed out the door. I drove to the hotel about twenty minutes out of the city and casually walked to the front desk.

"David Jones checking in," I said.

The person typed my name in the computer. "I have you right here. That'll be four hundred dollars."

I gave him cash, which caused him to raise an eyebrow.

"Can I have a credit card to put on file?"

I shook my head. "No. I'll give you this instead," I said, and counted out five crisp one-hundred-dollar bills.

"Sir, I need—"

I gave him a look that made it clear he wasn't getting a card. I slid another hundred to him. "Your tip."

He nodded and quickly typed on the keyboard before handing me a room key and giving me brief directions to the suite. I wasn't about to give him a credit card and leave a paper trail. Not to mention the name discrepancy was sure to raise some red flags.

I took my bag and headed for the elevator. She clearly hadn't arrived yet. The price of the room told me she had reserved one of the nicest suites in the place. I didn't mind. I was looking forward to another night with her. I had been trying to convince myself I would never have her sweet, naked body under mine again after we had left the yacht. My brain refused to buy the story I kept trying to sell.

When I let myself in the room I grinned. It was the honeymoon suite. There were rose petals scattered on the massive king-size bed and a bottle of champagne chilling. A bowl of plump red strawberries sat alongside it.

I dropped my bag and checked out the place. The huge tub in the bathroom had candles on one edge with an assortment of bubble baths in a cute little basket. I looked at the tub and grinned. It was definitely going to get some use tonight, I decided.

"Jack?" I heard her call my name, and I walked out of the bathroom.

"Hi, Mrs. Jones," I said with a wink.

She laughed. "I'm not so creative apparently."

I shrugged. "I gave the man enough cash that I don't think it mattered."

Her mouth dropped open. "You did too?"

I threw my head back and laughed. "He is going to be eating fine tonight."

"It will be worth every dollar."

I stepped toward her, enveloping her in my arms and kissing her like I hadn't seen her in years. "I missed you."

"I've been dying without you," she confessed, making me smile.

Her words warmed my heart. "There's one hell of a tub in there. I want you naked and wet."

She smiled. "Wet with water or wet because of you?"

"Both."

"I ordered room service while I was down there. It should be here in the next thirty minutes," she said and the coy smile on her face told me she was up to something.

"Should I be worried?"

Her cheeky grin promised many debauched things were headed my way and I couldn't wait. "Maybe a little. We'll feast tonight."

"I want to feast on you."

"Maybe later."

"That room service better hurry up or they are going to catch us in a very compromising position." I growled.

"Down, big boy, there's plenty of time," she cooed, running her hand over my crotch.

"Nat, don't tease me."

She cupped me through my jeans. "I plan to tease, tantalize, and titillate until it's you who is screaming my name," she whispered before moving her hand and walking away.

I didn't let her get away and snaked out my hand, grabbing hers and yanking her body against mine. "Damn it, woman. I'm hard and I need you now."

I guided her hand back to where my erection was straining against the denim. Her mouth opened, and I quickly took advantage, plunging my tongue into her mouth, sucking on her tongue while grinding against her.

A knock on the hotel room door stopped my attack. I was on the verge of taking her right there on the floor of the hotel room.

The waiter rolled in a cart with shiny lids covering various plates. Natasha gave the man his tip before he quickly exited the room. She lifted one lid to expose more fresh fruit and a dish of fresh whipped cream. There was another bottle of champagne and a bottle of wine as well. A platter of what I knew to be gourmet cheeses and meats along with several varieties of crackers was under the other dome lid.

"I figured we'd need lots of snacks." She winked.

I nodded. "Good thinking. Now get naked. I'll start the bath."

She giggled before walking to the door and throwing the lock. I watched her grab the champagne and two glasses before sauntering to the bathroom.

"I was going to let you see me strip, but you're being far too bossy."

"I'm going to watch you strip," I said firmly.

I followed her into the bathroom and as promised, she gave me a hell of a show while I lit the candles and tossed in the fresh rose petals before adding an entire bottle of bubble bath to the running water. I watched as she pulled her long black hair up in a messy bun on top of her head, little wispy strands following around her neck.

"Your turn." She breathed out when she was standing nude before me.

"Take off my clothes," I ordered her.

"Gladly," she said before undoing my pants and lifting my shirt as high as her small five-four frame would allow.

We held each other close, our heated skin pressing together before we climbed into the hot, aromatic water. We sat at opposite ends of the large whirlpool tub, sipping champagne and chatting about our week. I leaned over and pushed the button to turn on the jets, stirring the water up while massaging our bodies.

"Have you given my idea any more thought?" I asked, knowing I was beating a dead horse, but I really wanted her to agree to it. It was the closest I was going to get to an actual engagement.

Her coy grin told me she knew exactly what I was talking about but was going to play innocent. "Idea? You've had a lot of ideas and most of them have worked out very well for me."

"This one will too."

"I thought we already discussed your idea and I explained how much I didn't like it?" she said, sipping her champagne.

"You have to admit it's a good idea. We make our families happy by dating a few people and then when it doesn't work out, they can't be that upset that we chose each other," I insisted, completely confident with my plan.

"What if you or I happen to meet someone, and we realize they are the ones we want to be with? What if this little plan of yours backfires?"

I shrugged a shoulder. I seriously doubted that would happen. "Then so be it. If you love something set it free and all that, right?"

"You would just walk away?" she asked with shock on her face.

I nodded. "I would."

"Liar."

I grinned. "I would try, is that better?"

"And would we tell our families about this pact?"

I shook my head. "No way! I say we wait a year, do our best to stay apart and date other people. Go out with guys your dad fixes you up with. Give it a shot."

She wrinkled her nose. "I don't like the thought of you going out with other women."

"I don't like the thought of another man's hands touching your body." I snarled.

"Yet this is your idea," she mumbled.

"I'm thinking about our long-term happiness. I want to be with you, Nat. I want you to be happy and I can't think of a better way."

She sipped her champagne, her pretty pink toenails were poking through the mountain of bubbles around my chest as she watched me. "Okay."

I blinked, not sure I heard her correctly. "What? Okay? Really?"

She shrugged one naked shoulder. "I'm game. We'll try it and I guess we'll see what happens. If fate truly wants us together, then it will happen."

"I agree. Should we toast to the pact?"

She leaned forward, holding up her glass. The movement gave me a very nice view of her breasts. I nearly forgot what we were supposed to be doing as I stared openly at the soapy bubbles clinging to her skin.

"Hello," she said in a singsong voice.

My eyes drifted up to meet hers. "You're too sexy for words."

"To our pact," she said, and we clinked our glasses together before each of us took a drink, sealing the deal.

"Now that we have all that out of the way, I feel like you're too far away from me," I said, putting my glass on the edge of the tub.

"I agree."

She put down her glass and moved between my legs, kissing me before seating herself in front of me, her back pressed against my chest, my erection poking her in her back. I wrapped my arms around her waist, loving the feel of her naked, slick body pressed against mine. Between the scented candles, the rose petals, and the fragrance in the bubble bath, I felt as if I were caught up in a delicious bubble of fruit and flowers.

"We're going to be okay," she murmured, leaning her head against my shoulder as she looked up at me.

I nodded, giving her a quick kiss on the lips. "Damn straight we will be. This is too good to ever think about losing."

She sighed in contentment, my larger body cradling hers. I couldn't imagine letting her go, but I knew I had to do it if I wanted to be with her in the future.

CHAPTER 18

NATASHA

I dabbed on a bit of lip gloss and smacked my lips before grabbing my purse and heading out the door.

"Bye, Mom," I said with a wave as I strolled past the dining room where my mother was taking her lunch.

I kept moving, not giving her a chance to ensnare me in a conversation. I was already running late for my lunch with Ashley. My mom had a penchant for getting into long talks about anything and everything when I was headed out the door.

The driver was already waiting for me when I walked outside. I wasn't thrilled to be taking the limo, but I still hadn't bought a car. I needed to. I felt like I had one foot out the door. I did if I was being honest with myself. I had the romantic notion Jack and I would run away together.

When the limo stopped in front of the fancy restaurant, I smoothed down my short skirt and with a page taken from the *Limo Exiting 101* book, I carefully placed my purse at my knees, blocking any sneak peeks up my skirt.

"Thank you, I'll call when I'm ready to go," I told the driver before heading inside.

I gave my name to the hostess and was escorted to the table I had reserved earlier that morning. I sat down and ordered the cursory mimosa. It was a rule when one came to a place like this. People in my social circle were practically expected to drink from the moment they woke up.

"Hey," Ashley said cheerily taking her seat at the table.

"Hi." I smiled.

"I was wondering if you had run away from home. Where have you been?" she asked.

I shrugged a shoulder. "Doing research for my company and hanging out with Mom."

"I bet that made her happy."

"It did. She's planning a renovation to her master bedroom and wanted my advice. We did a lot of fabric shopping and even flew over to Chicago for a day to meet with some textile dude. It is mind-blowing how much work she puts into these renovations."

Ashley smiled. "I'm not that surprised. So, how's it going on the one-who-shall-not-be-named front?"

I rolled my eyes. "Same. Well, not entirely the same. We made a pact."

That seemed to intrigue her. She leaned forward. "A pact, like you're going to kill someone for him and he kills someone for you?"

My mouth dropped open in horror. "God no! What the hell have you been watching? You're nuts! Ash, you really have a very active and scary imagination."

She burst into laughter, earning us a few looks from fellow diners. "I'm teasing. I was watching old movies the other night and *Strangers on a Train* was on."

I rolled my eyes. "What is it with you and those old movies? Our generation might be horror freaks, but those old movies are scary in a horribly, creepy way."

She shrugged a shoulder. "It's good cinema. You should try watching a few."

"No way. I watched *The Birds* with you and nearly run screaming in terror every time I see them congregating in the park," I muttered, only a little embarrassed.

She waved a hand in the air, dismissing the movie topic. "What is this pact you speak of?" she asked, her eyes bright with laughter.

I cleared my throat, a little embarrassed to admit to it. "If neither of us has found someone to settle down with in the next year, we're going to get married," I announced, my chin up as I said the words.

Her eyebrow shot up. "You're joking. You have to be kidding. You would never—"

She stopped talking when I didn't smile or give any hint that it was a joke. I knew I should have expected her to think I was teasing. It was a ridiculous idea and not like me at all. Desperate times called for desperate measures and I was absolutely desperate to be with the man I loved.

I shook my head. "I'm not. We're going to give it a year. We'll try and date a few people and satisfy the family. After a year when we are both still single, we'll announce our love for each other and get married. They won't be able to ignore our wishes," I said, my voice quiet, not wanting anyone to overhear my plan.

She let out a long sigh. "A year? That's a long time. Are you sure you want to be in limbo that long?"

"I don't really have a choice. I mean, my options are to tell my parents right now and be disowned, or to try to make them happy by seeing other people for a few months before I drop my bombshell on them."

She wrinkled her nose. "But a year without seeing each other? That's a long time and your feelings might change."

"We were apart for two years and it was like we hadn't ever been apart, except for the sex. The sex proves we were apart for two years," I said with a grin.

"What if your dad still says no?" she asked in a soft voice.

I shrugged. "Then it's his problem. I will do what I can to ease him into it, but in the end, I want what's best for me. I want to be happy. He had my mom all these years. I want someone who makes me happy. He can't deny me that same happiness."

"Nat, your dad is a stubborn, powerful man. I think he can do anything he wants."

"I want to be with him. I've tried to stay away. This is the real thing. I can't ignore it. I want to be with Jack," I said firmly, wanting to climb to the top of the highest building and scream out my proclamation.

"I'm on your side, truly I am," Ashley said.

"Thank you. I appreciate it. I imagine the next twelve months is going to be difficult." I groaned, drinking my mimosa with gusto.

"It is going to be tough. Are you guys going to try and sneak around and see each other?" she asked.

I sighed. "I don't think so. I think the idea is to go cold turkey. I hate the idea of him dating other women and I know he feels the same way about me and other men. I trust him."

"Nat, I have to say this," she started, and I knew what was coming.

"Don't."

"What if he falls in love with another woman?" she asked in a gentle voice, her eyes soft and probing as she looked at me.

I nodded. "I know there's a chance, but I have to try. I don't see any other way for this to work. My parents are going to accuse me of making a rash decision. They're going to blame him for chasing me, and Elijah is going to get dragged into it. I don't want to lose my family, but I definitely don't want to lose Jack. I don't think I can ever be happy if he isn't in my life."

Our lunch orders were delivered, stopping the conversation. It wasn't long before Ashley got a wild smile on her face.

"What's on your mind?" I asked.

"There's a chance you might be getting married next year!"

"Shh." I hissed, not wanting to attract attention.

"We should go dress shopping. You can buy a dress and leave it at the shop. It'll take a good six months to get it made unless you want to have one designed for you. What kind of style are thinking?" she asked, excitement making her voice high-pitched.

My mind was boggled. "I don't know. I haven't even thought about it."

She shook her head with disgust. "Nat, you know it takes a year to plan a good wedding."

"I don't want to plan a wedding I don't know for sure is going to happen. Plus, don't you think my parents would find it suspicious if we announce we're together and hand them a wedding invitation for two weeks later? I think that's called premeditated," I said, joking.

"I'm so happy for you," she said.

"Thank you. Hopefully, it's all going to work out as planned. This whole thing could backfire in our faces."

She lifted her empty glass, summoning the waiter to get her a refill. "I've never seen you so happy."

"I am happy. Well, I am, but I'm also terribly afraid and nervous as hell."

We finished our lunches and left the restaurant, intent to do a little shopping.

"Remember the scuba diving trip when we were in Australia?" she asked conversationally.

I nodded. "I do. I don't think I've ever seen you as happy as you were that day."

She sighed and shook her head. "That was a good day. A great day."

"You walked around like a dog in heat," I said, unable to control my laughter.

"We were surrounded by the most gorgeous men in the world, shirtless, I might add, and you were not interested. They were every-where, and they were so attentive and kind and beautiful and abso-lutely every wet dream I've ever had," she said wistfully.

I couldn't help but laugh. "I think most women would have felt the same way. They were very attractive."

"Except you. You were the only straight woman on the planet who was uninterested," she grumbled, shaking her head with disgust.

"This is why the pact has to work. I don't know if I can ever be with another man. It's Jack. It's always been Jack. When I'm with him, I feel whole, like I can breathe better, and everything is just so much better. I don't know if I could ever truly be happy with another man," I explained, hoping she would understand.

"You've got it bad."

"I do. I know I do. I didn't plan it this way. I wanted to leave the city and go out and find a different man. I didn't want it to be him. I know this is going to tear my family apart." I sighed, picking up a blouse and holding it up to my chest before looking in a mirror.

Ashley was browsing the next rack over. "I know you didn't. I hope it all works out for your sake. I know you're head over heels for him. I can't imagine what your life will be like if you can't have him."

"Miserable," I muttered.

"Stay positive."

"One more year," I said, trying my best to sound cheery and hopeful.

Ashley had a few blouses in her hand as she headed for the dressing room. "A year. An entire year. Can you do it?"

"If it means getting what I want in the end, I'll have to. I'm probably going to be pretty cranky," I joked.

"Lock yourself in your room and don't come out. You're likely to eat a small human."

I burst into laughter and took my own selection into the dressing room next door. With each blouse I tried on, I couldn't help but wonder if Jack would like it. I had to stop thinking like that. I wasn't sure how I was going to do it, but I had to find a way to focus on the here and now and not Jack and our future together. Or lack of a future together.

CHAPTER 19

JACK

I wanted to tell myself I was kicking ass at the whole not seeing Nat thing, but that was a lie. I was struggling. Every morning I woke up and told myself it will be a little better today. The ache and the loss of not seeing her would ease and I could focus on work. It had yet to work. It seemed like the more I didn't see her, the more I thought about her. I wanted her so desperately.

I had thought about a million different ways we could still see each other. The pact had been a stupid idea. I didn't want to wait a year. We could keep sneaking around and in a year's time, we could make our big announcement. We'd have to go out on dates and all the other bull- shit during that year, but it would be better than not seeing her at all.

"You made it two years, Jack," I muttered to myself, burying my face in my hands as I sat behind my desk pretending to work. I had lost all ability to focus on anything. I had been slacking off and if I weren't who I was, I'd probably get my ass fired.

I inhaled a deep breath through my nose, trying to cleanse my soul of all thoughts of her. It had been just over two weeks since I had seen her last. I longed to have her in my arms. Every time I smelled roses, I thought of her in that bathtub. There were constant reminders of her throughout the day. Every time I felt like I had blocked her image from my head, I would hear a song, smell flowers, or see something that reminded me of her.

My iPad lay on my desk, the screen reminding me of what I couldn't have. As if I wasn't tortured enough, I had been browsing engagement rings. I wanted to get Natasha the perfect ring. I'd considered having one custom made for her, but I had no idea where to start. Nat's style and personality made me think of elegant while maintaining a sense of uniqueness. I needed a ring that matched that style. I didn't want anything garish that would look as if I were trying too hard.

I let myself get lost in the ring shopping, the computer screen with a spreadsheet outlining the profit and loss for one of the companies we were going to acquire ignored as I let myself dream about slipping one of the rings on Nat's finger.

I heard a knock on my opened door and two seconds later, Elijah was strolling through the door.

"Hey," I said, hoping I didn't look as guilty as I felt.

His eyes drifted to the iPad on my desk, one brow raised. "Ring shopping?"

I smiled. "No, company shopping."

He took a seat in one of the available chairs across from my desk and folded one leg over his knee as he eyed me carefully. "Company shopping?"

"Yes, we're considering acquiring the company and I'm doing a little research on them," I said, hoping he believed my lie.

"Oh."

I exited off the page and turned off the tablet. "What brings you by?" I asked easily.

He shrugged one big shoulder. "I wanted to see if you were available to go grab a drink."

I grinned. "Rough day?"

"Something like that."

I could tell something was off with him. "Is everything okay?"

"Just a really shitty day and I could use a stiff drink. I need to blow off some steam," he said, and I could hear the strain in his voice.

The guy didn't have an easy time of it. I knew he wanted to take over his father's company. At least, that's what he said he wanted to do. All through high school and college, Elijah had rebelled against his father. He had been the firstborn son and the heir to the Levy empire, a lot like Grayson. There was a lot of pressure put on him. He didn't feel like he had a choice in what he did with his life. His destiny had been decided the day he'd been born.

"Let me wrap this up and we can go," I told him, wanting to be there for my friend.

I quickly saved the spreadsheet, tucked my tablet into my briefcase, and shut down the computer.

"Thanks, I should have called but once I left the office, I kind of wandered and ended up here."

"You know I'm always up for a drink," I joked.

"You're a good friend, Jack," he said, putting his hand on my shoulder as we headed for the elevators.

I could feel the guilt in the pit of my stomach like a heavy ball. I hated lying to him. I knew if he found out about me and Nat, he would see it as the worst kind of betrayal. I hated the idea of hurting him or causing him pain, but he had to know I was the man for Natasha. My mind started on a path down memory lane, a path that included numerous one-night-stands and rather unbecoming behavior. That was in the past. That had been in my wild youth. I hadn't been that man in years. Elijah would have to see that.

"Corner bar?" I asked.

"Works for me," he said with a serious lack of enthusiasm.

We strolled down the sidewalk, ignoring the looks from the single, young female executives who were hustling by on their way to grab a cab or back to work. We walked in silence. I could tell he was in a seriously shitty mood. I'd wait until after he got the first drink in him before I began to pry into what was eating at him.

We sat at a small table pushed up against the window and were quickly delivered two scotches served on paper coasters. I sipped from my drink, staring out the window at the people moving up and down the street. I wondered what their stories were. Did they have someone they loved waiting for them at home? Is that why they were in such a hurry?

"My dad is really in a mood lately," Elijah said, breaking the silence.

I looked at him and could see the little lines of stress around the corners of his eyes. His brow was furrowed, and he looked much older than the thirty-four years I knew him to be.

"What's going on?" I asked.

He shook his head. "I'm not sure. He's been in a shit mood for a few weeks. When he's mad at something or someone, I get to be his proverbial punching bag. One of these days, I have a feeling it will be the real thing."

"What's got him fired up?" I pressed.

Elijah shrugged a shoulder before running a hand through his hair that looked so much like Nat's. "I don't know. I thought he'd be in a better mood when Nat came home, but it seems like things are worse."

"I thought he was happy to have her back?"

"I did too. Something's off."

I cleared my throat, trying to relieve the pressure of the guilt boiling in my belly. "Maybe Nat can talk to him," I suggested.

Elijah scoffed. "Nat has no idea who our father really is. She won't believe me when I tell her the guy is acting like a complete dick. She always takes his side and vice versa. She's always been treated like a princess and has never truly seen my dad pissed. He saves that for me. I don't even think my mom has seen that other side of him that he keeps hidden so well."

"I'm sorry. What do you think has him in such a bad mood?" I pried, hoping he didn't suspect anything about Natasha and me.

"I have no idea. It's seriously gotten worse since Nat has been back. I mean, the first week she was home, it was all good, but lately, my dad is acting weird. I can feel him staring at me, like he hates me."

"He doesn't hate you," I assured him.

"My dad has never held me in high regard. Granted, I didn't always give him a lot of reason to, but I never want to see him fly into a rage. Remember when we got caught spray-painting the football field at school?" he said, shaking his head.

I smirked. "We painted, then burned, but yes, I remember."

"I thought he was going to kill me that night. He yelled at me in front of my mom and Nat, but then they went to bed. I was in the kitchen making a sandwich and he flipped out. He pushed me against the fridge and freaked. I thought for sure he would kill me. My sister and mother have no idea how mean my dad can truly be."

"Are you afraid of him?" I asked, suddenly feeling horrible for potentially being the cause of Wayne Levy's shitty mood. I couldn't let Elijah take the heat for something I was doing.

Elijah finished off his drink before putting the empty glass on the coaster, his blue eyes looking directly into mine. "I'm younger, faster, and bigger than my dad. I'm not afraid of him anymore. He used intimidation when I was younger and dumber. He knows damn well that isn't going to work anymore."

That gave me a modicum of relief. "I'm sorry. I don't know what to say."

He looked me in the eye. "I guess there's nothing you can say, can you? This is my cross to bear. I was born a Levy. You were born a Bancroft. Was your dad anything like mine?"

I shook my head. "No. He raised his voice and we all tried his patience, but it was always my mom who scared me," I joked.

"Nat has no idea," he mumbled.

"What do you mean?" I asked, suddenly on guard once again.

"She thinks she can waltz around and do no wrong. She has this idea she's going to start her own company. Dad isn't going to let her. He's humoring her. He spoiled her rotten when she was younger and now she has this sanitized view of him. She doesn't know my dad— not like I do. I hope she never crosses him."

I had to bite back my own comment. If Wayne Levy ever treated Nat the way he treated Elijah, he'd be answering to me.

"I think your dad and Nat have a different relationship than the two of you. I can't imagine him ever yelling at her, let alone treating her the way he does you," I said, my voice solemn.

Elijah was still looking at me. I wasn't sure if it was my own guilty conscience making me nervous or if he knew something. If he knew about Nat and me, why wouldn't he just come right out and say it? He would be screaming at me and threatening to kill me. Unless, he was waiting to see if I would confess. I couldn't help but feel as if I was being tested.

I needed to talk to Natasha and find out if there was any way her dad and brother knew about us. I couldn't call her. It would put her at even more risk. I had to find a way to warn her. Elijah's description of his own father made me very concerned for Nat. Maybe they'd already found out and confronted her. A pit of fear opened up in my chest. I hadn't talked to her in over two weeks. What if—

I couldn't finish the thought. I schooled my features and ordered us another round. I couldn't give anything away. I had to play it cool. *Be normal.*

CHAPTER 20

NATASHA

I had spent way too long browsing my massive closet trying to find exactly the right outfit to wear. I wanted to look absolutely stunning tonight. Tonight would be the last time I got to see Jack for a year, and I wanted to make sure he had a good memory to fall back on. If he was out with another woman, I wanted him to think about me. I wanted it to be my body he fantasized about when he went home alone after a dull date.

I knew I'd probably run into him on occasion. We did tend to run in the same circles. I hoped I could stand the sight of seeing him dancing with another woman or holding another woman's hand as he led her into a restaurant.

Tonight, it was only going to be us. It was our last night together. Every time I said the words in my head, my heart clenched. It almost felt like a small heart attack. I had gone two years without him and I managed to survive, but it was different now. We were different. Our relationship, if that's what it could be called, was different.

When Ashley had called me yesterday to tell me she had a surprise for me, I had been expecting something like a new handbag or something like that. She'd been really excited but refused to give me a single hint about what it was. With Ashley, one never knew. When I showed up at her place, a little nervous about what her surprise could be, she handed me a box with a red bow. Inside the box, there was a phone. Then, she left me alone in her living room. Within minutes, Jack called the phone. It was all very James Bond-like, which was a crazy turn-on. We arranged to meet tonight at his place. He told me he would explain later about the phone. I was very intrigued; although, I would have gladly met him without all the cloak-and-dagger stuff.

"Focus, Nat," I mumbled, staring at the three choices I had pulled out of my closet. At least I had narrowed it down to three, which was a huge success, but everything had to be perfect.

I finally settled on a little black dress. The new black teddy Ashley and I picked out yesterday in anticipation of my big night with Jack would match perfectly with the dress. Add the new pair of black boots that took the lingerie from sexy to sultry and I felt like a vixen in one of those James Bond movies. I knew he loved me in boots. These had a killer heel on them, which added several inches to my height. With my makeup perfectly applied, I carefully headed downstairs, hugging the railing to keep from tumbling down the grand staircase in the killer heels.

I had just made it downstairs when I heard my father's booming voice. "Natasha!"

I knew he was going to comment on the outfit. It was a little skimpy and it was a little weird to have my dad see me in it. I sucked in a deep breath and headed for the study where his voice had come from, preparing myself for his lecture about the proper way to dress for a woman in my standing.

"What's up, Dad?" I asked in my best nonchalant voice, moving to stand behind one of the leather couches to hide the shortness of my dress.

I was convinced there was an arrow above my head flashing and highlighting my deception. I couldn't look guilty or act like I was up to no good. I had always gone out. Tonight was nothing new. I just had to play it cool. The whole parent judging thing shouldn't be happening at my age. I was setting myself up for these awkward moments by continuing to live in the house. Once again, I reminded myself I had to get my own place.

"Where are you headed dressed like that?" he asked, looking up from the brief he was holding in his hand. There was a cigar in his other hand, which seemed like a dangerous combination to me.

I steeled my nerves. "I have a date."

He grinned, his mustache moving with the action. He was clearly happy to hear the news I was dating. "Oh? With who?"

I waved a hand through the air and gave him a coy smile. "Someone I went to school with."

"Really? I didn't realize you were seeing anyone."

I shook my head. "I'm not seeing him."

"You just said you were going out on a date. Is this someone you're interested in?"

I sighed. My dad and I had a close relationship and usually his questions wouldn't bother me, but I hated lying to his face. The more questions he asked, the more lying I had to do.

I shrugged my shoulders. "I'm not sure. We're going out and we'll see how things go."

His smile slipped a little. "That sounds vague. You said you knew him? Did he call you?"

It suddenly felt like more of an interrogation than his usual fatherly interest. "We ran into each other the other day and he asked if I wanted to go out tonight, I agreed. I'm not headed down the aisle anytime soon, Dad," I joked, hoping to lighten the conversation, even if the intensity of it was likely all one-sided.

My dad was still staring at me and making me uncomfortable. I could see the scrutiny on his face. He was looking at me like he used to if he found a scratch on his prized car after I borrowed it. "Is he a good guy? I think I should meet anyone you are thinking about dating."

I nodded. "Yes, he is a good guy and, Dad, I'm thirty. You can't meet every guy I go out with."

"I don't want you wasting your time on losers who only want your money," he warned. "You're a pretty girl and with your name and wealth, some guys will see that as a target."

I shook my head. "He isn't like that. He has plenty of his own money," I assured him.

"Do I know him?" he asked, and I suddenly got the idea he was asking a question he already knew the answer to.

"I don't think so," I blurted out.

He was still studying me. "Why don't you let me set you up with Don's son. I bet the two of you would get along well."

I nearly stuck my finger down my throat. That would be juvenile. "Um, no, I don't think so. I don't need you setting me up."

"If you don't like Don's son, I'm sure there are other men out there worthy of you."

"Thanks, Dad. I'll keep that in mind. I need to get going. Are you okay with this?" I asked in my sweetest, most innocent voice.

He smiled, stood and smoothed out one of his many dark-blue suits, and gave me a quick kiss on the cheek. "Of course, princess. You know I'm only looking out for your best interest. Have fun," he said, moving to sit back in the chair he'd vacated.

"Don't wait up!" I said with excitement as I rushed out of the study. I popped my head into the limo, handed the driver a fifty, and told him to keep going.

Then, I headed down the driveway, sticking to the shadows as best I could. The boots were not great for navigating the pretty cobble-stone my mother had insisted be used for the long driveway. I made it to the gate and quickly slipped out without anyone noticing.

I saw the faint glow of taillights another fifty feet down the street and groaned. I was seriously regretting my choice of footwear. I managed to make it to the car to realize it wasn't Jack's car at all. I was about to turn and go the other direction when the driver got out.

"Miss Levy, Jack sent me," he said.

I breathed a sigh of relief and got in the back seat. Jack was taking the clandestine thing very seriously. When the driver stopped in front of Jack's building, I quickly exited the car. The anticipation of seeing him had me practically running through the lobby to get to the elevator.

As soon as he opened the door of his apartment, I fell into his arms.

"I missed you." I breathed out before inhaling the scent of him.

He looked completely casual in his black slacks and a black dress shirt with the top few buttons undone. His sleeves were rolled up to his elbows. He was the sexiest man alive. All the men they kept putting on the covers of the magazines had nothing on Jack. Jack had it all. He was tall, muscular, his eyes were intoxicating, and charm oozed from every pore. And he was mine.

"I missed you, baby. Come in," he said, shutting the door behind me.

I looked around and noticed there were no lights on. The soft glow was coming from what looked like at least a hundred candles of every shape and size placed around his huge open living and dining area.

"Jack, this is amazing." I gasped, looking around the luxurious space.

"I wanted tonight to be special," he murmured, coming to stand behind me, his mouth nuzzling my neck.

I noticed the dining table already set with a bottle of wine and two glasses had already been poured. "I'm impressed, truly."

"I made dinner," he said, taking my hand and leading me toward the table before pulling out a chair and instructing me to sit down.

"You made dinner?" I asked with real surprise.

He chuckled. "I did. Nothing too fancy, a simple lasagna my mom used to make all the time."

I took a sip from the red wine in front of me and looked around his home. The little flame on each candle danced and created shadows on the walls while giving the room a romantic orange glow. I committed every detail to memory, knowing that night would get me through many lonely nights in my future.

He was wearing a flowery pair of oven mitts on his hands, carrying a steaming pan of lasagna. The sight of a man like him wearing feminine oven mitts was a huge turn-on. I found myself staring at him as he placed the pan on the table before dashing back to the kitchen to grab a bowl of sliced bread. He took off the oven mittens and tossed them at the opposite end of the table before taking his seat.

"What?" he asked when I couldn't stop looking at him.

"You're so hot," I said on a sigh.

He leaned forward and gave me a quick kiss. "Baby, you are killing me with those boots. Eat. You're going to need the calories, so will I with what I have planned to do to your body tonight. We've got a lot of lovin' to do before we have to say goodbye."

His words dropped like a heavy blanket over the romantic meal. I could feel my heart squeezing. Tonight was our goodbye. It was hard to say what the future had in store for us. I knew there was a chance tonight could be our last night together—ever. Life wasn't kind. Things happened.

I stared into his eyes and smiled. "I don't want to say goodbye."

He reached out and cupped my face in his hand. "We'll be okay. We're going to get through this. Now, let's not spoil this meal. I want to enjoy every minute I have with you."

I nodded, blinking back the tears that were threatening to fall. "You're right. That lasagna smells delicious. I can't believe you made it. What other secrets are you hiding?" I teased.

He chuckled as he dished up a healthy serving of the cheesy meal onto my plate. "You're just going to have to stick around to find out."

I nodded, hoping I got the chance to uncover all of Jack Bancroft's secrets.

CHAPTER 21

JACK

I looked at her from across the table, watching her as she took a bite of the bread I had picked up fresh from the bakery.

"What? Am I totally pigging out? This is amazing. I cannot believe you cooked. I hope you know I will expect many more meals in our future," she mumbled around a mouthful of bread.

"I will gladly make you whatever you want. I don't guarantee it will be edible, but I will do whatever I can to keep you happy."

She grinned. "And I you. Except cooking. I'm sorry, that is just not a skill my mother felt I needed to learn. I guess it was decided from early on I would never be barefoot and pregnant. A Levy woman plans parties, looks beautiful, and knows just what to say—she does not cook, clean, or do anything else that would be unbecoming of a woman in her position," she said in a high-pitched, haughty tone.

"I'm sorry. I'm guessing you've heard that a time or two throughout your life."

She let out a long sigh. "Yes and no. I mean, it was never said exactly like that, but it was made clear I was expected to be proficient in table settings, proper greetings, and things like that. I was never asked to cook. Although, I remember my nanny teaching me how to make pancakes when I was younger. At least until my mother found out and nearly fainted at the horror of her daughter cooking over a hot burner. God forbid," she muttered.

"You were destined for greatness," I teased.

She laughed. "Elijah was destined for greatness. I was destined to marry well and breed perfect little Levy descendants. My dad wants to build an empire. I think it's because he came from nothing and built a fortune. I mean, don't get me wrong, I love my dad dearly, but sometimes I hate all the pomp and circumstance and all the flaunting of wealth."

"I understand. I do. You are destined for greatness. You're great in every way. You're smart, beautiful, driven, sassy, and determined. I love that you are fiery and, unlike your father, you are humble," I said, reaching over to hold her hand.

"Thank you. You are so sweet."

I wrinkled my nose and shook my head before taking my hand back. "I'm not sweet. Please don't call me sweet."

She giggled again. "You are a manly man. You're all caveman, alpha, sexy, and have a rocking hard body."

I nodded. "Thank you, that's more like it."

She rolled her eyes. "I'm going to clean this up."

"No! Sit. I've got it."

"Jack," she protested.

"Go sit. I'm just going to put this in the fridge and leave the rest for tomorrow," I said, helping her to her feet.

"Thank you," she said and sauntered toward the couch. I quickly cleaned up, not wanting to waste a minute of our time together.

I refilled her wineglass before carrying it to the sofa where she was sitting. Everything was absolutely perfect. It was all working out like I had hoped. The dinner had been good, which had surprised me a little. I wanted her to think I was a great cook, but the truth of it was, I really wasn't great in the kitchen. I could scrape by, but I would never be considered a gourmet cook. Mom's lasagna recipe was easy enough to follow.

"Thank you," she said when I handed her the glass.

I walked to the control pad and quickly turned on the gas fireplace. Within seconds, the soothing glow filled the room. With another push of a button, I turned on some jazz, turning it down low before rejoining her on the couch.

"Warm?"

"Perfect."

"Thank you for coming over."

She giggled softly. "You know I wanted to. I've missed you like crazy. Is it weird I missed you more these past few weeks than I did the two years I was gone?"

"No, it isn't weird. I feel the same way. I've been struggling to think of anything else," I confessed.

"How are we going to survive a year?" She breathed.

I wrapped my arm around her shoulder and pulled her against me. "We'll make it."

"Are we going to have these little sneaky meetings to help us get through it?" she asked.

I sucked in a breath. "I don't know. I know I should say no, but damn, woman, I don't know how I'm going to survive a year without touching you. I'm going to have the worst case of blue balls known to mankind."

She started giggling. "I'm sorry."

"Don't be. I'm going to invest in a serious supply of lotion. I see a lot of calluses in my future," I mumbled.

Her hand clapped over her mouth. "Jack! My poor ears!"

"I'm only being honest with you. You make me hot and hard and there is little I can do to stop it. You are the sexiest woman I've ever laid eyes on. Now that I've tasted you, touched you, and watched your face when you orgasm, I will never, ever get it out of my head. I don't want to."

I could hear her breathing pick up. She was nearly panting. "Jack, you are making me crazy."

"Good."

"So, tell me about the phone. I've been dying to know why," she asked.

I took a deep breath. I didn't want to tell her about my suspicions, but I needed to give her a heads-up. "Your brother came to talk to me the other day. He said your dad was acting different. The way Elijah was talking, I got the impression something was off."

She groaned. "How do you think they found out?" she asked.

"I don't know that they did find out. Something just felt off, like Elijah knew more than he was saying," I told her, hoping to calm her down.

She took a sip of wine before answering. "You're right. My dad has been different. They can't possibly know, but maybe more of a suspicion."

"I hope so. I don't want to make trouble for you, Nat. I would not be able to handle it if I knew I did something that caused you any problems," I told her.

"I know you don't. We'll get through this, but I'm going to hold on to that phone. I need a lifeline," she said, nodding.

"Works for me. Maybe I should get one too," I mused aloud.

"Yes! That way if Elijah finds the phone, he won't recognize your number," she said.

"I could just block my number," I offered.

"No, come on. It'll be so much cooler if we both have burner phones. It will be like a real-life secret affair."

"It is a real-life secret affair. At least it was," I grumbled.

"Let's not talk about the end. Not tonight. Tonight, is about us spending our last night together," she said.

"Baby, you and those boots make it pretty tough for me to think about anything."

She stretched out her legs, the short dress riding up on her thighs as she moved her feet back and forth. "I bought them with you in mind."

I laughed, reaching out to run my hand over her covered calf. "I can't tell you what these boots do for my imagination."

Her legs dropped as she turned to look at me. "What if I told you the dress is only half the outfit?"

"Baby, if that tiny dress is half the outfit, the other half can't be much of anything."

"It's not."

Breath hissed from my lungs. I reached for her hand, bringing it between my legs, letting her feel how excited the mere mention of her other outfit made me.

"Looks like you got something happening there," she cooed.

"I do. Right now, I want to drag you into my bedroom and fuck you until neither one of us has the energy. I've wanted to bury my face between your legs from the very moment I opened that door and saw you standing on the other side."

"What's stopping you?" she asked, somewhat out of breath.

I took the glass from her hand and put hers and mine on the table, before standing up and pulling her into my arms.

"I want to dance with you," I whispered.

"Dance?" she asked.

"Yes, stay here. Don't move," I ordered, walking to the wall pad and turning up the music.

I walked back to her, admiring her beauty in the little black dress, loving the way the boots brought her face closer to mine. I kissed her, wrapping my arms around her and slowly moving back and forth. It wasn't an actual dance, but more of a mating ritual. I could feel her heart beating against my chest, her breath washing over my neck as we gently swayed back and forth.

"I never want to leave this place," she whispered.

"Me neither."

We danced a while longer. Having her in my arms was pure bliss. I knew I was going to look back at that moment and cherish it for years to come. No, for the rest of my life, no matter how things turned out. I was never going to forget what it was like to hold her close.

I leaned down and kissed her. There was a change in the atmosphere in the room. The sexual tension had escalated and could no longer be ignored. I could feel the vibrations coming off her body. She needed me as much as I needed her.

The kiss grew in intensity and just when I was ready to kick things up a notch, she stepped away from me.

"Wait," she said, holding up her hand.

"Wait?"

"I told you I wanted you to see my outfit."

I let my eyes roam over her body, taking in the low-cut top that gave me a very nice view of cleavage. Her tiny waistline was accented by the cut of the dress and her legs looked amazing with the high hemline that left plenty of skin exposed. Then it was the boots. Damn, those were some serious fuck-me boots if I ever saw a pair.

"Baby, you're rocking that dress."

She grinned. "Then wait until you see what's under it."

Her arms reached up behind her and the sound of a zipper being pulled down ever so slowly filled the room. I watched, holding my breath as the dress loosened before she carefully pushed it down her body and stepped out of the dress.

I couldn't breathe. "Fuck me." I groaned, wondering how in the hell I had managed to get so lucky.

Her breasts were lifted with a thin, gauzy material stretched across the nipples. The lace teddy covered her torso but stopped just above her hips. The tiny pair of panties peeking out from under the garter she was wearing sent my heart racing. She turned slightly to the right and bent her leg, giving me a seductive pose.

"Do you like it?"

My eyes traveled back up her body to meet her gaze. "I feel like I've died and gone to heaven. This is what heaven must be like."

"I assure you, you are very much alive, and I plan on taking full advantage of your body in every sense of the word," she said, her eyes sparkling with devilish desire.

I nodded. "I'm going to let you."

She slowly spun around, pausing to give me a good look of her ass before casting a glance over her shoulder. "Now, Jack," she demanded.

My nostrils flared as I lunged for her, scooped her up and carried her to my room where I planned on exploring every inch of her body.

"You're mine, Nat, all mine," I declared, setting her on my bed while I quickly shucked my clothes.

I stripped to my briefs. If I was as close to naked as possible, there was going to be nothing stopping me from taking her. Whenever I was with her, all self-control was lost. I felt like a rutting buck. Not tonight. Tonight, it was going to be slow. I wanted to make love to her. I had to prove she was more to me than a beautiful body.

CHAPTER 22

NATASHA

He placed me on the bed as if I were a fragile piece of glass. I could see him holding back. I was used to the intense fucking that always seemed to erupt between us whenever we were alone. This time it was different. We were both more inclined to take things slow, since we knew it would be our last time together for a long while.

"I want you to lie back," he whispered, his eyes focused on my body as he stood at the end of the bed looking at me.

I nodded, sliding onto the bed a bit more, then lying back, propping myself up on my elbows, watching him intently, ready to do whatever it was he wanted.

"Now, open your legs," he ordered.

I had yet another surprise for him. When I spread my legs, his eyes widened before looking up at me. I gave him a cheeky smile, my eyebrows dancing.

"Crotchless?" He choked the word.

I nodded. "All-access panties," I quipped. "I wanted to make sure we could get right to the good stuff if we wanted."

I watched him suck in a deep breath and knew he was fighting for control. I wanted to tell him to forget about being controlled. I wanted him. I wanted that fiery, wild sex we shared. I wanted him fierce and feral. I loved when he lost all control and gave me every piece of him.

"Natasha, I want you so bad," he said, his dark eyes full of emotion as he stared at me.

"I'm yours. You have me. Take me."

He stepped forward, his hands moving to my knees, caressing his fingertips along the inside of my thighs before unclasping the stocking from the garter. He crawled onto the bed, ordering me to slide higher onto the pillows. With a gentle touch, he bent my knees, opening me wide to his view. When he dropped to his elbows between my legs, I gasped in anticipation.

One finger reached out and spread the panties a bit more giving him complete access to my core. His mouth closed over me, sending shockwaves through my body. My hands fisted the comforter as I held on for dear life. His mouth was moving, his tongue was plunging, and I was convinced I was dying with pleasure. I moaned, thrashing my head back and forth as he teased me with his mouth.

"Jack!" I screamed when his index finger slid inside me, his teeth nibbling at my clit.

I lost all hope of control and bucked up, my heels dug into the mattress as I thrust myself against his face. I was a wild woman, unable to stop my body from demanding more as he feasted upon me, lapping up every last drop. I sagged against the bed, my legs falling open.

"I love how sweet you taste, baby," he said, crawling over my body, his hot breath heating my skin as he moved.

His mouth closed over mine as his hands went between my legs, working me up to another fevered frenzy of lust.

"Wait," I said, pushing his hand away from me.

"What?" he said, surprise in his voice.

"Roll over," I ordered.

"Baby, I'm not finished with you," he said, his fingers moving back between my legs.

"And I haven't started with you."

He grinned and rolled to his back. I got to my knees, the boots making it a little difficult to maneuver. I moved to take them off.

"Don't," he said firmly.

I nodded. Tonight was for him. I could work my way around the boots. I grabbed his underwear and slowly pulled them down his legs, excitement coursing through my veins as I stared at his engorged shaft.

With his underwear discarded, I reached up, wrapping my hand around him, and slowly stroking up and down. I lowered my mouth to him and slowly sucked, bobbing up and down, loving him with my mouth in the best way I knew how. Each moan from him made me take him deeper, wanting to give the same kind of pleasure he gave me. I let my teeth graze over him as I slid up his hard cock.

"Nat." He groaned, pushing my shoulders.

"Not yet," I replied.

He growled and moved away from me, before ordering me to my knees. He shifted behind me, his fingers moving between my legs and spreading my folds, making way for his entry. I held my breath as he slowly pushed inside me. I could feel the coiled strength in his muscles as he fought to maintain that fierce control.

His body moved, in and out, pushing me forward with each thrust. I rocked against him, taking him deeper, meeting him thrust for thrust.

"I love you." He groaned, his hand lovingly caressing me through the sheer lace covering my body.

His words washed over me, stirring up something deep within me. The orgasm that bloomed was unlike any I had achieved before. It started out slow, a tingling in my toes that was chased by a warming sensation that completely enveloped my body.

"I. Love. You." I gasped as the wave building inside me crashed over, leaving me speechless.

"That's it, there you go," he said in the sweetest tone as he slowly rocked in and out, drawing out my pleasure with each move.

I collapsed face-first on the bed, helpless to move. I felt his fingers move to the inside of my thigh and then the sound of my boots being unzipped. He took off one and then the other, sliding each stocking down after the boots were removed.

I rolled to my back and silently asked him to remove the lingerie. I wanted to feel his skin on mine. If tonight was going to be our last night together, I needed that intimate contact. His hands worked at the teddy, untying, then pulling it down until I was completely naked on the bed. His body covered mine, the crinkly hairs on his chest rubbing over my sensitive nipples as he held his weight on his elbows, his face hovering above mine.

"I don't know how I will survive a year without you," he whispered.

I shook my head. "Let's not think about that now."

He nodded and slowly lined himself up before sliding inside me once again, his eyes on mine as he filled me completely. It was as if our souls were joining. I stared into his dark eyes and swore I could see into his heart. I knew he loved me. I felt so much love coming from him it was overwhelming. When he was deeply seated inside me, he lowered his weight just a little as his mouth closed over mine.

We were connected, mind, body, and soul in that very moment. It was unexplainable. It felt so right. Everything about him was mine and I was his in every way. My hands glided up and down his spine, moving to grab his ass and squeezing it hard, pulling him deeper inside me.

I groaned, the sheer pleasure of being so close to him brought me to the brink. I could die a happy woman in that very moment and have no regrets.

"I never want to leave this moment," I whispered.

He kissed the tip of my nose. "I want to say the same, but, baby, I'm on the verge of exploding inside you."

I smiled. "Explode. I want to feel you deep inside me. I want to watch your face while you take your pleasure in my body."

His eyes squeezed shut as he inhaled through his nose. "I can never get enough of you. I want you more every time I have you. I can't get through a year. I can't do it," he said, his voice strained as he moved his weight to his elbows once again.

"We can do it. We have to. The promise of being able to be together will have to keep you going," I told him, reaching my hand up to cup his hard jaw.

He nodded. "I have to move, baby."

I wrapped my legs around his waist, pulling him against me. "Move."

His body moved in and out before he did a little hip roll that scraped along the insides of my slick passage, sending shivers of ecstasy through my body. My response encouraged him to do it again and again. Soon, we were both worked up to a fever pitch. Both of us gasping and moaning as we raced for the finish line together.

"I can't hold back," he said, grunting.

I arched up, needing more, demanding more. He understood my cue and moved to his knees, pulling my butt onto his thighs as he pushed inside me once again.

I gasped, the new angle was stretching me. "Oh God," I cried out, feeling a combination of pain and pleasure streak through my body.

His finger moved to my core, touching me just inside where his dick had me completely stretched. The pressure was too much. My head thrashed back and forth on the bed, my body jerked. It was too much. The pressure was far too intense for my brain to process.

"Fuck me, you're so wet!" he shouted, his finger working deeper inside.

I screamed as the intensity became too much for me to keep bottled up.

"Give it to me!" he shouted.

My hands stretched out across the bed as my body was gripped in a strange limbo. I couldn't find my release. It was just out of reach. I wanted the pleasure to last forever while needing it to end at the same time. He moved his finger, tweaking the nub before swirling over it.

Lights exploded behind my eyes. I screamed out, this time it was joined by a flood of juices flowing. He roared with supreme male dominance as he grabbed my body, bringing me forward as he fucked me hard and fast, prolonging the most violent orgasm I had ever endured. I was convinced I would die. No human being should ever experience such pleasure. His hands were around me, hugging me tight against him, his mouth closed over one nipple, clamping down with his teeth.

I arched my back, pushing the nipple deeper inside his mouth as he bounced me up and down, his body erupting inside of mine with hot, explosive bursts of liquid heat. Once our bodies had finally drained each other of all energy, I fell backward on the bed, he fell beside me. I was convinced I was hyperventilating as I struggled to catch my breath.

"Holy shit." He moaned.

I nodded. "Yes. That. My God. I'm broken."

"Did I hurt you?" he asked, his hand coming to rest on my chest.

"No. Absolutely not. I'm broken. I will never be the same. That was intense," I mumbled, my thoughts muddled as I tried to express my feelings.

He chuckled near my ear. "Me too. Broken. Spent. I don't have a drop left to give."

I sighed. "Good. I couldn't do it again if I wanted to."

Neither of us moved. I knew we were both completely wiped out. I was so glad I was spending the night. I didn't think I would be able to walk under my own steam. I had zero strength. My body kept jerking as little aftershocks of pleasure whipped through unexpectedly. I had a feeling moving would spark another orgasm. Everything felt raw between my legs. Even the air brushing over me was too much.

"Covers," I mumbled.

"Okay," he said, not moving.

I smiled. I was too tired to move.

CHAPTER 23

JACK

My body felt like I had just gone through the most grueling workout followed by the most relaxing massage. I didn't want to ever move again. I heard her moan beside me and I smiled. She was clearly feeling the same way.

"You're good to stay over?" I asked, my words slurred from exhaustion.

"Mm-hmm," she replied, snuggling against my side.

I let my eyes drift closed, exhaustion pulling me under. Sleep was hovering at the edges when I heard a knock on my front door.

"What the hell?" I grumbled, half asleep and not entirely sure I had actually heard the sound.

"Someone's at the door," she muttered, slapping my bare chest.

I rolled over, having no idea where my underwear may have landed and just reached for the first thing I could find—a pair of sweats that I was pretty sure weren't clean. She was pulling on my shirt as I walked out of my room. I checked the time as I walked by the clock on the microwave. It was after midnight. I wasn't expecting anyone.

I heard her footsteps behind me and stopped. "Go back to bed," I whispered.

"It's fine." She hissed back.

The knocking was much more persistent. I opened the door to find Elijah standing there, a look of murderous rage on his face. Everything suddenly became very clear. I moved to close the door, but one of the four bodyguards flanking Elijah flung his hand out, stopping the door.

Elijah pushed the door open, his eyes landing on his sister. His lip curled in disgust as he took in her state of dress. "Goddamn it, Nat! What the fuck are you thinking!"

I tried to step in front of Nat, wanting to shield her body from the other men, but Elijah shoved me hard, sending me into the wall as he grabbed Natasha's arm.

"Stop!" I ordered.

"Elijah, stop," Nat cried out.

I moved to slap Elijah's hand off her arm but was stopped by two of the bodyguards. Elijah pushed his sister toward one of the guards who had stayed in the hall.

"Get her out of here," Elijah said, seething.

"Don't do it," I said, shaking my head.

"Elijah, don't do this. You don't understand," Nat said, her voice filled with sadness.

Elijah spun around to look at his sister. "I told you to stay away from him."

"You don't understand. Let's go inside and we can explain. We'll talk like rational adults. Your bodyguards can wait out here," she pleaded.

"I understand plenty. You hooked up with him after I told you not to. Do you know what our father is going to do?"

Nat was shaking her head. "Don't tell him. Elijah, please, I love him. We're in love. We've been in love. Let us be happy. Don't make this into something ugly. I'm a grown woman. I can decide who I want to be with."

Elijah turned to look at me with disgust. "I can't believe you. You were supposed to be my best friend. You're fucking my sister? How could you do this to me?"

"I am your best friend. That doesn't change. It's like she said. I love her, Elijah," I insisted.

Elijah glared at me before looking back at his sister. "Do you know what this is doing to Dad? Do you know how pissed he is going to be? You've opened up a can of worms you can't sweet-talk your way out of Natasha."

"Don't tell him! You don't have to. We can keep this between us," Nat pleaded, her eyes wide with fear.

I didn't have the heart to tell her. Wayne Levy already knew. It was the only way to explain Elijah's presence with the guards. He'd sent his son to do his dirty work. He couldn't be bothered to get his hands dirty. It disgusted me that the man could be so vindictive and controlling.

He shook his head. "You know that will never happen. You made your bed, now you get to lie in it. Is this what you really want, Nat? Do you really want to be on Dad's bad side? Are you ready to lose that little crown he's always had perched on your head?"

She looked at her brother, then me, tears flowing down her cheeks. I moved to comfort her, wanting to promise her that everything would be okay.

"Nat—" My words were abruptly cut off. One of the bodyguards lunged, punching me hard in the stomach, knocking the wind from my lungs. I doubled over, trying to catch my breath. Both of my arms were being pinned back by another guard.

I heard Nat scream and call my name. I looked up to see the bodyguard, who had been holding her, drag her down the hall toward the elevators. She was begging and pleading with her brother the whole time. Elijah kept his back to her. I knew how much he loved his sister. There was no way he was doing this on his own. His dad was pulling the strings.

"Stop! Leave her alone!" I shouted, earning another punch to my stomach. "Elijah, don't let them hurt her." I groaned.

"No one is going to hurt her. What kind of monster do you think I am?" he snapped.

I had a lot of ideas about the kind of monster I believed him to be.

He had just done his father's bidding, letting his sister be dragged out of my apartment in the middle of the night with nothing but my shirt on. Her purse was still in my house.

I watched the bodyguard shove her into the elevator before disappearing from my view. I pushed against the guy holding me back, throwing an elbow up, connecting with the guy's jaw. Elijah moved to close the front door and I knew shit was about to get real.

The guard holding me dragged me backward and into the living room. I stood at my full height, glaring at Elijah. I wasn't going to go down without a fight. I didn't care if it was four against one. I'd make damn sure I got in a few good blows. I hated the idea of fighting the guy I considered a brother, but I wasn't going to take his beating without fighting back.

"Don't look at me like I'm the bad guy," he said, stepping toward me.

"You're a dick. You just let them manhandle your sister. No, you ordered that guy to do it, you piece of shit. What kind of man are you? You jump to do your daddy's dirty work? Isn't he man enough to drag his ass over here and face me himself?" I sneered.

Elijah was seriously pissed. His face was red, and his eyes were mere slits on his face. "You don't know shit about me or my dad."

I scoffed. "I know everything there is to know about you and I know your dad well enough to know he talks a lot of shit about me and my family, but he can't back it up. He never says shit to any one of us. It's always behind our backs. He's spineless. So are you if you cower to his demands."

I knew I was digging a bigger hole for myself, but I didn't care. It was already very clear how my night was going to end. I was certainly going to say my piece before the beating began.

He shook his head. "I told you! Damn it, she's my little sister! My dad is a powerful man. He doesn't have to come over here."

I took a deep breath, prepared to try a different approach. I couldn't ignore that last twenty years or so of our friendship. We'd been through a lot.

"Elijah, I love her. I didn't want to. I knew that would be a problem for you, but I couldn't help it. You and I are friends and your dad is okay with it. Maybe we can work something out. She's happy with me. You have to see that," I said in a soft voice, not begging, but trying to appeal to that side of him I knew well.

He looked at me and I could see the hurt and betrayal in his eyes. I hated to see it, knowing I caused it. He was my best friend and I loved him like a brother. I knew that relationship was over. He would never trust me again. He was a good guy, and this wasn't like him.

He was shaking his head, his hand fisted as he moved it up and down. He looked a little crazed, which was not a good thing for me. "You could have helped it. You could have walked away. You could have had a hundred other women, but you chose her. I don't understand why you would do that," he said, his voice higher than normal.

I didn't answer. There was nothing I could say. "Where are you taking her?" I asked instead, needing to know she would be okay.

"To my dad."

My blood ran cold. Everything became very clear in that moment. "Your dad knows?" I asked, suddenly very worried about her.

He nodded. "I convinced him to let me come and get her. I'm not the villain here, Jack. You are. You made a horrible decision and now she's going to pay the price. I'm going to pay the price as well. I told you about my dad. You didn't value our friendship enough to stop seeing her. You're a selfish prick. This is why my dad hates your family."

"Elijah, you don't know my family," I spat.

I wasn't going to let him talk shit about my family. They were innocent in the whole situation.

"Do you know how this would have played out if I let my dad come over here and he found her half naked in your bed? He would have lost his shit. He was beyond pissed. I came over here to protect her from him." He growled.

"And yet you just sent her back there while you're here with me," I stated in a voice devoid of emotion.

Out of nowhere, he swung and hit me in the jaw. It took me by surprise, giving me no time to block it or move. I was helpless to do anything with the two assholes behind me, holding my arms. Elijah swung again, this time, I doubled over as he connected just below my rib cage. They released my arms and I dropped to the cold, hard tile floor in my apartment.

I made a move to get back to my feet. A boot slammed into my back. I refused to say a word. I knew I'd be pissing blood for a week. I just hoped I'd have the opportunity to pee again. I had no idea who Wayne Levy really was. For all I knew, he could have ordered my death or a beating that would leave me seriously incapacitated.

"Take care of Nat," I whispered, using the little air I had in my lungs to speak.

"She's not your problem," Elijah shouted from above me.

I closed my eyes, preparing myself for more pain. When she and I thought about the risks of being together, physical violence had never crossed my mind. I assumed Elijah would try and fight me, but I knew I could kick his ass. This was more than I could have imagined. I just prayed Natasha's father truly loved her and wouldn't lay a hand on her.

CHAPTER 24

NATASHA

I was practically shoved into the limo by the very ungraceful man who had pulled me from Jack's apartment. I was ever so grateful that the lobby in his building was empty and no one could witness the embarrassing scene. I pulled the shirt over my thighs the best I could.

"Where are we going?" I snapped when the bodyguard crawled in and sat across from me.

I pressed my knees together and pointed them at the window, trying to have a slight bit of modesty.

"To the Levy estate," he answered, slapping his hand two times on the privacy glass.

The limo began to move.

"Hey! Wait, what about Elijah?" I said, my voice full of panic.

"I'm instructed to get you back to the estate."

"You're leaving him here, with the other three?" I asked, my mouth dry as I had a very good idea of what was happening upstairs.

The bodyguard looked at me but refused to answer my question.

"Take me to my friend's house. I'm not going to the mansion," I ordered.

He smirked. "My orders are to get you back to the estate. That's exactly what I'm going to do."

"I'll pay you," I offered.

He raised an eyebrow. "With your daddy's money? You realize he's my boss?"

"I have my own money. I'll pay you double what he's paying."

He shook his head. "No thanks."

I leaned back in the seat, knowing I was fighting a losing battle. The man was not going to let me out.

"What about Jack?" I asked. "What are they doing to Jack?"

He shrugged a shoulder. "I don't know. I'm not there."

"You're a real peach."

"I'm not paid to be your friend."

I rolled my eyes. "You could never be my friend."

He ignored me, clearly not the least bit fazed by my insults. My heart ached, and my stomach twisted into knots. Jack was alone with four men. I knew he was strong and tough, but there was no way he had a chance against them. I had no idea who had ordered Elijah to Jack's door or what their plans were, but deep down I knew it wouldn't be good. They were going to hurt him. They were going to hurt the man I loved because he loved me. It was so unfair.

The driver of the limo turned in to the driveway of my parents' estate. The guard was doing his best not to look at me, but not doing a great job. Jack's shirt fell mid-thigh, protecting my modesty, but it was not the way I wanted to go walking in the front door. I had tried several times to get the man to let me go. He wasn't having it. He worked for my father and not me, he reminded me repeatedly on the long drive home.

When the limo stopped in front of the doors of the mansion, I could see nearly every light was on in the place. The foyer was glowing through the large picture windows that showcased the massive chandelier my mother had specially made and imported from Italy. The fact it was on was not a good sign. I stared up at the massive double doors and tried to come up with another escape route. I hesitated, not wanting to get out of the car, hoping there was a small chance I could convince the driver to turn around and keep going. I could beg the driver to take me to Ashley's.

I didn't get the chance to offer up money or anything else. The guard climbed out and reached inside, grabbing my hand and pulling a little harder than necessary, nearly causing me to tumble face-first onto the driveway as I fought to stay inside the car.

"Don't! Stop touching me!" I shouted to no avail, yanking my arm back.

The giant man forcefully pulled me out of the car, dragging me up the walk, and through the front doors. I considered making a break for it and racing for my bedroom, but the guard must have noticed my eyes drifting to the staircase. He shook his head and pointed toward my father's private living room.

"He's waiting for you."

"I just bet he is. I hope you're proud of yourself. What are you two hundred and fifty pounds? You just manhandled a woman half your size. I hope you sleep well tonight," I spat.

He chuckled. "Lady, I sleep just fine every night."

"You're a pig," I snapped.

He shrugged a shoulder. "Oink. Oink. Mr. Levy is waiting in the living room. If I were you, I'd get my skinny ass in there before he gets even more pissed."

I glared at him, wishing like hell I could fire him for his impertinence and general asshole-like character. I would make sure he was fired as soon as all this was over. I knew my father well enough to know he would not tolerate the manhandling I endured at the mercy of the man standing to my left, staring at me with a smug look on his face.

"Asshole." I hissed before looking down the hallway.

I had a choice to make. I could stand there and cry and cower to the men in my life or I could stand tall and proud, prepared to meet my punishment. I chose the latter. I thought about all the women throughout history who had endured their right to make their own choices throughout their lives. Some of my heroes had fought back against their oppressors. I would too. I was not a little girl and I didn't care if they took away everything they had given me. I didn't need their money. I would make it just fine on my own. If Jack would still have me after all this, he would take care of me.

I threw my shoulders back, quickly buttoned the two buttons on Jack's shirt, raised my chin up high, then walked barefoot over the marble floor toward my fate. I walked as if I owned the place. When I walked into the living room, I quickly took stock of the situation. My father was standing in front of the fireplace, his back to me, one hand resting on the mantel. My mother was sitting on the couch, her back ramrod straight and her hands folded in her lap, not saying a word.

I strolled in, acting as if I hadn't a care in the world. I could smell the acrid scent of cigar smoke in the room mixed with the sweet cloying smell of my father's favorite brandy. My mom took one look at me and my attire and gasped before shaking her head. It was then my father turned around to look at me, his lip curled as he looked at my bare feet and legs. I could see the revulsion on his face and had to fight back the urge to try and cover myself.

"What the hell were you thinking!" His voice boomed so loudly I thought for sure my mother's expensive vase on the mantel would shatter.

"Dad—" I started, but the subtle shake of my mother's head told me not to say a word.

I took a deep breath, waiting for my father to unleash his fury. I had never seen him so angry. I was seriously worried for his health. His face was red and the vein on the side of his neck looked as if it would burst. His hands were clenching and unclenching. His jaw was set so tightly I worried his teeth would shatter.

"I cannot believe you betrayed me, betrayed your family. You have made a terrible mistake and I will never forgive you. I always expected more from you," he said, disgust making his voice sound choked.

"I didn't betray you," I replied in a calm manner, not wanting to fight fire with fire. I knew it would only make things worse.

"You are sleeping with the enemy!" he shouted.

I stayed near the door, prepared to make a quick escape if needed. "Dad, you're being unreasonable."

His arm swung wide, knocking my mother's favorite vase to the floor. It shattered into hundreds of pieces. My eyes went wide as he picked up a glass figurine from the mantel that I knew was something expensive. He threw it, slamming it into the wall as he roared. My mom's hand covered her mouth, but not before an audible gasp escaped.

"Do you know what you're doing? Are you purposely trying to destroy us?" he raged.

I shook my head. I was afraid to speak. I had no idea what he was capable of, and I didn't want to find out. I was nearly frozen with terror. I felt helpless to fight back against his words or his anger. In the back of my mind, I thought about Jack. If my father was this angry at me, I couldn't imagine what he had ordered his goons to do to Jack. I choked back a sob. I would not let him see me weak.

"Wayne," my mother said, not getting up from the couch.

"You don't say a word! You know what she's done?" he shouted again.

My mom nodded. "I do."

"Then you know she's trying to ruin us!"

My mother turned to me, her horror over my father's temper tantrum vanished. She pursed her lips, staring at me as if I were a mangy stray dog that had just been dragged from the sewer. "You should be ashamed of yourself."

"Mom, Dad, you guys have to realize I'm old enough to make my own choices. I'm old enough to fall in love with whomever I choose," I said, trying to keep my voice calm.

My dad looked like he was going to vomit. His face twisted in disgust as he shook his head, his index finger waggling back and forth as he moved to walk around the couch toward me. "There will never be Bancroft blood mixing with ours. I forbid it."

I raised one eyebrow. "This is my life."

"You are my daughter and I will do whatever it takes to keep you and this family safe."

"He isn't a threat," I defended.

"Listen to your father. Do not sass him. This is something you know darn well will not be tolerated," my mother chimed in.

My dad was around the couch. He stopped and put one hand on the back of the couch as if he needed to support himself. I was immediately concerned for his health.

"Dad?" I said the word as a question.

"I expected better from you. Your brother, I couldn't stop him from befriending that jackal, but you, you knew better. You could have had any man out there and you chose to roll in the mud with one of my sworn enemies." He snarled.

I shook my head. "It isn't like that. You don't even know Jack."

"I don't have to! I know his type! I know his family! They are all the same!" he practically screamed the last.

I took a small step back, getting a little closer to the door. I wanted to escape. I wanted to pack my things and run away. This was not how I imagined this all happening. I knew he would be pissed. I expected that, but this was next level anger.

"Can we talk about this later, when we've all had some sleep and you've calmed down?" I suggested.

He shook his head. "There is nothing to talk about. It's over. You will not see that man again. I don't care if I have to send you away again. I will not tolerate you spending another minute with that man."

I was going to tell him he couldn't tell me what to do when his words sank in. I blinked, looked at my mother and then him again.

"What?" I asked, positive I couldn't have heard him correctly.

"Lose his number. If I hear of you two trying to sneak off together, there will be hell to pay," he threatened.

"Send me away?" I repeated the words that had been stuck in my head.

He looked at me, then my mother, then shrugged. I felt as if I had been hit with a sledgehammer. Everything was so much clearer. I couldn't decide whether to cry or rage.

CHAPTER 25

JACK

Elijah dropped low, squatting next to me before pushing my shoulder and rolling me over to look at him. I glared back at him. He was a coward. He couldn't handle the situation like a real man and had to use hired thugs to take me down. I sneered at him, refusing to give him any satisfaction in knowing how much pain I was in.

"Guess what, lover boy?" he asked, a smile on his face.

I defiantly stared back at him. "I have a feeling you're going to tell me, so save the drama and say what you have to say."

"He's sending her away—again," he said, taking great pleasure in the words.

"What do you mean?"

Elijah stood, forcing me to look up at him. "My dad doesn't want her around you. He's sending her away. She's going to get the chance to start her company and build a new life without you in it. You've messed her up. She's doing things she would never do. It's your shitty influence that's ruining her."

I shook my head. "He's making a mistake."

"No, in this one thing, I agree with him. It's better for everyone if she leaves. I knew you couldn't stay away from her. I thought you would out of respect for our friendship, but I should have known better," he said, and I could actually hear sorrow in his voice.

I moved to sit up and was met with another swift kick to my side.

"Get out of here!" Elijah shouted to the guard who kicked me.

Now he gets a conscience?

"Give me a chance to explain," I muttered, sitting up and hoping I could stand up without getting hit again.

I managed to do so, squaring off with Elijah. He was staring at me, shaking his head with disgust. "Leave it alone, Jack. Seriously. We can still be friends, but you have to drop this. You have to stay away from her. She's too good for you."

"We can still be friends?" I scoffed.

He shrugged a shoulder. "You knew I had to hit you for fucking my sister. That's the rules."

I rolled my eyes. "Whatever. The guards?"

Elijah looked at the two remaining guards in my apartment before jerking his head and ordering them out. I was thankful for that. I could handle Elijah.

"I don't understand how you could trick her into sleeping with you. She's my little sister. She is one of the only people I love in this world. I trusted her, and you made her betray me," he said, his voice low.

"I didn't make her do anything. She loves you and she trusted you before you barged in here and did this. Grow up, man. She's a woman with a good head on her shoulders. She knows what she wants. You out of all people should know nobody can convince her to do anything she doesn't want to do," I said, my hand going to my bruised side.

"You corrupted her. You made her think you loved her just so you could get her into bed. I *know* you, Jack. I have been your wingman for a long time. I know your tricks!"

I slowly shook my head. "Think about the last time I needed you as my wingman. Think about the last time you saw me going home with a woman or even flirting with another woman," I said, wanting him to see the truth that had been right in front of him the whole time.

I saw the moment things started adding up. "You've been fucking her for years?" he squealed.

"It isn't like that and quit talking about her like that. We've been together for years, yes. It isn't something dirty like you keep trying to make it out to be. It's the real thing. It's your father who is holding her back from what she wants," I snapped.

"She doesn't know what she wants. She is only going after you because you're the forbidden fruit."

I laughed, shaking my head. "You're crazy. You know that's bullshit."

"There are so many fish in the sea, why her?" he pleaded.

"I can't explain it. I didn't want to love her. It happened. I can't change how I feel. We tried to stay away from each other. We tried to go our separate ways. We knew your dad would freak out if he knew about the two of us. When she came back home, I hoped the feelings I had for her would have faded. They didn't," I said, being completely honest with him.

"Make them go away. Stay away from her. It's better for you and her. Give it up. Move on," he ordered.

"It isn't that easy. You've never been in love. You don't understand. I can't just walk away from her," I explained.

"She needs to focus on building this company. If you know her as well as you say you do, then you'll know how important this is to her. My dad is giving her everything she needs to get started. Don't ask her to stay. Don't hold her back," he demanded.

I looked him dead in the eye. "You're seriously going to let your father dictate her life?"

"Look, Jack, you and I are friends, but I will never trust your family. There is something between our families, you can't deny that."

I slapped a hand to my forehead, wanting to shake the man for being such an idiot. "I thought you were different. I guess you are you father's puppet."

"Don't say that to me! I came here to warn you. I'm telling you to back off. Move on for your own sake. You're never going to have her."

He straightened his suit jacket and turned to leave. "Don't let him ruin her life, Elijah. If you love her, you'll stand up for what she wants."

He spun around and looked at me. "Really? Let me put it to you like this. If you love her, you'll stay away from her."

"Why!" I shouted in frustration.

"Because it will destroy our family. Family means a lot to her. Don't take that away from her."

I took a deep breath. "You and your dad are taking it away because she fell in love with the wrong man. You're the one hurting her."

"Whatever, Jack. Stay away from her. Sorry about the guard kicking you, but you and I both know you deserved it."

I followed behind him. "Do you really think we're going to be friends after this bullshit?" I growled.

"I'm willing to be your friend, which is pretty magnanimous I'd say. You should be so lucky to call me your friend."

I laughed through my anger. "Bullshit. Don't ever call me again. We are not friends. I would never be friends with a man who could so willingly destroy the life of someone I love. The life of someone he proclaims to love. You don't love her. You love your dad and the wealth. If you truly loved Nat, you would do what was best for her. You're a selfish prick. You're doing what's best for you."

"Best for me?" He spun around as he opened the door.

I nodded. "Yep. You're too much of a pussy to stand up to your dad. You're doing his bidding because you're spineless. I bet you Nat is at home right now giving him hell. She's brave. You're a coward. You'll always be under his thumb."

"You don't know what you're talking about. You're nothing in your family. You're the second-born. You don't know what it's like to be held responsible for the family's business."

I shrugged a shoulder. "I guess that's the difference between our families. For all your talk about how great your family is and how horrible my family is, it seems to me your family is the one that has some serious issues. Your family is the one that controls and manipulates its members. My mother and my father would never do what your father has done. I have a feeling this little feud is because of something your father did. My dad would never stoop so low. Your dad is a double dealing, controlling, manipulative man."

He sneered. "And your dad was a fucking saint?"

I nodded. "He was compared to yours. I suggest you go home, tail between your legs, and ask daddy dearest again about this feud. I have a feeling you might get the truth. He hates the Bancrofts because we are better than he is. He will never be the man my father was. The way I see it, he's jealous. Now you're jealous."

Elijah raised one eyebrow. "You know that's a load of bullshit. My father's business is a hundred times more successful than your Bancroft bullshit."

I smirked. "Do you measure everything in currency? Is Natasha's happiness measured by the same means? If that's the case, how much will it cost for me to buy her off you guys?"

His mouth fell open. "Fuck you, man. My sister isn't a piece of meat you can buy."

"Really, because that is exactly how you're treating her, as if she has no say in how she lives her life. Your father is treating her like a piece of property, and you're going along with it. You disgust me. Get the fuck out of here before I have your ass thrown in jail."

I slammed the door in his face and locked it before going to the security pad. I was about to push the button calling the police but hesitated. Things were already bad enough. I didn't need to make it worse by having Elijah and his goons tossed in jail. Although, it would give me a great deal of satisfaction to see him taken down a peg or two.

I needed to call Natasha and make sure she was okay. I turned too fast, pulling the muscles that had been so violently bruised, and winced in pain. I moved a little slower and grabbed my phone, not giving a shit if they saw my number on her real phone.

I hit the number and waited. It rang several times before going to voice mail. I hung up and dialed again. I would call all damn night until I heard her voice. If I didn't hear her voice, I would storm the gates of the Levy estate and pull her out of there. I wasn't a coward like Elijah. I would do whatever it took to keep her safe.

I called again. "Don't fucking call her again!" Wayne Levy answered.

"I want to talk to Nat," I said in a low, dangerous voice.

"She doesn't want to talk to you. Don't ever call her again. I will be changing her number."

"You can't keep her from me," I spat.

"You made a fool of her tonight. You disgraced her. What kind of man are you?"

I took a deep breath. I wanted to tell him he was the one who had disgraced her by dragging her out of my apartment in the middle of the night.

"I want to talk to her," I repeated.

"She is far too good for the likes of you. Jack Bancroft, you and your family have been a thorn in my side for too long. Stay the fuck away from me and my family. You know you're no good for her. You know it, I know it, and she's going to know it by the time I'm through with you," he shouted.

"Don't do this," I warned.

"Stay the fuck away from her!" he shouted before ending the call.

I stared at the phone in my hand, trying to decide what to do next. Shit had just hit the fan in every way. I redialed her number only to have it go straight to voice mail. I retried it several times always with the same result.

"Son of a bitch," I muttered.

CHAPTER 26

JACK

I strolled down the hallway of the Bancroft home. Although it was a mansion, I never really thought of it like that. It was my childhood home and held many fond memories. It wasn't a cold, sterile place like many of the mansions I had visited over the years. We had been lucky like that. Our family was traditional with our mom staying home to raise all six of us boys, family dinners she cooked herself and placed on the table every night, and parents who attended every one of our sports games.

I could smell the familiar scent of lemon oil and knew the maid had finished her rounds. It was a scent I had grown up with and it always took me back to a time when life was so much easier. A time when I didn't have to think about the future beyond the weekend. I smiled, thinking about the many good times we had in the house. I was getting old. That's all there was to it. I sounded like my dear departed grandpa, always reminiscing and feeling nostalgic about the good old days.

I could hear the deep baritones of my brothers and followed the sound. Grayson, James, and Mason were all in the den. It was a mini-family reunion. My mom had spent the first part of the summer traveling and had only returned a few days ago. I had missed her and was anxious to finally have a day off to visit. Clearly Grayson and the others felt the same.

We were all mama's boys, but none of us would ever admit it. She was our rock. All of us tended to be wanderers and maybe a little on the playboy side, but when it came to our mom, she was the only woman in our lives who really mattered. Well, except for Grayson. He had a beautiful wife and the prettiest little girl on the planet. I hoped I would have that one day, but it wasn't looking promising.

"Hey," I said as I strolled into the room that had been my dad's favorite in the house.

It was strange how we always found ourselves congregating in the den. My dad was never the type to be a real sappy guy, but he was a decent man and we knew he loved us. Being in the room was like he was a silent listener. Sometimes, I could smell the scent of a cigar being lit and would look around, expecting to see him somewhere. I still missed him. We all did. My mom was pushing on and the trip had been the first time she'd gone anywhere without my dad. It was a good thing and we were all happy to see her moving forward with her life.

"Boys!" My mom walked in right behind me. "It's too nice of a day to be holed up in this dark room. Come on out to the patio. I've got cold lemonade," she said in a cheerful voice.

We did as she asked and followed Mom out to the patio, which was surrounded by tall trees that provided the perfect amount of shade on a hot summer day. The backyard was another place that held many fond memories. It was where Channing broke his arm in a rough game of tackle football. It was where we got to roll around, got dirty, and covered in grass stains like all the other normal kids in the world.

"Where's Channing?" I asked, realizing my brother was absent.

Grayson scoffed. "Who knows? France? Some island. We know he's with at least one woman, more likely several."

I chuckled. Channing was the second youngest brother and was definitely one of the wilder ones out of the six of us. He was a free spirit and traveled the world nonstop, always chasing the warm weather where women were more likely to be in bikinis. He claimed it was for his art, but we all knew better. He loved photography and was great at it, but never really took it seriously.

"Colt?" I asked, my other brother missing from our gathering.

"He stopped by when I got home," my mom answered.

I nodded, glad he had stopped by. My mom needed all of us. "Good."

"I'll be right back. Doris made some scones," my mom said, heading inside.

It was good to see her back to her old self. We had all been worried when she'd broken her hip the year before, knowing the injury could have waylaid her. It didn't. Mom was a fighter and she'd gotten right back up and moved on.

When she returned, she'd put the newspaper on the table before passing out the scones. My eyes fell on the blaring name in print and I felt my stomach plummet. It was the only name that had that much power over me. I casually leaned over and grabbed it off the table, my eyes focused on the headline before I tossed it back on the table. I didn't bother reading the article. I didn't care.

Mason snatched it off the table. Mom said something about needing one more thing and disappeared in the house.

"'Natasha Levy returns to New York City on a mission to follow in her father's footsteps,'" Mason read aloud, grabbing the attention of my other brothers.

"Ouch," Grayson murmured.

"Whatever," I snapped.

Mason was clicking his tongue, shaking his head. "Maybe Daddy got the little girl he's always wanted. She obeys and jumps when he commands her to. Sounds like she has her own company and Daddy is helping her." He whistled low.

"Now will she marry whoever Daddy picked for her," Grayson said, growling.

My secret had been revealed last year after the incident at my apartment. It was Grayson who'd taken me to the ER when I couldn't get Mason on the phone. From there, all my brothers had been made privy to my secret affair with the family's mortal enemy's daughter. It had been sticky business but when she'd disappeared, it solved the problem for the interim.

Now she was back.

Only I knew about our agreement. It had been a year. I had not spoken to her since that horrible night, but I had to believe she was sticking to the plan. I'd gone back and forth between being convinced she was out there waiting for me, then to being worried she had truly moved on. It had been a tortuous year, but I had managed to keep from chasing her down, which was a serious accomplishment in my opinion.

"I don't see anything about her bringing a man back with her," Mason commented.

"You know her daddy already has the perfect man for her, and it isn't a Bancroft. She's probably engaged or has someone lined up now that her exile is over," Grayson snapped.

James chuckled. "I bet he's going to marry her off to one of the Gordons."

We all made faces. The Gordons were notoriously ugly. They were wealthy, but they had all swam at the wrong end of the gene pool. I shuddered thinking of one of those overweight men touching my woman. I'd never be able to handle seeing that in person.

"She'd never go for that," I snapped, hating the very idea of her getting anywhere near one of those men.

We all fell silent when our mother returned. She did not need to know about the affair. It would hurt her and that wasn't necessary. Nat was out of my life, and I wasn't going to cause my mom stress for nothing if there was no chance of ever getting her back.

"What are you boys talking about?" she asked, taking her seat at the head of the table.

"Just how good these scones are," I lied easily, making it clear I didn't want my brothers saying another word about Natasha Levy.

I sipped the cool lemonade, my mind replaying the last night I was with Natasha. Her brother had done his father's bidding and yanked her out of my place. Elijah had been my best friend, but after that night, I had vowed never to speak to him again. The guy had steered clear of me and my brothers. The rage I had felt in the first few months had been blinding, but I'd put it in check and tried my best to focus on the endgame.

I had debated trying to find her but had to stick to the plan. If I chased her down, I knew we risked everything. We had agreed to wait a year while we gave our families time to get on board. When I devised the plan, it hinged on no one knowing about our relationship. That had all been blown out of the water when Elijah showed up at my damn door and ordered his thugs to beat the shit out of me.

"What's on your mind, Jack?" my mom asked, snapping me out of the reverie that always left me with a mixed bag of emotions.

I shook my head. "Nothing, I'm just enjoying the day."

She gave me a look that said she knew I was lying. I wasn't going to burden her with my problems.

"You need to relax, Jack. You're going to get wrinkles," she scolded, causing my brothers to snicker.

I glared at them. "Mom, I'm fine. I'm relaxed and enjoying your fine company," I said, pouring on the syrupy sweetness and earning an eye roll from her.

"Good, can I get you boys anything else to eat?" she asked.

"Mom, you don't have to wait on us," I told her.

She waved a hand. "Well, I want something salty. Those scones were sweet and now I need salty," she muttered, getting up and leaving the table again.

I shook my head, watching her walk away. She was a bundle of energy and loved to take care of us. Her entire life had been focused on taking care of her six boys and my father. When he passed away, we'd been worried about her and had been coming by regularly to make sure she never felt alone. I wasn't going to lie. I appreciated her doting and when she was in the mood, she cooked some spectacular meals.

"Are you going to call her?" Grayson asked.

I shrugged a shoulder as he picked up the dismissed conversation without missing a beat. "I don't know."

"Bullshit," Mason snapped.

I glared at him. "I'm going to wait and see where things stand. I'm not going to push anything and risk another war."

"Things stand right where they left off ... Elijah kicking your ass." Mason snarled.

"No, he didn't. He had a gang kick my ass," I shot back.

"Let her go, man. There's too much bad blood. Now you don't even have her brother to back you up," Mason lectured.

"I don't need her fucking brother." I glowered.

"It would have made it a little easier to win her father over," Grayson pointed out.

I rolled my eyes. "I don't care about her dad."

"But she does," James chimed in.

"What about Mom?" Grayson asked.

I shrugged. "I don't know. I think she'll be more open than Wayne Levy. Mom doesn't hold grudges like that."

Grayson shook his head. "But Mom is loyal to Dad. Dad did not like Wayne Levy."

Mason threw his head back and laughed. "That's an understatement."

"And none of you know what the beef is about?" I asked, still in disbelief no one knew what it was that had caused such animosity between the two families.

All my brothers shook their heads. It was one of the great mysteries of the universe, I surmised. We would likely never know the real reason why our fathers hated each other so much. The sins of the father had been bestowed upon his son. It wasn't fair. I knew life wasn't fair, but not being able to be with the woman I loved seemed like it went against the cosmos. Hopefully, fate would step in and right the wrong. If it didn't, I was going to die a lonely man.

CHAPTER 27

NATASHA

Being back home was a little surreal. When I had been sent away to the other side of the country a year ago, I had pouted and raged for weeks, vowing to never step foot in my parents' mansion again. It had taken some time, but I slowly learned to accept my fate and embrace it. My father had kept his distance those first few months. It was then I realized I couldn't live without my dad in my life. I had been alone and miserable, and the exile had given me a lot of time to think about Jack and the entire situation.

I pushed the thought to the back of my mind. I was not going to think about Jack. Those days were gone. I was home and it was time to embrace my future with my dad's company. I took a deep breath and began to unpack my suitcases. Unlike the last time I had returned home, I didn't have a new wardrobe to unpack.

There was a quick knock on the door before it pushed open.

"Hi, Daddy," I said with a smile on my face when I saw my father poke his head in.

"Do you have a minute?" he asked.

"Sure, come in. I'm just unpacking," I told him, putting some things into the chest of drawers.

"I just wanted to check in and see if you needed anything," he said, looking around the apartment my mother had designed for me for my last homecoming, a year ago.

I shook my head. "Nope. I've got everything I need."

"I'm very proud of you, princess. You've made huge strides this past year and I would hate to see you go back to old ways and bad habits," he said in a serious voice.

I knew exactly what he was referring to but chose to ignore the subtle lecture. "Thank you, Dad. I'm excited for the next chapter. I've been working hard, and I am ready to make my own name in Levy Industries. I've got a ton of ideas and can't wait to get started."

He held up a hand. "Slow down, you've been home a few hours. Take a few days and relax before you dive into work."

"I will," I promised.

"Natasha, do we need to talk about the Bancroft situation?" he asked bluntly.

My back was to him when he said the words. I took a deep breath before turning to look at him. "No, Daddy. That's all in the past."

He raised one of his bushy eyebrows. "Are you sure about that?"

"I am. I'm ready to move on with my life. I have big plans and that is going to be my focus."

"I hope you understand why it had to be done," he said in a tone laced with guilt.

I shrugged. "I've moved on," I assured him, not wanting to talk about the subject anymore.

He slowly nodded. I could tell he wasn't completely convinced by my words. I couldn't really blame him. I had put up quite a fight those first few months after he sent me away. I had begged for him to understand that I loved Jack Bancroft, but there had been no changing his mind.

"Good to know. I don't want to hear about sneaking out or any of that nonsense. I won't allow that man or his family to sully my daughter's reputation," he scolded.

"He won't. It's over," I said firmly, barely holding my own frustration in check.

I looked him in the eye, giving him the reassurance he obviously needed.

"If he tries to contact you, I want to know."

I inhaled a deep breath. "I can handle it."

He held up his hands. "All right, I don't mean to keep bringing it up, but with you back in the city, I'm sure there's bound to be some old business kicked up. I only want to make sure you have your head on straight."

"Daddy, I have far more important things to worry about. I want to get my business off the ground and I want to buy my own house," I told him, already knowing what he was going to say.

"Princess, there's no need for you to move out. You have your own apartment here with plenty of privacy. Save the money and the stress of moving. Your mother loves having you around." He cajoled.

I smiled. "Dad, I'm too old to be living with my parents. Elijah hasn't lived at home for a long time," I pointed out.

"He's a man," my dad shot back, which I had expected. Elijah and I had always been treated very differently. Elijah was capable of making his own life decisions and doing as he pleased, as long as he knew he would one day take over the company. I was expected to marry well and be a dutiful, devoted daughter.

"I want to have my own place, my own kitchen, and move on. I'm grateful to you and Mom for doing this for me, but it's time for me to leave the nest. You've always encouraged me to be independent and that's what I'm doing," I said gently, not wanting to hurt his feelings.

"Okay, I'll leave you to it. Dinner will be ready soon. I hope you'll join us," he said before leaving me alone once again.

I released a long sigh. I had expected the uncomfortable conversation to come up, but no matter how much I prepared myself, it still had a tendency to hurt a little. I had done my best to move past Jack. After seeing how badly I had hurt my father, I knew I couldn't do it again.

I closed my eyes, praying Jack had forgotten all about the pact. I couldn't go through with it. I couldn't live without my family. I had thought I could and had gotten caught up in the romance. Seeing my dad's anger, the look of betrayal on Elijah's face, and the disgust in my mother's eyes had proven to be too much for me. I loved my family and I couldn't sacrifice my relationships with each of them to be with Jack.

Part of me hoped he'd given up on me and moved on. The other part of me nearly died inside thinking about never being with him again. That was the selfish part of me, only thinking about my wants and needs, and not considering what was best for my entire family. I had to believe I would find someone else to spend my life with. Someone who wouldn't drive a huge wedge between me and my family. It was a small sacrifice I was willing to make to hold onto the relationship with my father. Things had been going so well between us the past six months, I didn't want to rock the boat. I would avoid Jack and the entire Bancroft clan.

My dad had made it clear he would never accept a Bancroft into his family. If I were to marry Jack and have children, they would never know their grandparents or uncle. My father would truly disown me. I couldn't live with that and had come to the conclusion that the only thing to do was move on.

It hurt. I couldn't deny it had carved out a large chunk of my heart and left my soul feeling a little lost, but I would make it. I was strong. This was my lot in life. I was born a Levy and I needed to accept what that meant. It wasn't a horrible life. I had privileges other people could never imagine. I had the love of my family and in general, I was happy. Dwelling on what I couldn't have would get me nowhere.

After unpacking, I made my way downstairs. I didn't want to be rude and keep my parents waiting.

"There she is." My mom walked to me as I headed toward the dining room.

She wrapped her arms around me, hugging me tight, before looping her arms through mine and walking with me into the formal dining room. Every meal was a grand affair at the Levy mansion. My mother insisted.

"Wow, Mom, you redid the dining room?" I asked with surprise.

She shrugged a shoulder. "I grew tired of those muted black and white tones. I wanted something a little more traditional," she said with a smile.

As always, my mother had outdone herself with her interior design. "It is gorgeous. I love all the cherry wood tones in this room. It feels very regal in here. I feel a little underdressed," I joked, smoothing down my plain blue dress I had on.

"Oh, don't be silly. It's only us," my mother assured me.

I smiled and nodded, her own elegant pantsuit was a testament to how underdressed I was. She loved to change clothes for dinner, something I found to be tedious and a very dated practice, but it was what my mom enjoyed. No one, not even my father, ever tried to discourage her.

"Did you get settled?" my father asked, coming into the room with his customary drink in one hand and the unlit cigar in the other.

"I did."

We all took our seats. Elijah's absence was a good thing. I still wasn't ready to hang out with him and pretend nothing had happened that night. While I could understand my father's irritation, I couldn't help but feel betrayed by my own brother. He could have given me five minutes to dress instead of having me paraded through the building in nothing but Jack's shirt. His actions were unforgiveable in my mind. I didn't care if it was my father's orders. Elijah was a grown man and could have defended me.

"It's so nice to have you home," my mom said, beaming.

I nodded, not wanting to break it to her that I was dead set on moving out at the first chance I got. I loved my parents, but I had to get out of the house.

"Don't smother her," my dad lectured.

My mom shot him a glare. "That's your department," she snapped.

It was an age-old argument. My mother and I didn't have an overly close relationship. It was my dad and I who were close. I was his baby girl and like him in more ways than I liked to admit. Being away for the last year, and focusing on my business plan and getting things set up, had shown me how much like him I truly was.

"I'll have my team at your disposal whenever you're ready," my father said, pride written all over his face.

"Thanks, Dad. I'm going to take your advice and take a day or two off before I dive in. I have a feeling once things get started, it will be a long time before I have some free time," I said, smiling with excitement.

"You are just like your father," my mother muttered.

My dad was grinning proudly. I was a lot like my dad. It took the year away for me to understand why he had been so against me and Jack being together. He believed I would be stifled. I knew in my heart Jack would have never intentionally held me back, but I would be inclined to work less and want to spend more time with him, maybe even start a family. My dad had wanted me to pursue my dreams of having my own company.

His methods were not exactly kind or gentle, but that was how my dad was. He was firm-handed, and his anger tended to get the better of him when he was truly passionate about something. In many ways, I had to believe I had deserved his harsh treatment. I knew what I had been doing with Jack was wrong, but I did it anyway. I'd lied and deceived him, and he had every right to be mad. Elijah had his own reasons for being angry with me. Maybe one day we could be close again, but there was still a lot of healing that needed to happen.

CHAPTER 28

JACK

Sundays were not typically the day I woke up and decided I needed to go pump iron, but today wasn't an average Sunday. I had a lot of pent-up energy and when Mason had called and asked me to join him at the gym, I had decided to take him up on the offer. I couldn't sit around all day, worrying and wondering what Nat was doing. I had to stay busy. I had to try to keep my mind off her and avoid calling her.

The receptionist had enthusiastically greeted me when I strolled through the doors of the elite gym. She commented on not seeing me for a while and we chatted for a few minutes before I pulled myself away and headed beyond the double doors, or the inner sanctum of the gym. It was all very private, making sure no one walking in off the street could see the exclusive clientele sweaty and grunting. Celebrities and models frequented the gym and were promised privacy.

My eyes scanned the area. I could see Mason leaning against the wall next to the juice bar, flirting with the pretty blonde working the counter. I knew damn well he wasn't interested in a smoothie or anything else available at the counter. He wanted her.

"Hey," I called out across the gym, snagging his attention.

He looked at me and grinned, waving me over.

I weaved through the many weight machines in the gym, saying hello to the people dedicated enough to be working out on a Sunday. Mason had convinced me to meet him at the exclusive gym, even though I would have much preferred hanging out at home, feeling completely miserable about the situation with Natasha.

"Good morning." I greeted the woman with a friendly smile before looking at Mason and raising an eyebrow.

"Relax, Jessica here was just telling me about the new smoothie they got in," Mason said easily, flashing that grin of his that we had dubbed his "panty dropper smile" a long time ago.

"Great, how about we actually work out before we start thinking about replacing calories we haven't burned?"

Mason didn't allow my comment to bother him. "You'll have to excuse my big brother. He's been in a bad mood for a year."

Jessica stared and gave me a little pouty lip with it. "Oh, I'm sorry. Is there anything I can do to cheer you up?"

I didn't want to be rude, but I was not in the mood to flirt. "Thanks, Jessica, but I'll be okay. A good workout will help me get rid of some of the frustration."

She leaned forward, making sure to give me a clear shot of her obvious surgically enhanced breasts squeezed together in the tiny workout tank she was wearing. "I'm really good at relieving tension," she said in blatant invitation.

Mason was snickering in the corner, watching me fend off the rather aggressive female. "I'll keep that in mind. Mason, are you ready?" I asked, anxious to escape Jessica before she could make any more passes at me.

He shrugged a shoulder. "I'm a little frustrated, maybe you'd like to help me relieve some of it," Mason said, reaching out to touch Jessica's hand.

She grinned and turned her attention back to my little brother. He was the bad boy every girl wanted. Clearly, Jessica wasn't picky.

"Why don't you stop by when you're finished?" she said in a sultry voice.

"I'm probably going to be all sweaty," Mason said, staring at her breasts.

She grinned. "That's exactly how I like my men."

Her eyes drifted over the tattoos on his arms, which were bared in a tank top, another thing the ladies liked. Not all the ladies, but the women looking to walk on the wild side with a man who wore his hair too long, broke all the rules of the upper-crust society, and bucked every tradition he could.

I walked away. Mason could follow or stay behind. We all had memberships to the club that was the most elite in the city. Not just anybody could walk in and buy a membership. You had to be a part of the country club and be referred or vouched for by another member. As Bancrofts, we'd been welcomed with open arms. It afforded a level of privacy and security I couldn't find at the standard public gym, which I greatly appreciated, especially when I didn't want to be recognized.

Generally, the employees at the club were far more reserved in their dealings with the clients, but clearly Jessica was new, and Mason had encouraged the heavy flirting.

"She's hot," Mason said, coming to stand beside me as I selected a few dumbbells.

I rolled my eyes. "She is not my type."

"Does it matter? She's gorgeous and she was into you."

I shook my head. "That's usually not the problem. It tends to be *me* not being into them. I like a woman who plays a little harder to get," I told him.

"What's the point? It's all going to end up the same way?" He chuckled.

"There is a point, besides, not interested," I said in a growl.

"You're holding out for her," he said, shaking his head.

I shrugged. "Maybe."

"Has she called?"

"No. I don't expect her to call or reach out. She just got back. We need to give it some time, let the dust settle a little before we go stirring shit up again," I explained as if it weren't bothering me and driving me crazy.

I heard Mason suck in a breath through his teeth and looked up to meet his eyes in the mirror. "I don't know, man, I think you're setting yourself up for a heartbreak."

I shook my head. "It's part of our plan," I insisted.

Mason reached for two weights and began to do curls. I followed suit, sticking to a much lighter set. Mason was ripped, there was no doubt about it, but I preferred to be able to wear suits that didn't tear at the seams.

"A lot can change in a year," Mason said, foreboding in his voice.

"No, it didn't."

"Not for you, but maybe for her," he replied.

I thought about his words but couldn't believe them. My heart and my head refused to believe she had moved on. I couldn't believe that. I wasn't sure how I would go on if that was the case.

"It'll work out. I have to be patient," I said more for myself than Mason.

We continued to work out with Mason seeming to have accepted my explanation about Natasha. I could see his roving eye, using the mirrors in the gym to check out the women who were in a Zumba class in an adjoining room. The man had a roving eye, far worse than I did. It would be offensive if the women weren't the ones initiating the leering.

"You can't tell me that hot brunette doesn't catch your eye?" Mason muttered as we switched positions on the weight machine.

I shrugged a shoulder. "She's pretty," I agreed.

"Pretty? How can you not think about sex when you look at her? Look at that mouth, big full lips. She's checking you out. She's been watching you for the last ten minutes. She wants you. What would it hurt to take her out, maybe have a little after-dinner sex?" he said with a smile.

"Not interested."

"Too late, she's coming over with her friend. Don't blow this for me," he said in a low voice.

"Mason, I don't want to go out or hook up with anyone. I'm here to work out." I hissed.

He was ignoring me. I looked over to see the two women walking toward us, their eyes roaming over us.

"Good morning, ladies. You both look gorgeous," Mason said in a smooth voice.

"Hi, guys. We haven't seen you around before," the brunette said, her eyes hungry.

Mason made a strange face. "Really? I'm here quite often and my brother here, well he gets here when he can."

The ladies continued to eye us. I was beginning to get uncomfortable. "We should probably finish this set," I mumbled to Mason

The women looked at each other, then us again. "What are you guys doing after your workout?" the brunette asked, her eyes staring straight at me.

"We have a lunch date with our mother," I replied, earning a look from Mason that said he did not appreciate my lie.

"That's right," Mason said, turning to look at the women.

The practiced pouts on their lips was ridiculous. They were grown women, not babies. I hated the silly nonsense, which was yet another reason I was drawn to Natasha. She didn't play the stupid games. That kind of shit was cute and funny about ten years ago—not so much now.

"Have a great rest of your day, ladies," I said and returned to the machine to finish my workout.

Mason sauntered over a minute later. "You're a shitty wingman."

I shrugged. "I thought we came here to work out. I didn't know it was going to be a damn meat market. This place is worse than a club. At least there, alcohol can be used as an excuse," I grumbled.

"Any warm-blooded, straight guy would be thrilled with the attention," Mason pointed out.

"I'm not interested. Now, can we finish this. I need to take a shower and get home."

Mason chuckled, not the least bit bothered by my bad attitude. I was happy to be found attractive and usually I could flirt a little better, but knowing Natasha was back was making me a little anxious. Why hadn't she called or stopped by? I knew it had only been a day or two, but if the roles were reversed, I would have gone from the airport straight to her. The longer she waited to contact me, the more I had to believe Mason could be right.

I had to give her the benefit of the doubt. I knew how she felt about me. That didn't just go away. We had the real thing and had survived a two-year separation and come back even stronger. One year was child's play.

"Ready?" Mason asked as we both finished our showers and had changed into street clothes.

I nodded. "I am."

"Want to grab something to eat?"

I looked at him, one eyebrow raised. "From the juice bar?"

He laughed. "I want actual food. We'll sneak out the side exit."

I nodded in agreement. I did not want to fend off the likes of Jessica or any of the others who were crowding into the gym for a late morning workout. Mason was the kind of man used to attracting attention. I believed it was why he had the tattoos and wore his hair a little long. He stood out in a crowd. His muscular body was also eye-catching. I preferred to be a little more less obvious. As Bancrofts, we had notorious reputations and I preferred not to trade on it. Not Mason. He may not have wanted to be a Bancroft and had done everything in his power to shuck the image of a wealthy trust-fund baby, but he loved attention in general.

"She's going to call," I blurted out as we strolled down the street toward a small café.

"Okay," he replied.

"Don't placate me. She's going to call. Everything will work out," I reiterated.

"Okay. I believe you. But if something does throw a wrench in your perfect plans, I'm here for you. I've got your back," he assured me, slapping one beefy hand between my shoulder blades with a little more force than was necessary.

"Thanks," I mumbled, shrugging off his hand and heading into the restaurant to eat all the calories I had just burned.

CHAPTER 29

NATASHA

I was happy to have a day off, with my dad out of the house and my mom out doing whatever it was she did all day. It was hard to pretend like everything was okay. I had thought it would be easier. I had spent so much time convincing myself that my father was right that I had almost bought into all of it. For the most part, I was on board with his plan of staying far away from Jack. Unfortunately, there was a tiny little part of me that still ached for him. That part had been tamped down about a million times. Being back in the same city was making it worse. I had to keep my mind off him. I would not disappoint my family and fall back into old habits.

"Hey," I said when Ashley answered the phone.

"Hey, what's up?"

"Want to hang out today?" I asked hopefully.

"Sure. You want to do some shopping?" she asked.

I shook my head, even though she couldn't see it. I didn't want to go into the city and risk running into Jack. "I was thinking we could hang out here, a little pool time."

"It's cold," she said bluntly.

"The indoor pool silly," I replied.

She giggled. "I thought you were confused about which coast you were on. I'll be over in an hour or so."

I hung up and crawled out of bed, showering before putting on one of the many bikinis I had picked up during my time on the West Coast. I had loved the heat and the sand, but New York was my home. It would always be my home.

I threw on a pretty blue swimsuit cover-up and headed downstairs to the kitchen to throw together some snacks for our day by the pool. It wasn't exactly a sunny beach, but I had developed a real fondness for swimming. I preferred swimming as a workout to running or Pilates. It was so much more freeing and enjoyable.

"Can I get you something?" one of the housekeepers asked, coming into the kitchen while I was rooting around.

"I got it. I'm just grabbing some snacks and drinks for Ashley and me," I said, then smiled.

"Natasha, you know I can do that. Please, go, I'll bring it out," she lectured.

I shook my head. "You have other things to do. I got it. Thank you," I said, taking my bag of loot and striding down the long corridor that led to the indoor pool.

The moment I opened the door, I could smell chlorine. There was always a muggy feeling to the room, which made it feel like you were on a Florida beach in a lot of ways. My mom had an assortment of potted trees and tropical flowers all around the area to give more of a beach feel.

"Just need a little sand, Mom," I joked as I set my bounty from the pantry on one of the tables.

I switched on the surround sound, quickly flipped through the satellite radio stations, and put on a Jack Johnson station to help set the beach vibe. With the mood set, I stripped off my cover-up, quickly put my hair up, and dove into the water. I swam several laps before I came up for air, feeling better already.

"Did you turn into a mermaid while you were over there?" Ashley quipped, watching me from the edge of the pool.

I crossed my arms on the pool edge, my body weightless in the water as I grinned up at her. "Maybe. Come on. It's like being in a huge bathtub. It's so warm," I told her.

She stripped off her own cover-up and daintily stuck in a few painted red toenails before moving to the stairs and walking in. I giggled as I watched her slowly glide through the water.

"It does feel good," she said with serious appreciation in her voice.

We swam a bit before climbing out and retiring to the lounge chairs to feast on the cheese and crackers along with the grapes I had hijacked from the kitchen.

"Have you heard from him yet?" she asked, and I knew exactly who the "he" she was talking about was.

"No and I don't plan to."

"What? Come on." She cajoled.

I shook my head. "It's over. It was a mistake from the very beginning. I was rebelling and have learned my lesson. Jack Bancroft is off-limits."

"Nat, you love him," she said in a soft voice.

I turned to look at her. "I can't."

"You can't because your dad says so, but I know you still care for him," she replied.

I shrugged a shoulder. "It doesn't matter. A year is a long time. I'm sure he's moved on, especially after the way things went down. I think he got the message loud and clear that my family would never accept him. This is for the best. Jack and I had fun while it lasted, but now I'm focused on getting my company off the ground."

Ashley turned her green gaze on me, eyeing me carefully. Without the shield of sunglasses, I couldn't hide what I knew she was seeing. "Liar."

I heaved a sigh. "Ash, I have to move on. I can't do that to my dad. I have to leave Jack in the past."

"What about him?"

"What about him?" I asked.

"Do you think he is willing to move on?"

"I don't think it's up to him. This is a joint thing, if I say no, then

177

it's over," I said, trying my best to sound committed to my decision but failing miserably.

She was silent for a bit, popping grapes into her mouth. I knew she had more to say and was waiting to hear it.

"Jack was crazy into you. I don't think he's going to simply let you walk away without a fight."

"It isn't his choice," I reiterated.

"He loves you."

"A year is a long time. There is a good chance he is seeing someone. He's a wealthy, attractive, kind, sexy man. Women have been after him for a long time. With me out of the picture, he was free to move on," I said, the words souring the grapes in my stomach.

Ashley burst into laughter. "Gee, I can totally tell you're over him. Are there any more adjectives you'd like to use to describe him?"

I turned my head and shot her a glare before closing my eyes and pretending I was on a tropical island far away from my worries. We spent the afternoon swimming, relaxing, and catching up on the happenings around the city and in our social circle. She'd been out to Los Angeles to visit me a few months ago, but a lot could happen in three months and as it turned out, I was seriously behind on the gossip.

"Thanks for hanging with me today," I told her as we headed down the long corridor into the main living area.

"Duh, what else am I going to do when my best friend returns after a year away," she said with a warm smile.

I walked her out to her fancy little red Miata in the driveway, the cool fall air in stark contrast to the humid environment we had just left.

"I'll call you in the next day or two. I'm trying to figure out my schedule," I told her.

"Hey, there is a charity ball for the children's hospital this weekend. I know Elijah is going, are you?" she asked hopefully.

"I don't know. I hadn't heard about it."

"You have to go, please. I've had to attend so many of these without you. I need you there to keep me entertained," she insisted.

"We'll have to go shopping," I said the words as if I were talking about doing something dreadful.

She grinned. "I know. Tomorrow?"

I nodded. "I'll skip and go back to work another day."

I waved as she drove off and had just made it back inside the mansion when the front door opened. I turned to see what Ashley forgot and saw Elijah standing there. We stared at each other for several minutes before he walked toward me and wrapped his arms around me.

"I'm sorry," he muttered.

I sighed against him. I had missed my big brother. We had always been very close, and the year apart had been difficult. I'd seen him a couple times, but I had been very cool toward him despite his many apologies. I decided in that moment all I had was my family. I needed to cherish every single one of them.

I hugged him back and felt him sigh with relief.

"Oh, this is great!" my mother squealed walking through the door.

We broke apart and I had to wipe a tear, which had slithered down my face, from my cheek. "Hi, Mom."

"I'm glad you're both here. I need to talk to you both about something. Come into the living room," she said, her heels clacking across the marble floor as she moved.

"I guess that means we better follow," Elijah said with a smile, wrapping his arm around my shoulder as we trailed behind my mother.

It felt good to have finally closed the chasm that had been between my brother and me. He was only looking out for me, trying to steer me in the right direction. It was better for all involved if I went along with the family's wishes.

"So, Levy Industries will be donating a large amount to the children's hospital. We've been asked to give a speech at the fundraiser this Friday," my mom said, her eyes dancing with excitement.

"Congratulations, Mom," I said, knowing how much she loved the public eye and any chance to show off her wealth and status among the rich and famous in New York City.

She shook her head. "I've just left your father's office and we want you to present the check and give the speech."

"Me?" I squeaked.

She was absolutely beaming. "Yes, this is a great time for us to reintroduce you to society. Your father thinks this is a great chance for you to get your name and face out there as you prepare to launch your own company."

"I don't know, Mom. I wouldn't know what to say. Maybe it would be better for Elijah to present the check," I suggested.

"Nonsense! This is an excellent opportunity for you to get yourself out there. It would make your father and I very proud to see you do this," she said, pulling out the card she knew I couldn't refuse.

Elijah looked at me, grinning. "I guess now you know you have to do it."

"Fine. I'm going shopping tomorrow. I wasn't planning on standing in front of a crowd," I said already feeling nervous.

"Perfect! Your dad will be so pleased," my mother said, clapping her hands together.

I stood and left the room, heading upstairs to change and call Ashley. I was going to need the perfect dress, which meant some serious shopping ahead of us. She would need to be fully rested. I heard my phone beeping, telling me I had missed a call. I checked the display and felt my heart speed up. It was Jack. There was a voice mail. I couldn't hear his voice. I quickly checked and cleared the voice mail without listening to the message.

He knew I was back. He was calling. Did he actually think I was going to hold him to the promise he had made? I hoped not. I didn't want to hurt him, but I couldn't be with him. I had to do what was best for my family. My happiness was going to have to sit on the back burner for now.

CHAPTER 30

JACK

As usual, the first thing I thought of when I opened my eyes was Nat. I checked my phone and wasn't all that surprised to discover she hadn't called or texted. Feeling very zombielike, I went through my usual morning routine, showering and shaving before throwing on a tailored suit and heading off to work at the office. I sometimes felt like I was stuck in my own version of *Groundhog Day*. It was the same old shit, different day.

I glanced up at the clock and realized it was after ten. I had accomplished nothing in the two hours since I'd been sitting at my desk. I looked at my computer screen. It was the same email I'd been returning to for the last hour. Staying focused on anything was a real struggle. I was trapped in a horrible limbo, unable to move forward or do anything until I knew what was happening.

Nat was back. She hadn't called me and wasn't answering my calls or texts. I had a bad feeling about it. She would have reached out. She would have found a way to get a message to me if she wanted me. I kept pushing away the bad thoughts, telling myself she had a plan. She'd call me when she could. There was no way she would listen to her father and cut me out of her life.

I closed my eyes, willing away the doubt and demanding my brain stay on task. It was like I could sense her in the city. I wished I had never seen the paper announcing her return. When I knew she was gone, there was always the idea we were sticking to the pact. I didn't have to wonder if she had changed her mind. I knew she was back and now it was eating at me, driving me absolutely insane with both hope and doubt commingling in my brain and taking up way too much space.

"Damn it!" I slammed my hand on the desk and stood up.

Sitting in my office wasn't doing any good. Something had to give, or I was going to lose my damn mind. I stomped down to Grayson's office, looking for a distraction. Everyone I passed was hard at work. I could see some executive meeting happening in the conference room and hoped I wasn't supposed to be in there. My secretary hadn't mentioned it, so I was going with no. I'd be useless anyway. I knew Grayson would probably be working hard, like I should be. Maybe he would inspire me. I hoped. Or maybe he'd give me some important project that had to be done right away and I could devote all my time and energy to it. I smiled at his secretary as I passed. She didn't bother trying to stop me. I knocked once and headed inside.

He looked up from whatever it was he was reading and making notes on, an eyebrow raised in question. "What's up?" he asked.

I walked in, flopped in one of the leather chairs, and sighed. "I'm bored. Give me something exciting to do."

He looked at me, both brows raised now. "You're at work. It isn't exactly a death-defying kind of job."

I curled my lip with disgust. "It's boring. I want to do something exciting."

"Are you saying you want to leave for the day or you're contemplating retirement?" he asked, confusion written all over his face.

"No and no," I answered, not really knowing what I wanted.

Grayson nodded. "Okay, so, do you want me to entertain you? I don't juggle," he said dryly.

I groaned with irritation at his attempt to be funny. "No."

Grayson stared at me a few seconds before throwing his hands up. "Then watch me work. I have to get this report reviewed and back to the acquisition team. I'll try my best to do it in a way that is exciting and entertaining. I don't do tricks. I could sing," he said, the smart-ass tone nearly pulling a smile from me.

Clearly, Grayson wasn't understanding of my plight. I was thankful he didn't ask me about Natasha directly, even though we both knew that was my problem. Simply being out of my own office and with him in his helped me climb out of my head a little.

I sat in the chair, staring out the windows for a bit, listening to the sound of his pen making scratch marks on the paper with the occasional tap on the calculator displayed on his tablet. My big brother looked relaxed and completely at ease in his chair, acting as the head of Bancroft Estates. There was no tension in his body. He looked content and happy. I wanted that. Before, Grayson was always stiff and edgy. The love of a good woman had changed him.

"Thanks," I said, actually feeling better and got to my feet.

He glanced up. "Uh, glad I could be of help. Stop by and stare at me anytime."

I chuckled, shrugging a shoulder. "You are pretty funny looking."

He rolled his eyes at the rather juvenile joke. "Go away."

I laughed, feeling better and ready to face the day like a grown-up. I walked out of his office, determined to keep my head in the game, but first I needed a heavy dose of coffee and maybe something sweet. I headed for the break room, hoping there were some doughnuts or those little treats someone was always bringing in. The room was empty, because everyone else was actually working, except for me.

The TV mounted on the wall was on, the background noise all but ignored as I stuck a K-Cup in the coffee maker and waited for my hot brew to be finished. I glanced around and found some healthy granola bars sitting right next to a box of doughnuts. That's what I needed.

"Natasha Levy has just been announced as one of the guest speakers," the newswoman said from somewhere above my head.

I froze. Did the news lady really say Natasha's name or was it my brain playing tricks on me? I truly had Natasha on the brain if I could actually hear her name being spoken. That was some next level shit I didn't even want to try and figure out what it meant. I turned and looked up at the TV and sure enough, her name was running across the ticker tape along the bottom of the screen. It was a slight relief to know I wasn't completely losing my mind.

I stepped closer, reading the information being reported, barely listening to the man and woman news anchors as they jabbered on about the exciting new venture and blah, blah, blah. My eyes were glued to the screen as a picture of Natasha popped up on the screen. She was launching a new branch of Levy Industries. I smiled thinking about her getting her chance to start her own company. It wasn't exactly her own. Her daddy was obviously footing the bill on the start-up, which I was sure made Wayne Levy a very happy man. He got to keep her under his thumb a little while longer.

Everything started to become very clear. Natasha was being given what she wanted, but I had a feeling there were some caveats attached to the project. She could have nothing to do with me if she wanted to fulfill her dream of starting her own company. Now, she wouldn't only lose her family if she chose to be with me—she would also lose everything she worked for. I felt the cold realization wash over me, my heart aching with the understanding that I may have truly lost her for good. I couldn't compete with that.

"Go," Grayson said, clapping a hand on my shoulder, nearly causing me to squeal like a teen girl.

I turned and looked at him, my brain still processing the news announcement. "What?"

"Go to the event. We have an open invitation. You could represent Bancroft Estates. We'll give a big fat check and you'll get a chance to talk to her," he said smoothly.

I shook my head. "I don't know if it's a good idea for me and Wayne Levy to be in the same room. I'm sure Elijah will be there as well."

"I can't go, but I'm sure Mason or maybe Colt will go with you. You need backup in case there's trouble again," he groused.

I looked back at the monitor, her picture still in the corner of the screen as they talked about the charity event that was supposed to be a big deal. Usually Grayson or Colt, as the head of the charity foundation set up in the Bancroft name, went to the big shindigs aimed at getting the wealthy to write big checks. I usually managed to avoid them, but this could be my one chance to talk to her. She was avoiding me, that much was clear.

"I will," I blurted out, my mind made up.

"Not alone. We can have security go along as well," Grayson said.

I appreciated him looking out for me, but I wasn't too worried about Wayne or Elijah sending their guards after me in a public place. They had an image to uphold and wouldn't want anyone to realize they were nothing but a bunch of thugs.

"I'll be fine."

"Try not to cause too much trouble," Grayson said with a chuckle.

I shrugged a shoulder and turned back to my coffee. "They started this war. I'll walk away if I need to."

"You can't go in there already prepared to give up," Grayson said, shifting to stand a little closer to me.

"I'm not planning on giving up, but if she doesn't want me and has decided to do as daddy dearest has ordered, there's not much I can do about it," I said, blowing on the coffee before taking the first sip.

"Bullshit," Grayson spat.

"Excuse me?"

"You're a Bancroft. We don't take no for an answer because the challenge is too big. If you want this woman and you know she is the only one who will make you happy, you won't give up so easily."

"Grayson, I don't want to make her life miserable. I won't push her. I'm man enough to accept defeat if it saves her a lot of heartache. She is really close with her family. I won't be the one who divides them. That isn't cool. If she tells me to my face that she wants to move on, I'll let her. It isn't like I can't find another woman," I said, trying to sound cavalier.

"Keep telling yourself. Remember, I've been there before. It isn't quite so easy," he said, a small smile playing on his lips.

"Completely different situation. You were a dick. I'm the good guy in this version," I said, laughing as I teased him.

"Whatever. I got the girl."

I shook my head. "Barely. If she had better sense, she would have run far away from you."

"Go back to work. Earn that giant paycheck." He growled.

I laughed, feeling a little better about my plight. I would go to the ball, find Nat, and get a few moments alone with her. I needed to know if she wanted me to wait while she worked things out or if she was well and truly kicking me to the curb. I kept telling myself I could accept the last, for her sake, but deep down, I knew it would rip my heart out to never have her again.

CHAPTER 31

NATASHA

I smoothed the tight black dress over my hips, making sure there were no wrinkles. I felt a bit like a glamorous Morticia Adams. The form-fitting gown had lots of sparkle and would certainly attract a great deal of attention. I wasn't typically prone to wearing gowns that were quite so flashy, but tonight was a big night. When I saw the dress at the shop, I initially passed on it. It was swanky, sultry, and a little daring. I was the girl who stuck to the conventional. I liked my own style, but I didn't like to draw a lot of attention to myself.

Ashley was the one to convince me to try it on. I had agreed to do it more as a joke to show her it wasn't for me. The moment I slid the fabric over my body, I knew I had to go for it. It made me feel like a woman. Like a grown-up and not the little girl my father tried to insist I was. I wanted to rebel just a little against my father. I knew the gown was over the top and not exactly the subtle classy style he always preferred, but it was elegant. Sexy but not sleazy.

There was a long slit up the side, which was the only way I was able to walk in the dress. I turned to check the slit, making sure there was no risk of things being exposed that shouldn't be. I did not want to be flashing anyone. I had opted to go commando for the night—another daring risk. There was no room for a panty line. I put in the diamond earrings my father had given me for my birthday a couple years ago. They matched the necklace he gave me last year for Christmas. It was the perfect amount of ice to match the dress. My hair was in a twist, keeping the hair off my neck, showcasing the jewelry.

I heard a soft knock on my bedroom-slash-apartment door and stepped out of the huge closet, carrying my shoes with me as I moved to my vanity. "Come in," I called out, expecting my mother.

Elijah stepped through the door, wearing a tuxedo and looking like a true Levy. He was a handsome guy. I briefly wondered about his love life and why he wasn't married. He was wealthy, attractive, and I thought he was a good guy, minus the Jack incident.

He smiled when he saw me. "You look beautiful," he said.

"You're looking very handsome yourself. Is that a new tux?"

He winked. "This old thing. Yes, it's new. Mother insisted. They all look the same to me, but she said tonight was special and it had to be new. They're always so uncomfortable when they're new," he said, tugging at the collar.

I laughed. "You're such a baby. At least you don't have to wear heels," I complained, strapping my shoes on my feet.

He flopped down in one of the chairs against the wall. He suddenly reminded me of his ten-year-old self when he was being forced to dress up and go to one of our parents' many social obligations.

"I'm leaving as soon as I make my appearance."

"You're staying for my speech," I told him.

"Of course."

"Are they waiting on me?" I asked, turning back to the mirror to put on the finishing touches of makeup.

"Mom said to give her five minutes. Dad's enjoying a cigar."

I laughed. "Of course, he is."

"Are you nervous?" he asked.

I grabbed the red lipstick I had selected for the night. It was bold and a stark contrast to the all-black ensemble I was wearing, bolstering my confidence a little more.

"I'm not nervous. It isn't like I haven't been performing for wealthy people since I was five years old. This is what we've been groomed to do. We're the perfect Levy children, molded in our parents' likenesses. You poised to take over the company, and me branching out to be a little Levy, just like a good daughter should," I said, knowing I sounded snarky, but unable to control myself.

He threw his head back and laughed. "Damn, you're fierce."

I smeared on the lipstick before turning to face him. "I feel fierce. I feel like I've come a long way, and nothing is going to get in my way now."

He shook his head and rose from his chair, walking toward me. He placed a hand on each of my shoulders and looked directly into my eyes. "You're going to do great. I'm proud of you."

I winked. "I know."

"Damn, you're a little spitfire."

"I was taught by the best. Now, are you ready to do this? We are going to kick ass and take names tonight," I said with all the confidence in the world.

"We're going to a charity event. This isn't the fight club. Relax and try to have a good time. No one is coming after you," he said, the playfulness gone.

I took a deep breath. "I know, but I have to psyche myself up. This is my one chance to make a good impression. I don't want to be seen as little Nat Levy, tugging on her daddy's coattails. I want to be taken seriously. I want people to see I've grown up and I'm serious about my business."

He nodded. "I understand. No one doubts your determination or your ability to be successful. Me, Mom, Dad, we're all behind you."

I gave him a quick hug, making sure not to get any makeup on his crisp white shirt. "Thank you. That means a lot."

"You're welcome. I promise you, I will always have your back," he said, his voice serious.

I stepped away and smoothed down my dress once again before walking out of the apartment. I was very grateful to have my big brother back in my life. It had been hard not being able to call him up and chat about nothing. The horrible business with Jack had nearly torn my family apart. It was only now that I realized Elijah was only looking out for me. I knew he and Jack had not spoken since that night. Elijah had lost his best friend because of me.

Thinking about Jack and that night stirred up other memories that I wished I could have kept buried. I didn't want to have feelings for him. I wished there was a switch I could flip. I wanted to stop feeling anything for him. All the missed calls, voice mails, and texts were killing me. Hearing his voice on the voice mail had pulled my heart-strings. It literally took my breath away.

"You okay?" Elijah asked, pausing at the stairs to take my arm.

I smiled. "I'm great."

"Hold on to that rail. I don't want you tumbling down the stairs in those heels," he teased.

The heels were killer, but they were perfect for the dress and made my legs look longer than they actually were. Being petite had its bene-fits, but in a dress like I was wearing, I needed every inch of height I could get.

Our parents were waiting in the foyer as we descended the stairs. I did love moments like these. Our family had been to plenty of swanky balls and other formal events, but it was always exciting and fun to dress up.

"Princess, you look absolutely stunning." My dad gasped.

"Thank you, Daddy," I said, happy to please him.

"I love the dress, even if it is a little risqué," my mom said, staring at the fitted gown.

I smiled. "You look very pretty, Mom."

"Thank you, dear."

"Are we ready to go? The limo is waiting," my dad said, moving toward the door.

"Ready," I said, and carefully stepped off the last stair and made my way to the door.

I wasn't used to wearing such high heels, but once I got my bear-ings, I felt better. I felt confident. This was going to be a good night, I silently vowed. We crawled into the back of the limo, all of our various colognes and perfumes creating a bit of a toxic environment in the closed-up car. My dad cracked a window, his unlit cigar in his pocket. I could smell the tobacco fighting for the top spot in the cloying smells.

My mother poured champagne for each of us. "I want to toast new beginnings," she said with a smile.

"It is going to be a great evening. Nat is going to be spectacular and kick off this new profitable venture," my dad said, clinking glasses with my own and then the others.

"Was it you who put out the press release?" Elijah asked our mother.

She grinned. "I wanted to make sure we sold the rest of those tickets to the event and gave Nat the audience she needs."

I laughed. "You are a sneaky lady. Thank you."

"I'm more than just a pretty face," she said, beaming with pride at her contribution to the family business.

"Of course you are, dear," my father assured her.

The car navigated slowly through the traffic on a busy Friday night in downtown New York City. I looked out the window, watching people moving along on the sidewalks and those sitting in traffic alongside us. I loved people watching and imagining what they were doing in their busy lives.

"Oh my." My mother gasped.

I turned to look out her side of the car and saw the line of limos. "Wow, I didn't realize how big this was."

"Now you're nervous," Elijah teased.

I shook my head. "Nope."

"Liar."

Our limo got in line and came to a stop. We watched as one group after another climbed out of their limos and made their way across the red carpet. Whoever organized the event had gone all out. I couldn't remember something quite so elaborate in the past. They were literally rolling out the red carpet.

The flashing of cameras from paparazzi as well as people who were interested in seeing if any Hollywood people would climb out of one of the limos. My mom was primping, as the limo crawled closer to the exiting point.

The car stopped and before I knew it, the back door was opened. My dad went out first, as was his custom. Then my mom followed by Elijah, who reached in and helped me out of the car. The flashing lights blinded me at first, but I quickly adjusted my line of sight to look over the flashes and not directly at the damn things.

My arm was looped through Elijah's, using his steady body to support mine and keep me stable. We all stopped and posed for pictures together. I was asked to step away for a single picture, which I accommodated once. I didn't like all the attention on me. As we made our way inside and away from the cameras and the crowd, I breathed a sigh of relief.

"This place is packed," Elijah commented as we stepped to the side of the hall.

"It is," I mumbled, smiling and nodding at a couple of women I had gone to college with years before.

"I wonder if there will be any other familiar faces here tonight," Elijah said in a low voice.

I knew exactly who he was talking about. I knew Jack wasn't usually the type to attend such showy events and hadn't really thought much about him showing up. Colt Bancroft was the one who attended the various charity events and was generally the face of the Bancroft charitable deeds. Now that Elijah had put the thought in my head, I couldn't stop scanning the faces passing in front of me.

"We should go in," I said, noticing our parents slowly begin their way into the ballroom.

With Elijah beside me, we walked in and were quickly given glasses of champagne as we began to make the rounds, mingling and making nice with some of the wealthiest people in the city—the state really. I felt comfortable and confident, and every minute I didn't see Jack, I relaxed a little more.

CHAPTER 32

JACK

I put on the cuff links before slipping into the jacket of my tux. It was a big night. I could almost feel the weight of my future sitting on my shoulders. Whatever happened tonight would likely decide my future. I knew I would see her. I was going to make damn sure I got a minute alone with her. I wasn't in the mood for games and wouldn't waste time asking her silly questions. I wanted the truth.

I checked the clock before using my fingers to smooth the hair above my ears. I had gotten a cut that morning, wanting to make a great third first impression, if that was a thing. I couldn't believe how long I had been waiting for Natasha. If I were any one of my brothers, I would laugh at them for being so ridiculous. I would tell them to move on and to quit playing games. Unfortunately, I couldn't seem to follow my own advice.

I grabbed my keys and headed out the door. Mason was going to be meeting me in the lobby of my building. I had managed to talk him into going with me, which hadn't been easy. I couldn't remember the last time I had seen him in a tux—if ever. I was a little worried he would be waiting for me in a sleeveless tux. I would kill him if he tried anything like that.

At first, I didn't recognize my younger brother, standing with his back to me as he chatted with another man wearing a suit. When he turned to look at me, I stopped walking. Mason, the notorious black sheep of the Bancroft family, willingly the black sheep, looked like he had just stepped off a Wall Street trading floor.

"Don't say it." He growled when a grin broke out on my face.

I shook my head. "I have to. Hold on," I said, grabbing my phone from my pocket.

I had to get a picture. If I didn't have a picture, I couldn't prove it. I already knew my other bothers—no picture and it didn't happen.

"Don't you fucking dare," he said in a voice that would have terrified the average person, but I knew he was all bark and very little bite.

I took the picture anyway, grinning when he tried to snatch my phone. "Holy shit. I didn't know you could clean up. You look—normal. Mom is going to be so damn happy. Do you know how long she's waited to see you in a tux?"

He rolled his eyes. "Keep it up and you'll be going stag. I don't need this shit."

I raised an eyebrow. "I am going stag. You're not my date."

He smiled, his bushy brows bouncing above his hazel eyes, which were exact replicas of my own. "You know you think I'm sexy."

"Please don't talk for the rest of the night," I grumbled, striding toward the doors.

The limo was waiting to take us to the hotel. I had planned to arrive about thirty minutes late. I didn't want to go through the whole red-carpet ordeal. I didn't need that kind of attention.

Mason climbed into the limo, his designer tux stretching around his huge biceps as he sat across from me. "We could tell the driver to keep going. We can go to Atlantic City and forget all about this whole thing. Let's go get drunk, gamble, and find a couple women to pass the time with."

I shook my head. "I have to do this. This is important. I have to see her."

"It's a bad idea. This is a new tux. I don't want to get it dirty," he said, dusting off an invisible fleck of lint from the sleeve.

"Not everything has to be violent. We're not going to a biker bar or wherever it is you hang out. No one is going to be hitting anyone," I lectured.

He smirked. "You are dragging me to this thing because you are worried it will get violent. You wanted me because you know I can handle my business."

I sighed. "Again, this isn't a tavern. You can't break bottles over people's heads or whatever it is you do in those places."

He was genuinely laughing. "One of these days you're going to have to strip off that suit and visit one of those places. It might help get that stick out of your ass."

I didn't bother acknowledging his insult. When the limo pulled up to the side entrance at my request, we quickly exited and slipped inside without any of the onlookers noticing. The affair was in full swing when we walked through the double doors. Mason immediately attracted the attention of several young ladies. They recognized the bad boy thing and were drawn in like moths to a flame. I wasn't exactly ignored, but I was doing my best to fend off advances in case Natasha happened to see me.

A man in a black suit gently tapped us on our shoulders and asked us to find our table. Fifteen minutes later, we were sitting at a table surrounded by others who had paid the five grand for a plate. The lights dimmed in the room before the podium up front was lit up.

The event coordinator gave a short speech before announcing Natasha. I held my breath, anxious to see her after a long year deprived of her.

There was a rolling hush as she walked on to the makeshift stage. My table in the back didn't give me the best view. I pushed my chair back, giving me a direct line of sight to the stage. It felt as if I had been kicked in the ribs.

"Oh my God," I said on a breath.

"Damn, I guess I can see why you're so hung up on this woman." Mason hissed.

I couldn't pull my eyes away from her. She was absolutely stunning. The dress hugged her curves, reminding me of what was underneath. I briefly closed my eyes, controlling my rolling emotions and primal response to seeing her.

I wasn't sure how it was even possible, but she had grown more beautiful. Every time I saw her after one of these long stretches, she took my breath away. I was a lucky man to have even had the chance to be with her. I hoped to have her back in my life, but I would cherish every minute I had spent with her if she decided to walk away.

She began to talk, but I didn't hear the words. I was watching her lips, my eyes roving every inch of her face, remembering the way her lips felt against mine. Her lips stopped, I looked up to her eyes, and saw her staring at me. I saw the flush spread over her cheeks. She managed to pick up her train of thought and pulled her eyes away from mine. I immediately felt the loss and wanted to demand she look at me again.

The second her speech was finished, she rushed off stage. It was my chance.

"I'll be back," I said, ignoring Mason's protests not to do it.

I made my way out of the room, dashed down the hall, and went through the door I suspected led behind the stage area. I saw her walking away and took a brief second to admire her fine ass in the gown before rushing toward her.

"Stop," I called out.

She spun around, her eyes wide, shaking her head. "No. You can't be here," she said.

I stepped closer, using my body to push her away from the crowd. "I need to see you," I told her.

She drew in a breath, her chin rising. "You've seen me. Go."

It was not the reaction I had expected. "Nat," I protested.

"No, you should go, seriously," she insisted, backing away from me.

"Nat, come on, it's me. You know we have unfinished business," I said, using a low voice I knew turned her on.

I could use my charm just as well as the next guy. She wasn't immune to it, no matter how much she pretended otherwise. I stepped closer, my hand reaching out to cup her cheek.

She jerked away. "Don't."

I dropped my hand, staring into her blue eyes, trying to find the Nat I knew and loved. "Natasha, what's wrong?"

"Jack, we can't," she said, shaking her head.

"We'll go upstairs. I'll get a room. We can talk, that's all, if that's what you want," I pressed.

"Jack, this isn't a good time. I need to get back. My family is waiting."

I watched her, studying her mannerisms and expression. She was truly pulling away from me.

"Will we talk? Are you going to tell me what's going on?" I asked, a little frustrated.

She looked over my shoulder. "I need to go."

I was stunned. No matter how much I had tried to prepare myself or the possibility she would truly dump me, there was a part of me that refused to believe it could actually happen. I thought about what Mason had said and couldn't believe he could have been right. No way.

"Can you call me later?" I asked.

"No. Goodbye, Jack," she said the words and brushed past me.

I turned, with total confusion, to watch her walk away. She'd never truly denied me. We'd played games, but she always ended up coming back to me. I had the stark realization that wasn't the case.

"Well son of a bitch." I groaned, walking back into the hall.

I wanted to leave. My goal had been to see her and talk to her. I had done both. There was nothing more for me to do. I walked back into the ballroom, ignoring everyone. I found Mason, flirting with a woman.

"I'm ready," I said in a low voice.

Mason looked at me. "Ready? To leave? I was just starting to have a good time," he said, smiling at the woman waiting a few feet away.

"Yes, I'm ready to leave. Stay. I'm leaving." I growled, turning and heading for the door before the night got any worse.

I had managed to avoid the rest of the Levy clan and I wanted to keep it that way. The last thing I needed was to see Wayne Levy gloating or the smug look on Elijah's face knowing he'd won. They had managed to persuade Natasha to stay away from me. It was a hard pill to swallow. By the time I made it to the limo, Mason was on my heels.

He took off his jacket, removed his bow tie, and unbuttoned the top few buttons before climbing into the back alongside me.

"Goddamn, how do you guys wear those damn things so often," he grumbled.

I ignored his comment, reaching for the bottle of scotch in the small bar. I didn't bother pouring a glass and drank a long slug straight from the bottle.

"Don't even say it." I growled when he looked at me with pity.

"I take it things didn't go well," he said, grabbing the bottle out of my hand and taking a long drink.

I yanked it back. "Not exactly."

"I'm sorry. I know that doesn't mean shit, but I am sorry."

"Thanks," I said, staring out the window.

"Let's go out. I'll show you how real people have a good time," he said with a grin.

"I'm not in the mood."

"You keep slamming that bottle of scotch and you will be," he quipped.

My response was to take another drink from the bottle. "I just want to go home."

He shrugged a shoulder. "Suit yourself. I'm going out."

I nodded, my mind kept replaying the brief conversation with Natasha. She had seemed so different. She wasn't her usual, warm self. Hell, she'd even dressed differently. It was like she came back an entirely different woman. Maybe I had lost her for good.

CHAPTER 33

NATASHA

I knew I had better get my butt downstairs to eat breakfast with the family or risk one of them coming up to check on me. I never said a word about the encounter with Jack last night, but I had a feeling my guilt was written all over my face. Jack wasn't the kind of man who blended in. I knew my family had to have either seen or heard that he was in attendance. I hadn't seen him after our backstage run-in.

I slipped on my new cashmere sweater and pulled my hair into a loose-up style before making my way downstairs. I could smell bacon and immediately perked up. How bad could life be when there was bacon?

"Good morning," I said, breezing into the dining room where everyone else was already seated.

"Good morning, princess." My dad greeted me with a friendly smile.

That smile, and his overall happiness, was why I had pushed Jack away the night before.

I took my seat and was quickly delivered a plate with bacon, fluffy scrambled eggs, and a couple pieces of wheat toast. A second later, a plate of French toast and another plate of two golden pancakes was placed in front of me. My eyes grew wide as I looked up at the woman serving me a breakfast that would feed three people.

"Thank you," I said, wondering what they expected me to do with all the food.

"I wasn't sure what you would be in the mood for, so I had the cook prepare several dishes," my mother explained.

"This is amazing," I said, using my fingers to pick up a piece of crispy bacon and earning a frown from my mom.

"You did great last night," my dad said.

"Yes, she did," my mother chimed in.

I looked at Elijah. "What? You need me to bolster your ego?" he joked.

"Nope. I kicked ass," I shot back.

"Natasha!" Mom gasped.

I laughed and dug into the breakfast, doing my best to appear normal. I didn't want them to know I had seen Jack. I did not want to stir up that hornet's nest. Inside, that familiar ache was burning a hole in my belly. It was a fire only Jack could ignite and only he could put out. I had dated, or attempted to date, and no man had come close to measuring up to Jack. I shoved a piece of bacon into my mouth to distract my brain from going down that very dangerous road again. I had to stay focused. Keep my eyes on the prize. My company and a good, healthy relationship with my family was my main goal.

We finished our leisurely breakfast, none of us having any real plans for the day and in no hurry to go anywhere.

"I'm going up," I said, after drinking the last bit of orange juice.

"Are you going to be home today?" my mother asked.

I shrugged. "I think so. I need to call Ashley. We talked about doing a little shopping," I said, wanting an excuse to have a little time away.

"Oh, that sounds fun," she answered.

I managed to extract myself from the dining room and practically ran upstairs. I felt horribly guilty and kept expecting one of them to call me out. I couldn't believe none of them knew about my meeting with Jack. Maybe they were waiting for me to confess. It was probably all in my head.

I made it to my room and headed for my phone, plugged in on my nightstand. I was almost afraid to look at it, afraid to see Jack's number on the screen. I grabbed the phone, heard a noise behind me, and nearly screamed with alarm.

"You scared me!" I scolded Elijah.

He shrugged. "Sorry. What's wrong? You ran up here like the hounds of hell were on your heels."

I shook my head. "Nothing. I was just grabbing my phone to call Ashley," I said, holding up the phone to prove my story.

He eyed me carefully. "Liar. Something's up."

"I don't know what you're talking about," I said, walking past him and heading back into the living area of my apartment.

He followed me, not the kind of guy who would ever give up that easily. "Nat, I can tell something is on your mind. You can talk to me."

I flopped down on the settee while he took a seat across from me in one of the chairs my mother had moved into the room.

"I saw Jack," I blurted out.

I saw his eyes narrow and his jaw clench. "You what? When?"

"Last night. After my speech. He found me backstage."

He was slowly nodding. "And?"

"Nothing. Nothing happened. I didn't talk to him. We exchanged a few words and that was it. I told him I couldn't see him or talk to him ever again," I explained, hoping Elijah would keep my secret.

I wanted to believe my brother was loyal to me and I wanted to trust him, but after the last incident, I wasn't quite so sure I could rely on him. He was my dad's son first and foremost. That was where his true loyalties lay.

"You did the right thing. You can't start with him again. It would tear Dad up. I don't want to see you hurt, Nat. Please promise me you'll stay away from him," he asked, his voice low.

I didn't detect anger. In fact, I thought I could hear a little regret and sadness.

I nodded. "I am. Now, will you please go away so I can call Ashley."

"Ashley?" he questioned.

I cocked my head to the side and shot him a glare. "Yes, Ashely. I'm not going to explain my every move to you. Remember, I'm a grown adult. I'm only telling you who I'm calling to be nice. I don't have to tell you anything."

He grinned. "All right. I'll leave you alone."

"Good."

"I'm sorry," he said, stopping at the doorway.

"For?"

He let out a long breath. "For all that Jack business. For what it's worth, I am really sorry about everything."

"Thanks. It's over. It's in the past and I don't want to talk about it ever again."

He walked out, closing the door behind him. I breathed a sigh of relief. It felt good to get it off my chest. I truly hadn't done anything wrong last night, but I felt horribly guilty for not telling them I had seen Jack. I was stuck in this weird limbo. I felt like a sixteen-year-old girl who'd been busted sneaking around with the boy from the wrong side of the tracks and was now on lockdown. It was hard to reconcile that feeling with the fact I was a grounded thirty-year-old woman.

I looked down at the phone in my hand and called Ashley. I couldn't wait to tell her about the run-in with Jack. She'd been so busy dancing and having a good time last night, I hadn't wanted to ruin it with more of my drama, but now I needed her advice. I needed her to tell me I was doing the right thing.

"Good morning," she answered in a singsong voice.

"Hey there. How's your head?" I teased.

She giggled. "Not bad at all. I drank a gallon of water before I crawled into bed for the night—or the morning I guess."

I laughed. "Did you go home with that guy you were dancing with most of the night?"

She gasped. "Natasha Levy! What kind of girl do you think I am?" she asked with exaggerated shock.

"I think you are the kind of woman who spent the night dancing with a really hot man, and I think you are the kind of woman who doesn't let a man like that get away."

She burst into laughter. "Well, I didn't go home with him, but I did get his number. He was hot, huh?"

"He was."

"What about you? Did you have fun?"

I cleared my throat. "Did you happen to see Jack at the ball?"

"No. He was there?"

"Yes."

"Oh, Nat, did you?" She didn't finish her sentence.

"No. After the speech he found me backstage. He wanted to talk, but I told him I couldn't," I said the words, feeling the hurt of the moment all over again.

"How did he take it?" she asked in a soft voice.

"Not well. The look on his face … it was horrible," I muttered.

"I'm sorry. You know this is for the best. Did you agree to talk with him later? Should I be expecting him to show up with a secret phone again?" she asked.

"No, I don't think so. I told him I couldn't talk to him. I think I made it clear it was over," I said.

Ashley was quiet for a few seconds. "You don't sound convinced."

I groaned. "I'm not. Jack is not the kind of man who backs down easily. We only talked for a minute. I think he thought I was pushing him away because we were at the ball with my parents in the area. I have to make him understand we can never be together."

"I think you're right. It has to be firm. You can't lead him on or have him waiting in the wings for you," she agreed.

I could feel the hurt in my heart growing with every beat. I was dreading the moment I had to tell him. It was something that had to be done sooner rather than later. We had been in this yo-yo relationship for so long, I knew he would think this was one of those moments where I pushed him away only to pull him back. Not this time. This time I had to make it crystal clear there was no pact. There was no chance.

"It's going to hurt." I choked out the words.

"Yes, it is. Think of it like a Band-Aid. Rip it off. Get it over with. Give yourself a chance to heal and then you can move on with your life. Both of you can. This whole thing is a disaster waiting to happen. I'm sorry to say it, but you two together is a recipe for something close to a nuclear meltdown. You weren't meant to be together. What you had was good, but it wasn't real. You were young. He's an attractive, slightly older, powerful man. And, he's the forbidden fruit. There's no wonder why you wanted him, but now it's time to move forward," she lectured in a friendly, gentle way.

I nodded, wiping a tear from my cheek that had slid down my face. I knew she was telling me what I needed to hear, but it hurt. She'd always been in my corner, backing me up and promising to stand by me if I wanted to be with Jack.

"Thanks, Ash. I appreciate your support," I muttered.

"I'm here for you. I'm sorry. He's a great guy, he really is. Another lifetime, another place, another world, and the two of you would be perfect together."

"I know," I replied, feeling the tears pouring in earnest.

"Let me know if you need me to cover for you," she said, already knowing what I had to do.

I wiped my face, took a deep breath, and steeled my resolve. "We're going shopping and then out for drinks," I told her, setting up my alibi.

"Got it. Good luck and call me if you need me," she said before hanging up.

I stood and walked into my bathroom to clean up my face and hide the evidence of my aching heart. My family would never understand how much pain they were causing me. Part of me wanted to scream, rage, and demand they accept Jack as the man I loved, while the other, more rational part of me knew that would never happen.

I had everything in the world. Why did it feel like I was completely alone and empty?

CHAPTER 34

JACK

I had to admit it wasn't horrible. The liquor wasn't great, but it got the job done. The bar was a little smoky and the smells in the place Mason had dragged me to were very different from the upscale bars and clubs I was accustomed to and generally frequented. I could smell cheap cologne, cheap liquor, and sex. It was an odd combination and made me wonder if there was a whorehouse above the bar.

"Quit scowling," Mason said, returning with two fresh drinks in his hand.

"I'm not scowling," I retorted.

"You are. You got that look on your face like something stinks."

I smirked. "Something does stink. You don't smell that?"

He shrugged a shoulder. "You get used to it. It's the smell of real people having a good time, none of those uptight people you always hang out with."

I didn't get a chance to respond. A body slammed into the table next to ours, followed by a lot of shouting and the sound of a glass breaking. I watched the scene with mild horror. Mason didn't seem to notice anything was happening and continued to drink from his glass. It was a rough bar. Mason seemed to be in his element, which gave me a little more insight to how he'd been spending the last ten years of his life when he all but ditched the family.

"They need security," I grumbled.

Mason chuckled. "They've got it handled. Not everyone needs babysitters."

I rolled my eyes. "If anything, this place could definitely use babysitters."

"These people are acting like grown men, working shit out the old-fashioned way. They'll be friends by tomorrow," he predicted.

I nodded, seriously doubting his opinion. Mason had demanded I go to the bar of his choosing in exchange for him dressing up in a tux and going to the ball the previous night. When I had agreed to the deal, I had expected to be in a much better mood.

A couple women sauntered over, bringing us two bottles of beer. "Hi, boys, you look lonely," one of the bottle-blondes cooed, her red fingernails matching the thick red lipstick painted on her lips.

She was not my type. She was pretty enough, but fast and loose wasn't my thing. I didn't care if they had a million dollars in the bank or nothing at all. It was a turn-off. I liked to do a little chasing. This woman oozed sex. I had to keep from shuddering and offending the woman.

"Are you offering to keep us company?" Mason said, staring directly at the huge boobs right at eye level, purposely thrust in his face.

The deep V-neck, tight shirt she was wearing made it impossible to look at anything else but her tits.

"We are," she replied.

I kicked Mason under the table, telling him without words he better send the women packing or I was leaving. I was not in the mood for that kind of company. I didn't come out to hook up with anyone. I was only out because I had made a deal.

"Oh, sweetie, my brother here is married, and I have to make sure he doesn't do anything stupid. Maybe another time," he said in a gentle voice.

The lady on my right purposely looked at my empty ring finger before rolling her eyes. The women did not like being rejected and were clearly very offended. They picked up the beers and stomped off. I felt a twinge of guilt for acting so rudely.

"Thanks," I muttered.

"You're killing my vibe, man. Lighten up. That woman has got you torn up and inside out. She isn't the only woman in the world. I don't get your problem," he grumbled.

"You wouldn't understand. She is the only woman in my world," I protested, a little embarrassed to hear the words coming out of my mouth. I sounded like a sop.

"Quit your damn moping," he lectured.

"I'm not moping," I shot back, clearly lying.

"You are. Move on. There are other women out there. She's moved on. Why can't you get that through your thick skull?"

I shook my head. "Because she has said the same thing about a hundred times in the last four years."

"I think she means it this time. Let. It. Go."

I sighed, knowing he was right, but struggling to listen to the solid advice.

"Look, check out the hot blonde over there," he pointed to a woman at the bar, wearing an outfit that made me question what she did for a living.

"I'll pass."

I finished my drink and waited for another one to magically appear, then remembered I wasn't in that kind of place. I was going to have to go chase down a damn drink if I wanted one.

"I'll get it," Mason said, rising from the table.

I could feel a good, strong *drunk* coming on. It felt good to take the edge off all the harsh feelings. I was staring at a neon sign, lost in thought when I felt someone sit down at the table. I assumed it was Mason and turned to grab my drink only to come face-to-face with Elijah.

I smirked. "I should have known you'd show up sooner or later. Big, tough brother rushing in to save the day. Oh, wait, she isn't here, dumbass."

"Nope, she isn't, and she never will be." Elijah glowered, his mission clear by the way he was glaring at me.

I laughed. "You thought you were going to catch her disobeying daddy dearest. Oops, guess your intel was wrong. Maybe you should hire smarter security who know the difference between your sister and the women in here."

"My sister would never step foot in a place like this." He sneered with disgust.

I smiled. "I don't think you know your sister very well at all. You have no idea who she really is," I said in a low voice full of innuendo.

"I know she doesn't want anything to do with you," he shot back.

"What the fuck do you want?" I snapped, immediately noticing the three men standing behind him and smirking.

"I wanted to make sure you got the message. I'm not sure if your brains got a little rattled after our last encounter," he said, a smile on his face.

I rolled my eyes. "Seriously? That's your big threat. What was it, five on one? I hope you feel like a big man. I guess your daddy is still holding onto your balls."

"Stay away from her," Elijah said, his voice low and menacing, his eyes shooting fire.

I knew I got to him. He hated that his father treated him like an inept child. Elijah had always felt less than a man and it was because of his dad. I knew him well enough to know his weak spots and I wasn't above taking advantage of them.

The alcohol was pumping through my veins, tickling my temper. "And if I don't? What, are you going to have your goons beat me up?"

Elijah shook his head. "I'm serious. Don't push this. Leave her alone. Don't call. Don't show up where she is. Stay away from her. She doesn't want you. She's too nice to be a bitch to you," he said and rose from the chair he had just sat down in.

"Oh shit, is there a party and I wasn't invited?" Mason said, his voice sinister as he set the two fresh drinks on the table.

Mason and Elijah faced off, neither of them saying a word as the heated, silent exchange made the air around the table thick. Elijah knew my little brother could mop the floor with his ass. We all knew that, and the funny thing was, Mason would enjoy doing it.

"He was just leaving," I said to Mason, not wanting to have a bar brawl that would land all of us in jail for the night.

Mason stayed standing until Elijah left the bar. He was bigger than my ex-best friend and was a hundred times more intimidating.

He sat down and shook his head. "Guy has some balls showing up like that."

I curled my lip in disgust. "He looks and acts just like his dad. His father should be so proud. He's created two spawns in his likeness."

My night took a deeper dive into a shit pile. I knew I was horrible company and left Mason at the bar with a couple of his friends. By the time I got home, I could feel a headache coming on as my buzz faded. I wanted to pass out. I stomped into the kitchen and poured myself a whiskey neat before heading to my room and stripping off the jeans I'd worn in an attempt to blend in. I slid on a pair of sweats and headed back to the kitchen to refill my glass.

"Fucking Levys," I mumbled, taking a sip of the strong whiskey.

I heard a soft knock at the front door and rolled my eyes. It had to be Mason. I swore if he showed up at my door with strange women I was going to kick his ass. He could take them back to his own place.

I pulled open the door to find the source of my shitty mood, standing there in a pair of skinny jeans, knee-high black boots and a long sweater, her black silky hair loose around her shoulders. Of course, she looked hot as hell.

"What do you want?" I snapped, looking around to see if her brother and his thugs were waiting to jump me. It was all a little déjà vu. Hell, I realized I was wearing the exact same thing the last time I'd been standing at my doorway with her on the other side.

"Jack ... I ... uh." She licked her lips, stammering over her words as her eyes roamed over my shirtless body.

I stood there, watching her cheeks flush until she was done with her perusal of my body. I took a drink of the whiskey, drawing her attention back to my face.

"What do you want, Nat?" I asked again, not inviting her in and making it very clear I was not happy to see her darkening my door.

"I came to tell you it's over. We're really over. No pact, nothing," she said, her voice strained.

I guffawed, my eyebrow shooting up. "Really? Wow. After you said the exact same thing last night, I was confused. I'm so glad you came over here to clear that up for me at—what?—eleven o'clock at night? Is this your twisted way of rubbing salt in the wound?" I sneered, having zero patience left to deal with her or any of the Levy family.

I was tired of being fucked with by members of that family, and I wasn't going to act as a punching bag for them to get their jollies out on any longer.

"I'm sorry, Jack, we knew it was never going to work from the very beginning," she said the words as if I were a child being told I couldn't have chocolate for dinner.

"Thanks for making it clear."

She stood there looking at me. I could see pity in her eyes. "I'm sorry. I didn't mean to hurt you."

I shrugged a shoulder, casually sipping from my glass. "If you're not here to fuck, you should probably go," I said, not caring if I offended her with my crassness.

Her mouth dropped open, but instead of spinning away on those killer heeled boots she was wearing, she stared at me. The woman was playing with fire. She had pushed me too far. I wasn't that nice of a guy.

CHAPTER 35

NATASHA

I should walk away. I should have already been in the elevator on my way downstairs, but I wasn't. I was still standing in front of him, staring at his naked chest that I had missed so much. His hazel eyes looking at me with such anger and hurt filleted me to my very core. There was something compelling me to stay right where I was. He was in a horrible mood and for some crazy reason, it turned me on. He was rarely ever in such a bad mood. It didn't deter me. All I could think about was sex. Not just sex, but sex with him. I was dangerously close to begging him to have his way with me.

"We don't have to do this," I said, my words getting jumbled in my head. I wanted to tell him we could be friends, but that would be a blatant lie. We couldn't be friends or lovers. I could never be with him like I wanted.

"It's already done. You made damn sure of that, didn't you." He snarled, sipping the dark liquid from his glass.

I closed my eyes, begging for strength to walk away. "You know it would never work. The marriage pact was nothing more than a young lover's fantasy. We live in the real world. It was cute, but it wasn't realistic."

He continued drinking from the glass, watching me with disinterest. "Okay."

"Okay?" I asked, caught off guard.

"Okay." He shrugged.

I didn't know how to reply. I think I wanted him to fight for me. He had given up on me. "Oh," I said, my heart in my throat as I stared at him.

"I'm not going to tell you again. You keep standing there, and I'm going to remind you why you keep coming back," he said, his gravelly voice holding that hint of danger that was making me crazy.

"Jack," I said his name, not sure what I wanted to tell him.

"Don't fucking say it." He growled.

My shoulders slumped forward. "Jack," I said his name again, this time I knew exactly what I was saying. I was resigned to what I really wanted.

"I fucking warned you," he said a split second before stepping toward me, one arm snaking my waist, jerking my body against his as his mouth slammed down on mine.

He kept moving, pushing me backward until I felt the hall wall behind me. I kissed him back, pressing my lips hard against his.

"Fuck," he snarled, and I heard his glass hit the floor.

He dragged me back into his place, his mouth hot against mine. I could taste the whiskey and savored every drop on his tongue as it languished inside my mouth. His hands shoved my arms upward, yanking the sweater over my head before unsnapping my bra in record time.

"I warned you," he repeated, his mouth hovering above mine as his hands began to work at my jeans.

"I know," I replied, pushing his sweats over his hips, grabbing the erection that was freed.

"Fuck these goddamn jeans," he shouted, finally pushing them down my hips only to get stopped by the boots.

"Wait." I gasped, prepared to take off the boots.

"No!"

He spun me around, his hand pushing against my back, forcing me to bend over. I had a brief moment of wondering how it would work with my knees nearly locked together with my jeans acting as a vise.

"Jack, my—"

I cried out when my answer was the head of his dick probing at my core before shoving inside my body with no warning. My desire for him was evident as his passage went unblocked without any stopping.

"Fuck me. Why fucking deny me? Why? Feel me in you. You're fucking wet. You're wet for me." He was cursing loudly as he pushed in deeper.

I was almost embarrassed to have my secret so blatantly exposed. I was wet. When he opened the door wearing nothing but a pair of sweats, I felt my panties grow damp almost instantly. He was a fucking Adonis. All my senses had awoken and reminded me of how good it felt to be in his arms, to have him deep inside me. I would always want him like this, I knew that deep in my soul.

"I have to," I cried out when he was fully seated inside my body.

The clamped knees made him feel bigger inside me. I squirmed, trying to adjust to his girth pushing against the walls of my body, demanding entry. I gasped as I felt the first tightening of muscles clamping down on his hard cock.

"And I have to fuck you hard. That's what you want, right, Nat? You want my dick, just not me?" He growled, pulling out and slamming back in.

My fingertips tried to gain purchase on the smooth wall as he drove into my body with fierce passion. I wanted to fight the orgasm, somehow prove to him I didn't need him or want him in my life. It was futile. My body was betraying me, bursting into flames around him, soaking him with my passion as my head fell backward, my back arching to the point I feared it would snap as I came apart.

"You're not finished yet," he snarled, pulling out of me, leaving me gasping for air as I leaned on the wall.

I saw his sweats fly before my boots were unzipped. He yanked one foot up, then the other, not being gentle in the least as he shoved my jeans down, pulling them over my feet. I stood, before turning to face him. The anger in his eyes was replaced with passion. There was a dangerous look about him that excited me. I knew he would never hurt me, but he would definitely dominate me in every way.

"What now, Jack?" I asked defiantly, wanting to poke the angry beast in front of me.

He shook his head. "You're playing with fire."

"Burn me."

He responded with a searing kiss that left my knees shaking and my body dripping with desire. He lifted me, sliding me up until I was seated against his body, my legs wrapped around his waist. I opened my eyes, staring down into his. Our connection was indescribable. Without speaking, I moved, finding him and taking him within my body, our eyes holding together as I descended upon him, letting him fill me again.

In a flash, he changed. "No. We're not doing that." He growled.

That brief, tender moment where our souls touched vanished and the man, the snarling beast intent on fucking and nothing more was back. I went with it, understanding the need to keep things on a basic level.

He began fucking me, pushing me up against the wall once again as I bounced up and down on his body, my breasts bouncing in time with each thrust. I could feel his pent-up passion with every stroke inside me. It was making me crazy, driving and pushing me toward another violent orgasm. I stiffened, my legs locking around him, holding him close to my body as I let the waves of ecstasy roll over me.

"That's it. That's why you're here. You know I can fuck you just like you want it. Like you need it," he was saying from somewhere far away.

I nodded, moaning in place of the words I wanted to say but couldn't form as he continued to push me higher and higher. My eyes slowly opened when he began moving down the hall. We were going to his bedroom. I wrapped my arms around his neck, dropping my mouth to his and leisurely kissing him as he moved, still deep inside me.

He unceremoniously dropped me onto his bed. I looked up at him, watching him as his eyes roamed my naked body, covered with a sheen of sweat. I stared up at him, my hunger for him growing with every breath. His erection jutted forward, glistening with the evidence of my last orgasm. I wanted him.

"I'm here," I said, looking up at him.

"You are."

"What are you going to do with me?" I asked, flirting and feeling extremely sexy and daring.

He shrugged. "I've been fucking you. Where have you been?"

"I'm not done."

"Maybe I am."

I looked down at his erection and smiled, raising an eyebrow. "I don't think so."

"Roll over," he ordered.

I rolled to my side, looking over my shoulder at him before rolling to my stomach and going up on my knees, waiting for him to finish what he'd started. He reached out and slapped my ass once, then again, stirring up the fire burning low inside my belly.

He worked his fingers over my folds, probing and rubbing, stoking the fire until I was squirming and begging for him to take me.

"Jack, I'm ready," I told him, hoping he'd get the hint.

He slapped my ass hard and before I could stop myself I was coming, my body rocking, pushing back, searching for something to impale myself on. I was begging him, pleading with him to give me more.

"Now, you're ready." He growled.

He reached out, fondling my sensitive core with his fingers before using his hand to spread my thighs. I could feel him behind me and had to turn to see it with my own eyes. I could see the determination on his face, his hands holding my hips steady. I held my breath, antici-pating his body filling mine. When he made contact, I gasped, drawing his eyes to mine.

The look on his face was stone cold as he slid inside, excruciatingly slow, one tiny, little bit at a time. When he was to the hilt, I closed my eyes, hanging my head low as he slowly moved. It was too good. How had I lived a year without the man? His body was made for mine. There was no man on the planet who could ever satisfy me like he could.

The sheer enormity of the realization took me to an entirely new level of sweet, agonizing ecstasy. I let myself get lost in the moment, blocking everything else out. It was just the two of us. No one else mattered.

"Goddamn it, Nat." He grunted, his fingers digging into my hips.

I couldn't reply. I just let him do what he needed. I was his. I could feel the tension spiraling within, like a spring being pushed down, ready to explode. By the way he was breathing, I could tell he was feeling the same. I braced myself knowing his orgasm would be explosive. I wanted to give him the same pleasure he had given me.

"Jaaack." I drew out his name on a gasp as the lights behind my eyes began to explode.

"Fuck," he said, the word slipping between gritted teeth.

I rolled my head back, his orgasm pumping deep inside, his cock pulsing with each hot spurt as he cursed under his breath, his fingers gripping my flesh as he pummeled me with his body. The orgasm stretched on, pulling from every cell in my body.

He stopped moving, his head falling forward and resting against my back, both of us rapidly breathing. It was a sweet moment that I wished we could stay in forever. When he moved away from me, I rolled to the side before sitting up on the edge of the bed. We stared at each other for a long while. There were no words to describe what had just happened. Words would ruin it. Words would mean we had to acknowledge everything that was wrong.

CHAPTER 36

JACK

I sat down on the bed next to her, not touching her as we both sat naked, staring at the carpet under our feet. I could feel the guilt radiating off her. I knew she was having second thoughts and a whole bucket of regrets. I didn't. Not even one. I, unlike her, had no doubt we were supposed to be together. I wasn't prone to have regrets, especially when it was something that I felt was right down to my very core. I refused to feel bad for loving a beautiful woman who I knew loved me as well.

To be fair, I had warned her. I knew what would happen if she stuck around. Obviously, she did too. There was a chemistry between us that was undeniable. The only way to avoid it was to stay on opposite ends of the country. Even that wasn't enough to really dampen the fire that would always be burning between us.

"Are you okay?" I asked, hoping things hadn't gotten too out of control.

"I'm fine," she replied, not looking at me.

A man only had so much self-control. I had given her plenty of warning. She knew I was helpless when it came to her. She was my kryptonite. I knew I gave her too much power. It was like some kind of chemical reaction. She was the catalyst to my hormones, sending me over the top. It wasn't just the sex. She was so much more to me.

"It's chilly," I mumbled, moving to get more comfortable in the bed.

I moved to put my feet up on the bed, dragging her with me. She didn't fight it. Her head rested against my chest as I reached down to pull a blanket over our bodies. Everything was different between us. It wasn't the usual post coital bliss we usually shared. There was something, heavy, dark, and dirty hanging between us. It felt like we had cheated. Neither one of us was doing anything wrong. We were following our hearts and for anyone to make either one of us feel guilty about that was wrong in my book.

I was ready to fight. I was prepared to stand up to Wayne Levy and let him know I was in love with his daughter and he could kiss my Bancroft ass.

"We can't do this again. It was a one-time thing," she said, her words brushing over my chest, dumping a little icy coolness on my desire to tell her dad to fuck off.

I shrugged one shoulder. "You said that before. It's always a one-time thing until we do it all over again."

"I mean it this time. This, this was a mistake. I mean, I don't regret it and I don't blame you, but we can never do that again," she said.

"Fine, but it wasn't a mistake." I refuted her ugly word.

I wasn't going to argue with her. I was done groveling at her feet, begging her to stay with me. It was the basis of our entire relationship. I had learned a long time ago it was something she needed to say, maybe to assuage her guilty conscience for ignoring her family's demands. If she really wanted to stop, she could say no or stop coming to my place. I wasn't exactly aggressively chasing her. It was very much the opposite.

"Jack, I'm serious. The pact isn't going to happen. I can't risk everything. This is all very important to me. I'm moving on," she said, pulling back a little to look up at me.

"Moving on?"

She nodded. "Yes. What we had, it was amazing, and you know

how much I care about you, but it's time for us both to accept we'll never be happy together. Our families mean too much to us to keep sneaking around. It's too risky. I don't want to get caught."

I took a deep breath. "Screw your family. I don't give a shit what they think, especially your punk-ass brother."

She slapped my chest. "Don't say that."

"I'm sorry, but it's the truth. I'm not going to let your family dictate my life. You're an adult. I'm an adult. I don't understand why we're giving them so much power," I said, firm on my decision.

"I won't destroy my family so we can be together. That's wrong and selfish. It would hurt my dad," she protested.

"Then, don't," I snapped.

"You've changed," she said, looking up at me, searching my eyes.

I shook my head. "Nat, you know I love you. You know I'm crazy about you and I want to be with you. I've not changed, but I'm tired of the game. I can't keep waiting for your dad to come around to the idea of you being with me. What is that getting us? We lost another year of our lives because of it. How much longer should we wait? Do you really see anything changing?"

"What about your family? Are you saying you're willing to hurt your family? Tear your family apart?" she asked, frustration in her voice.

"I'm not saying that, but I am saying I won't let your father dictate my life. I have to believe my mom would be okay with it. My brothers all know."

"What? All of them?" she asked in horror.

"Well, I had to tell Grayson. He was the only one who could drive my ass to the hospital the last time we were together. Mason has known all along. Then the others just kind of found out. They're not beating the shit out of me because of who I love," I said coolly.

She took a deep breath. "Your mom won't be so open."

"She might be."

"It isn't just my dad I have to worry about hurting," she defended.

I smirked. "That's right, we have your brother in our business as well. We can't have poor little Elijah getting bent out of shape because his little sister fell in love with a man his father hates for no good reason."

"Stop, it isn't like that."

I scoffed. "It is exactly like that. You were dragged away. After you left, it was made crystal clear Elijah was doing his father's bidding. He doesn't have an original thought in his head." I snarled.

"I'm sorry about that night. It was a mess. Please don't be mad at Elijah. I mean, I get why you're mad, but he was doing what my dad ordered him to. He was put in a terrible position as well," she defended.

I raised an eyebrow. "You think he had a rough night?"

"Were you hurt?"

I wouldn't admit anything. "I was fine. What about you? What he did was completely disrespectful to you."

"I was fine, Jack. It was humiliating, but I brought it on myself."

"Bullshit. We did nothing wrong. Neither of us deserved what we got that night," I said, still thinking back to the blows I endured and the fear I had felt for her safety as she was dragged away.

Her hand rubbed over my rib cage as if she could smooth away the pain that had been physically done that night. I had endured a couple cracked ribs. They had long healed, but the other scars remained. Those were the scars that were not likely to be forgotten anytime soon.

"The year apart is something we agreed to."

"Not like that," I shot back.

"We were supposed to try and meet someone, date, and go out with others," she said accusingly.

"I didn't want to."

"But that's what we agreed to," she insisted.

"Nat, what does it matter? You've told me, several times now, the pact was stupid, and you aren't going through with it."

She looked torn. "I don't know. I hate this," she whispered.

I reached up and cupped her cheek. "Let's not worry about it. That doesn't matter. You're mine. You know that. I know that. That's all that matters. The two of us, and how we feel when we're together, is what I want to focus on."

I could see the resignation in her eyes and leaned down to kiss her. It was tender and sweet with plenty of promise. I felt her give in to what was happening between us and deepened the kiss, sucking her tongue into my mouth as I stoked that fire burning deep inside her like only I could do. She could say all the right words, but I knew her better than she knew herself. I knew it was me she wanted. I was the only one who could give her the pleasure she craved.

My hands moved to cup her breast, gently rubbing and refamiliarizing myself with her body. The first time had been too fast. I hadn't taken the time to enjoy her body. I was going to this round. I wanted to tease and tantalize her in every way and remind her how much she needed me. I tweaked her nipple, pulling a gasp from her before reaching between her legs. She subtly opened her legs, giving me better access to rub that sweet spot. She was still wet and swollen from our earlier joining.

Her hand wrapped around my swollen cock, already ready for round two. She rubbed and stroked, taking me to the point of no return. I scooted down, pulling her with me.

"I can't," she said, rolling away from me.

"What?" I asked, my brain a little slow with the lack of blood flowing south.

She shook her head, climbing off the bed. "We can't. I have to go."

I jumped off the bed. "You don't have to go. We're working through it," I said, my cock hard and aching.

"Jack, we're fooling ourselves. Sex is just sex. This isn't a relationship. We could never go out. We could never marry, have a family, live together, all of that is off the table. That isn't the kind of life I want," she said, walking out of my bedroom.

I followed her out of the room, my erection leading the way. "You're letting them control you."

She was frantically dressing, jerking her clothes on. "Don't call me."

"You came to my house," I pointed out none too gently.

"That was a mistake. One I won't make again."

She zipped up her jeans before quickly trying to finger-comb her hair. It was useless. Her hair was good and tousled.

"Nat, quit fucking around!" I said, frustration making me crazy.

She pulled on her sweater and jerked open the front door before walking out, not bothering to look behind her or to even shut the fucking door. I stood there, still stark naked, my erection flagging. I stomped to the door and slammed it shut.

"Goddamn it!" I shouted, banging my hand against the wall.

I walked back into my room and dropped on my bed, staring up at the ceiling. I had no idea what had just happened. She'd come over to my house, let me fuck her with all the pent-up passion I'd been holding just for her for over a year. She let me get hard and on the verge of getting another chance to pull the pleasure from her and feel it wash over me.

What kind of woman did that? She teased me. She got me fired up and walked away. That was nothing but pure torture. If nothing had changed, why in the hell had she bothered to come over? Why would she kiss me, touch me, and lead me down the path of ecstasy and then leave me high and dry?

It wasn't right. I just knew she had ruined any chance of me moving on and not looking back. Maybe that had been her plan after all. I wasn't going to be kept dangling. I loved her, but that wasn't something I could let myself keep doing. I had more self-respect than that.

CHAPTER 37

NATASHA

I couldn't believe it. It was finally happening. My dream of having my own company was finally coming true. I had been planning and thinking about this day for nearly four years. My parents had insisted I take my two-year vacation to enjoy life before I got into the business world. I knew they had thought I would change my mind or find a man and get married, forget all about the idea of having my own business.

I hadn't. I had been focusing on it for the last year as I tried to move past the Jack thing. I had spent many long nights planning and jotting down a million ideas and now, here I was in the future offices of my company.

I had insisted on a separate building away from Levy Industries. Yes, I was under the Levy umbrella, but this was going to be all mine.

"Hey, Nat, we have everyone set up in the conference room," my new assistant said, walking toward me in what would be my new executive office.

"Thank you. I'll be right there. Hey, Bonnie, do you think I should leave all the windows in front or have walls put up?" I asked her, staring at the space.

She shrugged. "I like the openness of the glass, but it does nothing for privacy."

I nodded. "Exactly what I was thinking. I think I'll go with walls. The windows on the other side are plenty," I said, happy to have made a decision.

I quickly walked over to the contractor, who was busy taking down a few walls to make the space a little bigger, and told him what I wanted. The man looked a little put out but noted it on the yellow pad where he had been writing down all my other requests. I planned on being hands-on from the very beginning.

I headed for the conference room, excited to have my first investor meeting. I wanted to grow beyond the limitations of Levy Industries and this was how I was going to do it. My speech at the charity event had the desired effect and drummed up plenty of interest. I walked in, feeling confident with my hair slicked back into a tight, serious bun and my black pantsuit perfectly tailored.

"Good morning, everyone. Thank you so much for coming," I said, taking my seat at the head of the table.

The meeting went great, with lots of promises of support. As I was walking out, I was stopped by a couple other people who were coming in on the ground floor of the company with me. I had handpicked every person after talking with them and making sure our personalities all meshed well. The last thing I wanted was a lot of drama and interoffice politics.

I was the boss and I did demand respect, but I also gave respect, and I valued the opinions and advice of the people I had surrounded myself with.

On my way back to my office, I heard a familiar voice and turned to see my father walking through the offices, his eyes roaming the construction zone.

"Hi, Daddy," I said with a smile.

"Hi, princess. It looks like you have things under control here," he said.

I smiled. "I hope so. The contractor promises me everything will be done within two weeks."

"Is this your office?" he asked, looking at the huge corner office that took up a huge chunk of the space.

I grinned. "It is."

"Good. You deserve the best."

"Come in," I said, walking through the door and gesturing for him to have a seat on the one couch that had been moved in.

"I can have my decorator come by if you'd like," he suggested.

I shook my head. "The furniture will be in within the next day or two. What brings you by? Checking up on me?" I teased.

He turned to face me on the couch. "I wanted to talk to you about the other night."

I immediately froze, panic welled inside as I stared at him. "The other night?" I squeaked.

He smiled. "It's okay."

"It is?" I asked, wondering what had made him change his mind. For a brief second, a glimmer of hope filled my soul, giving me a glimpse of a happy future with Jack by my side.

"I'm glad you told him to leave," he said.

I blinked several times. "What?"

"That Bancroft character. I know he tried to talk to you at the charity ball."

"Nothing happened, Dad. I told him not to bother me ever again," I quickly assured him.

He smiled and nodded. "I know and I'm proud of you. I'm happy that you've seen reason. I'm sorry for all the hurt and pain it caused you, but this is for the best."

I saw my moment and I took it. "Dad, please, I want to know. Why are you so adamant I not be with Jack Bancroft?"

His lip curled with disgust. "Because those Bancrofts are a blight on society."

"That's a bold statement. Why? What happened that has made you hate them?" I asked, hoping he would tell me the truth.

He sucked in a deep breath and just when I thought he would ignore the question, he grabbed my hand and began talking.

"Art Bancroft and I used to be in business together. We were just starting out. Neither of us really knew what we were doing, but I knew I wanted to go after the renewable energy niche. I knew it would be big. Art agreed, and we were just scraping by at first. It wasn't a big thing thirty, forty years ago," he explained.

I nodded. I had suspected it was business gone bad that had led to the fight. "You were always cutting edge," I told him, coaxing him on.

"Things weren't easy, but I was in it for the long haul. Art, he wanted something bigger and better right away. We'd been trying to find people to invest, to help us grow, but there wasn't much interest. Art was a smooth character. He could talk to anyone and get them to listen. I found out he was having meetings behind my back. I did some digging and found out he was shopping our company around to sell it."

My mouth dropped open. "Seriously?"

He nodded. "Yep. He wanted to make a quick buck. No one wanted to give us money to get it off the ground, but he managed to find someone interested in buying the company and growing it. When I found out, I was adamantly against it. I fought hard, telling him no way. It was my baby. I had the idea. It was my vision and he was ready to sell it to the highest bidder."

I waited, afraid to hear the end of the story. I couldn't imagine how that would have made my father feel. "I'm sorry."

He smirked. "That's not the worst of it. One day I got to the office and noticed a man in Art's office. I popped over to see what was going on just in time to see them shake hands. They'd made a deal, selling the company right out from underneath me. I was cut out of the deal. Art made millions on it," he said, his lip curling again.

"What? I don't understand," I asked.

He nodded. "You see, it was Art who had the capital to start the company. It was Art's name on all the paperwork. I had the intellectual side of things while Art had the money. I was a fool back then. I didn't know I was getting into bed with a snake. Art tried to convince me it was a good thing and how he could use the money from the sell to funnel back into a new company focused on building the equipment for the renewable energy. It was a bullshit story. He was trying to soothe things over by lying to me."

"Wow. So, you left him and started Levy Industries?" I asked in confusion.

"Yes. I still had the company, but no money. I had zero capital. I had to start from scratch. I moved out of the office and took everything I had and worked from home for years. Bancroft tried to make things right over the years, but I wanted nothing to do with that greedy man. Fool me once, shame on me; fool me twice, and I don't deserve to be the head of my company," he said firmly.

I could see the pain in his eyes and began to understand the situation a little better. "I'm sorry, but look how successful you are now and it's all on you. You did it. You managed to take a bad situation and make it into something awesome. That has to be worth something."

"What he did to me was bad and it certainly caused some bad blood between us, but that wasn't what turned me against Bancroft to the point I wished him dead on more than one occasion," he hissed.

"There's more?" I gasped in horror.

I couldn't remember meeting Art Bancroft, but I knew Jack, and I was vaguely familiar with his brothers. They didn't seem evil or vindictive, but maybe they were better at hiding their true selves.

"Kathy was my girlfriend at the time. We had been seeing each other for about six months. I was ready to ask her to marry me when Art sold the company," he said, a wistful tone to his voice.

"Kathy?" I asked, confused all over again.

He looked at me. "Yes, *Kathy.*"

Then it slammed into me like getting hit upside the head with a bus. "Oh my God. Kathy Bancroft was your girlfriend?"

He nodded. "Yes. Art stole my company and my future wife. He married her. He even had the audacity to invite me to the damn wedding. Then that woman started pumping out sons every damn year to add insult to injury."

I couldn't begin to wrap my head around it. In some weird, parallel universe, Jack and I could have been brother and sister or some weird shit like that. I couldn't believe it. The thought of my dad and Jack's mom being together was almost unbelievable. From what I knew of Kathy Bancroft, she was the polar opposite of my mother. Maybe that's what had drawn my father to her. It was too crazy to consider.

"Dad, that was a long time ago. You have Mom, you have your company, and you have a ton of success. Don't you think it's time to let the past go?" I suggested gently.

He shook his head. "No way."

"Dad, come on. You have to see it isn't fair to the sons of the man who cheated you. You don't know that they are like their father," I said, hoping he didn't get pissed that I was trying to make him see reason.

"Sons follow in their father's shadow. Like father, like son. That man was a vile human being and there is no way in hell any of those boys could have escaped that gene. They're all tarnished. They're all his spawns. Look at them. Look at that Grayson character. He buys up companies and sells them for a profit. That is exactly what his father did to me. The apple does not fall far from the tree."

He did have a point. "I'm sorry you had to go through all that, but I think your life turned out pretty okay, don't you?"

"I do. I'm happy with everything I have, but that doesn't mean I'm going to start making friends with the Bancrofts. It is human nature for children to follow in the footsteps of their parents," he insisted.

I wanted to tell him there were about a hundred studies that disproved that theory, but I knew he would only shoot them down. Once he was set in his ways, that's all there was to it. I knew in my heart Jack wasn't like that. He would never willingly hurt anyone. It wasn't in his nature. He was a good man.

CHAPTER 38

JACK

It was my day with Mom. Everyone else was either out of town or busy, which meant I didn't have to share her. I looked forward to hanging out with her, just the two of us. It was always so much easier when we could chat or just sit by the fire in the living room without saying a word. My brothers tended to be rowdy. There was always a lot of talking, joking, and general mayhem when several of us were in the same room. I was looking forward to a quiet afternoon that didn't require me to be on my toes, fending off brotherly jokes and jabs.

I pulled through the gates, parking my car in the front drive before heading inside. The moment I opened the door, I could smell something delicious wafting from the kitchen. Mom had cooked. I smiled, strolling toward the kitchen in search of whatever it was that smelled so good. I inhaled the scent of herbs and what I thought was chicken. The closer I got to the kitchen, the easier it was to peg the smell.

"Chicken potpie," I said walking into the huge kitchen.

"Oh, Jack, I didn't hear you come in," she said, leaning over so I could kiss her cheek.

I gave her a quick peck before lifting the lid on the pot bubbling on the stove. She slapped my hand away as she always did when we tried to grab a peek.

"This smells amazing, Mom. You know I can't resist your cooking."

"You need a wife to cook for you," she replied.

I pretended to check my watch. "Gee, Mom. It took you an entire two minutes before you brought that up. That must be a new record for you."

"I worry about you. I want you to be happy and settled. You need a good woman cooking you dinner or serving you breakfast in bed on a Sunday morning," she lectured.

"Like Grayson."

She grinned. "I'm not going to lie, I would love to have a few more grandkids."

"Subtle, Mom, very subtle."

"I'm too old to be subtle," she said, going back to her cooking.

I meandered around the kitchen before moving to stare out the window. The backyard was showing its fall colors. It always reminded me of football. My dad had loved football. When we were younger we had spent many Sunday afternoons roughhousing with one another and my father. Life had been good for us. I wished we could have seen it back then. Of course, we were too busy hating everything and feeling like we needed to constantly rebel. I smiled thinking about how much you try to get away from your parents for the first half of your life only to spend the latter half wishing you could have them a little longer.

It wasn't long before Mom announced lunch was ready. We opted to eat in the kitchen at the small breakfast nook instead of the formal dining room. I liked the smaller, more intimate space.

"Amazing as always, Mom," I said after a couple bites.

"Thank you, son."

"Planning any more cruises?" I asked her, hoping she was going to keep up the new zest for life she had found.

She smiled. "I am. Myself and a few friends have been talking about taking a longer trip this spring. We are thinking about heading across the ocean this time."

"Really?" I asked, a little surprised to hear her thinking of staying gone for so long.

She shrugged. "I don't know if I'll do it. My friend Hettie wants to do one of the around-the-world cruises. I'm not sure I could be away for that long."

"How long?"

"Several months."

I was immediately put off by the thought of not seeing my mother for that long of a stretch. She was waiting for me to tell her it would be okay.

"Good. You should do it if you want to. Around the world, that's very ambitious. I imagine that would be a lot of fun. Just think of everything you would see," I told her, hoping I sounded enthusiastic.

She ate a few bites. "Jack, really I want to see you happy. I hate to think about leaving when you're so unsettled."

"None of us are," I pointed out.

She waved a hand. "You're different."

I laughed. "I'm more selective than my brothers."

"Why aren't you dating anyone?"

I shrugged a shoulder. "Mom," I protested.

"You have so much to offer. You're wealthy, you have a steady job, and you are an attractive man. You should have many prospects. I would expect there to be a long line of women waiting for the chance to date you."

I looked down at my food. "I don't have time. I'm not interested in the dating scene."

"Jack, are you seeing someone?" she asked pointedly.

"Why do you ask that?" I said, trying my best to hide the guilt I knew would be written all over my face.

"A mother knows."

I looked up, fearing she did know and that I was caught in one of those situations where the truth could set me free or get me in a world of trouble. "What?" I gulped.

Her eyebrows shot up. "Jack, now I know there's something going on. You were never a very good liar."

I shook my head. "Lying? What are you talking about?" I said, playing the innocent as best as I could.

I started ticking off the names of my brothers in my head. One of them had told her. I was trying to think of which one it could be. I was betting it was Mason. He had no qualms about rocking the proverbial boat. He didn't understand the need to keep my relationship a secret from my mom. While he didn't mind shocking her and airing his disapproval, I did. I was already plotting what I was going to do to get even with him.

"I want you to be happy, Jack, that's all. I don't want to meddle. Please don't take it the wrong way. I know the last thing you want to do is talk about your love life with your mother, but it's only because I care," she insisted.

"Thanks, Mom. I know you do. I'm just not interested in all of that right now. I promise you'll be the first to know when I'm ready to marry someone."

She laughed. "You're not getting any younger. By the time I was your age I had three children."

"Those were different times," I said.

"Is there someone you have your eye on and are biding your time?" she asked, a slight lilt in her voice.

I laughed. "Mom, I'm focused on work these days."

"All work and no time for love is going to leave you a lonely, old man."

"Sheesh, Mom, you are on a roll today. I don't think I'm headed to my grave quite yet. Do you do this to all your children, or am I the lucky one?" I teased.

That made her laugh. "I'm not blind or naive. I know my other sons are sowing their wild oats as far and as fast as they can throw them. You have never been that way."

That wasn't entirely true, but I was a little more discreet about my sowing I guessed. "Thanks, I think."

"You were always more grounded, the one who seemed so much wiser and far more mature than the others. Grayson has always had that sense of duty and responsibility, but you have always just seemed like you were more interested in stability than the constant running around. Don't think I don't know about the hijinks you and that friend of yours got up to—I do. Your father did as well, but we let you think you were getting away with all of it."

I thought back to the many nights I had sneaked out and had suspected they had known, but since they never said anything, I thought I was the smartest kid in the world getting away with it all.

"Well there goes my entire childhood," I quipped.

Speaking of the old days gave me an idea. Maybe I could get her to open up a bit about the Levy family. I knew she didn't care for them, but it had always been my dad who was vehement we never have anything to do with them. When it became clear Elijah and I were going to be good friends, my mother had been resigned to the fact. There weren't any invitations to the dinner table, but she hadn't been blatantly awful about it either.

I had to think my mother would be a little more understanding than Wayne Levy. She was an easygoing woman and would be more inclined to understand our situation. Nat and I had fallen in love. We couldn't have controlled it. It happened. The heart wants what it wants, I told myself.

"I ran into Natasha and Elijah Levy the other night at that hospital charity," I started.

"Oh," she said through pursed lips.

I nodded. "Yes."

"I thought you and Elijah were on the outs for a reason no one will tell me about," she said, her eyebrow up as she stared at me.

I shrugged a shoulder. "We just kind of went our separate ways."

"Good. It's about time. I put up with that weird friendship the two of you had for too long. I'm happy to have that family out of our lives for good," she snapped, taking me by surprise.

"Mom, what is it with our families? Why do you hate them so much and vice versa?" I asked, hoping to get an answer so I could finally start to try and work through whatever the problem was.

She stood up, taking my half-finished plate, and began to clear the dishes. Clearly, I had upset her.

"That family is bad news. I hated that you befriended that man's

ALI PARKER

son. I tried to rise above, but good Lord I hated you hanging out with that brat," she said vehemently.

"I had no idea. You never really said anything," I said, moving to stand beside her at the sink.

She shrugged a shoulder. "I knew you were friends with that boy to irritate your father and me. I didn't want to give you the satisfaction. I'm just glad it's over."

"Why? What did they do? Why do you hate them so much?" I asked, growing frustrated by the evasiveness.

She shook her head. "I don't want to talk about it. Suffice it to say, it is not a subject I like to revisit. Just stay away from that Levy monster. You'll be better for it."

I nodded, not wanting to upset her. She wasn't going to tell me what happened, which only heightened my curiosity. I couldn't imagine what the man could have done that was so horrible it had made even my mother despise him. Whatever it was, it had to be serious.

"Okay, forget I said anything," I muttered, returning to the small table to grab the last of the dishes.

I spent the next two hours hanging out with Mom, hoping to have properly smoothed things over and make her forget all about my Levy question. We browsed some of the cruises available, talked about the different lines, and how long she could feasibly be away. By the end of my visit, I felt everything was back to normal and took my leave.

She never mentioned Natasha, so I had to assume she didn't know it was Natasha who had my heart. She knew there was someone, but she didn't know who and I planned on keeping it that way. If there was no chance Nat was ever going to go against her father's wishes, I didn't see any reason to upset my own mother any further. I would leave it alone.

CHAPTER 39

NATASHA

The car stopped in front of a newly renovated building in the downtown area. I could feel butterflies in my stomach as I stepped out of the car and looked up at the classic building, which oozed luxury from the ground floor to the very top of the seventeen-story building.

Ashley climbed out and stood next to me. "Wow. I think I've driven by this place at least a hundred times and never knew it was here."

I nodded, agreeing with her. "Me either. The realtor insisted it was exactly what I was looking for. I guess I always thought it was old and run-down. Now that I look at it, I can see it has been updated."

"Let's go in. I'm excited to see this place."

"The realtor told me to meet her in the bar," I said.

Ashley raised an eyebrow. "The bar?"

I pointed to the double doors on the left of the building. "That's a bar."

"Wow! You have a bar in your building? How amazing is that?"

We burst into laughter and pulled open the door, heavily tinted to provide plenty of privacy for those inside. It was an upscale bar, complete with lots of dark woods and low lights. The bartender was wearing a suit and looked like he had stepped off the cover of a magazine. I spotted my realtor chatting with a couple and waved. I watched as she handed the young couple her card and made her way toward us.

"What do you think?" she asked.

"I'm more interested in the apartment, but so far, I'm impressed."

"Great, let's go up. Now, to access the residences through this door, you'll need a special key," she explained, holding up a key card before sliding it into the lock.

The door opened to the other side of the building's ground floor and revealed a luxurious lobby area. Ashley and I followed behind her as she moved to the elevators.

"Is there full-time security?" I asked, noticing two security guards milling around the lobby area.

"Yes," the realtor acknowledged.

We stepped into the elevator and watched as the realtor used the card again, taking us to the top floor of the building. I could feel the nerves in my belly making me anxious. I shifted from one foot to the other. This was a huge step for me. I had rented a much smaller apartment in the past, but now I was looking for something long term. Something I could settle into and live in for years to come.

The moment the elevator doors slid open, I knew I was in love.

"Oh my." Ashley gasped as we stepped into the open greeting area of the penthouse.

The realtor smiled as she walked toward a set of elegant double doors and opened them into the main living area of the home. I was immediately taken back by the huge open floor plan with windows that lined the two corners, giving me a full view of the city below. I shook my head in wonder.

The realtor began her spiel, showing us around the five-thousand-square-foot penthouse with three bedrooms and four bathrooms. When she opened one set of French doors to lead us onto the patio, I was sold. There was a hot tub bubbling in the corner. I immediately pictured myself relaxing in the hot tub after a long day at work.

"This kitchen is amazing," I said, walking through the large space, the breakfast counter stretching on for a good ten feet. The gorgeous granite countertop with flecks of gold in it caught the light. Every tiny detail had been addressed.

"What do you think?" the realtor asked after we spent a good thirty minutes touring the penthouse, checking out the closet spaces and admiring the huge bedroom suites.

"I'll take it," I said, feeling bold and brave for making such a huge decision on my own.

The realtor grinned. "Great, I'll get the paperwork started to put in an offer."

"Pay full price. I want it," I said firmly, not willing to wait months for negotiations. I had the money and I wanted the place. It was that simple.

I saw the woman's eyes light up and knew she was already thinking about the fat commission she was going to make.

"Okay, I can do that," she said.

I turned to Ashley, who looked shocked by my impulsive move. I was about to blow her socks off.

"I want the keys, today. What will it take?" I asked, taking a page from my father's book.

"What?" the realtor asked with shock.

"I want it now. I understand there is some paperwork and all that, but I want the keys. I will wire money to the owner this minute," I said, pulling out my phone.

The realtor looked at me before pulling a set of keys from her pocket. "This will be our little secret. You can't move in until the paperwork is filed, but I'm sure you'll be responsible."

I snatched the keys. "Of course. I'll be waiting for the paperwork. I want this done as soon as possible," I reiterated, feeling more and more like my father.

"I'll have it to you by Monday," she assured me.

"Tomorrow works better," I said, not holding back.

"Okay, I will get right on it," she replied.

I knew the amount of money she would make from the sale was

worth spending a Saturday afternoon doing paperwork. I didn't feel the least bit guilty about my demands.

"Want to grab a drink in the bar, in my new building?" I asked Ashley with a grin as we left my future home.

She burst into laughter. "Yes, I do."

I said my goodbyes in the lobby to the realtor, who promised me she would be emailing me documents to sign by tomorrow afternoon. Ashley and I headed for the bar, ready to celebrate my first home-buying experience. It had been too easy, but I supposed money tended to grease the wheels.

"I cannot believe you just did that," Ashley said, shaking her head in awe.

I shrugged a shoulder. "I needed my own place. I wanted to buy this time."

"Yeah, but you didn't haggle or anything."

"I looked at so many places online and the few around the city. I don't want to waste another minute. Besides, you saw the place. Those floor-to-ceiling windows sold me the second we walked through the door," I said, still in disbelief.

"They were amazing. I loved the dark wood floors. It gives it a very dramatic look. I can already imagine you living there. It is so you," she agreed.

We ordered a couple glasses of wine and were chatting about all the things I needed to buy for my new home when a couple guys we were acquainted with sauntered over to our table.

"Good evening, ladies," Devon said as he greeted us.

"Hi, guys," I said with a smile.

"Can we buy you ladies a drink?" he asked.

I looked at Ashley who had a gleam in her eye. "Sure, you'll join us for that drink?"

"I thought you'd never ask," he said, as he and his friend Sebastian sat down at our small table.

The bar was fairly quiet. It catered to an upscale clientele. There wasn't loud music blaring in the background or obnoxious flashing lights. It was a nice place to kick back, relax, and have a real conversation.

"Are you still working for your dad?" I asked Devon.

He nodded. "Yep, he's getting ready to retire next year and I'll be taking over the company."

"Wow! Congratulations!" I said, happy to see he was doing well.

We had all gone to college together and essentially grown up together. Our families were all part of the same social circle.

Sebastian was gazing at Ashley, the two of them whispering back and forth. They had dated a little in college and by the looks of things, there was still some interest on both sides.

"I saw you give your speech last week. You were amazing, as always," Devon said with a wink.

"Thank you. It was a last-minute thing," I told him.

"I would have never guessed. You are always stunning, Natasha," he said, flirting as he usually did.

I slapped at his arm. "Stop. You're embarrassing me."

He playfully grinned. "Don't pretend you're shy now. We all know better. Remember that keg party at that frat house?"

I could feel myself blushing. "That was the tequila's fault. I would have never done that if it had been any other drink."

Ashley burst into laughter. "To this day, she will not drink tequila. I've tried to tell her tequila doesn't actually make your clothes fall off."

"In my case it does," I said, still a little embarrassed about the flashing of my breasts.

"You made a lot of guys very happy that night," Devon said, then laughed.

"Thank God most of them were so drunk they didn't remember," I said, shaking my head at the ridiculous antics of a college junior.

"And someone had been smart enough to confiscate all cell phones at the door. Your dad would have flipped out if he had seen pictures floating around," Ashley pointed out.

"Or big brother would have kicked some ass. How is Elijah by the way?" Devon asked.

"Good. He's working with my dad and hopes to be taking over one day as well. My dad is too stubborn to retire, though."

Devon shrugged a shoulder. "Tell Elijah to enjoy his freedom while he has it."

"I've tried. He doesn't see it like that. What else have you been up to? I don't see a ring on the finger," I said, pointing to his left hand.

He purposely looked at my hand. "Me neither."

"I've just gotten back into town. I was gone for two years, home for a couple months, and then gone for another year. A girl needs time to catch her breath," I said, my excuse well-practiced.

"I think we need to toast to your return," Devon said, holding up his hand to get the attention of a waitress.

When she came over, he ordered a bottle of champagne and four glasses. I was going to protest but champagne was perfect. We were celebrating after all.

"To the return of Natasha Levy and Ashley Cooper," Devon said as we all clinked our glasses together.

His arm went across the back of my chair in an easy way. He was a good friend and it was nice to relax with people I had known for a long time. We chatted about some of the people we'd gone to school with and what everyone had been up to over the summer.

"Next summer, you ladies need to come out on my family's yacht," Sebastian said.

Ashley was clearly very excited about the prospect. "Oh, that sounds exciting. Will it be an overnight visit?" she teased, heavily flirting with Sebastian.

"It can be," he replied in a low voice.

"You two are good together," Devon pointed out.

"I agree. Why did you guys break up in the first place?" I asked, not worried about putting either of them on the spot.

Ashley and Sebastian exchanged a look. "I don't know. I think we just kind of got bored with each other. We're friends," she said with a shrug.

"But we could be friends with benefits," Sebastian said, laying it on thick.

I burst into laughter, as did Devon. "Damn, man, you don't hold back. I think you're supposed to ease into that," Devon lectured.

"Like you?" Sebastian shot back.

Devon looked at me and I could feel my cheeks growing hotter. "No! That is never going to happen!" I said, sending the table into another round of laughter as the champagne began to make us all a little giggly.

"Hey now, that's only a little insulting. You never know until you try," Devon said leaning in close and trying to flirt.

I rolled my eyes. "Devon, I don't have to know. Every one of my friends in school knew."

He grinned. "So many ladies, so little time."

We all laughed again as Devon refilled our glasses with champagne. The day was ending on a high note and I couldn't have been happier. Well, that wasn't entirely true. The only thing that would have made it better was ending it with Jack.

CHAPTER 40

JACK

I t was good to unwind without a lot of people around. Grayson had told me about a new bar that had recently opened not too far from the Bancroft Building. After a long, boring day of meeting after meeting, he promised to hang out with me for a bit before rushing home.

"How'd you find this place?" I asked, following him to a dark corner in the new place.

"Someone at work told me about it. It's not overly popular and keeps a low-key profile," he said.

I nodded in agreement. "I would say so. There wasn't even a sign on the door."

"They just started selling the apartments in the building. The bar is mostly geared for the people who live in the building," he explained.

I wrinkled my nose. "This building has been here forever."

"It was recently renovated and went from something like sixty units to twenty or something like that. With this address, they had to keep up with the neighborhood. So they went from catering to the middle class to only the rich and famous could afford to live here," he said with disgust.

I shrugged, not all that interested in the real estate world. I had enough shit of my own to deal with. "I like it so far," I mumbled.

The waitress, wearing an outfit I would expect to see in a lawyer's office, appeared at our table and took our order. She was pretty, smart, and seemed completely out of place in the bar. I automatically assumed she was working her way through college.

"I'm going to be a dad," Grayson blurted out.

I raised an eyebrow. "You are a dad."

He laughed and shook his head, holding up two fingers. "Hannah's pregnant."

"Damn! Congratulations! How far?"

"She just crossed the three-month mark. We were waiting to tell everyone. I'm still in shock. I guess I thought it would happen later."

"Is she excited?" I asked.

He grimaced. "Yes and no. Those first few months of morning sickness were really hard on her, but she seems to be doing a little better now."

"Damn, Mom is going to be thrilled. Maybe this will get her off my back. She wants an entire fleet of grandchildren. You and Hannah are on track to do that," I teased.

"What about you?" he asked.

"I'm not having a baby," I replied dryly.

It was as if thinking about Natasha conjured her up. I heard her laugh. I knew it was her laugh. I turned to look around the bar and there she was. I felt the immediate kick to my stomach when I saw her sitting at a table, laughing and having a great time with another man.

"Why don't we go somewhere else?" Grayson suggested.

I shrugged a shoulder and turned back around to look at him. "No."

"Come on, there's no reason we have to stay here. We can get a drink anywhere."

"I'm not going to run away every time I'm in the same place she is. It's bound to happen. We tend to run in the same social circles. This isn't high school. I can handle myself." I growled.

He slowly nodded, clearly not believing me. The waitress returned at that exact moment to deliver our whiskey and Cokes. I ordered another one, knowing the first one was going to be going down fast. I needed to dull the pain I could feel blooming in my heart and alcohol was my best shot at that.

"Any chance you're ready to give up on that?" he asked.

"There's a very good chance of that," I replied, not committing to anything.

"I'm sorry. I know it isn't easy. When you think you've found the one, it's hard to let go and move on. I tried, it didn't work," Grayson mumbled.

That made me smile. "Don't I know it. But that was you. You pushed her away."

"True, but I do know what it's like to want what you don't have," he reiterated.

"I don't think I'm quite ready to give up. I know she wants me. She keeps coming back," I told him.

"Be careful, that's all I can say. I won't tell you to not see her, but I've got to tell you it could get very ugly. I'll support you either way," he said, reminding me how glad I was to have my big brother back in my life.

"Thanks. I'm not sure what I'm doing, but I'll figure it out," I grumbled, listening to the sound of her laughter echoing across the half-empty bar.

Grayson and I had another drink before we decided to call it a night. Being that close to her and unable to be near her was brutal. Listening to her laugh and have what sounded like a great time with another man was conjuring up a pit of jealousy in my belly.

"You ready?" Grayson asked.

"Yep," I said, throwing a twenty on the table and standing up.

Grayson and I began making our way out the door when someone I knew called my name.

"I'm going home," Grayson said, leaving me to talk with the guy I vaguely remembered from some business meeting I had attended.

I was polite, made small talk for a few minutes before making my excuses to leave. I had just made it around the U-shaped bar when I looked up to see Nat headed my way. She hadn't seen me. She was fidgeting with something in her hand and was on a collision course with my body. Instead of moving, I stayed right where I was, letting her slam into me.

"Oh." She gasped, looking up to find me staring down at her.

Her perfume assailed my senses, stirring up different emotions along with the most basic of them all—lust.

"You should look up when you're walking," I said in a low voice.

"I ... uh ... I was," she fumbled over her words, looking behind her to the table where her date was still sitting.

I raised an eyebrow, waiting for her to say something coherent. "You were what?"

"I was—I needed." She shook her head as if she could pretend I wasn't standing there.

"Don't let me interrupt your evening. I was on my way out," I said coolly.

"Jack, it isn't like that," she said in a small voice.

I stared at her, wanting her so much it hurt. "You look stunning as always," I whispered.

"Thank you. I should probably go," she said, not making a move to walk away.

I nodded, still holding her gaze. "You don't want to keep him waiting."

"Jack, he's a friend," she protested.

"He might be a friend, but he isn't me. Keep trying to fill the hole I'm going to leave in your life since you kicked me out of your bed," I said, my voice husky as I stepped a couple inches closer, crowding into her personal space.

Her lips parted a little. "He's not," she said, her voice raspy.

"He can't."

"Jack," she said my name, the single word said so much.

"What's the matter, Nat?" I asked, smirking as I watched the first shivers of lust wash over her body.

I knew her well. I knew when she was aroused. She still wanted me. She might be trying to tell herself otherwise, but I knew how much she needed me. I could see it in the way her eyes grew hooded with passion, her lips parted, and her tongue darted out to dampen her suddenly dry lips. They were all signs I knew well. I wanted her too. I wasn't done with her. She could keep telling me it was over, but until it was made loud and clear that was the case, I wasn't going to go away quietly, not when she did this every time we saw each other.

"Ashley's here," she blurted out.

I shrugged a shoulder. "I don't want Ashley. I want you."

"We can't."

"Why? You want it. I can see it in your eyes. Right now, you're thinking about me buried between your legs. I bet you're already wet," I said, not releasing her gaze from mine.

I used my body to slowly back her away from the bar. We were barely moving at all, just a few inches here and there until I had her cornered in a dark, more secluded area of the bar. I was thankful it was a quiet bar, with few people, giving me plenty of privacy to work with.

She bit down on her lower lip as I stepped closer, her back against the wall with nowhere to go. "This is a huge risk." She gasped.

"I like risks. I like you. I want to taste you," I said, my eyes dropping to her mouth.

I reached up and brushed my fingers across her jaw before using my thumb to open her mouth a little wider. Her sharp intake of breath told me she was hot and ready. I could take her in the bathroom if I wanted.

"I have a place," she said the words so low I almost didn't hear them.

"I have a place," I replied, rubbing the pad of my thumb across her jawline as I moved my hand down her neck, applying a little pressure as I moved.

She shook her head, her breath coming fast. "No, here."

I raised an eyebrow and smiled. "Here? Okay, but I think we might draw some unwanted attention."

She squeezed her eyes closed. "Not here. It's close. We can go right out that door."

I turned to look behind me, noticing the door for the first time. "That door?"

"Yes!" She practically screamed the word.

I looked at her mouth, enjoying the game. She was desperate for me. I could see it in her eyes, the way she was breathing, her twitching as she tried to stay perfectly still.

"Show me the way," I ordered, my hand moving to the back of her neck as I lowered my mouth toward hers.

I hovered there, not kissing her, letting her feel me, heightening the anticipation of what was to come. She pushed away from me, her hand in the center of my chest. I grinned when she stepped to the side and made a beeline for the door so fast she nearly knocked over a chair during her hasty exit.

"I have to text Ash," she mumbled, pulling out her phone, her fingers flying rapidly over the keys before sending the message.

"Where are we going?" I asked her as she slid a card into the elevator.

She looked at me and grinned. "You'll find out soon enough."

Oh, now she wanted to tease me. I stepped toward her, backing her against the elevator, my body pushed against hers, my forehead resting on hers. "Don't play games you can't win," I warned her in a gravelly voice.

I was still aching from the last time she'd gotten me hard and wanting before up and leaving me high and dry.

"No games," she whispered.

I closed my mouth over hers, slowly kissing her, tasting the champagne on her lips, fueling my jealousy at the thought of her out with another man. My hands moved to either side of her face as I held her steady, my mouth covering hers, devouring every bit of her. She was mine and one day she was going to learn that. For now, I would show her the best way I knew how.

CHAPTER 41

NATASHA

I shouldn't be doing it, but here I was, right back in Jack's arms. I wanted him and no matter the long list of reasons why I should stay away, I couldn't deny that strong pull that always brought me to the man. I felt possessed by him and I didn't care. I wanted him to control me, use me while dominating my body and mind, blocking out all the reasons why I couldn't have him. When the elevator stopped, I pushed him back, grabbing his hand to lead him into my new penthouse.

"What's this?" he asked, looking around the empty space bathed in the light pollution streaming in through the windows.

"My new penthouse," I replied, feeling very proud of myself.

"Yours?" he asked.

I nodded. "Mine."

Without furniture, it looked huge and a little cold and uninviting. The wall of floor-to-ceiling windows provided a twinkling nightscape that looked like something pulled straight out of a landscape photo. I watched as Jack moved into what would be the living space before turning toward the open kitchen.

"Nice," he murmured and turned to glance back at me.

It was then I realized it was a little awkward. There was no furniture to speak of and the dark hardwoods weren't exactly inviting. Judging by the way he was eyeing me, that wasn't a problem for him. He moved toward me, his eyes holding mine captive. I knew I would do anything he asked. Damn the discomfort. I would take the man anywhere and had nearly done so right there in the damn bar. He had a way of getting me so fucking hot and worked up I lost all sense of control.

When he was inches in front of me, I had to look up to accommodate his height. I challenged him with my eyes, waiting to see what he would do next.

His hand reached out, turning me around before moving to the zipper on the back of my dress and slowly pushing it down. The cool air in the room washed over my skin as the dress gaped open, a million goose bumps spreading over my flesh. I casually stepped out of it, then turned to face him, wearing my matching black bra and thong that I had worn for the day.

In the dim light, I could see his nostrils flare as he looked over my body. I loved how he looked at me. It always made me feel like the most beautiful woman on the planet. I reached out to loosen his tie before undoing it all the way, then pulling it from around his neck. He stood still, letting me unbutton each of the tiny buttons on the pale-blue shirt he was wearing. My hand brushed inside, touching the soft cotton under shirt, feeling his defined pectoral muscles that led into the sexiest abs I had ever seen. In an instant, I was ravenous for his skin on mine. He must have felt the change as well and shucked his shirt, yanking his T-shirt over his head before unfastening his belt and pants with record speed.

I touched his chest, my hand splayed over the hardness of his body before I stepped closer and rubbed my bra-clad chest against him like a cat rubbing against its owner's legs. His hand quickly released my bra, freeing my breasts and giving me that skin-to-skin contact I was desperate for. My erect nipples scraped over his chest, the crunchy hairs rubbing against my sensitive skin.

My hands moved to push his pants down his body, wanting all of him against all of me. He stripped my thong from me, leaving us both standing naked in the dark room with only the bright lights of the city all around us.

"No blinds," he muttered, cupping my breasts.

I gasped, my head dropping back. The open windows were an additional thrill. I knew no one could see in. It was heady and erotic to think we were in the open, exposed and yet completely concealed at the same time.

"Take me," I whispered.

His mouth moved to my neck, sucking and biting as his hunger amped up. He reached down, cupping my ass before lifting me and carrying me to the ice-cold granite countertop that spanned the length of the kitchen. My heart pounded faster as he stepped away from me.

"Lie back, I'm hungry." He growled.

I closed my eyes as desire flooded my body, reclining to rest my back against the hard, cold surface. It was so naughty, so bad, and so fucking good I could feel my juices pooling between my legs without a single touch from him.

I arched, opening my legs a little, needing him desperately. I felt his silky hair against the sensitive skin on the inside of my thighs and moaned in anticipation of what was to come. At the first lap of his tongue over my folds, I cried out in sheer pleasure.

"Slow down, I'm just getting started." He growled, the words vibrating over my core, sending heat waves over my body, instantly warming the once cold countertop.

"I can't stop." I gasped as he lapped again, his tongue splitting my folds and finding my core.

I had no control over my body. I was completely at his mercy. His tongue delved inside me, his teeth scraping over me as I searched for something to grasp on the slick counter. I felt as if I were going to float away.

His mouth worked me into a frenzy, my head thrashing back and forth, my legs pulled up and dropped open wide as I greedily begged for more. When the explosion I had been striving for finally happened, I screamed out his name. He didn't give me a second to wind down, standing, and pulling me to the edge of the counter before sliding inside my spasming body, sending me straight up into heaven again as he began to move inside me.

"That's it, keep coming, don't stop," he grunted, stroking deep inside.

I couldn't stop if I had wanted to. A million needle points of glorious ecstasy slammed into my body with each thrust. I heard myself moaning and threw caution to the wind, relishing every second I was with him.

"Don't stop," I chanted, mindlessly repeating his words.

"I'm not going to stop. I can't stop. I can't get enough of you. I see you and I have to have you. You're mine, Nat. All mine. This is mine." He growled, reaching for my breast, squeezing as he continued his steady rhythm.

"Yours," I repeated, my mind blank. All I could think of was him, him filling me and loving me so deeply.

I moved to sit up, wanting to taste him. The shift in position created a series of new sensations flooding my body. I grabbed his face, holding him as I used my tongue to spread his lips open, thrusting inside, and thoroughly exploring every inch inside his mouth. His tongue dueled with mine before I grabbed it with my teeth, pulling a loud groan from his mouth.

My hands dropped, squeezing his firm ass, yanking him against me.

"Slow down." He growled near my ear before his mouth opened wide, sucking my neck, then biting.

I returned the favor, still holding his ass in my hand as I sucked hard on his neck, knowing I was leaving a mark. I wanted to mark my territory.

"Harder," I ordered.

"You don't know what you're asking for." He hissed.

I slapped his ass, letting him know I knew what I wanted. "Harder," I repeated.

He roared, a feral, primal sound scraping over my nerves and taking me to a new level of ecstasy. He hammered into my body, pushing me across the counter only to jerk me back hard against him and start the process all over again. It was hot and loud as we each expressed our desires through moans and shouts.

In a split second, our bodies erupted at the same time, tumbling over the crest into sweet surrender. His body arced into mine, giving me every drop he had as I willingly absorbed him into me. His head dropped to my shoulder as he struggled for air. I wrapped my arms around him, holding him close as I slowly came down from where he had taken me. I looked to my right, gazing out at the city and sighed in pure contentment.

Jack stepped away from me, moving to pick up his clothes. Without a word I followed suit, picking up my bra and underwear and quickly dressing.

"This is a nice place. Do I get the grand tour?" he asked, buckling his belt before quickly pulling on his shoes.

"I'd love to show you around," I said excited to show him my first home.

I moved to turn on the lights, flooding the open living space with light from above.

"Where's your room?" he asked.

I giggled softly and strolled down the hallway to a set of double doors at the end, pulling them open in a grand gesture. "Tada!"

He flipped on the light and whistled low. "This is really nice," he said, walking into the huge space, opening the connecting bathroom door and then walking in.

I followed him, marveling at the beautiful room. I loved it. It looked like something out of a magazine with black-and-white marble all over the floor leading to an elevated garden tub that I just knew I would be taking advantage of.

He walked past me, barely brushing me as he continued to tour my home. We ended up back in the kitchen.

"What do you think?" I asked.

"It's a great place. Did you buy it?" he asked with disbelief.

"Well I didn't rent it."

"This is a big move for you. You're moving out of your parents' house?"

I smiled. "I am."

"Good for you. This place is perfect for you. I could see you living here. I know you'll put your own personal touch on it, make it your own."

I sighed with satisfaction. "Thank you. I'm excited. It's my first step to freedom."

He walked toward me, putting his hands on my hips as he looked down at me. "I can see me coming over, bending you over the back of the sofa right there," he said, shifting his gaze to a place in front of the windows.

"Don't," I whispered.

He shook his head. "I'll take you in the shower, before carrying your wet, limp body to your huge bed and then fucking you again there."

My heart clenched, knowing it couldn't happen. "Stop," I told him, not wanting to let myself think about a future that couldn't happen.

"I'm not going to stop," he said firmly, staring directly into my eyes with fierce determination before turning and walking out of the penthouse without saying another word.

I stood in the kitchen, turning to look at the counter and groaned. Every time I thought I could find the strength to push him out of my life, he showed up and all that resolve dissolved in an instant. All it took was a look or a single word, and I was putty. I buried my face in my hands, trying to figure out how I was going to get myself out of the mess I had created.

I quickly cleaned up the place before letting myself out and then heading home. I felt a little guilty about ditching Ashley, but in that moment, nothing else mattered except being alone with Jack. She'd understand, and I really didn't owe Devon an explanation. It hadn't been a date. That thought brought up a whole new list of worries.

How was I ever going to date anyone? If I saw him out, it was going to be impossible to focus on the man I was supposed to be with. Even if I didn't see Jack, I would be thinking about him.

"You're screwed," I muttered, getting into the back of the car I had ordered.

CHAPTER 42

JACK

At some point during the afternoon, I realized Nat's new place was not all that far from mine. It was a weird thought that popped into my head without warning. It didn't matter if she lived in Jersey or Manhattan, I would always find a way to her. Her close proximity only made it a little nicer. It would be a short drive after work or early in the morning after spending the night with her. And I had no doubt in my mind I would be spending many nights with her.

I was feeling much better about things, even if nothing had truly been resolved. It was good to know she still wanted me. After the night at the charity ball, I had questioned everything. I had been ready to throw in the towel and move on, but then she'd shown up. She wasn't ready to toss me out just yet. That meant I still had a chance to convince her to stand up to her father. I realized I was going to have to tell my mom at some point, but I was still counting on her taking it a little better than the Levy family. I had to believe that.

I finished fixing my tie before reaching for the black Armani jacket. Tonight, was a business meeting Grayson had asked me to attend with him. We knew the deal was in the bag, but whenever we bought someone's company, we tried to treat them with the respect and dignity they deserved. The two men who were selling us their start-up were long-time acquaintances. They were a lot like Grayson and me. They found fledging start-ups that were on the brink of burning out and infused new life into them, growing them into a business that could be taken even further with the kind of capital our company could bring in. We took the seed and helped it flourish, I liked to think.

I was taking a car to the restaurant, knowing there would be drinking involved as we sealed up the deal. When I arrived at the waterfront restaurant, I was taken to the table where Grayson was already waiting, a folder on the table as he reviewed the contract.

"Is it not neat and tidy already?" I asked, taking my seat on his left.

"It's good, I just want to familiarize myself with the terms. I've closed a lot of deals this week and I want to make sure I've got the details straight," he said absently as he read.

"I know it forward and backward," I assured him.

He looked up from the contract. "You do?"

I shrugged. "I put this deal together. Of course, I do."

He sighed and took a drink of the ice water in front of him. "Thank God. I've read the same sentence four times."

"Hannah still struggling with morning sickness?" I asked, noticing the dark circles under his eyes.

"Morning, noon, midnight, all day, all night." He groaned.

I shook my head. "Isn't there something they can give her?"

"She takes a couple things, but I think she's dealing with a flu on top of everything. She was at the park and that place is nothing but a germ fest. Now the baby—sorry—she's not a baby, she's a big girl, is sick as well."

I grimaced, not envying him in the slightest. I thought I wanted a family, but the man looked like he'd been through hell. "I'm sorry. That really sounds bad. You're taking care of them yourself?"

"Yes." He growled.

"Why?"

He rolled his eyes as if the answer were obvious. "If she'd let me hire a damn nanny she wouldn't need to wear herself out trying to keep up with everything, and I wouldn't have to be cleaning up puke," he grumbled.

I chuckled and shook my head. "You know she won't do the nanny thing. She's hands-on. Mom was the same way. Remember when we all came down with that flu? Mom didn't sleep for a week and Dad bitched the entire time about hiring a nanny. She refused."

"I know and I'm usually grateful for it, but right now, I really wish she'd admit defeat. She did let me call a sitter for tonight while she rested. And although I'm here, I have strict orders not to stay out late."

"We'll get this tied up quick. You can go home. I can handle the schmoozing," I assured him. "Hell, you can leave now."

"No!" he said a little too quickly. "Trust me, I want to be here. I want to eat a meal without the sound of retching."

I covered my mouth to hide my snicker. "Okay, you can eat dinner, but then you better go. I'm not answering to Hannah if you are late. I can handle this. You can trust me."

"Thank you. I know you can handle this. I'm only here as decoration. I trust you. Seriously, I cannot imagine how this company could run without you. Don't even think about retiring or running off to chase your lady," he warned.

"I won't leave you hanging," I promised him.

It wasn't long before Bill and Carl showed up, both eager to finalize the deal and celebrate. I took lead, giving Grayson the chance to act as second chair. It had been my deal from the beginning and I was perfectly capable of handling the situation. I knew I didn't have to prove myself, but I did like when I could show him I was more than the spare keeping the VP's chair warm.

"Good evening, gentlemen," I said, greeting both men before ordering a round of scotch for the table.

We went through the usual pleasantries and small talk before quickly getting business out of the way.

"You feeling okay?" Carl asked Grayson halfway through dinner.

Grayson wiped his mouth and nodded after scarfing down half of his meal in record time. "My wife is expecting another child and she has the flu on top of the morning sickness," he explained.

Carl, who was a man in his sixties, grimaced. "Sorry to hear that. My wife breezed through each of her eight pregnancies, but my youngest daughter is pregnant and having a hell of a time."

The conversation switched from business to the joys of fatherhood. Bill, a lifelong bachelor, and I remained silent, nodding, but having nothing to add to the conversation.

"What about you, Jack? Isn't it about time you started to think about settling down?" Carl asked.

I smiled and shrugged a shoulder. "I don't know, Bill seems to be happy enough."

Bill grinned and held up his glass before taking a long drink. "I enjoy the single life."

"Liar. You are still pouting over what's her name leaving you," Carl said.

"Easy come, easy go. I bet you know what I'm talking about," Bill said to me.

I rarely talked about my private life with business acquaintances, but the family had known Carl and Bill for decades. They knew me when I was just getting started in the company.

"I'm taking my time," I said, hoping to satisfy the invasion into my private life.

Grayson gave me a look filled with apology. "Guys, I hate to run out on you, but I am leaving you in the very capable hands of my brother. I've got to get home and hopefully get some sleep tonight."

"Take care of yourself and your family," Carl said, standing and shaking his hand before Bill followed suit.

I ordered another round of drinks, not wanting them to feel dismissed. "You have your eye on anything new?" I asked the men casually.

Bill nodded. "We have a couple in the works we might be bringing to you in the next few months."

"You know I'm always ready to see what you've got," I assured him.

"Yes, you are. Your father would be proud of you and your brother. You guys have done a great job growing your company. I hate when you guys turn us down on a deal, because I know that means we're about to get our asses handed to us by a less-than-honest company."

I shrugged a shoulder. "You know we have to stick with sure things."

"Oh, we know it, which is why it sucks when you shoot us down, we know we've got a lemon on our hands," Bill replied before bursting into laughter.

"Sorry guys," I said, lifting my shoulders.

The waitress appeared with a glass of scotch. I looked up, questioning her.

"The woman over there," she said, pointing to an attractive woman in a red dress sitting at the bar.

I smiled at the woman before turning back to the waitress. "Can you politely decline for me?" I asked gently.

"I will," the waitress said and walked away with the full glass.

"That's a beautiful woman," Carl said in a low voice.

"She is," I confirmed.

Bill casually turned to look at the woman who'd just been informed I denied her drink. I didn't want to be an ass, but I wasn't interested in another woman.

"Man, I would have taken the drink. That woman is sexy as hell," Bill said under his breath.

"If only you were thirty years younger," Carl said with a chuckle.

"Thirty, hell, I only need to go back about ten years and twenty pounds," Bill joked.

We all got a good laugh before both men focused in on me. "Are you seeing anyone?" Carl asked.

I had grown so tired of hearing that question. Why in the hell did everyone think my dating life was up for discussion?

"I'm not seeing anyone at the moment," I replied, not technically lying.

"He's probably playing the field," Bill defended my lack of a ring or a girlfriend.

"Then I'd be playing whatever game she is in," Carl joked.

"Ha. Ha. I don't mix business with pleasure and I'm enjoying my evening with you fine fellows," I said, hoping to shut down the beginning of an interrogation.

"We'd never want to hold you back. If you want to take that woman up on her offer for a drink, don't let us stop you. We're old, not dead," Bill replied.

"Thank you, but trust me, I'm fine. I'll be going home alone tonight with phone numbers in my pockets," I told him, trying to keep it light but quickly growing irritated.

Carl held up his hands in surrender. "No more. We'll leave you alone. A man gets enough pressure from his mama about things like this, am I right?"

"You would be dead-on," I confirmed his suspicions.

We finished our drinks, chatted about our plans for the holidays, and possible business deals that we could potentially work together on. It was eleven when we said good night and parted ways. It was a long, lonely ride home. Returning to an empty apartment did little to lift my spirits. I was growing tired of going home alone.

It was making me second-guess a lot of things in my life. I didn't want to overthink things. If I started thinking about the future, I would get pissed or completely bummed. I didn't want to think about what it would mean if things didn't work out. I had to hold on to the hope that there was a chance for a normal life with Natasha. It had to happen soon, or I was going to lose my damn mind.

I climbed into bed and thought about calling her. I couldn't. I knew that. I wondered what she was doing and who she was doing it with. I couldn't stand the thought of her on a date with another man, laughing and flirting. Her new home was a good step in the right direction. Although, I'd much prefer if she were moving into my place. Time. I had to be patient.

CHAPTER 43

NATASHA

The moment I stirred awake, all I could think about was how I would soon be in my very own penthouse, in the bed I chose. My second thought was what the hell had I drank the night before? My stomach was angry and my head was pounding. I closed my eyes and lectured myself for drinking too much the night before. Then my eyes popped open. I didn't drink the night before. I had stayed in last night, choosing to do a little online browsing and shopping for my new penthouse.

I must have picked something up. It was that time of year when everyone had some kind of cold or flu. I groaned and rolled out of bed, pulling on my robe and sliding my feet into my fuzzy pink slippers before heading out my door and down the stairs. It was a slow journey. Every step jostling my stomach and threatening to upset the very careful balance I had managed to achieve.

When I made it to the kitchen, I grabbed some sparkling water from the fridge and took a cautious sip, letting it flow down my throat while the little bubbles combated the nausea rolling in my belly. A few more drinks and things were getting better. I headed for the bathroom, located off the kitchen, and found some Advil in the medicine cabinet, popping two in my mouth and washing them down with more of the sparkling water. Today was going to be spent in bed with my laptop, I decided, and headed back to the kitchen to grab supplies.

With another bottle of sparkling water and a sleeve of crackers in my hand, I prepared to make my great escape to solitude when Elijah appeared out of nowhere, scaring me half to death.

"What are you doing here?" I gasped.

"I wanted to talk to you. You look like shit," he commented.

"Thanks. Now you've talked to me, move out of my way, I'm going back to bed."

He folded his arms over his chest and leaned against the wall, effectively blocking my escape. "What do you want, Elijah? I'm really not in the mood," I grumbled.

"You're seeing him again."

I froze, my eyes going wide as I stared at him, an accusatory look on his face. "What?"

"Don't try and deny it. I know you're seeing Jack again."

"Don't say that!" I hissed, looking around the kitchen to make sure my parents weren't lurking around the corner.

He shook his head. "Don't lie. My friend saw you the other night with him."

My mouth dropped open before snapping closed. The other night I had dragged him up to my penthouse. Where in the hell had his friend been? What did his friend see? The calm I had managed to achieve in my stomach was gone and back was the bubbling nervousness threatening to make me ill.

"Elijah, it isn't like that," I protested.

"What's going on? I thought this had been taken care of." He glowered at me, anger in his eyes.

I sighed, not up for a fight. "Nothing is going on. Ashley and I were celebrating my new place. I ran into him at the bar. It was no big deal."

"Do you still love him?" he asked pointedly.

"No. It's just ... I don't know." I waved a hand through the air, hoping to make him go away.

Elijah stepped away from the wall and toward me. "It's just what? You know you're playing with fire."

"Elijah, it isn't so easy to walk away from someone. Old habits die hard. Whether you want to believe it or not, he and I had something special. It was meaningful to both of us. Walking away because you and Dad said so has been the hardest thing I've ever done," I said, emotion making my voice raspy.

Elijah looked at me, studying my face. "You know Dad will make you regret seeing Jack if he hears about this."

I immediately bristled. "Are you threatening me?" I demanded.

"No, I'm telling you Dad isn't going to keep giving you a free pass. I don't want to see you hurt again," he said, before wrapping his arms around me and hugging me tight, threatening to crush my crackers.

"I'm not doing anything," I assured him again.

"Good. I'm only trying to protect you and that asshole. Believe it or not, he was my best friend for a long time and I don't want to see either of you get hurt. You're getting in too deep. I won't be able to protect you if you don't back off this thing," he said.

I took a deep breath, waiting for him to let me go before stepping back and looking at him. "I'm moving out as soon as my penthouse is ready. That will give me some breathing room."

"Don't do anything stupid, Nat. Dad is not the kind of man you want to betray," he warned again.

"I know. I'm not," I said and left the kitchen, feeling sicker than I had when I made my way down.

I should have known better. There were eyes everywhere. I could never be with Jack in secret. People knew me, and they knew him. People loved to gossip about the latest hookups. Jack and I weren't safe anywhere. If anyone saw him going into my building, it would get back to my family. I felt as if I would never escape their watchful eyes.

Once I had reached the safety of my apartment in the mansion, I closed the door, hoping everyone would leave me alone. It was impossible to be alone in the place. They may have given me my own space, but my mom was always stopping by to ask me this or that, or to check on me in general. I was beginning to feel claustrophobic in that place and couldn't wait until next weekend when I could start moving into the penthouse.

My mom was loaning me two of the housekeepers to pack my things. Everything else was staying in the mansion. I was starting over, starting new with my own things handpicked by me. With a few more sips of sparkling water, I began the process of calming my churning stomach all over again. The headache was subsiding a bit as well.

With my laptop, crackers, and bubbling water, I relaxed on my bed, browsing some of the home interior designs I thought would be best suited for the space and for those that spoke to me. I knew I could ask my mom for help, but this was something I wanted to do all on my own.

My thoughts kept drifting back to Jack and how much my family hated him. It seemed so unfair. Jack had done nothing to any of them. He was a good man. He was kind and considerate and despite what they thought, he was honest. Sometimes brutally honest, but I knew I could always count on him to tell me the truth. He didn't like lies and deceit. He had nothing to hide. Why my father thought Jack was like his father was beyond me. It wasn't as if Jack inherited the deceitful gene. It didn't work like that, but my dad was convinced all the Bancroft men were carbon copies of their father.

It was stupid and archaic to hold Jack responsible for something his father—and apparently his mother—had done. I knew Jack had no idea about the situation. I couldn't imagine how he would feel knowing his mom and my dad had once been a thing. That was weird to even think about.

There was a soft knock on the door. I did my best to put on a serene expression when my mom popped her head in.

"Good morning, dear," my mom said, coming into the room.

"Hi, Mom."

She looked at the water and crackers sitting on my bedside table. "Oh no, are you sick?" she asked, coming right over.

I shrugged a shoulder. "I'm fine. I think the worst of it is over. I'm sure with all the people I've been interacting with all week, I managed to pick up some virus."

"Well, you stay in bed. I'll have some soup brought up."

"Mom, I'm fine, really. I'm just going to take it easy for the day," I assured her.

She nodded. "That's a good idea. Are you working?" she asked, looking at the laptop.

I grinned. "No, I'm doing a little shopping."

"Oh, for?"

"Furniture," I said, then smiled.

She clapped her hands together. "Scoot over. I want to see what tickles your fancy."

I giggled and scooted over a bit on the bed. I showed her what I was looking at and waited for her opinion. Surprisingly, she kept it reined in, offering little suggestions here and there about how to create a more intimate space for conversation without taking away from the room. They hadn't seen the penthouse, but I had shown her the online listing. She was as taken with the windows and huge open concept as I had been.

For the next hour, my mom and I planned out the living room area, complete with a beautiful rug and furniture. She told me to choose artwork in person and to never rely on a computer screen to give me the full colors of any piece. I happily took her advice. She did know a thing or two about making a home feel comfortable and inviting.

"I'll let you rest. Don't overdo it. You know you don't have to move out right away. You have a lot going on with the new office. Maybe you need to slow down," she lectured.

"I'm fine. I'll rest today," I promised her.

"Okay, I'll send up the soup in a couple hours," she said before leaving me alone once again.

I would miss them, but I was ready to be a big girl. I didn't need my mom coddling me when I didn't feel good. Millions of adults managed to survive on their own, I could too. Of course, if I kept up with Jack, I would be well and truly alone. I wouldn't have to worry about my mother coddling me. She wouldn't even be speaking to me.

That was the problem. That had to be it. The more they told me I couldn't see him, the more I wanted him. It was as if something was wired wrong in my brain. I was stuck in some fourteen-year-old rebellious teen stage and couldn't quite move past the idea of doing exactly what my parents didn't want me to do. It was a little stupid, immature, and a lot embarrassing to admit, but that had to be it.

No matter how many times they told me and how many times I tried to tell myself, I couldn't seem to put the idea of Jack and me together out of my head. Deep inside, I knew he was the only man who I would ever love the way I did. Maybe there was different kinds of love. That had to be it. My dad loved Kathy Bancroft but in a different way than he loved my mom. I hoped that meant there was a chance for me to love another man, even if it wasn't with the same fiery passion that I loved Jack with.

"You can't have him, Nat," I whispered.

"Can't" was a strong word. It was the word that triggered the rebellious side of me. I could have him but having him wasn't worth the cost. I needed to look at it with a less emotional view and look at the situation with a clear eye. Being with Jack would cost me everything and everyone else in my life. I knew the divorce rate was high. Was I willing to sacrifice everything with the possibility of losing Jack in the future?

I shook my head. There was no way I would ever lose Jack. He and I had a connection that would stand the test of time if we allowed it to flourish.

CHAPTER 44

JACK

She was so beautiful, her black hair flowing around her as she raced through the trees. It was where we had agreed to meet, where her brother wouldn't find us. She was young and carefree as she raced down the path that wound through the tall pine trees in the park. She loved to play this little game of hide-and-seek. I managed to catch up to her, grabbing her and wrapping my arms around her waist, staring down at the creamy white skin that had been untouched by freckles despite her time in the sun. Her petite body in my arms felt so right.

"I have to be home soon," she whispered.

"I know. I had to see you before you left," I told her, brushing the hair away from her face as the breeze kicked up.

She leaned up on her tiptoes and gave me a quick kiss. "I'm going to miss you like crazy."

"I'm going to miss you too. Are you sure you have to go? What am I going to do without you for two years?" I whispered, my heart in agony at the thought of never seeing her again.

"You'll think about me and I'll think about you when I'm lounging on some beach in the South of France," she teased.

"Are you going to be wearing a tiny bikini?" I playfully growled.

"Maybe I'll wear nothing at all," she teased.

"You're killing me." I groaned, my body reacting to the idea of her lounging nude on a sandy beach, the sun reaching down and caressing the length of her body.

"We could pretend we're somewhere far away," she suggested.

I raised an eyebrow, intrigued by her idea. "Really? Here?"

"Why not? No one is around. We're all alone. It's just me and you."

It was not a suggestion I would ever turn down. I kissed her, took her hand, and led her to a grassy spot surrounded by trees. Together, we sat down in the grass, our shoulders touching as we stared out over the small lake nestled in the trees.

"Do you think we'll be able to do this again one day?" I asked her, already knowing the answer but wanting to stay in our world of make-believe.

"Absolutely."

I reached out and held her hand in mine, holding on to it like I would never let go. She sighed as she rested her head against my shoulder.

"I never want to leave this place," she said on a sigh.

"Do you ever think about what it would be like to wake up and be someone else? I mean, wake up and be normal, free to be with whoever you wanted?" I asked, knowing I had thought of that very thing almost daily since I realized I had fallen for the one woman I could never have.

She laughed softly. The sound still reverberating in my ears, even in my dreams. "No, but I think about waking up in your arms all the time."

"Maybe I'll sneak over and visit you," I suggested after some deep thought.

She laughed softly, the sound carrying over me, making me smile and warming me from the inside out. "I'll be waiting for you."

I leaned down and kissed her. It was going to be the last time we were together, and I wanted to make it special. Her soft lips beneath mine spread wide, giving me access to plunge inside her mouth. I kissed her, pouring every unspoken emotion into the kiss. Her body was pushing against mine as we gave ourselves to each other. I gently laid her back on the grass and made love to her in the sweetest way I knew, telling her with my body how much I loved her. Her body arched under mine, spurring me on as we joined together.

I lost myself inside her sweet body, giving her my heart and soul and taking hers to carry with me always. Her gasps of pleasure and moans of sheer desire still haunted me in the best way possible. I could feel her beneath me, my body on the verge of a powerful climax as her fingernails dug into my back.

My eyes popped open as my heart fluttered in my chest. My body was tense and my dick hard as the remnants of the dream clung to the outskirts of my conscience. The memory of our last night together before she had left on that trip was one I frequently revisited in my dreams. It always left me with a raging hard-on and the need to relieve the ache in my balls. It had kept me company on the many lonely nights I had endured since she left that first time. Back then, we knew our love was forbidden, but it was so much easier.

Neither of us was thinking about our futures and just kind of assumed things would get better. I don't think I realized then how much I loved her. I had no real understanding of what it meant to want to be with a woman for the rest of my life. I would have never guessed I would never touch another woman. We had both laughed and said we would date and have fun. That had been naive. Our souls were melded together long before we ever knew it.

I had fallen asleep on the couch, watching a football game that was clearly not all that entertaining. As always, Natasha had been in my dreams waiting for me. She always was. I got up and splashed water on my face, looking at the clock. It was only eight o'clock. After my little power nap, the last thing I wanted to do was go to bed or beat off.

I wanted Nat. I wanted her body under me, enveloping me as I slid inside her. She was too close for me to take care of the problem myself. When she was halfway around the world, I could take matters into my own hands, but when she was a short thirty minutes away, I wanted her.

"Fuck it." I growled. I went to my room to throw on a pair of jeans before grabbing my jacket and keys and heading for the garage where my Porsche was stored.

It was stupid and dangerous, but I was going to the Levy mansion. I had to see her. It wasn't like I didn't know my way around the place. Wayne Levy had no idea how many times I had sneaked in back when Elijah and I had been friends in school. There had been some wild, drunken nights that ended up with me sneaking in through his window to drag his ass out.

I parked outside the gate, went around the back where I knew there was a gap in the fence that I could easily maneuver through, and headed across the dark yard, my destination one of the tall oaks that grew outside her old bedroom window. I knew it was stupid. I knew it was juvenile, but I was doing it anyway. It had been the dream, reminding me of those days when things had been so much easier between us.

I made it to the tree and almost burst into laughter. I was a thirty-five-year-old man about to climb a damn tree to sneak into the bedroom window of the girl I was in love with. It wasn't quite as easy as I remembered, but I managed to pull myself up to the first branch and from there, it was a lot easier. I heard a rip.

"Shit," I muttered.

The dark made it a little difficult to navigate, but her window was just another foot up. I hoisted myself up on the thick branch and caught my first glimpse of her. She was sitting cross-legged on her bed, her laptop in her lap. Her hair was pulled up into a loose pile on her head. It looked like she was dressed for bed, wearing a pair of tiny shorts and a T-shirt. I watched as she stared at her screen, not realizing I was a few feet away.

I reached out, holding onto the branch above me and hoping like hell I didn't fall out of the damn tree. I tapped on the window. I watched as her head shot up and looked around the room. I tapped again, a little harder, drawing her attention to me. Her eyes bulged as she saw me at her window. She jumped off the bed and rushed over to open the window.

"What are you doing?" she said on a hiss.

"I wanted to see you."

"You can't be here! Are you crazy! Go!" she ordered frantically.

I shook my head. "No."

"Jack!"

"Move, I'm coming in," I ordered, turning to put one leg inside the window before climbing in as she stood back and watched, horror on her face.

"What are you doing, Jack? Do you know how stupid this is?"

I shrugged a shoulder, not caring a bit. "I don't care."

"You're lucky my parents are out for the night. If my dad catches you he's going to kill you."

"I don't care. I wanted to see you," I repeated.

"Be right back." She disappeared and returned a few seconds later. "I locked the door," she explained.

I stared at her, as I always did, but noticed something was a little off. "Are you okay?" I asked her, looking at her skin and noticing she was a little paler than normal.

"Just a little under the weather. You're lucky. I was supposed to go to dinner with them but stayed home because I wasn't feeling well."

I walked to her, reaching out to cup her cheek as I stared into her blue eyes. "Are you okay?" I asked with concern.

"I'm fine. It's past now, but I didn't want to risk going out and exposing anyone else."

"You can expose me," I told her leaning down to give her a chaste kiss.

She sighed against me. "I cannot believe you just climbed through my window. I really feel like a child now."

"I thought it would remind you of the old times," I said with a grin.

"The old times when I was a young woman, uncaring of what her parents would think. I'm a little older now and a lot more cautious," she scolded.

"You shouldn't be. Throw caution to the wind," I replied.

"Easy for you to say," she mumbled, moving to her bed to close her laptop.

"What were you doing?" I asked.

She looked a little embarrassed. "Shopping. I've been shopping all day."

"For?"

"Furniture. House stuff," she replied.

I nodded in understanding. "Sounds fun."

"It is."

We stood staring at each other. The tension palpable. We were alone in her room and she was wearing a tiny pair of shorts that showed off the curve of her ass. She was braless under that T-shirt and her nipples were standing at attention.

I leaned down and kissed her again, this time telling her exactly what I wanted. She kissed me back before pushing me away.

"We can't," she whispered.

"Oh, we can, and we can do it very well," I told her.

She shook her head. "What if they come home?"

I shrugged. "I'll hide under the bed."

"Jack, it's too risky."

"Risky is going to make it better," I promised.

It was a weak protest. I knew she wanted me as much as I wanted her. She could try and deny it, but I could see it in the way she was breathing, the way her eyes were roaming over my body. She wanted me.

I leaned down and kissed her again, this time, I didn't stop to give her time to protest. I was going to have her.

CHAPTER 45

NATASHA

My heart was pounding with a mixture of passion and adrenaline. I couldn't believe he was in my bedroom in my parents' house. It was so wrong, but what he was doing to my body was so right. I arched into him, rubbing my hard nipples against his chest. Everything felt heightened, more powerful, each rub of my breasts over his hard chest sent shock waves through my body.

"I had to have you," he whispered, pulling my shirt over my head.

I moaned as the air hit my sensitive nipples, reaching down to grab the hem of his shirt to lift it up enough to give me that skin-on-skin contact I craved.

"We can't get caught. My dad would kill you and me, literally, I think," I said, wrapping one leg around his, rubbing myself against his hard thigh.

"We won't get caught. Your door is locked," he assured me, his hand moving to the back of my neck and holding me steady as he gave me a deep kiss full of longing.

I whimpered in ecstasy, loving the way he tasted against my lips. "They'd be so mad. Maybe throw you in jail for trespassing," I whispered against his lips.

"I'll go to jail. I don't care. I had to be near you. You haunt me in my dreams. I can't go a day without thinking about you," he said, kissing over my jaw toward my earlobe where he sucked and nibbled at my flesh.

"My penthouse." I gasped.

"What about it?"

"There. It will be safer there," I told him, trying to remember what I was going to say. He had a way of making me forget everything when he was kissing me.

He sucked on my neck. "I'm not waiting until you fucking move out. I'm here now."

"But, if they—"

He growled. "Do they usually tuck you in?" he snapped in frustration.

"No."

"Then let me love you," he commanded.

I sighed, loving the way he could be so forceful and, yet, so sweet and gentle. I knew he would never hurt me. I loved when he got like he was now, all fired up, his hands jerking as they squeezed and rubbed over my body as if he couldn't get enough of me.

"Love me," I whispered, leaning my neck to the side to give him the access he was seeking.

His mouth clamped down, sucking on my jugular vein as he nibbled with his teeth before kissing away the stinging sensation. The action sent goose bumps covering my body and heat pooling at my very center. He was going to make me orgasm with foreplay alone. I rubbed myself against his leg again, grinding and groaning as the hard muscle pressed against my clit. He stepped forward, giving me better access to rub against him.

"I dreamed about you. Feel this," he whispered grabbing my hand and moving it between his legs.

I could feel the erection straining against his jeans. I rubbed over the long length, loving the steely rod I could feel beneath the denim. He jerked, making me grow more excited. I quickly returned to the hem of his shirt to yank it over his head as the fire in my belly burned out of control. I was the one frenzied. I couldn't get close enough to him. I wanted to crawl over him, cover myself with his body.

"I want you," I told him, speaking exactly what was on my mind.

"And you'll have me," he stated matter-of-factly, his tone the exact opposite of my far more desperate one.

"We have to be fast, they'll be home soon," I told him, gasping as his bare chest pressed against mine, clawing at his back, trying to pull him closer.

"I don't need long. I'm ready to explode right now," he said with a groan.

I shook my head, moving my mouth to his left nipple and suckling. "Not yet. I need you first."

"You'll have me. I'll make you come, baby, you know I will," he promised, his hands running up and down my rib cage before moving to the elastic waistband of my shorts and pushing them over my hips.

I pulled my mouth away from his sexy chest and stripped off the rest of my clothes, standing before him in the muted light of my bedside table, the window still open and creating a chilly breeze.

"Take off your pants," I ordered, moving to the window to close it.

He quickly peeled them off. I stared at the erection jutting proudly from his body and smiled. I wanted to taste him like he had me so many times.

"Sit on the bed," I told him.

I kind of liked the control, although he did it better. He sat on the bed, his dick twitching as I watched. I dropped to my knees in front of him, looking up at him. His hand reached up and pulled the scrunchie from my hair, letting my hair tumble down around my shoulders before he gently ran his hands through it.

"I'm waiting." He growled.

I leaned forward, gently wrapping my fingers around his dick, pulling a gasp from him as I stroked up and down, my mouth hovering near, but not touching him.

"Take me in your mouth." His voice came in a rasp.

I looked up to meet his eyes and stuck my tongue out, circling the head, watching him clench his teeth together as I slowly ran my tongue around the top and over the slit before closing my mouth over him. His grunt sounded as if he were in pain as I slid my mouth over him, sucking as I moved up and down.

"I can't." He groaned, pulling me up in one sudden move.

He jumped off the bed and spun me around, pushing me onto the bed before climbing up beside me, his body stretched out alongside mine as his hand moved between my legs. His swift invasion with his finger shocked me, pulling my own cry of pleasure from low in my throat.

His finger worked inside me before a second one joined, stretching and readying me for him. I was beyond ready and told him, begged him to mount me. When his heavy body slid over the top of mine, I reached up, pulling his mouth down to mine to languish in the joy of kissing him as he joined his body to mine.

He slid inside, ever so slowly, taking me higher and higher on the climb to sweet ecstasy, his tongue plunging in and out of my mouth as he held his weight over me. I groaned with pleasure as his hips connected with mine, filling me completely.

"Open your eyes," he whispered.

I hadn't even realized they were closed. I opened them to find him staring down at me with such love it made my heart feel full and completely whole. As he began to move inside me, his intense gaze made me feel as if he could see right into my very soul, see the feelings and emotions bubbling inside me as he made love to me. It was a sensual, emotional experience far different from our usual passion-filled joinings that were more desire than emotion.

Seeing his pleasure, the unspoken love touched me in new ways, triggering a sweet orgasm that started slow and gently crested with him gently rocking in to me, holding my eyes with his before he dropped his mouth to mine and made love to my mouth with his.

I felt the moment everything changed, his body felt harder, tenser as he pulled away from my mouth and rolled over, pulling me onto him.

"Ride me," he said through gritted teeth.

I happily obliged, giving him the slow ride that he had given me, taking my time, loving every inch of him wrapped inside my warmth before I couldn't hold back. I found myself riding him as he bucked below me, holding on to one of his hands as my body moved in a frenzied pace that threatened to spill me off him and onto the floor. I held on, riding harder and faster until I cried out in pleasure, quickly snapping my mouth shut to keep from alerting anyone who might be in the house.

"There you go," he coaxed, his fingertips running up and down my spine as my body slowed and floated back down to earth from where I had been rocketed to the stars with a violent explosion of passion.

"Oh, Jack." I sighed, feeling so complete with him.

"Off." He moaned, gently pushing me off him.

I rolled to my side, knowing instinctively what he wanted and moving to all fours, letting him position himself behind me. His hand lovingly followed my spine before moving over my hip and thigh.

"You're so beautiful," he whispered before using his hand to guide himself into me.

I moaned as he filled me once again, pushing back against him and pulling a loud groan from him. I rotated my hips, scraping against him, shuddering with excitement as he groaned again, breath sucking between his teeth.

"Harder." I gasped when he thrust once.

"Shh, I'm barely holding on." He panted.

"Don't hold back," I demanded, loving the tone of his voice, which told me he was losing all control.

"Damn it, Nat." He growled, grabbing my hips and thrusting hard into me, once and then again, pulling a cry of ecstasy from deep within my body.

"More." I moaned.

"Fuck, you turn me inside out." He rasped, his body moving deep inside me as he took his pleasure, my body willing to give him all he needed.

"Baby, I need you. All of you," I said with a whimper, desperate for more.

I was selfish. I wanted another orgasm and I knew he could give it to me. He was a generous lover, always giving me so much pleasure while holding back his own. He commanded my body with little effort, knowing right when to go hard and when to pull back. He knew my body better than I did.

"I'm giving you every drop. You're mine. All mine. Never forget that." He grunted each word as he thrust deep inside me, possessing me with his body.

"I'm yours," I chanted, giving up all control to him.

He moved inside, pumping and grinding his body against mine as he took his fill. The orgasm building hot in my belly, spreading out like a slow-moving fire over every nerve, every inch of skin feeling too hot, too tight as the shattering of my body and soul left me a crumpled heap with him pounding into me.

I heard him cry out, his passion palpable as he gripped my hips, driving into me with so much force I began to slide across the bed. Intense passion like I had never felt before sent me spiraling upward again as his orgasm stretched on and on, his body vibrating inside me, spasms rocking through our joined bodies.

"Damn, baby, you have no idea what you do to me." He gasped as he fell beside me, one arm flung over his face as he struggled to draw breath.

I giggled, landing on my side as I cuddled next to him. "I do. You do it to me."

"Good. I wasn't lying."

"What?" I asked.

"You're mine in every way. I don't know what the future holds, but you will always be mine."

I knew he was speaking the truth. I felt the same way. I would always be his. I wasn't sure if we would ever be able to take our relationship out of the shadows, but no matter what happened, he would always be the one my heart, mind, and soul belonged to.

CHAPTER 46

JACK

I wrapped my arm around her, bringing her naked body to my side. I knew I was pushing my luck, but I didn't care. I didn't want to leave her. I wanted to stay right where I was until I was ready for another round, which judging by the way my body was responding to the mere thought of having her again, would be much sooner rather than later.

"Want to see the furniture I picked for my living room?" she asked.

I grinned. "I would love to. I need an image to go with the fantasy I've already conjured up in my head. I want to know the fabric and color of the couch I'm going to bend you over," I said in a low, husky voice.

"Stop!" She gasped, feigning shock at my crude words.

She rolled away from me, climbing off the bed and quickly throwing on her clothes, tossing mine at me.

"You better get dressed," she said with a sexy smile.

"Why, it will only take longer to get you under me again."

She rolled her eyes. "You have a serious issue. What is the word I'm looking for?"

I shrugged. "Nymphomaniac?"

"That seems fitting. Although, I believe it is only a woman who can be a nymphomaniac."

I wrinkled my nose. "That seems wholly unfair. Are you a nympho?" I asked, waggling my eyebrows.

She gave me a cheeky grin. "Maybe."

"When it comes to you I can never get enough. I'm not out there chasing every woman I see—only you. You are the only one who has this kind of effect on me."

That cast a serious tone over the conversation. She had to know it was only her I wanted. It was only her I fantasized about. Only her body I wanted to plunge myself into.

"At least put your pants on. I don't want to be tempted. This is serious business," she joked.

I grinned, folded my hands under my head, and looked at her. "Are you saying my nudity distracts you? Tempts you?"

"You know it does."

I bobbed my hips up and down. "Is it my dick that is making it difficult for you to think straight?" I asked, trying not to laugh.

She giggled and pounced on top of me. My arms wrapped around her, holding her close while I kissed her, stirring things to life once again.

"Uh-oh," she murmured as my dick hardened under her body.

"I told you. Now you're dressed, and I have to waste precious time getting you undressed again," I said to her, laughter in my voice.

"Technically, it's only my shorts in the way," she replied, kissing me before escaping my grasp.

"Tease!"

She was giggling as she moved farther away from the bed. "You are insatiable. I think you have some kind of sickness. No one can want sex that often."

I raised an eyebrow. "I don't see you saying no. And if I remember right, you're the one who nearly climbed me at the bar that night."

Her cheeks flushed. "That was different, we hadn't been together in a while."

I shook my head. "I will always want to be with you, even if I have just had the best sex of my life, I'm going to want it all over again. I want to top the last best time."

She chewed on her lower lip. "Stop. You're tempting me."

"Good. I want to tempt you. You don't have to deny yourself. Come over here. Climb on top of me and have your way," I said, only slightly kidding.

"You're so bad." She groaned and walked away from the bed.

Realizing I wasn't going to get another quick tumble in bed, I sat up and pulled on my briefs, not bothering to dress the rest of the way before propping myself up on the mountain of pillows she had on her bed. She sat next to me, opening her laptop, and giving me a full tour of her living room or what it was going to look like once she was finished. I loved listening to her talk about her future. She was so excited and so animated it was contagious.

"I'm thinking to keep things warm, like dark blues and maybe some dark browns to go with the floors. What do you think?" she asked me.

"Baby, I don't have the first clue, but I trust you to do exactly what you want and make it exactly what you like and will make you feel at home. Don't trust anyone else to tell you what you want. I'm a guy with zero taste. I hired a decorator and she came in and did my whole place. I couldn't even tell you what color anything was, except my sofa. That's black."

She burst into laughter. "Way to pay attention to your surroundings."

I shrugged a shoulder. "It doesn't matter to me one way or another. All I'm interested in is making sure the sofa is comfortable and the TV is big."

"You're such a man."

I leaned down and kissed the top of her head. "Damn straight and that's why you love me."

She got off the bed and moved around her room, picking up odds and ends. "I don't know if I want to take any of this with me. Is that odd?"

"You're a grown woman, Natasha. This is your childhood room

with your childhood things. I think you're ready for a new chapter in your life," I told her honestly.

"I am. You're right. I was going to have all this stuff packed up, but I think I'll leave it. I'm sure there are going to be nights I stay here. If my parents don't remodel and turn this place into a movie theater when I move out, it will be nice to visit now and again. Kind of nostalgic," she said with a hint of wistfulness.

I smiled, watching her move, loving the way we could be so at ease with each other. I loved that we could talk as friends and not strictly lovers. Sex between us was amazing and all-consuming, but I liked being able to just hang out with her as well, even if somewhere in the back of my mind that raunchy side of me was thinking about all the different ways I could fuck her.

"What about your mom? Did she renovate your rooms once you moved out?" she asked.

I shook my head. "Nope. They are just as they were. She keeps them cleaned and there aren't any linens on the bed, but I know exactly where to find my collection of Hot Wheels."

She smiled. "I love that. I love the idea of holding on to that little piece of our childhood. It's better than any picture. I want to bring my daughter back to my room one day and show her all the things that made me feel comfortable when I was little."

The thought of her with a daughter did a number of things to me. I imagined me as the little girl's father. The girl would be a spitting image of her mom but have my height. Then my brain turned evil and I imagined someone else fathering her children and a streak of jealousy surged through my body at the mere thought of another man touching her.

"That's a good idea. My mom always says she's going to turn our rooms into guest rooms or her sewing room, but she's never done it."

"Your mom sews?" she asked with amazement.

I grinned. "Nope."

She threw her head back and laughed. "I guess I can see why you're not worried."

"Exactly."

I relaxed on the pillows and watched her as she sat down in a chair and began to surf the internet again. I could watch her all day. I wanted to commit this night to memory as well. It would join that other memory, but I had a feeling this one would take over in the number one position in my brain. Tonight had been different from that night nearly five years ago when she'd been about to leave on a two-year world adventure.

Back then, we hadn't really given much thought to what the rest of our lives meant. We'd both grown a lot since then and thinking about our future was far different. It was a much more serious topic. We were forced to choose between truly being happy with each other and giving up our family's love and support or choosing blood over love. Back then, I would have chosen the first, but now, with a little maturity and wisdom, I could understand her decision to choose the latter. I had only seen a glimpse of my mother's anger at the mere mention of the Levy name. Would she be like Wayne Levy and disown me if I dared commit my life to Natasha?

"What's on your mind?" she asked.

I blinked and focused on her sitting in the chair, watching me. "I was thinking about us."

She smiled. "I do that a lot."

She closed her laptop and walked toward me, sitting on the edge of the bed and putting her hand on my chest. "It's time for you to go. As much as I would love to spend the night with you, we can't, and we definitely can't do it here."

"You're right. I know. It was nice while it lasted, right?" I said, putting my hand on top of hers.

Her sad smile was my answer. "It was."

I stared at her a minute longer, committing every detail to that memory I planned on relying on later before getting up and pulling on my clothes. She moved to the window and opened it.

"No."

"What?"

"I'm leaving out the front door. If someone sees me, so be it."

Her mouth dropped open. "Jack! You can't!"

"I can, and I will."

I gave her a quick kiss before unlocking her bedroom door and stepping into the hall. I could see the staircase on the right and headed downstairs, tempting fate to step in and expose our secret. I almost wanted to be found out. I wanted to force the hand of fate and make something happen. I didn't want to be the one in control of walking away or staying and causing her pain by losing her family's love.

I paused on the bottom step, tempted to head toward the den, wanting to run into Wayne face-to-face and deal with the situation like a real man. I closed my eyes, knowing that would take it too far. I headed in the opposite direction and walked right out the front door, strolling down the long driveway without a care in the world.

I was almost a little bummed to walk out the side gate without anyone saying a word. The Levys should really think about hiring some security, I mused. That would have pushed the hand of fate for sure. Unfortunately, or fortunately, I wasn't sure which, there was no one to see me, no one to witness me leaving the bedroom of Princess Levy.

I got into my car and slowly drove past the gate, heading away from the mansion that caged my love. I had actually been hoping we would get caught. If I were being honest with myself, it was why I had lingered so long, well after when she expected them to show up. She hadn't pushed me out the door. I had a feeling she also was almost hoping to be caught and get everything out in the open.

I wasn't sure if it would make our situation better or worse, but the stalemate we were stuck in was driving me crazy. It was going to take something big to push us one way or another. I had to be willing to trust fate to push us in the right direction, even if it wasn't what I thought I wanted.

CHAPTER 47

NATASHA

Ashley and I strolled down Fifth Avenue, our coffees in hand as we blended in with the other shoppers crowding the sidewalks. It was obvious who the tourists were. They were the ones holding cameras or clutching their purses to their bodies as they gawked at the windows of the high-end shops and storefronts lining the streets. Like a good New Yorker, I casually stepped around the lingerers, intent on my destination.

I'd been in my penthouse for a week and was on the hunt for some pretty art and other decor to help fill up the place. I loved the openness, but it felt so empty and hollow. I needed things. All kinds of things. I wasn't exactly sure what, but I would know it when I saw it. Ashley, always up for a day of shopping, had agreed to come with me.

"I've got to have a cinnamon bun," I blurted out, the scent of fresh baked cinnamon buns filled my senses as we walked by a bakery.

"Really?" Ashley asked with surprise.

I nodded, following my nose inside the bakery. "Yes, just a few bites. Come on, they smell too good to pass up."

"You're killing me. I'm going to have to do an hour on the tread-mill when I get home," she complained.

I shushed her. "Then you can watch me devour one. I have to have one."

We ordered two before sitting down at a small table in front of a window. I took the first bite, moaning as the flavors erupted in my mouth.

"So, have you heard from him?" she asked around a huge mouth full of cinnamon bun.

I shook my head. "Nope."

"Are you upset by that?"

I shrugged a shoulder. "I don't know."

"Liar."

I took a deep breath, taking a drink of my latte to help wash down the sticky, sweet bread in my mouth. "I'm not sure what's going on. I haven't seen him since he walked out of my bedroom. Isn't that odd? I mean, before he wouldn't leave me alone and now he's up and vanished," I lamented.

"It's what you wanted, I thought?" she questioned.

"Yes and no. I know, I'm a mess. This flu bug kicked my ass and I just feel completely scatterbrained. I know it's the move and trying to get the new business off the ground, but I feel like I'm losing control of everything."

She smiled. "You're the one who insisted to have all these major life changes in the same week. You could have waited to move," she lectured.

I rolled my eyes and shook my head. "Now you sound like my mom."

"She's right and you know it. Has Elijah said anything else to you about Jack? Maybe he scared him off or threatened him with some-thing," she suggested.

I laughed as I took another bite of my treat. "I doubt that. I don't think Jack is ever going to be afraid of Elijah. If anything, Jack would kick his ass this time around, assuming my brother was alone."

"He doesn't have to use violence. He could have told Jack your dad would take away your company or send you away if he found out the two of you were seeing each other again," she said in a low voice.

I stopped chewing, a sick feeling in my stomach as her words sank in. "Oh my God. Do you think that's what happened?"

"I don't know. I'm just putting it out there. I think we can both agree Jack is madly in love with you and would never do anything to hurt you or destroy something you cared so much about. It's why he stayed away before," she pointed out.

"I swear, if my family did anything like that, I will be furious."

I reached for my phone, flipped it over to stare at the dark screen. There weren't any missed calls or texts. I'd been checking my phone constantly for the past two weeks, expecting to hear from Jack.

"And you know he's alive?" she joked. "Maybe he never even made it out of the house that night. Maybe your dad or brother was lying in wait and attacked him when he was walking out!" she exclaimed.

I shoved in another bite of the bun. "Yeah, right. There would be a missing person's story all over the news if a guy like Jack Bancroft went missing."

She smiled. "Then you know he's fine," she said, satisfied to have made her point.

"So, basically, you're saying he's not into me anymore?"

She made a face, a mixture between a grimace and a smile. "I think that is what I'm saying. I'm sorry. I know you still care for him, but maybe he realized you weren't lying when you said you two could never be together. He's a little slow, but I think he finally got the message."

I let out a long, depressed sigh. "Is it terrible that I feel horrible about it?"

She reached out and touched my hand. "No. You loved him. Of course you're going to feel sad over losing him."

"But I didn't lose him. I shoved him away. I made him stay away when all I really wanted to do was pull him closer. I hate how I feel. I feel like I've lost a little piece of my heart. I'm not joking, my heart doesn't feel like it beats the same anymore. I keep getting these little flutters and it physically hurts when I think about never seeing him again or kissing him," I whispered, putting it all out there.

"I'm sorry, hon. It sucks. You know I like Jack and I like that you feel so good with him. I will support you in whatever you do, but just make sure you know what you want. You've struggled for years to get over him. Whenever you were about to move on, he showed up and pulled you back in. Maybe this is for the best. You'll eventually feel better and it won't hurt so bad."

I shook my head, wiping the tear that had slid down my cheek. "Promise?"

"Time heals all wounds. I'm not saying you won't love him anymore, but it won't be what it is right now. You'll be able to move on one day. You have to give it time and give it a chance," she said.

I stared down at the cinnamon bun. It no longer looked appetizing. I pushed it away. "I don't think that's true."

"What isn't true?"

"I don't think I will be able to move on, not completely anyway. I can't help but feel like I'm missing a part of me. Nothing has felt right these past couple weeks. I should be enjoying every minute of my life. I have a new home, a new job, and I am building the company I have always dreamed about, but yet, I feel like something huge is missing. I can't truly be happy when I am missing a piece of my heart," I explained, hoping she could understand how serious I was.

I knew I probably sounded completely ridiculous and she probably thought I was overdramatizing it, but I couldn't help how I felt.

"Nat?"

I looked up and met her eyes. "What?" I pouted.

"Do you want him?"

"Of course I do, but I think it's too late. The back and forth was too much. I knew that night when I showed up at his place he was at his wit's end with me. I had pushed him too far. The last night we were together, he was different. I should have seen it then. I should have really listened to what he was saying. I have gotten so used to him always coming back, I never really expected him to truly leave me alone and stay away." I groaned.

She laughed. "You're a woman. You're supposed to be a little neurotic and change your mind every five minutes."

I shook my head. "Jack isn't the kind of man who likes games."

"I bet you could show up at his place right now and he'd be more than willing to play a little game with you," she said with a wink.

I wasn't quite so sure of that. "I don't know. I think he was telling me goodbye that night and I ignored it."

She shrugged. "You won't know unless you try, but Natasha, be sure this time. The back and forth is getting old," she said bluntly.

"I know. For me too. I'll think about it before I do anything. I don't want to be the wishy-washy woman. That's annoying," I said, feeling a little guilty about my past behavior.

"You said it, not me. Now, can we please toss these things and go back to shopping?"

I nodded in agreement. The overly sweet dough was making me sick all over again. I should have known better than to try and eat something that rich on my revolting stomach. I knew it was the stress of all the life changes making me sick. The day of shopping was supposed to help me get my mind off things, so I could go to work on Monday and be all there.

Lately, I'd been distracted and unable to concentrate on things that needed my full attention. That wasn't the way I wanted to start my company. I had to make a real decision about Jack. The limbo wasn't healthy for anyone. It was literally making me sick and I could tell by the way he'd been the last few times I had seen him, it was wearing on him as well.

"Let's do this. I've got a credit card burning a hole in my pocket!" I said, doing my best to infuse my voice with excitement.

We set out, intent to spend a ton of money as we decorated my apartment. We filled the next several hours meandering in and out of shops before heading to a gallery opening we'd been told about on our quest for a few good pieces. I knew almost nothing about art, but my mother had told me to pick something that spoke to me whether it was an expensive piece or something cheap. That's exactly what I was going to do.

We walked in to the gallery and were immediately handed a glass of champagne.

Ashley leaned over to whisper in my ear as we stood in front of a rather ugly sculpture of what I assumed was a woman. "Do you think they try to ply you with alcohol the moment you step through the door to make this stuff look better, like beer goggles?"

I slapped my hand over my mouth to keep from laughing out loud and insulting the curator and potentially the artist. "I think you might be on to something. Let's keep looking. I'm convinced that thing is watching me." I hissed, looking over my shoulder at the hideous sculpture.

"What about this?" Ashley said, standing in front of an abstract piece.

I wrinkled my nose. "Not for me, but if you like it, go for it."

"It hurts my brain," she mumbled under her breath.

Once again, I found myself laughing. I took a drink of the champagne. "Does this taste bad to you?" I whispered.

She took a drink from her glass. "Nope. Tastes fine to me."

I shook my head. "Yuck. I think my stomach is still angry about that cinnamon bun," I said, putting my glass on a tray as a waiter walked by.

She eyed me carefully before slowly nodding. "That must be it," she murmured.

Together, we did manage to find two pieces for me and one for her. The day of shopping had left me exhausted. We parted ways and I headed home, anxious to kick off my heels and settle in with a hot cup of tea on my new sofa. The moment I sat down, my eyes closed and then I passed out on the couch.

CHAPTER 48

JACK

The only way to stick to my guns was to stay busy. I was giving Nat the space she kept demanding. She kept telling me to go away—to stay away—and that we couldn't be together. I was going to do as she asked, even if it was killing me. It had been a lot easier when she was in California or in some foreign land. I had to stop myself from going to her penthouse every night this last week. I couldn't. I needed her to see I wasn't going to be there whenever she snapped her fingers.

I grabbed the keys to the Porsche and set out for Mom's house. I was feeling reckless. I found myself blowing through yellow lights and taking corners far too fast as I made my way out to the Bancroft property. Ever since that night I had walked out the front doors of her house, I had been waiting for something to happen. It was like feeling an electrical storm in the air, but not knowing when lightning would strike. I was pushing fate at every turn, taking risky deals at work, drinking too much, and now, driving too fast.

The wheels screeched as I cranked the wheel to the right, zipping into the driveway before coming to a halt at the front door. I could smell the rubber burning when I stepped out of the car. I stalked through the door, stomping down the corridor toward the sitting room where I expected to find my mother. It was long after lunch and early enough before dinner that I knew she wouldn't be cooking.

When I found her, she was in the sitting room as I expected, but James was there as well. I was in a shitty mood, glowering at my younger brother. "Can you give Mom and me a minute?" I snapped.

James looked surprised. My mother looked a little concerned. "Sure," James grumbled, walking past me.

I sat down in the seat he had just vacated, leaning my elbows on my knees and staring at my mother, as she placed the magazine she had been reading on the table next to her.

"What's wrong, Jack?" she asked, a line of worry creasing her forehead.

"I need to ask you something and I'm begging you to please be honest," I said.

She nodded. "Okay."

"Tell me about Wayne Levy. Why does he hate me and our family so much? Why do you hate him?" I blurted out.

She took a deep breath and leaned back into the couch. "Jack, that is old history. There's no reason to bring all the skeletons out of the closets."

"Yes, there is Mom. I want to know. I have to know. What happened that made you and Dad hate him so much and vice versa? Was it Dad? Was it Wayne? What happened?" I all but begged.

She sighed, shaking her head. "I don't know why it matters now. You and Elijah are no longer friends."

"It matters, Mom. It matters a great deal."

In the back of my mind, I could tell by the way she was acting and avoiding the subject, it had been my father's fault. My dad was to blame for the feud. It was hard to imagine him ever doing something that would be so bad he could create a decades-long feud, but her reluctance to tell me was obviously out of loyalty to my father. She didn't want to damage his reputation.

"Fine," she finally agreed.

"Tell me!"

"Your father and Wayne were in business together. It wasn't a long business relationship. They had only just gotten started. Your father's family had money and he used his connections to fund the company. The concept was Wayne's idea. Your father was more of the brains on the business side of things while Wayne was more of the thinker, the inventor," she said with a faint smile.

I nodded. "Business gone bad. Never going into business with family or friends," I said, repeating the advice my father had given each of us a number of times.

"Exactly. Your father, well, he could see the business was struggling. They weren't making any money and he was worried they were going to lose everything. Elijah's father was an excellent business man and your father didn't want to look bad in his eyes, so he did something he probably shouldn't have," she said hesitantly.

"Dad did?" I asked, wanting to clarify.

She nodded and continued to speak, "Yes. An investor came around, offering to buy part of the company. Your dad knew there was no way Wayne would ever agree to the deal, so he went behind his back. He was going to use the money he got from the sale to breathe new life into the company and focus on a new product Wayne had been working on. Actually, it was one of those solar things that made Wayne famous."

"Okay, I don't understand. What aren't you telling me," I said, anxious to hear what had gone so terribly wrong all those years ago.

"Wayne found out about the sale, and before your father could explain what his plan was, things got very ugly. Your dad kept all the money, leaving Wayne with nothing more than an idea. Things were very tense back then," she said, and by the way she said it, I could tell she was holding back.

"What else? You're not telling me something. Why would that be something that had to be kept secret for so long? That's part of doing business. Sometimes it doesn't work out," I said, shaking my head.

She looked down at her hands. "You're right, there is more. Wayne and I dated for several months. We were together when your father and Wayne were in business. Shortly after everything fell apart,

Wayne changed. He was a different man. I didn't love him and ended up falling in love with your father."

My mouth dropped open. "You and Wayne were together, like a couple?" I gasped.

She smiled. "Yes, we were."

"Why?" I said, my face twisting with disgust.

I couldn't imagine what she ever found attractive about the man. Maybe it was because I had been jaded from the moment I had been born, but Wayne and my mother would never make sense to me. My mom was kind and loving, and Wayne was a dick. A selfish, arrogant dickhead in my book.

She released a soft laugh. "He was different back then. It wasn't until after the business fell apart. He changed. Anytime I opened my mouth, I was told to shut up. He didn't want me to give my opinions or talk to him about the business at all. I realized I would never be happy with him."

My mind was reeling as I listened to her tell her story. "Wow, I had no idea. You just left him and hooked up with dad?"

She laughed again. "It wasn't quite like that, but the more I started to see how Wayne would never make me happy, the more I started to see how well your father treated me. We knew each other through Wayne. When your father left the company, we stayed in touch. He knew all about Wayne's volatile temper and encouraged me to get away. Your father was a slick man, too, you see. You boys didn't get your charm from me." She winked.

"I understand. I'm shocked. I can't imagine you with Wayne, and boy am I glad you left him."

"Me too. I've had a very happy life and there is nothing I would change about it."

"Well, I guess that explains a lot," I said, leaning back in the chair and trying to figure out what to do with the information I had.

"Jack are you in love with Natasha Levy?"

I sat up. "What?"

She smiled. "Are you?"

My first instinct was to lie, but I knew that would be wrong. I couldn't lie to my mother. She would see right through it if I did try.

"Yes," I said the one simple word I knew had the potential to make my mother furious with me.

She let out a long sigh, her shoulders slumped forward, and I could see the look of disappointment on her face. I hated knowing I did that to her.

"I thought so," she said quietly.

"It's not so bad. Like you, I think I've come to realize having Natasha in my life might not be good for me either. Or her." I confessed the thing that had been plaguing me for the past two weeks.

I had kept blaming Natasha for the push and pull when in reality, I was just as guilty. I could have walked away a long time ago. I was responsible for my own happiness. I had let myself be played and I had played her. I was beginning to wonder if our relationship was toxic. I couldn't see it because I was caught up in it. I was caught up in the amazing sex and wanting to rebel against Wayne Levy. With a little reflection, I was able to see the bigger picture. Nat and I were always in this strange bubble where we couldn't really be together, which drew us to each other.

Take all that away, and what did we have?

"Jack, why do you say that?" she asked.

I shrugged a shoulder. "I don't know. It's just something I've come to realize recently. For too long I gave Wayne Levy all the power. I think I just realized that if I was to choose to be with Nat, he would always be a dark shadow in our relationship. I don't think I want that. I want to love a woman who isn't embarrassed about who I am. I want a woman I can bring to family dinners and I want to be able to go to family dinners with her. What kind of life would we have if her family hated us together? Our children, they could never be with their maternal grandparents. I would never trust Levy to be respectful toward them and me. It's more trouble than it's worth," I said on a sigh.

My mom stood up, looking at me. I left my seat and stood in front of her. "Jack, only you know what's right for you. I don't care for

Wayne or his wife, but I would never stand in the way of your happiness. If you chose to be with her, I would support you. You're right, things would be difficult, but if she's the one you love, you have to decide if that fight is worth it."

I hugged her, so damn happy to have her in my life. "Thanks, Mom. I'm sorry I didn't tell you earlier. I didn't know what I was doing, and I didn't want to upset you if I didn't have to."

She laughed against my shoulder. "It's cute that you think your mother doesn't know things like this."

I burst into laughter. It was the same thing she'd been telling us for years. She always gave us a chance to confess and usually, if we didn't, things would be far worse for us. I had hoped all that was behind us, but as it turned out, my mom was still the all-seeing mother. It was a little spooky at times, but in this case, I knew one of my dear brothers must have divulged my secret. Whether it was on accident or on purpose was hard to say, but I was glad to have it all out in the open.

Now, I just had to figure out what to do with my life. I needed to make a decision and quick. The sooner I could put this behind me, the sooner I could move on and hopefully find another way to be happy in life.

CHAPTER 49

NATASHA

My stomach was not being kind to me at all. I was tired of feeling sick and at the very strong urging of Ashley and my assistant at work, I decided to take the day off. I was doing too much and burning myself out. I hadn't given myself adequate time to rest and recover from the illness I had gotten a couple weeks ago. It was either I take the day off or Ashley threatened to take me to the hospital. I wasn't that sick, but she had insisted.

The nausea came and went, but it was the general feeling of ick that was wearing me down. I wanted to be my old self again. I wanted to feel energetic and happy. I missed being me. Everything had just felt so wrong. Nothing felt right. My new home wasn't bringing me the excitement and satisfaction I had been expecting. I found myself crying more often than I cared to and blamed it on Jack, then my dad, and then Jack. The men in my life were making me miserable. I was strongly considering running away to somewhere tropical and without cell phone service.

I heard the phone ringing and managed to get off the couch and grab it from the kitchen counter where I had left it. I was tired of looking to see if Jack had called. Obviously, I could call him, but I couldn't really. If I called him, it meant I was ready to say screw my dad and be with Jack. I felt like I was trying to break a bad habit. I already had a full seventeen days under my belt and if I went back, I'd have to start all over again. It took twenty-one days to break a habit. I could stick it out a little while longer.

I already knew by the ringtone it was Ashley, so getting up was more of a necessity. If I didn't answer, she would keep calling. She was probably checking to make sure I was actually home and not at work. I wouldn't be the least bit surprised to know she had some kind of GPS on my phone, checking my whereabouts to make sure I didn't leave.

"Yes, Mother. I'm home and I was resting," I answered.

She laughed. "Good. I'll stop by in a bit and bring you some soup."

"I don't want soup. I'm not hungry," I said, knowing I sounded like a petulant toddler.

"Too bad, I'm bringing it anyway. Do you need anything else?"

"Fine. Will you please bring me some more ginger ale as well?" I asked.

"Of course. Rest and I'll see you soon."

I hung up, taking the phone with me to the couch where I lay down and snuggled under the blanket. I wasn't feeling any better. I didn't feel sick, but I was still miserable. The day off had done nothing but give me more time to dwell on the fact I had not heard from Jack in almost three weeks. Staying busy was what I needed, but it was also what knocked me off my feet.

It was another hour before Ashley showed up, letting herself in using the spare key I had given her. It wasn't like I had anyone else to give it to. The moment she stepped through the door, I could smell the herbs in the chicken broth. I didn't think I was hungry, but the smell coming from the paper bag in her hand had my stomach growling. It smelled delicious.

"I'll put some in a bowl for you," Ashley said, carrying the bag of soup into the kitchen.

"It's fine. I'm not an invalid," I complained, taking the six pack of ginger ale from her and then putting it in the refrigerator, keeping one out to drink.

She shook her head, opening the cupboard where I had put my new dishes. Since she had helped me set up my kitchen, she knew exactly where everything was. She pulled out a bowl and set it on the counter before turning to look at me.

"I'm going to do this, while you do something else," she said, both hands resting on the counter.

The way she was looking at me made me nervous.

"What am I going to do?" I asked her.

She walked where she had deposited her purse on my new dining table and pulled out a purple box. She put it behind her back, heightening the intrigue.

"Before you freak out, I want you to hear me out," she started, instantly putting me on guard.

"Why would I freak out? What are you holding behind your back?" I asked nervously.

She sucked in a deep breath, winced, and stuck her arm out. "This," she said, handing the box to me.

"What's that?" I said, snatching the box from her hand and immediately knowing what it was.

"You know exactly what it is. You need to do it. I think you have to recognize there's something going on here," she said, gesturing to my stomach.

My eyes went wide as I shook my head. "No way. I'm not doing that. There's no point. I'm on the pill. I don't need this," I said, handing the test back to her.

"Are you sure about that?"

I nodded. "Of course I'm sure! I'm not pregnant. It's not possible."

"Natasha, you have to acknowledge your body is telling you something. Just stop and think about it," she said, pushing the box back in to my hand.

In the back of my mind I immediately started listing off all the days I had forgotten to take my pill. Hell, for several days I had completely spaced it. Things had been so hectic once I moved back. I had the company, house hunting, and life in general. My normal routine had been off, and I had forgotten to take them a time or two or five, I admitted.

"I forgot to take my pill once or twice," I confessed.

"That's all it takes," she said in a knowing voice.

"A few times I forgot. That cannot mean I'm going to get pregnant. It isn't like I was having a lot of sex. It was here and there, like twice, maybe three times," I said, trying to remember exactly when the first time was and matching up dates in my head.

"There it is. I see those wheels turning. It's all coming together, isn't it?" she said, nodding with satisfaction.

"Ash, you don't understand. I can't be. Do you know what my father will do to me?" I said in a high-pitched voice.

She shrugged a shoulder. "You're a grown woman. You have a job and you are more than capable of taking care of yourself and a child financially. Even if your dad cuts you off, you have money and I'm sure the baby daddy would be pitching in."

I shook my head. "It isn't about the money. I can't have a baby. My dad would kill me," I reiterated.

"Daddy may not get a say in it," she pointed out.

I closed my eyes, feeling the shame and guilt wash over me. I couldn't imagine what my father would do if he found out. If I was pregnant, it was pretty obvious he would find out. I could lie. I could tell him it was someone else. No, I couldn't do that.

"Oh my God, this can't be happening." I groaned.

"I think you need to take the test. If it's negative, then I'm hauling your ass to the doctor to find out why you've been sick forever. If it's positive, well that's a whole other can of worms we will deal with if we need to," she said, her hands on her hips as she stared me down.

I rolled my eyes. "This is stupid and a waste of time. I refuse to believe I'm pregnant," I said, taking on a new stance. I refused to be, therefore I wasn't.

Ashley was laughing. "You can choose not to believe it, but when your belly swells, along with your ankles, you may have to consider it's a possibility," she joked.

I stomped my foot. "No, no, no! It's impossible!"

"I don't think it is. Think about your symptoms," she said, moving back to pour the soup in a bowl.

I stood in the kitchen watching her and mentally ticking off all the symptoms I had been suffering for the past few weeks. The upset stomach, most of the time in the morning. My breasts were sore and I was always tired. The crying moments could also be attributed to a pregnancy I realized.

"Oh shit. How did I not see this sooner?" I mumbled.

"Exactly. Now, take your ass into the bathroom and pee on that stick," she instructed.

"But what if it's positive?" I whispered.

"It isn't like if you don't take it, it will just go away. You need to know so you can start taking better care of yourself. You have to eat better, sleep more, and quit working so damn hard. Be like me; relax and just be an heiress," she said with a smile.

I shook my head in denial. "I can't do it. I can't take the test. I'll do it later."

"Sure, you can. Sit on the toilet and pee on the stick. It's pretty simple. Don't tell me you've never taken a pregnancy test before?" She gasped in shock.

I shook my head. "No, I haven't. I've always been on birth control. I've never needed to. You have?"

She laughed. "Birth control isn't a hundred percent. Haven't you gotten that lecture? Sheesh, girl, I feel like you just hatched. Welcome to the world of sex and consequences."

"I've heard all the statistics, but I've never worried about it."

"Count yourself lucky you haven't had one of those scares in the past but worry about it now. Your man must be very potent."

"Don't say that." I moaned, thinking about Jack and sex was not helping the situation.

"Hurry up and take the thing. I'm anxious to know if I'm right," she said, gesturing toward the bathroom.

I stared at the box in my hand, in shock that I even had to take the test. With a great deal of reluctance, I made my way to the bathroom, dragging my feet and trying to think of excuses to explain all my symptoms. I wasn't having any luck and accepted the fact there was a real possibility I could be pregnant. I read the instructions on the stupid box, even though it was as basic as she had said. I didn't want to risk messing it up and giving myself a false positive.

With all the courage I could muster, I peed on the stick, stared at it, and put it back in the box. I couldn't look at it. I didn't want to know. I turned and left the bathroom, hoping it would vanish.

"Well?" she asked when I reappeared in the kitchen.

I shrugged. "I didn't look."

"What! How did you not look? You are crazy!"

"I don't want to know. I can't deal with that right now," I murmured.

"Damn it, Nat. Let's go look."

I followed her back down the hall. "Wait, I'll do it," I said, pushing her out of the bathroom and closing the door.

"I'll be right here," she called out from the other side of the door.

I took a deep breath and pulled the test out of the box, staring at the two pink lines in the window. "Oh shit."

I gave myself a few seconds to pull my thoughts together before opening the door.

"Well?" she asked.

I held out the test. "I have to go talk to Jack."

Ashley snatched the test out of my hand, a grin spreading across her face. "Told you so."

CHAPTER 50

JACK

"You headed home?" Grayson asked as I walked past his office.

I stopped and went inside to chat with him for a few. "I am."

"You seem to be in better spirits today. Did you and Natasha make up?"

I smiled and shook my head. "Actually, more the opposite. I haven't seen her in a couple weeks."

He raised an eyebrow. "And yet you're happier?"

I shrugged. "Mom knows. She kind of gave me permission to do as I pleased."

He smiled and nodded. "Good to know. I'm happy for you," he said, and I took my leave.

I didn't tell him there wasn't a lot to be happy about, but I did feel more settled. That was reason enough to be happy I supposed. Thankfully, the car was waiting for me when I exited the building. I couldn't wait to get home and block out the real world.

It had been one of those days where a glass of scotch or whiskey wasn't what I was craving. I wanted an icy cold beer. I felt like kicking back, feet up with a cold beer, and something good on TV. I grabbed one out of the fridge, kicked off my shoes, and walked to the couch to fulfill my wishes for the evening.

I had just put my feet up and got the remote in my hand when I heard a soft knock on my door. That was strange. I never really got company and when I did, it was usually one of my brothers and their knocks were anything but dainty. I had met my new neighbor the other day. I hoped she wasn't taking me up on my offer to stop by for a drink sometime. I hadn't actually been serious. It was more like one of those things you said but didn't actually expect someone to take you up on.

I put the beer down, a little irritated my night had been interrupted, and opened the door to find Nat standing there.

"Nat?" I asked, as if I wasn't sure it was her.

"Hi," she said in a soft voice.

I looked her over, trying to find the reason for her visit written somewhere on her face. She looked exhausted and a little pale. I knew that feeling well. I hadn't slept great since the last time we'd been together. Reality had crashed down on me. It wasn't a great feeling.

"Are you okay?" I asked her, wanting to reach out and hold her, but stopping myself.

She was off-limits to me. If I touched her, I'd be tempted to do a whole lot more. I needed to keep my emotions under control as well as everything else. With her, it was always all or nothing. I needed to keep it in the nothing zone. I took a step back, needing a few extra inches between her and myself.

"I need to talk to you. Are you busy?" she asked in a quiet voice.

I shook my head. "Nope, just got home. I'm glad you stopped by. I need to talk to you as well. Come on in," I said, holding the door open for her to walk past.

"Thank you."

I noticed she turned to the side, as if to avoid brushing by me as well. I realized she had probably come to tell me we were over. She didn't want to touch me. It hurt a little, but I knew it was for the best.

"Can I get you a beer, wine?" I asked, moving toward the kitchen.

I had a bottle of Merlot on hand, which I knew she loved. I grabbed it, anticipating her saying yes.

She shook her head. "No, thank you."

That was unexpected. I put the bottle down and felt the tension in the air. This was not going to be a long visit. She kept her jacket on and had an air about her that was standoffish as well as nervous. She had never been nervous around me before.

"All right, come on in. I was just sitting down to a cold beer myself," I said, easily, grabbing the beer and sitting in one of the armchairs. She may not want a drink, but I sure as hell did.

I didn't want to sit on the couch and have her sit next to me. That was too tempting. I needed her several feet away. I didn't want to smell her perfume or be tempted to touch her. Even now, being in the close proximity to her, I was struggling to keep my libido in control. I could smell the fruity scent of the shampoo she used. I had to fight the urge to close my eyes and inhale. She sat on the couch and looked down at her hands.

"Thanks, I'm sorry to show up without calling, but I really needed to talk to you," she said, smiling when she looked at me.

"You know I don't mind. I'm glad you came by," I said, nervously taking another drink from my beer.

"What did you want to talk to me about?" she asked.

I shrugged. "Go ahead and go first. I can wait. You came all the way over here."

She smiled. "No, please, you go first. I'll wait."

I took a sip from the beer, wishing I had already downed a few more before I took a deep breath. "I've been doing a lot of thinking about everything these past couple weeks. I think you were right. Of course, you were right. When haven't you been right?" I joked, trying to lighten the mood while gathering the courage to say what I needed to say.

"I was right?" she asked. "What was I right about?"

"Yes. You were right about us. We'll never work out. I know we thought we had something special and it seemed like it would be enough, but when it comes right down to it, it isn't."

"It isn't?" she squeaked.

I shrugged a shoulder. "You love your family and I love mine. I respect you enough to recognize that. I love you enough to know it's time to walk away. I've seen how much it has hurt you and torn you up each time you think about your father disowning you. I was being selfish and only thinking about what I wanted. That was wrong. As much as I have said it doesn't matter or conjured up stupid plans to convince your father to like me, it isn't going to work. The Bancrofts and Levys were never meant to be together," I said, watching her face as I delivered the speech I had been practicing in my head for the last few days.

In my imagination, I had pictured her being relieved, clapping her hands and thanking me profusely for finally seeing the light. I had mentally prepared myself to accept the fact she would be relieved to be rid of me. I didn't exactly like it, but I knew it was what she had been trying to say all along. I should have listened to her that first night at the ball. I had been a stubborn ass and insisted I was right.

"Oh, really?" she said in a voice so low I almost didn't hear her.

I nodded and leaned forward just a little in the chair. "I'm sorry I kept pushing you for so long. I should have left you alone when you came back from California. You were right. You've always been right. Our families will always hate one another. We could never have a normal, happy life. We could never have family gatherings or have children who would get to grow up with a big family like they deserve. Our fling has to end. It isn't worth losing our families and causing serious turmoil. I've been selfish, but I wanted to tell you that stops now. I'm not going to bother you ever again," I said firmly.

She was nodding. "Oh, I see. Well, that's … uh … that's a relief," she muttered.

"Natasha, I am so sorry I didn't listen to you in the beginning. You knew it would never work, but I kept pressing you. I was certain the feud between our families could be forgiven. For that, I'm sorry."

"You're sorry." She repeated my words as if she weren't sure of their meaning.

I fought the urge to reach out and hold her hand. "I don't regret a minute of our time together. You will always hold a special place in my heart. You are a beautiful, smart, and dangerously sexy woman," I said with a grin.

"Uh, thanks," she mumbled.

"I wish I could have seen it sooner, but I kept hoping there would be some way, some miracle that would make it possible for us to be together in a normal relationship with the blessing of our families. I guess I kept thinking that nothing could be that serious. That Romeo and Juliet thing we always joked about. I kept thinking that was all fictional and no families could actually hold onto a blood feud, especially in this day and age. I know better now," I said, trying to read her expression, but she kept her eyes focused on the floor.

I had a feeling she had been coming over to tell me the same thing. I hoped I was making it easier for her by saying it first and sparing her the trouble. Lord knew I hadn't listened to her the countless other times she had tried to tell me. I could admit I was stubborn, and I had been convinced she was what I wanted. I hadn't really given her the chance to say what she had really felt. I now knew the ultimate goal in life was to be happy. The two of us together could have been happy, but the outside influences would have eventually been too much. We would have been torn apart. I didn't want to end things with her on a bad note. I wanted us to part as friends or at least friendly toward each other.

"Okay, well, thank you," she said, still looking down.

"Nat, what is it? What did you come to tell me?" I asked.

She finally looked up at me and I thought I saw tears shimmering in her eyes. "You've said it all."

I could see something was very wrong. "Nat, did I say something wrong?"

She got to her feet and shook her head. "No."

"Where are you going? You just got here."

"Like you said, this is over. We're going our separate ways."

I reached out to touch her shoulder and she flinched. I snapped my hand back. "Sorry," I murmured, reminding myself of the no touching rule.

"I need to get going. Sorry, I just remembered I was supposed to be meeting someone about something for work," she said, rushing toward the door.

"Can we talk for a minute?"

She looked at me and smiled. "I'm sorry, I really need to get going. It's kind of an emergency. I've been such a scatterbrain lately with all this work stuff going on."

"I hope this means we can still be friends. I know we can't exactly hang out, but you mean a lot to me. I want to be friends. I want to be able to talk with you. Is that okay?" I asked as she reached for the door.

She stopped, turned, and looked me dead in the eye. "I don't think I can do that."

She swung the door open and walked out, leaving me staring at her back as she headed toward the elevators. That was not how I expected that to go. Maybe I should have let her go first, I thought to myself, before closing the door and then going into the kitchen. The beer was no longer going to do it. Whiskey was in order for the night.

CHAPTER 51

JACK

S itting in my father's den with James, Colt, and Mason was a great way to start a week, or end a week, depending on how you looked at it. It had been a month since I had last seen Natasha and I felt myself finally climbing out of the dark hole I'd been mired in for too long. It was time to focus on my family, my career, and my future.

Grayson strolled into the den and for the first time, I realized how much he looked like our father. He even walked like him. I knew we all pretty much looked alike with our hazel eyes, tall stature, and the same thick black hair my father had. I smiled thinking about my mother's response to the constant stream of comments about how "the boys all looked like their father." She was only the incubator and contributed nothing to our DNA, she would joke.

"You made it," I commented as Grayson poured himself a drink and sat down in one of the leather armchairs.

He nodded. "Hannah is feeling a lot better."

"You mean she's loosened the noose," Mason quipped.

"Whatever. You can't get a noose. You're jealous," Grayson shot back.

"I don't want a noose—trust me."

I could hear my mom's low heels clacking across the floor and knew she was headed our way. She appeared in the doorway and smiled. "I'm glad to see you're all here. Dinner will be ready in about ten minutes. Don't drink so much that you're too full to eat. I made a roast with potatoes and an apple pie for dessert."

"Sounds delicious, Mom," I told her.

She walked away, leaving us to finish our drinks.

"Are you back in town for good?" Grayson asked Mason.

He shrugged a shoulder. "I don't know. I've got no plans."

"Good, then you can help me out with the holiday auction I've got coming up," Colt said with a smile.

Mason laughed. "I don't think so."

"Come on. You're here, you may as well make yourself useful. This year is going to be the biggest ever. Mom insisted we go big. She wants to give every kid in the city a gift," he mumbled.

I laughed, knowing that was pretty close to accurate. She loved Christmas and without my dad and with all of us out of the house, she got lonely. She had thrown herself into the family charity with Colt and had been working hard with organizations that assisted with homeless kids and those in foster care. It was the perfect niche for my mom and I was glad Colt was letting her help out.

"We should probably head to the dining room," I suggested.

We all put our glasses on the bar and filed out of the den, proceeding to the formal dining room. We all took our seats around the table while my mother carried in one dish after another. Offering to help would be an insult. This was her thing. She loved to prepare big meals and dote on her family. I was certainly not going to try and stop her.

With the meal underway, we talked about our plans for the next couple of months and who was going to be in town for the holidays. Mom was practically glowing as we all sat around, taking our time and enjoying the fabulous dinner.

"Jack, I forgot to tell you, I ran into a friend of mine. Her daughter has recently moved back to the city. I was thinking you could take her out, show her a good time. Maybe take her to a show or something like that," mom said.

My brothers burst into laughter as I was put on the spot. My mother was setting me up with her friend's daughter.

"You know it's bad when your mother has to start searching for dates for you," Colt teased.

I rolled my eyes. "It isn't bad."

Grayson was holding back his own laughter. "I can count the number of times Mom had to set me up. Zero," he said making a circle with his fingers.

I knew I was going to be teased for at least the next several months over the offer to set me up.

"Mom, I thought I was your favorite?" Colt pouted.

"You are, dear, but you don't need my help in the love department." She cajoled him.

It had been a running joke throughout our entire lives. We always accused Colt of being a mama's boy. It was the dimples. He had a look about him that fooled people into believing he was a sweet and innocent child, but he was just as wild as the rest of us. All he had to do was flash those dimples and my mother's heart would melt. He would be forgiven on the spot.

"Mom," I started.

She shook her head. "Come on now, I think we all know the other relationship has run its course. I want you to be happy. It's time for you to get out there and see what life has to offer. You've been holding back, waiting for that girl for too long. It's time to move on. There are plenty of women who would love the chance to date you."

My brothers stopped their ribbing and grew silent. The worst kept secret in all of New York was my forbidden relationship with Natasha Levy. It had spanned nearly five years. In five years, I hadn't dated or been interested in another woman. It wasn't until recently my brothers had all learned about the forbidden relationship. They had all thought I was saving myself for marriage or some shit.

"It's over? For real?" Mason asked, one eyebrow raised.

I shrugged a shoulder. "It was never going to work."

"I'm sorry, really, I am," Mason said in an uncharacteristically genuine tone.

I offered a small smile. He'd been trying to help me out with the Nat situation. "Thanks for everything. I guess I was a little slow to figure it out."

Grayson reached over and patted me on the shoulder. "And now you have Mommy to help you heal your broken heart," he teased, immediately lightening the mood.

I laughed. "It isn't like any of you are going to be of any help."

"I'm certainly not sharing any women with you," James replied.

I hadn't exactly announced it was over, but after the conversation with my mother, when she told me all about the feud between our families, I had realized it was a relationship doomed from the very start. For too long, a part of me was convinced love would conquer all. That had been naive and immature and certainly not realistic. Neither Nat nor I would ever be happy if we kept trying to force it. I had ended it and that was that. It wasn't like she protested or tried to persuade me otherwise. She'd been relieved. That had stung, but I couldn't have expected anything different.

"Mommy is trying to marry off Jack. First comes Mommy's date, then comes marriage, then comes a whole horde of grandkids," Mason teased.

"Mason, stop it. You're next, mister," my mom scolded.

Mason's eyes widened. "Oh no. I don't think so. Don't even think about setting me up with any of your friends' kids. I'm not cut out for that life."

Mom rolled her eyes. "Oh, please. We all know that would never do. I'll have to get creative to find you a woman. I'll have to put on some boots and start trolling those bars you frequent."

We all burst into laughter, even Mason grinned. The thought of my mother wearing a pair of boots and stepping into a bar Mason would hang out in was laughable. He was rather unconventional and did not conform to the rules of the society we belonged to. One of the ladies from the world of the New York elite would scream and run the other way if she saw him standing at her front door.

"You may as well do it, Jack. She isn't going to stop fixing you up until you're married," Grayson lectured.

I thought about it for a second. "Okay. I'll do it."

Everyone stopped what they were doing. "Did you just agree to let your mommy set you up?" James asked, aghast at the thought.

I glared at him. He had the least amount of room to talk. He lived with my mother. Granted, it was more of a favor to the rest of us, but my youngest brother was the last one I expected to tease me. My mother was always setting him up, but he didn't realize it was happening. He assumed the young women who came over for tea or dinner were there to see her. I thought about filling him in, but I knew my mother would kill me if I let her little secret out of the bag.

"What can it hurt? It will save me time. I don't care for the dating scene. At least this way I already know she isn't a gold digger trying to hook up with me just because of my last name. The hard part is out of the way," I reasoned.

My mother was smiling. "She is a good girl. Her family has been solid and never involved in any scandals. She is very pretty and seems to have a good head on her shoulders."

"Then she's too good for our family," Mason interjected.

"No one is too good for my family," Mom said in a stern voice.

Colt took a drink of his wine before looking at me. "Don't you want to know what she looks like?" he asked in a low voice.

"Looks aren't everything, young man," Mom immediately answered.

I grinned. I had known that was coming the second he said the words. "Yeah, Colt. Looks aren't everything," I teased.

"True, look at some of the women you've dated, Colt. Attractive and shallow. What a combo," Mason teased.

"As if you have any room to talk," Colt shot back.

"Enough talk about the women you've all conquered. Jack, she's a lovely girl. I'll talk to Miriam and get her phone number. I'm glad you're getting out there. It'll be good for you," she said, a knowing smile on her lips.

I nodded. "Thanks, Mom."

"Really? You're really going to go out with the woman? Are you just saying that because Mom's sitting right in front of you?" Grayson asked.

I shrugged a shoulder. "Why not? What's it going to hurt to go on a date? It isn't like I've got anything better to do."

"You're right. I'm happy for you," Grayson commented.

I took another bite of the roast, letting the juices explode in my mouth as I thought about going out with another woman. It would be strange, but it was time to move on. I hadn't seen or heard from Nat. It had been rough, and I thought about her constantly, but now that I had made up my mind, I was going to keep moving forward. I couldn't look back. Looking back would take me right back to that place where I was stuck in a horrible limbo.

This was a good thing. I needed to start dating. She was probably already seeing other men. I had seen how much fun she'd been having with that guy at the bar several weeks ago. She was ready to move on. I had been holding her back. It was the right thing to do, I told myself for what felt like the millionth time. She deserved to be happy and that meant being with a man she could take home to Daddy.

Once dinner was over, we retired back to the den for another round of drinks. We all knew better than to drive to Mom's house for Sunday dinner. It always ended with whiskey in the den as we reminisced about Dad. My mom liked it and none of us minded talking about our late father. It was cathartic and helped us grieve his loss.

CHAPTER 52

NATASHA

I had seriously debated canceling the shopping trip Ashley had planned for us today. I wasn't up for it, which is exactly why she insisted I go. I didn't want to do anything. I wanted to sit in my penthouse and wallow in self-pity. In this particular situation, misery did not want company. Misery wanted to be left alone to think about how unfair life could be.

Instead of canceling, I had dragged my ass out to meet her and had not been pleasant since I had been out. I was being a pouty bitch and completely unfair to her. I knew it, but I couldn't seem to snap myself out of the funk I was stuck in. I was not good company.

"What about this?" she asked, holding up a pretty pink flowing shirt that would hide the belly I was sure to have very soon.

I shrugged. "It's not bad. I like it. I'll take it," I said with no real enthusiasm.

"Oh, gee, you sound thrilled. I'll put it back."

"No! Really, I do love it," I said, snatching it from her and adding it to the other hangers I had in my hand.

"I'm hungry and I think you have low blood sugar, you're cranky," Ashley said matter-of-factly.

"I'm thirsty and could use a coffee," I replied.

"Nope. No coffee for you."

My mouth dropped open. "Come on. One little coffee. It can't be that bad," I argued.

She shrugged a shoulder and pursed her lips. "I guess when you make that first appointment with an ob-gyn, you can ask."

It was a not-so-subtle dig at the fact that I had not made my first prenatal appointment yet. I was only a couple months along. I reasoned most women didn't even know they were pregnant until at least then. I had time.

"I said I was working on it."

"These things require scheduling. You need to actually call and make an appointment. Have your assistant do it for you," she said as we made our way to the register.

I stopped in my tracks. "No! I can't do that!"

She burst into laughter. "Then I guess you are going to have to do it yourself, aren't you?"

"Sometimes I really hate you," I grumbled before putting my items on the counter.

I smiled and did my best to be polite to the sales clerk, but I had a feeling I was failing. Her smile slipped as I snatched the bag and left the store. We walked down one block until we came to a place where she could get food and I could get something to drink. I wasn't ready to try eating and shopping. I wasn't sure how well the two would mix. We ordered and sat down. I found myself daydreaming, staring at the window, and watching a young woman push a stroller down the street. That could be me one day soon, I thought to myself.

Ashely was staring at me—again.

"What?" I snapped.

"I was looking for the glow."

"What glow?" I asked irritably.

She was grinning like a fool. "The glow pregnant women are supposed to have."

I rolled my eyes. "I think I have a green glow. I probably resemble the Incredible Hulk or the Green Lantern. Green. That's how I feel."

She held her arm up next to mine. "No green, but you are a ghostly pale. You need some sun. And you probably should eat more. Iron—that's what I think you're lacking."

"I'm always this shade of white and it's fall in New York. We're a little short on beach weather. When did you become a doctor?"

She shrugged. "It isn't rocket science. You're pale. You've been sick every morning and you're not eating enough. You're eating for two. Your body needs some nutrition," she lectured.

I knew she was right. I had been feeling weaker than usual and a little dizzy. I made a decision right then to listen to her in that respect. "I'll buy some vitamins today," I told her.

"Good."

"I am a little tired, though. Maybe we should call it a day and I'll just go crawl in bed."

She shook her head. "No way. You need fresh air and exercise. It helps lift your spirits."

I gave her a look that said I didn't believe her. "I'm trying."

"Come on, snap out of it. We're shopping. Shopping is supposed to be fun. It's a way to blow off steam." She cajoled, pushing my strawberry smoothie toward me.

I sighed, looking out the window and getting lost in thought as I watched people hustling and bustling up and down the sidewalk. Everyone was in a hurry it seemed like.

"I'm really trying. It seems pointless to shop for clothes when I'm not going to be able to wear them in another month or so."

"You've got a few months before you're going to grow out of everything. You've gotten a couple cute things that don't look like maternity clothes at all. We can search for actual maternity clothes if you want."

"No way. I am not wearing a tent."

She burst into laughter. "Have you seen some of the stuff they have nowadays? It's cute and doesn't look like tents at all."

"I'll wait until I absolutely cannot fit into anything else before I buy that stuff," I said, dreading that moment.

"We could shop for baby stuff?" she suggested.

I wrinkled my nose. "That will set the rumors flying. I am not ready to deal with any of that just yet. Can you imagine the hell that would rain down? Jack would find out. My family would find out."

"Are you going to tell your parents?" she asked.

I scoffed. "I don't think I really have a choice in the matter. What am I supposed to say when they ask why I'm as big as a house? I swallowed a basketball," I snapped.

She shrugged a shoulder, ignoring my crappy attitude. "You could try, or you could just wear really baggy sweaters. It is the right season for it. Carry a huge purse and wear jackets. If actresses can get away with it, you can too."

"And when I have the baby?" I asked, curious as to her solution to explain an infant magically appearing out of nowhere.

"You can say you adopted!"

I laughed. It was so ridiculous I had to laugh. I was a grown woman and here I was trying to hide a pregnancy from my parents. It wasn't the fact I was pregnant, it was the baby daddy that would send them over the edge. They would be absolutely livid when they found out I was having a Bancroft child.

"I was thinking about going back to California," I said in a quiet voice.

Her mouth gaped. "No way. You can't leave me."

"You could tag along," I offered.

"Nat, you can't just up and run away. Like that isn't going to raise suspicions, especially since you just got back, bought a penthouse, and started a business. They are going to know something is up," she pointed out all the flaws in my plan.

"I think it might be for the best. I won't have to face my parents and see their disappointment and anger. I can open an office in Los Angeles or just live off my inheritance. I think it might be easier," I said, resigned to the idea that running away was my best option.

She looked at me. "What about Jack?"

"What about him? He already made it very clear we were through. I'm not going to tell him about the baby just to get him back. He's gone. He called it quits for real this time."

"Because you wanted it that way. Are you ever going to tell him about the baby?" she whispered in case anyone in the place overheard.

"I don't know. I don't want to drag him into this mess. It might be better if he never knew. It would save us both a lot of misery," I reasoned.

She burst into laughter. "Sweetie, he is very much in the mess. He made the mess. He would want to know. I think he gets to decide if it's better he didn't know, and we both know that isn't going to happen. Jack is a good guy. No matter what your family thinks, you know in your heart, he's a good man."

I shook my head. "I can't tell him. If he knows, he's going to want to claim it. He's going to push marriage because that's the kind of guy he is."

She chuckled, shaking her head. "The horrors of a good man."

"Then my dad would find out. Look how he reacted when he found out I was seeing Jack. If he finds out I'm carrying his child, it is going to be so much worse. I'm terrified of what he might do. He'll disown me. I'll end up having to move out of the state just to get away from him. I mean, look at what happened to Jack. What if my dad hires someone to hurt him as a way to make him pay? I could never live with myself if Jack was actually hurt because we were together," I said, the thought making me feel sick to my stomach all over again.

"Your father needs to get over it, seriously," she said adamantly.

I tended to agree, but it didn't change things. My dad was a stubborn, old codger and there was no way he would ever welcome a Bancroft child into his life. I had thought about it for the past month. It was all I had thought about. I wasn't worried about raising a baby on my own, but I was scared to death to see my father's reaction to the news.

He'd been so angry that night Elijah had me dragged home. I had never seen him so disgusted. It was hard for me to imagine a world where I disgusted and ashamed my father. He had always called me his princess and always made me feel like royalty. I wasn't convinced I was brave enough to face him once he knew the truth. I felt like a coward.

"I wish it were that easy. I'm not going to make any decisions today. I need to think about all the options and the consequences," I told her.

"Yes, you do, but remember, you need to take care of yourself and that little peanut growing in your belly. Ultimately, this is your life and I know you will do what's best for your child. With that said, I think it's important you give Jack the chance to be in the child's life," she said gently.

I groaned and leaned my head back to look up at the ceiling. "I know. I'm just such an absolute mess right now."

"It's okay. You have some time. No matter what you decide, you know I'll be right here by your side. I've got your back no matter what. If you move out to LA, hell, I might just go with you. I could get used to living on the beach and being able to sunbathe all year round," she said with a friendly smile.

"Thank you. I appreciate that. Now, let's go shopping. I want to decorate that guest bedroom and maybe get a few more things for my own," I said, feeling a little better about everything.

"Amen! I'm ready to spend some money!" she said, rising from the table and grabbing the few bags stored underneath.

I felt a little better and was hoping I could block out all the other drama in my life and have some fun shopping. A little time, a little perspective, and a little shopping could solve all of life's problems—at least that's what I was hoping for.

CHAPTER 53

JACK

It was an average Monday, with the monthly board meeting wrapping up. Things were feeling a little more normal in my life. Every day I woke up, I reminded myself I wasn't going to see Nat and I was damn sure going to do my best not to think about her. I was doodling on my yellow pad as everyone else filed out of the room. Grayson and I stayed behind as usual to discuss things that had been brought up during the meeting.

"What'd you think about that business George brought up?" I asked Grayson after the room was cleared out.

He shrugged a shoulder. "I'm on the fence. Know anyone you can reach out for more information?"

I nodded. "I'll touch base with a few people I know and see what they say. It could be risky."

"But it could also be very profitable," he replied.

"I'll send out the emails now and let you know what I hear back," I said.

"Thanks. How's everything else going?" he asked casually.

I knew exactly what he was talking about. "It's all good. I'm keeping my distance and so is she."

"Sorry to hear, but happy to know you're moving on. My kids are really going to need some cousins to play with," he said with a cheesy grin.

"I'll get right on that," I said, rising from my chair and then heading down the hall toward my office.

I immediately noticed my secretary wasn't at her desk. That wasn't all that unusual. I assumed she must have gone to the break room or something like that.

I was making a mental list of the people I would email as I pushed open my office door and headed for my desk without actually looking at where I was going. It was the sound of breathing that alerted me to the presence of someone else in the room.

"What the hell are you doing here?" I growled, staring at Elijah who had made himself comfortable behind my desk.

He was sitting there with his phone in his hand and staring at the screen.

He looked up and smiled. "I was hoping we could talk."

I walked back to my door and shut it. I didn't want the entire office privy to my personal business with the Levy family. It was a lot of dirty laundry that I considered to be in my past. Things were likely to get loud and potentially violent. That was not a show I was willing to be a star in for the entire office to watch.

"Talk? Really? Why in the hell would I want to talk to you?" I said, stalking back toward him.

He rose from my desk and stood in front of the window, his hands in his pockets as he stared out the window at the bustling city below. His shoulders were relaxed, and I didn't sense anger or animosity. It was like nothing had happened between us.

"I want to talk to you about Nat. There's something wrong," he said before turning around to look at me.

I felt a bolt of fear race through me. "What's wrong with Nat?"

"I don't know," he said on a sigh.

"You don't know what's wrong?" I asked, wanting to make sure I was following the conversation. I felt very lost.

"No, I don't. Something is wrong, and I wanted to find out what."

I shook my head, confused by what he was saying. "I don't understand. Why are you here? Why are you asking me about Nat?"

"Can we sit down for a minute?" he asked, and I could tell he was bothered about something.

I knew him well enough to know when something was truly wrong and if it concerned Nat, I wanted to know. We may not be together, but I still cared a great deal for her. "Fine," I muttered, moving to the couch in my office.

He took a seat in the armchair and leaned back, crossing his ankle over his knee. "Something is off with her, like really off," he started.

"What does that mean—specifically?" I asked.

He took a deep breath, running a hand through his hair. "I don't know. Like she's sick, depressed, withdrawn. She's not her usual happy self. She won't talk to me. I know her well enough to know when something is wrong."

"Maybe she's working a lot," I suggested.

"It's different. I thought maybe you could tell me what was going on with her," he mumbled, as if he hated having to ask me for anything.

"Well, let me assuage your fears. I haven't seen or spoken to Nat in a month. I haven't the first fucking clue what's wrong with her," I stated, a little irritably.

"What? Really?" he asked.

"Yeah, really. Isn't that what you wanted? Didn't you very clearly tell me to stay away from her?"

"I just thought, I mean, the last time I really talked to her she told me you two were seeing each other. Well, she didn't come right out and say it, but I knew about it. I warned her to be careful and that was it," he explained.

I shrugged a shoulder. "That was over a month ago. Like I said, I haven't talked to her. I ended it. She hasn't called, and I haven't run into her around town."

Elijah looked lost in thought. I could see he was truly worried about his little sister. I knew he loved her and took care of her. Their parents were not like mine. Elijah had it rough and had done his best to shield Natasha from her father's violent temper. He looked out for her the best way he could and if he was worried about her, it was for good reason.

"Something isn't right," he said, more to himself than me.

"I'm really sorry. I have no idea. Have you tried asking her directly?"

He smirked. "I'm sure you can imagine how that went. She told me everything was fine, but it was the way she said it that worries me."

"Elijah, I think you have to take her word for it. She's had a lot to deal with the last couple months."

He ran his hands over his face and I could see the strain he was dealing with as well. "How about you and I go out for a drink sometime?" I heard myself saying before I even realized what I was doing.

His eyebrows shot up. "What?"

"Yeah, why not," I said, hating to admit to myself that I missed him.

We had been best friends for nearly two decades. It had been hard to lose him out of my life with almost no warning. I had felt betrayed, but that was in the past. Now that Natasha and I were over, there was no reason Elijah and I couldn't be friends. I doubted I would ever trust him like I had before, but I didn't want to completely lose him as a friend. It wasn't like I had a long list of friends to count on.

"Seriously? Are you setting me up?" he asked hesitantly.

I laughed. "How would I set you up? I didn't even know you were coming by. It's cool. I understand if you want to leave things as they are."

I could tell he was going to say no but at least I tried. I had extended an olive branch and he rejected it. I could go to my grave knowing I had tried to make things right between us.

"Okay," he said.

Now it was my turn to be surprised. "What?"

"Yeah, I'd like to meet up. I could use a drink and a friend," he admitted.

I stared at him again and noticed the wrinkles around his eyes were a bit more pronounced. He didn't have that exuberant energy I was used to seeing in him. The guy looked like he'd been beat down and was dragging his feet through life. I felt bad for him and wished like hell I could be there for him to lean on.

"Good. You know my number," I said, leaving it to him to pick the day and time so he wouldn't think I was setting him up.

"How about tonight?" he said enthusiastically.

I grimaced. "I can't tonight. I have a date," I announced, feeling a twinge of guilt but knowing it was exactly what Elijah needed to hear to know I had truly moved on.

"Wow. Congratulations. You and Nat are really done?"

"Yes, we are. You and I both know your dad would never change his mind. Nat loves your dad. She couldn't stand the thought of disappointing him or being disowned. I'm sorry it got so ugly," I told him.

He nodded. "My dad has only gotten meaner in his old age," he mumbled.

I looked at Elijah, studying his face. Wayne Levy was a mean son of a bitch. I had seen him nearly hit Elijah when we were busted for the graffiti incident. I had a feeling it had been rough for Elijah. I'd always felt bad when we got in trouble. I'd get grounded or would have to listen to one hell of a lecture, but I never worried about getting hurt at the hands of my father.

"I'm sorry to hear that. I'm free any other night," I offered.

"I'll give you a call," he said, standing up and reaching out to shake my hand.

I took it and gave it a firm shake. "Call me. Really, and let me know if there's anything I can do to help Natasha. I know I said we're done, but I still care about her. I always will," I told him.

He smiled and nodded. "I know you did. Who's this date with?"

I shrugged. "My mom set me up. I figured I'd better get to dating. I'm not getting any younger."

He laughed. "Your mom set you up? Damn, you must be desperate."

"Not desperate. She asked me to do it and I agreed. I've not dated anyone since your sister and I started seeing each other. I can tell you I've rejected women, feeling like I was cheating on her, but I have to accept that it's over," I stated.

I did feel guilty. I didn't know how the date would go, but I wanted to at least try. I had to for my own sanity.

"I'm sorry about that. I know you cared for her, but it would never work. I'm glad you're getting out there. I'll give you a call. I'm sorry about barging in. I had thought you'd be in here." He grinned.

I walked him to the door and shook his hand, saying goodbye before moving back to sit at my desk, loosening my tie as I sat. That had been unexpected. When I first laid eyes on him, I had assumed the worst. I half expected him to have a posse in the shadows waiting to jump me. It was odd Natasha hadn't told him we were over. She'd been pretty damn adamant about ending things. I figured she'd tell her big brother and get the pat on the head she'd wanted.

I pulled up the email program but couldn't stop my guilt from forming a pit in my stomach. I told Elijah I didn't feel guilty, but I did. I had been trying to find a way out of the date since the day I agreed to it. She had my heart. I wasn't sure if I would ever get it back.

"You're not cheating," I told myself again.

I owed her nothing. I didn't have to be faithful. I didn't have to feel guilty. We were completely over. I could go out with an attractive woman, have a good time, and not feel like an asshole cheating on his girlfriend. I closed my eyes and tried to block out the image of her, which was always hovering. It was going to take a while before I ever really felt like we were over. It was going to take serious commitment.

I could do it. I had to do it. For her and for myself.

CHAPTER 54

NATASHA

I was actually happy with my purchases. The clothes were cute. We found a lot of stretchy pants, flowy shirts, and plenty of warm, bulky sweaters that would help disguise my stomach while looking very fashionable. My hand ran over the soft cashmere as I thought about what boots I would pair it with. Thinking about boots reminded me of Jack.

I wasn't going to quit wearing boots simply because they stirred up memories that I hadn't quite decided were good or bad. It was boot season and I was taking advantage of it. I looked at the tall stiletto heels on one pair of boots and had to admit that may not be the best option if I was a little top heavy and wobbly on my feet. We'd have to see when that day arrived, I surmised.

I hung up the last sweater and grinned when Ashley, who was in my kitchen making some grilled fish dinner she'd looked up, hit a particularly high note in whatever song she was singing. There was no fear Ashley would ever be a music star. She loved to sing, but all those voice lessons she'd taken as a kid had done little to help her.

I smiled thinking about how great a friend she was. She had called me earlier and told me she was coming over to make me a healthy meal, full of iron and other vitamins. She was taking care of me. I loved that she cared enough to go out of her way.

"Oh no," I whispered when I felt the tears start.

I sat on the edge of my bed and covered my face with my hands, demanding my emotions to stop. I was tired of crying at the drop of a hat. It was futile, like trying to stop a runaway train with my hand. The tears began to flow with gusto as all my regrets bubbled to the surface. My life was a mess because I had pushed away the one man I truly loved. I had put my dad ahead of him. It was no wonder Jack had finally grown sick of being ignored and truly left me.

I couldn't blame him. I wondered where he was, what he was doing, and who he was with. I knew, I just knew he would start dating. Why wouldn't he? He wasn't pregnant and swelling up. He wasn't the one whose life had been forever changed. I couldn't blame him. He didn't know, and I almost felt like I owed him. I owed not telling him about the baby. He could move on and live his life without worrying about me. He would have more children with his future wife.

The thought brought on more tears. The bed shifted as Ashley appeared beside me, her arm wrapped around my shoulders as she quietly sat there, offering me comfort while I bawled my eyes out.

"What's wrong?" she asked.

I shook my head, wiping my cheeks. "I was thinking about how badly I messed things up."

"You didn't mess anything up."

"Jack is probably out there right now with a pretty blonde." I sobbed.

"Honey, you know it's you he loves. Call him. All you have to do is say the word."

I shook my head again. "No way. I can't keep doing that to him. It doesn't change anything. My dad still hates him. I don't want to tell him about the baby just to make him come back to me. I don't want it like that."

"Listen, we've had this conversation several times. You need to give yourself some time to work this out. Right now, you need to eat. Dinner is ready and I'm guessing cold fish is not going to taste good."

I smiled. "We eat sushi all the time."

She laughed. "Not anymore. Not with the baby in your belly."

I wrinkled my nose. "What? You're taking that away too?"

"Read, lady, read. You need to eat right for your baby."

I followed her out to the kitchen, feeling a little better after the release of tears. I was tired of crying all the time, but it did leave me feeling a little better. We sat at the table, the twinkling lights of the city catching my eye as we ate the fish and rice she had prepared.

"This is really good," I told her.

"Thank you."

"Thank you for coming over and cooking me dinner. You have gone way above and beyond the duties of a best friend," I said after I finished my last bite, then placed my fork on the plate.

"Of course. I'm here for you," she said and began to clear the table.

I helped her put everything away before we sat on opposite ends of the couch. The TV was on, but muted.

"I so wish I could go back and change the way things were," I muttered.

"You can't, but you can change the way things are," she said.

I looked at her and shook my head. "I don't think I can."

"Natasha, you have to tell Jack about the baby," she said firmly, grabbing my attention.

"Why? Why tell him and ruin his life?"

"It isn't going to ruin his life. You know it's the right thing to do. It isn't cool for you to try and hide this from him. He has a right to know. You have to tell him," she repeated.

I knew she was right, but I dreaded the drama that would unfold the second he knew the truth. "He's going to want to be in the child's life. He's going to want to be with me."

"You say that like it's a bad thing."

"It is a bad thing. He told me we would never be happy together. I don't want him to be miserable for the rest of his life because I got pregnant. He would want to be with me because he felt obligated, not because he actually wanted to," I told her, speaking my fears aloud.

She shrugged a shoulder. "But that is his choice."

"What about my choice?" I shot back defensively.

"You have a choice. You can tell him about the baby but insist you two co-parent without being in a romantic relationship. It doesn't have to be all or nothing. All I'm saying you need to do is tell him. Let him decide what he wants to do. Don't take away his choice," she insisted.

I looked down at my flat stomach and thought about what she was saying. It was the same thing I had been mulling over. I knew she was right, but I was trying to figure out how I could convince Jack not to admit the child was his. I knew I was still trying to figure out how to keep all the men in my life happy. It wasn't going to work. I had to choose one or the other, and that terrified me.

"I'm thinking about it," I muttered.

"Remember back a few years ago when Regina got pregnant?" she said, reminding me of one of our former friends.

I nodded. "I do, but that was a totally different situation. She cheated on her boyfriend."

"Not that different. Remember how pissed you were when she lied to her boyfriend?"

"I do."

"Well, how can you not see this is a similar version of that same story," she explained.

I wrinkled my nose. "I didn't cheat."

"No, but not telling Jack is exactly what Regina did to that other guy. I heard he found out later and she was forced to give him a paternity test. The guy got partial custody and her boyfriend dumped her. What I'm trying to say, it's going to come to light regardless. Look at the Bancroft men. There is no denying their parentage. What if you have a little boy and he looks just like Jack?" she asked.

I smiled thinking about the possibility. "That would be so cute."

She sighed and narrowed her eyes at me. "Yes, it would be adorable, but that is not the point of my story."

I held up a hand. "I know, I know, I get it."

Ashley looked at me, disappointment was in those green eyes. "Do you really get it? You're playing a dangerous game. Someone is going to get hurt. In this situation, I think a lot of people are going to get hurt."

"This isn't a game!" I shrieked.

"Then quit treating it like one. Quit trying to analyze all the pieces on the board and trying to figure out what your next move will be based on the best possible outcome for you. You want to win. I get that. That is why I love you. You're driven and competitive, but this is different. You are making decisions that could cause irreparable harm not only to yourself and your child, but Jack as well. Say you don't tell him. What are you going to tell that child ten, fifteen years down the road? Are you going to lie to him or her?"

Her words stung, like being slapped. "I know. You're so right. I am not purposely trying to hurt anyone. I'm trying to do what's right for Jack. Honestly, he is the one I'm thinking about. He's the one I want to protect the most."

She smiled, stretched out her hand, and rested it on my knee. "Because you love him."

I shrugged a shoulder, feeling the tears welling once again. "I do."

"Then tell him. Talk to him. I think you know he is a reasonable man. Tell him your fears. Let him help you through this," she said gently.

My heart ached. "It is so hard. I don't want him to be with me because I'm pregnant. His words from that night, they keep replaying in my head. I want him to be happy. I don't want him to be obligated to me, and we both know that's exactly what will happen. He will feel like I'm his ball and chain, holding him back."

"I'm sorry. I really am, but I think you will feel better once you tell him. If you don't want to be with him, you tell him. I think you guys can work this out," she insisted.

I nodded. "You're right. I will. Now, I just have to find the right time."

She laughed. "Well, I don't know that there is ever a right time."

"How should I do it? Should I take another test and send him a picture of it?"

Her laughter was my response. "You could call him."

I gasped in horror. "No way!"

"Go to his work?"

"No! Are you crazy!"

"You are seriously thinking about texting him the news?" she asked, her face a mixture of shock and horror.

I shrugged a shoulder. "It seems easier. I don't want to see his face when he hears."

"Nat, I think this is one of those things that needs to be explained in person, in private."

I sighed. "You're probably right, but I'm being a big baby. I'm nervous."

"That's okay. Be nervous, but please don't send him a text. That's very cold and not your style. You are a brave, strong woman and I know you'll be able to tell him face-to-face," she said, giving me the encouragement I needed to hear.

"You're right. I will."

She grinned. "Great, when?"

I rolled my eyes. "Damn, you're pushy."

"Soon?"

I nodded. "Soon. Now turn up the TV, I like this show," I said, hoping to change the subject.

She did as I asked and fortunately, the subject of the baby and Jack was put to rest for the night. I was relieved to have somewhat of a plan. I was going to tell Jack. That part I knew for sure. Now, I just needed to figure out how and when.

CHAPTER 55

JACK

I was acting like I was headed to my own funeral. I knew it, but no matter how hard I tried to look forward to the night, all I could think of was about a million different shitty excuses to cancel. I should have been excited and looking forward to spending the evening with a woman who was completely available to me. Our families would be thrilled to have us get together, marry, and live happily ever after.

My mother insisted she was attractive and smart, but I would be the judge of that. My mom's idea of attractive was a little different from mine. I was picturing a woman wearing something my mom would wear. Pink and full coverage with no heels, little makeup, and zero sex appeal.

"Is tonight the big night?" Grayson asked as I met him on the way to the elevator.

I nodded. "It is."

He chuckled softly. "Good luck. Who knows, maybe Mom has really good taste. If this thing works out, I feel sorry for the rest of our brothers. She is going to be on a mission to set them all up."

I groaned and shook my head. "I'm only worried if this doesn't work out, because then, she is going to keep setting me up."

"I'm glad I don't have to worry about any of that." He grinned, rubbing a little extra salt in the wound, reminding me he was lucky enough to be with the woman he loved.

He didn't have to worry about Hannah's father hiring a hitman to take him out. I had no doubt in my mind that was a real possibility with the way Wayne Levy had acted. The bodyguard beatdown was nothing compared to what he would do if I tried to marry Natasha.

"Thanks for that. Now, I feel so much better," I groused.

"Where are you taking her?"

"I've got reservations downtown."

"Fancy?" he asked, one brow raised.

I shrugged a shoulder. "It's a decent place. I don't think I can get away with a trip to McDonald's. Mom would kill me and accuse me of not really trying."

He nodded. "Try and keep an open mind. I know we gave you some shit about it, but you never know. She could be a really great woman."

I groaned. "Now you sound like Mom."

He chuckled and slapped me on the back as the elevator doors slid open. "Have fun!"

Grayson walked out the front doors where his chauffeured car would be waiting while I headed for the parking garage. I was meeting Annie at the restaurant. That left us both with a quick way out if we needed it. I hated blind dates. I hated first dates in general. They were always so awkward, and I was of the firm belief you knew whether it was worth sitting through an entire meal within the first five minutes. If she hated me on sight, which was a distinct possibility, I wanted to leave her an escape. She could have her friend call her and say there was an emergency or whatever. It wouldn't hurt my feelings.

I drove my Porsche through town, not bothering to go home and change first. I was wearing one of my better Armani suits and figured it would pass muster at the upscale restaurant. I handed my car over to the valet, straightened my tie, and sauntered inside. As I followed the hostess to the table, I nodded to the few people I knew from various business associations. In the back of my mind, I was already planning my excuse for leaving early.

I was the first to arrive and ordered a club soda. I wanted to keep my wits about me. No way did I want to get drunk and end up taking the woman home. I knew it would only be a one-night stand and my mother would kick my ass if she found out. This had to stay right here in the restaurant. I would not let it go any further than the door. If things somehow managed to go really well, we'd have a second date and things would be different.

"Jack?" A woman's voice snapped me out of my thoughts.

I stood up. "Annie, I presume," I said with a friendly smile.

She smiled, and I had to acknowledge she was a very pretty woman. I guessed her to be in her late twenties, blond hair, and light-blue eyes—not the dark-blue pools I was used to seeing when I looked at Natasha. She was slim and tall and had that patrician look about her. Her skin was a little freckled under her fading summer tan.

"You would presume right," she said, awkwardly shaking my extended hand.

It had been a reflex. I felt like an idiot but quickly got over it. "Have a seat, please."

The waiter took her drink order—a glass of white wine—before leaving us alone. I could immediately feel that weird strain in the air and was silently berating my mother for setting me up on the damn date and myself for agreeing to go.

"Thank you for doing this. I know this is weird. My mom, she's convinced I will die an old spinster if I'm not married by the age of thirty," she said with an easy smile.

I relaxed a little. At least she could recognize how strange it was for both of us. "It's no problem. Thank you for agreeing to go. My mom is beginning to think that same way."

We both laughed, and I felt the first proverbial break in the ice.

"So, tell me about yourself. All I know is you are one of the Bancroft boys, which, by the way, is a little intimidating for someone like me who grew up very isolated and only heard stories about the Bancroft bunch," she said with a small laugh.

I groaned. "I want to tell you to ignore everything you heard, but unfortunately, most of it is probably true. I can't say I'm fully responsible or a part of all the stories, but there have been some shenanigans."

She didn't seem the least bit scared. "That's okay. I think we've all done some wild things in our past. Although mine came much later in life and far away from the watchful eyes of the New York society gossips."

"Good thinking. Are you living in New York full time?" I asked, trying to make conversation when all I could do was compare her to Nat.

"I am. I was in Chicago for a bit, then Miami, and now I'm back here."

"What do you do?" I asked, wondering what kind of job had her moving around the country.

She shrugged a shoulder. "I don't really do anything. I went to Chicago, hoping to find some new, exciting adventure. Then I decided I wanted sandy beaches and sun. Unfortunately, that included hurricanes. Not my thing." She giggled.

I nodded and pretended to understand. I didn't. She seemed smart enough, but I got a bit of a ditty vibe from her. "Do you work for your family's business?" I asked, trying to remember what it was her family did.

"No. I do attend various ribbon cuttings and stuff like that, but I have no interest in sitting in some office and counting money."

I smiled, hiding my initial impression of her. "That does sound boring. What is it your family does?" I asked.

"Construction, new developments ... that kind of thing," she said, waving a hand through the air.

It was then her family name rang a bell. They tore down depressed properties and built fancy condos and subdivisions. "I remember now," I said, hoping I sounded interested.

I wasn't. Not in the least. She wasn't Natasha. She would never be a Natasha. While Annie was refined and pretty, she had more of a *Stepford Wives* thing going. I could see her hosting dinner parties and being the dutiful wife. She wouldn't give me that excitement Natasha did. Nat was driven and always had a gleam in her eye that kept me guessing. I didn't see me doing a lot of guessing with Annie. I liked that Natasha wanted to forge her own path. She wasn't content sitting in the shadows.

We chatted a bit more, talking mostly about our families, recent events, and things that one would talk about with someone they met at a party. It was all very much on the surface. There weren't really any personal or deep topics I was comfortable sharing with her. Once again, I thought about Natasha. We shared everything. I knew her, and she knew me, my hopes, dreams and even those things that worried me. I couldn't see myself ever opening up to Annie. She was more superficial and less inclined to understand what I was feeling.

I spent most of the dinner wondering what Natasha was doing. Was she okay? Was she really sick? Elijah had been worried about her, which was telling. She had looked a little pale the last time I had seen her. I should have pressed her for an answer about what was wrong.

"Don't you think?" Annie's voice cut through the worry clouding my brain.

I blinked, trying to focus on what Annie was saying. I felt like a jackass. She was nice and in any other set of circumstances, I could see myself being attracted to her. Unfortunately, it was Nat I was thinking about.

"Um, I'm sorry, what did you say?" I asked.

She smiled and repeated her question. We managed to get through dinner without me being a total dick. Annie seemed happy enough and hadn't seem to notice my mind was elsewhere.

We stopped outside where I handed my ticket to the valet. Annie had a car service waiting nearby.

"Would you like to go somewhere for a nightcap?" she asked.

I smiled, feeling bad, but knowing there was no way I could. "I'm sorry. I have an early morning and need to be getting home."

She wasn't going to give up. "You could come to my place, have a drink, and then be on your way."

A dark-black car pulled up to the curb. "I think that's your car," I said softly.

She nodded. "Indeed it is."

I walked with her to the car and opened the back door for her. She was looking at me, waiting for me to give her a kiss. Now I knew I was an asshole. "Take care of yourself, Annie. I had a nice time," I said, effectively ending the date.

She gave me a look that said she wasn't happy to be rejected and climbed into the backseat. I closed the door and waited for the car to drive away. I could already hear my mother bitching at me for not giving the woman a kiss good night, but I had exceeded my ability to cope with the guilt clinging to me like a hair shirt. I wasn't ready to date. I still felt connected to Natasha. I couldn't kiss another woman. It had been hard enough to sit through dinner with another woman. All I could think about was what Nat would have said or what she would have worn. I couldn't even remember what Annie had worn. I barely remembered what she looked like. Hell, if I were to run into her on the street, I probably wouldn't recognize her. I had paid that little attention to her.

My own car pulled up. The valet jumped out and handed me the keys, complimenting me on the nice car. I nodded and tipped him before sliding in my car and taking off. Once again, I found myself driving too fast through the city streets.

CHAPTER 56

NATASHA

I smiled, looking at the mess Ashley and I had made. Her dinner had been amazing, but there was something to say for junk food. We had gotten involved in some ridiculous show on Netflix and binge-watched as well as binge ate. Thankfully, it had been somewhat healthy. Packs of nuts, sunflower seeds, and some popcorn.

Ashley had been exhausted and kept dozing off. I had finally told her to go home. She was trying to be a trooper for me, which I appreciated, but I was perfectly capable of being alone. Ashley was making good on her promise to be there for me.

I tossed the empty wrappers into the trash and fluffed the pillows on the couch. Ashley had tried to stay and clean up, but I insisted on doing it myself. She had cooked, it was only fair I cleaned up. With everything put back in place, I decided to make myself a cup of tea that would hopefully help me sleep. I knew the pregnancy was partially to blame for my exhaustion, but it was also stress. I hadn't been sleeping at all. I kept thinking about Jack, the baby, and my dad and the combination of all three things was making me crazy.

I filled up the teapot and was about to turn on the burner when I heard what sounded like a knock on the front door. That was odd. I was in the penthouse. People could walk right into my living area, assuming they had the key or had been given a pass by security. I assumed it was Ashley and walked around the corner to see what she needed. Instead of coming right in, she actually knocked, which was strange.

"Ash, what are you doing? Did you forget something?" I called out.

I opened the door and gasped when I saw Jack standing there.

"Hi," he said sheepishly, looking devilishly handsome.

My eyes soaked in the sight of him standing at my door. It was so unfair he could be that good looking. Sex on a stick is the first thing that came to mind. I had forgotten how damn hot he was. It had only been a month, but it felt so much longer. The two years I had been gone hadn't felt this long.

"Hi," I whispered, still stunned to find him standing there in what would be my foyer.

He blessed me with that sexy smile that could make my panties wet in an instant. "Hi," he said again.

I shook my head. Oh no way was I going to fall for that Jack charm. He was off-limits to me. It didn't matter that there was sexual chemistry electrifying the very air we were breathing. It didn't matter that there was a pool of warm goo in my belly spreading throughout my body as my senses were flooded with the sight and smell of him. Memories of him naked and gasping as he rode me through one of his orgasms.

"Jack. What are you doing here? How did you get up here?" I asked with total confusion, snapping my attention out of the gutter and back to the present.

He shrugged a shoulder. "I have my ways."

I immediately decided the security guards in the building needed some serious counseling about how to do their jobs. My hand went to my hair, which had to be a complete mess. Add that to my zero-makeup, combined with what I was sure was puffy eyes, and I knew I probably looked like death. I looked down to confirm I really was wearing a loose, ugly T-shirt and my leggings. Yep, I was not the picture of beauty, and Jack was standing there looking handsome as hell in a nice suit and tie. Fate was a bitch.

"What are you doing here?" I asked again.

"I wanted to check on you. I gave the security guard a good story and a hundred-dollar bill and here I am," he said as if it were the most normal thing in the world.

I looked at him in the suit again and realized how terrible I looked. I felt horribly self-conscious. "I should go change or put on a robe," I muttered, realizing how dumb that sounded.

He reached out and put a hand on my shoulder. "Nat, you don't need to change or cover up," he said, his tone husky as his eyes roamed over my braless chest and down to the tight leggings hugging my hips and legs.

"I ... uh ... well, I wasn't expecting anyone," I muttered, begging for the earth to swallow me whole.

He smiled when his eyes met mine again. His sweet hazel eyes gave me that warm and tingly feeling all over my body. Damn, I missed him.

"I just wanted to make sure you were okay. I didn't mean to bother you and I hope I'm not interrupting," he said, his eyes drifting over my head to look behind me.

I shook my head. "I'm not bothered. I was just cleaning up," I mumbled.

"Good."

"Wait, you said you wanted to check to see if I was okay?" I asked, wrinkling my nose.

Did he know? Why would he wonder if I was okay? The only person that knew I was pregnant was Ashley. I quickly replayed the conversation with Ashley. She was insistent I tell him. There was no way she would go and tell him—would she?

"Yes. I wanted to make sure you were well, doing okay," he repeated.

I realized we were still standing in the doorway. He kept glancing around me, as if he were checking to see if someone were there. I moved out of the way and gestured for him to come inside. I had a feeling he was going to push me out of the way at any second if I didn't invite him. He walked in and looked around the place, running his hand over my sofa as his gaze roamed over the art I had on the wall. He moved to the windows, which spanned the wall, before turning back to look at me.

He nodded with approval. "It's nice. I knew you would make it perfect. It suits you. It looks very homey and yet, modern," he said.

"Thank you. Uh, go ahead and have a seat," I said, feeling a little weird having him in my personal space.

He moved around the sofa, looked out the windows for a few seconds, then turned back to me. I walked over and took a seat, keeping my distance and hoping like hell he couldn't tell I was pregnant.

"Are you feeling okay?" he asked.

I shrugged a shoulder. "Fine. Why do you ask?"

He cocked his head to the side, studying me. "Elijah came by to see me today."

My eyes bulged. "He did? Oh my God, I'm sorry. I thought he was over all of that. Did he hurt you?"

Jack smiled. "No, he didn't hurt me. He stopped by to ask me if I knew anything about you."

"Oh," I said, very confused.

"He's worried about you."

I waved a hand through the air. "I'm fine. You didn't have to come by."

He was still staring at me. He knew me too well. I knew he could see right through me.

"Nat, what's wrong? I noticed it the last time I saw you."

"Noticed what?" I snapped, running a hand over my hair.

He shrugged a shoulder. "You looked a little pale. Are you sure you're okay?"

I rolled my eyes, a little irritated to have him scrutinizing me so carefully. "That's really not nice."

"I'm not trying to be mean. I'm worried about you. Your brother said he noticed you've been a little off."

"I don't care what Elijah said. I'm fine. You didn't have to come over here," I repeated, growing more nervous by the second at the thought of him seeing too much.

He was watching me in that way again. It was the way he looked at me after we made love. It was unnerving. I wondered if he suspected something. He scooted over a few inches on the couch, getting closer to me where I sat in the comfortable chair I had picked out last week.

"Natasha, you don't look well. You look like you've been ill. Have you seen a doctor?" he asked.

I gulped down the lump of guilt in my throat. He suspected me of something. I could tell he didn't know what, but he did know something was wrong. I inhaled through my nose and did my best to look normal and healthy.

"Jack, it's rude to tell me I don't look well. I wasn't expecting company. I didn't exactly go out of my way to dress up. Please forgive me," I said sarcastically.

He grinned. "You know you always look beautiful. That has never been a problem for you. I'm only telling you because I care."

I scoffed. "It isn't your business to care."

He scooted over a little more before reaching out and grabbing my hand. "Natasha, I know we can't be together, but that doesn't mean I stopped caring about you. I do care about you."

I thought about the last words I had said to him. I had told him we couldn't be friends. Despite that, he was there checking on me. It was why I didn't want him to know about the baby. I knew he would be just like he was now. He would care and would want to be there for me, which was not a bad thing. I just didn't want his pity.

"Jack, this is really unnecessary. While I'm glad you and Elijah don't hate each other and can bond over your mutual opinion that I am sick and in need of saving, I don't need you to swoop in and rescue me. I'm fine. You can go now. You've come and checked on me. You can tell Elijah you did," I said, taking my hand away from him.

I knew he didn't believe me. I didn't care. This was not how I was going to tell him I was pregnant. I wanted it on my terms and I wanted to feel like I had the upper hand. In that moment, I felt as if he was at the advantage. He was dressed up and sexy as hell, while I looked like death warmed over. I leaned away from him and jumped up from my chair.

"What are you doing?" he asked when I walked into the kitchen.

"I'm making tea. I'd offer you some, but you don't drink tea, and I'm sure you have better things to do than sit around here. Plus, I'm tired. I'm going to bed soon," I said in a haughty voice.

He sat there, looking at me, but didn't move. He wasn't going to leave. I quickly went behind the counter, doing what I could to shield myself in case he noticed the changes happening to my body. Ashley told me they weren't noticeable, but Ashley didn't know my body as well as Jack did. Hell, I barely knew my body as well as he did.

"I'd like a cup of tea if you don't mind," he said in a soothing voice.

With my back to him, I squeezed my eyes tightly closed. He wasn't going anywhere. I should have known better. Jack wasn't the kind of guy who took anything at face value. I was going to have to sit with him and do my best to lie to his face for at least the next thirty minutes. Then, I would absolutely pull the tired card and send him away.

CHAPTER 57

JACK

I watched as she moved around the kitchen and knew something was off. I could tell she was lying to me—holding something back. I had no idea what it could be, but Elijah had been right to be worried. She did look pale and just didn't seem to be her usual vibrant self. The fact she was making tea was a big clue something was off. I had never known her to drink tea. Usually she would have a glass of wine or even brandy, but tea—that was a new one.

I waited until she was finished with the tea to question her further about what was really going on. I occupied myself by watching her and checking out her place a little more. I loved the way she softened the stark lines of the place with a fur rug and furniture that was dark and cozy looking. She carried both steaming cups into the living room and sat as far away from me as possible, back in the chair she had vacated earlier. I couldn't really blame her. Whenever we were near each other, there was an undercurrent that hummed between us that made it impossible to think of much else.

"How are things going?" I asked, hoping to get her talking a bit, then maybe I would learn a little more about what was going on.

"Good. Maybe that's why I look so unwell," she quipped.

"You look unwell because things are going good?" I questioned.

"Well, things are good but stressful. Starting a company takes a lot of time and energy. We had to go through a minor remodel in the office and things were just a little chaotic for a while. I've been kept very busy with meetings, investors, and trying to cut deals with various manufacturers," she explained, her hand moving a lot as if she were nervous. Her speech reflected her nervousness as well.

I nodded. "I can imagine, plus moving in here and getting this place just perfect. That's a lot of work," I agreed.

Her head was bobbing up and down. "Exactly. See? That's it. I'm fine, just a little stressed! Nothing's wrong. No one needs to worry. I swear my brother is worse than my mother."

Her voice was higher than usual, and her movements were jerky. I knew she was hiding something. I studied her face a bit more looking for some clue that would tell me what was really going on. She wouldn't look me in the eye. She blew on her cup of tea, keeping her eyes turned down as she looked anywhere but at me. She was sitting ramrod straight instead of the usual relaxed way she leaned back as if we were hanging out.

"Natasha, if there's something I can help with, I'm here. I hate to see you so stressed," I said in a quiet voice.

"I'm really fine. I have no idea why my brother would say anything. I mean, a girl can't always be at the top of the world. I'm a little tired and stressed. I'm not the first person to get like that. This is all part of starting a business. I'm sure you and Elijah have had days where you were really stressed and worn out too." She was rambling on.

I held the hot cup of tea in my hand before grabbing a coaster and setting it on the coffee table situated in front of the couch. She stiffened when I moved down the couch toward her again.

"Nat, are you seeing someone? It's okay if you are. I mean, I don't want to make you uncomfortable being here if you're worried a boyfriend will be jealous or something like that. Please, tell me to leave if my being here is what is making you so upset," I told her, having a sudden realization of what it could be that was bothering her.

"Oh God no! No! Absolutely not! Nothing like that. I'm not seeing anyone!" she blurted out.

I didn't say anything. I let the relief of knowing she was still single wash over me. I had no business being jealous, but I knew I would be when that day finally came. I would have to ignore it and pretend it didn't bother me, when it was going to tear me apart. I watched her. She looked as if she were in an interrogation room rather than her own living room. I simply sat, not talking, giving her a few minutes to relax. She sipped her tea before finally looking up to meet my eyes. I gave her a soft smile. I could see it in her eyes. There was something on her mind, but she wasn't going to tell me.

"I've missed you," she said, a sadness enveloping her that broke my heart. Her normally sparkling deep-blue eyes were dull and full of pain.

"I've missed you. I knew it would be hard, but I don't think I knew how hard," I confessed.

Another watery smile. "Definitely hard."

"We miss each other. That's normal. It's to be expected, but we can't go back. This thing between us is just bad for everyone. It will never work. You'll be hurt, I'll get hurt, and our families are going to be hurt if we try and pursue this. We've made it a month. I'm sure it will get easier," I said, not wanting to take a step backward.

She sat there, nodding, her lips set in a thin line. "I know. You're not telling me anything new or anything I haven't been telling myself. It's the way I feel, and I can't change that," she whispered.

My heart was clenching. My chest felt too tight as I struggled to draw in air. I hated seeing her suffer. I hated knowing I was the one doing it to her. "I'm sorry," I told her.

She shrugged one shoulder. "It's not your fault."

"In a way it is."

"It's the situation. I don't blame you at all. You tried. You were more than patient. I'm so sorry it ended like this." She said the words with so much emotion I could feel it in my very soul.

"How've you really been this past month, Nat? Please tell me," I asked again.

She let out a long sigh. "It hasn't been great, but I'm getting through. I'm stressed. I'm sure that's what my brother is seeing, but it can be helped. I've not been sleeping very well and just have a lot on my mind."

I nodded. "I can understand that. I wish there was a way I could make it better. I hate seeing you suffer like this."

"It's not so bad. What about you? Anything new and exciting in your life?" she asked with a soft smile that didn't meet her eyes.

I shrugged a shoulder, not wanting to make it sound like I had it easy, but not wanting her to worry about me either. "No, nothing exciting really. Same old thing. Mom is talking about taking a three-month-long cruise this spring."

I left out the part about dating again. There was no point in hurting her. I knew it would make her sad and I had no intention of twisting the knife in her heart. It was bad enough as it was. I was hoping to keep things light, friendly, but I had a feeling I was failing miserably.

"That sounds exciting. I've always wanted to take a cruise," she replied easily, falling into her old ways for just a second.

"Is your company getting off the ground?" I asked her, wanting to keep the conversation going. I didn't want to leave yet, and if we were talking, it was a good reason to stay.

She smiled, shrugging a shoulder at the same time. "I've got a lot of work ahead of me, but I feel confident it will get rolling along soon. I've got a good team working with me. I expect to be pretty busy over the next several months, getting everything settled. My dad tells me it will take at least a year before things really start to mellow."

"Good. I'm so happy for you. I know this is something you've wanted for a while. I'm glad it's finally coming together. You are going to do great. I have no doubt in my mind you will be successful."

She nodded and I could see the tears welling in her eyes again. Her hands were twisting in her lap. I knew the struggle she was going through. I knew what it felt like to have everything feel so wrong and being helpless to fix it. I couldn't stand to see her so miserable. I loved her. I didn't stop loving her the moment we officially called it quits on our relationship.

I reached out, leaning forward to grab her hand, and gently pulled. She jerked back at first, but eventually she came to sit beside me on the couch. I wrapped my arm around her shoulders and pulled her against me. She didn't talk. I could hear her breath catch and knew she was struggling not to cry. I wished I could scream and rage at her father. He was to blame for her pain and suffering as far as I was concerned. My dad had been a jerk, but Natasha didn't deserve to pay for his sins and neither did I.

"I'm so sorry it has to be this way. It seems so unfair," I whispered, running my hand up and down her upper arm.

She didn't say anything at first. I could hear her short gasps of breath and knew she was struggling to keep her emotions in check. "I know. I don't blame you," she mumbled against my chest.

"You could blame me. Maybe this would be easier if you hated me. Do you want to hit me? Yell at me?" I teased.

I heard a tiny laugh and felt a little better knowing I had given her some relief from the seriousness of the situation. We sat together, me holding her, listening to the sound of her breathing, her warm breath creating a hot spot on my chest.

She leaned back and looked up at me. Her eyes had so much pain in them as she stared up at me. When her eyelids fluttered closed and she leaned forward to kiss me, I didn't pull away. Her soft lips pressed against mine in a gentle joining. I realized I should stop the kiss. I needed to get up and walk away. We were crossing a line that both of us would regret.

I didn't stop. I kissed her back, pressing my lips against hers until her lips parted, giving me access to her sweet mouth. I groaned when my tongue swept inside. It was like coming home after being away for years. I could taste the herbal tea as I leisurely ran my tongue over hers. Her soft moan told me she was feeling all the same things I was. It was impossible for us to deny each other. We wanted each other so badly. How could it be so wrong? It wasn't all lust and passion. It was love. It was two people connected on a spiritual level, drowning in a world where we couldn't be together.

She turned her body, facing mine as her arms wrapped around me. Her hands moved up my back, picking up speed. The kiss was quickly changing into one of pure lust and desperation. I tried to stop. I kept telling myself not to let it go any further. When her hand reached between my legs, stirring my erection to life, I knew I was gone. There was no way I could stop. She was practically begging me to take her. Her boldness turned me on and stole away the last thread of self-control I had.

Fuck the line in the sand. In that moment, all I wanted was her. I didn't give a shit about anything else. It was me and her, and that was all that mattered.

CHAPTER 58

NATASHA

His body was mine. That was the one thought that kept running through my head as I ran my hands over every hard inch. I was desperate for his hot skin and began struggling to remove his suit jacket. He leaned away from me, jumped off the couch, and quickly pulled off his jacket, before loosening the tie and dragging it away. I stood, wanting to be near him almost afraid he would change his mind. I knew better, but I had made up my mind I was going to have him. I didn't want to give him a second to pull his wits about him and leave me. I wanted his body. I needed that connection with him.

My hands were yanking and tugging at his shirt, growing frustrated by my fumbling fingers and the stupid tiny buttons. I yanked hard, popping the last few stubborn buttons from his shirt before pushing it over his arms.

"Slow down, baby," he said, leaning down to kiss me as I went for the hem of his undershirt.

"Too many damn clothes," I cursed as he stood up and tore his shirt off.

I sighed in supreme satisfaction when his bare chest was before me. My hands caressed his pecs, moving over his biceps before heading straight down and working at the button on his slacks. I would pop the damn thing off if it gave me any trouble.

His hands moved to the hem of my shirt and tugged it upward. I stopped fumbling with his zipper and let him lift the shirt over my head. For the briefest second, I hoped he wouldn't notice the change I felt in my breasts or the tiniest swell in my stomach. I reminded myself it wasn't visible. He couldn't see the changes happening within. My secret was safe.

"Damn, girl." He groaned when I slid my hand under the waistband of his boxers, gripping his erection in my hand and squeezing.

"I need you." I gasped as he cupped me between my legs through the leggings I had on.

"Okay, okay," he assured me, moving his hands to the waistband of my pants and pushing them down.

I was ever so thankful for elastic waistbands in that moment. He stripped me naked while I held onto his dick for dear life. I never wanted to let go.

"Baby, you gotta let go of me. This only works if you move your hand." He cajoled.

His mouth closed over mine, and my hand holding him tightened as I began to stroke him, up and down, envisioning him inside me, pumping in and out.

"I need you," I rasped against his lips.

"Shh," he said, stepping away from me and quickly removing his pants.

I stood, watching, mesmerized by his body. I loved every inch of him. He was my man. I knew that as well as I knew the sun would rise in the morning. He stood before me, completely nude, staring at me before his eyes moved over my body. I involuntarily turned, not wanting him to stare at me too much out of fear he would notice something was different.

"I want you," I said, passion making me feel flushed.

He stepped toward me, his hand moving to the back of my neck as he held me close, his mouth devouring mine. I reached around and grabbed a handful of his ass, wrenching him against me. His erection pressed against my stomach.

"Come over here," he said, taking my hand and leading me around the couch.

I was expecting to have him take me to my bedroom. He didn't move toward the hall. He stopped and turned me around to look out the picture windows lining the wall, the cityscape and the dazzling lights beyond.

I smiled, thinking of the last time we were together in my penthouse. He had told me what he wanted to do and here we were. I rested my hands on the back of the couch, leaning my head to the side as his body came up behind mine, his mouth moving to the side of my neck. I leaned forward, staring at our reflection in the glass. His dark head covered my neck, my nudity concealed by his arm stretched across my breast, and the couch hid my lower body.

I watched the erotic scene, gasping as his hand moved over my stomach and between my legs. I watched the scene, my breath hitching as his head came up, his gaze focused on mine in the reflection. His finger stretched out, spreading my folds before his long index finger slid inside. I moaned, leaning my head back against his shoulder, my own hand moving to fondle my sensitive breasts, needing more stimulation.

He stepped back, lining himself up before slowly pressing the head of his engorged cock to my core. My legs spread, giving him better access to slide inside. He scraped across raw nerves, pulling small gasps and moans from me as he moved. I could feel my body weeping with ecstasy. The longing I had felt was nearly appeased. I needed more.

As usual, Jack instinctively knew what I needed. His body melded with mine, giving me all I could ask for. Sparking a beautiful orgasm that bloomed deep inside and spread throughout my body, touching every nerve.

"I've missed you," he whispered against my ear as he began to move again, taking me higher and higher as I felt the crest of another orgasm.

He pulled out, stepping away from me. I cried out and spun around to face him. His hands grabbed my face, holding me firmly as his mouth moved over mine. His tongue plunged in and out, working me into a frenzy, needing him inside me once again.

When he walked away, sitting on my couch, I straddled him, knowing exactly what he wanted. He rested against the couch as I slowly moved up and down on his shaft, my hands roaming over his chest, exploring every hard inch as my hips rocked back and forth. I could feel his excitement growing. I opened my eyes to stare into his. It was Jack. I loved looking at him as we made love. His hand swept up my arm, his fingertips trailing down, sending goose bumps to cover my body. I kept riding him, wanting to watch him lose control.

It didn't take long. His hands moved to my hips, dragging me back and forth in long, hard strokes. I heard him grunt as he thrust again, much harder, pulling another loud grunt of pleasure from him. I dropped my head back, my breasts thrusting up, the cool air in the room brushing over the sensitive nipples as I rode him. I could feel another orgasm preparing to burst over me and moaned low in my throat. His hand reached between my legs, finding the sensitive nub that always sent me over the edge, and rubbing, gently at first and then much harder. My body quaked over him before sweet rapture finally exploded. I cried out in ecstasy, never wanting the feeling to end.

He moved forward, his arm going around my back as he scooted to the edge of the couch. I heard the coffee table sliding away. His strong arms lowered me onto the fluffy white rug. I looked up and smiled at him as he rose above me and began to glide in and out all over again. I wrapped my legs around his waist, pulling him deep inside me, watching him as he watched me. We were so connected. I knew in that moment I would never have that same connection with another person for as long as I lived.

"You're so beautiful," he managed to get out, his voice guttural as he made long strokes inside my body.

I reached up to cup his cheek, feeling the hard jawline pressing against my palm. He closed his eyes and began to move faster. I could feel the intensity in every stroke and dropped my hands to hold onto the rug, knowing I was about to come with him. His arms were steady as he held himself above me, his body jackhammering against me, moving my body.

He threw back his head and shouted as he exploded deep inside me, giving me the last little bit of himself to take me along with him on the sweetest ride of my life. I gasped and arched below him, sucking him impossibly deeper inside my body as we both rode out the orgasm together, gasping and groaning as our bodies sealed together.

He dropped beside me on the rug, rolling to his back, one arm across my thighs as we both stared up at the high ceiling above. I thought about telling him about the pregnancy. Now was the right time. I couldn't find the courage to say the words. I felt completely vulnerable lying naked beside him.

Without looking at me, he let out a long sigh before moving his hand to his forehead as if he had just made the biggest mistake of his life.

"I should go," he muttered.

The moment was ruined. I had so wanted to tell him I was pregnant, but I couldn't. We'd had sex. That's all there was to it. It had been a quick round of sex to relieve our tensions and now he was going to leave. We were back to square one.

I had to fight the tears that sprang to my eyes. I rolled my head to the side, looking at the couch instead of him. I felt ashamed of what had happened. I had never felt shame before, but this was my fault. I had practically begged him to have sex with me. He didn't want it. He had come over to check on me because he cared, not because he wanted to resume our affair.

"I guess you probably should," I finally managed to get out around the lump in my throat.

I felt the cool draft the second he moved away from me. I rolled to my side and quickly got up, dressing much faster than he was able to with his many layers. I took our cups into the kitchen, wanting to put distance between us. I couldn't believe I had managed to have sex with him again.

Once he was dressed, he grabbed his keys, looking at me, but not speaking. "I'm sorry. I didn't mean for that to happen," he muttered.

I shrugged a shoulder. "I know. It's fine."

He nodded once and walked to the door to let himself out. I didn't follow him. I couldn't. I was afraid I would burst into the tears I was barely holding back. I heard the door close and waited a few minutes before moving to shut off the lights and go to bed. Tears were streaming down my face as I crawled between the sheets.

"What are you doing?" I asked myself in the dark room.

I had no idea what I was doing—that was the problem. I couldn't see him again. I knew it would always be like that between us, at least until I was big and pregnant. Then, he wouldn't find me attractive. He'd move on and have a skinny woman to take to bed at night. He'd be the kind gentleman, stopping by to drop off a check or to check on his child, but he and I would never work. I didn't think I could ever be with him once he had another woman. Some part of me hoped he did move on. That was the only way I would ever accept it was truly over. I needed him to dump me and leave me for good. I couldn't handle him caring about me. It was too tempting.

CHAPTER 59

JACK

Thank God work had been absolutely crazy all week. We were in a rush to get as much business handled before the holidays. We all wanted to take an extended vacation and give our employees all the time off they deserved, but we also had to pay the bills, which meant a lot of work for everyone. I had one meeting after another. It had been difficult to keep everything straight. I had flown down to Florida on Wednesday and returned late last night. It was a quick spur-of-the-moment trip to meet with a man who was interested in selling to us. I had been putting the guy off, but then figured why the hell not, so I booked a flight and headed down. The busy week was exactly what I needed to keep my mind off Natasha.

Working from sunup to sundown was the best way to keep from calling her or showing up at her place in the middle of the night. I had tried like hell to keep my distance in the past, but I always managed to find my way right back into her arms. Not anymore. I couldn't do it. I couldn't keep putting us through the torture of having to walk away over and over again. It was a dangerous attraction. We both knew it and no matter how dire the consequences, we couldn't seem to stay apart.

I could have walked out of her place without touching her. I was sure I could have done it, but the moment she kissed me, it was all over. Somewhere, in the back of my mind, I had known exactly what would happen if I went over there. I knew that powerful bond between us would make it impossible for me not to touch her, kiss her, and plunge into her body over and over.

I had known it, but I'd gone over anyway. I had tempted fate and lost. I had truly been worried about her after her brother's visit. Elijah had been right. There was something different about her. I couldn't quite put my finger on it, but I sensed a sadness within her that went beyond us not being together. She didn't have that sparkle or that little fire I was so used to seeing burning bright within her. Something was seriously bothering her, and she wasn't going to tell me. I had tried to get it out of her, but she held firm. I'd seen the tears and had been hesitant to push it any further. I hated to see her hurting.

"Hey, how did it go in Miami?" Grayson asked, walking into my office near the end of the day.

"Good. I'm doing some research and will put together a report for you to review. It's out of our normal wheelhouse, but I think it's an option. We could branch out," I told him, not hiding the excitement I felt.

He sat down in the chair and nodded. "You think?"

"Why not? We need to evolve with the times. The internet marketing world is hot right now. I think it would be good to show we aren't limited. This could open up a whole new lane for us," I said.

He smiled, agreeing with me. "You know I trust you. You've not failed the company yet." He grinned.

"Thanks for the vote of confidence," I said with a smirk on my face.

"So, is it tonight you're meeting up with Elijah?" he asked, and I realized that was the real reason for the visit.

He was worried about me. Mason had offered to stick close in case there was another attempt to jump me. I assured him that was all behind us, and that Elijah and I were good friends once before and I hoped to have it again one day.

"It is. It'll be fine," I assured him before he could give me the big brother lecture.

"Keep Mason's number handy. I'd hate to hear the guy kicked your ass again."

I rolled my eyes. "He didn't kick my ass," I said for what I knew had to be at least the tenth time in ten years.

"All the same. I don't trust that family. They're shady."

"Natasha isn't," I immediately defended.

Grayson slowly nodded. "But she isn't defending you now, is she?"

I wasn't going to get all into it again. I wasn't sure how I felt about the situation. Part of me was a little pissed she wouldn't stand up to her father to defend me, but the other part of me knew why and understood. I had seen what Elijah had gone through with his father and I would never wish that on Natasha. It was one of the main reasons I chose to end things. I kept imagining violent family gatherings. I would never expose her—or our children, if we were ever lucky enough to have any—to that environment.

"Just be careful and call me if you need me," he said before standing and walking out.

It was nice to know he cared. Things were very different between us nowadays. I was so glad we had finally managed to work our shit out and be brothers once again. I finished up the report and got ready to leave. I was going straight to the bar to meet Elijah.

I saw him at a table, but before I headed in that direction, I looked around. I was still a little nervous it was a setup. I didn't notice any of his bodyguards. He appeared to be all alone. He looked up and put up his hand as if I hadn't noticed him.

"Hey," I said taking the empty seat at the table.

"Thanks for showing up. I didn't think you would."

I chuckled. "I wasn't sure you'd show up alone."

He smiled. "I deserved that."

"It's in the past, right?"

He nodded. "It is. Is it all in the past?"

I knew exactly what he was getting at. "I'm trying. I really am. She is too."

"It's a tough situation. I was only looking out for her. You've got to know my dad isn't a kind man."

"I do know that, but it isn't what Nat wants. I would never disrespect your sister. You have to know that," I said, looking him straight in the eye.

He took a drink from his glass. "I do know that. I've been doing a lot of thinking and I'm man enough to admit I may have been wrong."

The waitress delivered me a rum and Coke before disappearing.

"Wrong about?" I asked.

"She's not happy," he mumbled.

"I agree."

"Is it because of you?"

"Me?" I asked, my brows raised.

"You said you weren't seeing her anymore. I think it was about that time I noticed something changed in her. There is a profound sadness in her. I don't know if my dad sees it. I should have kept my mouth shut," he grumbled, running a hand over his face.

"What do you mean?"

"I told her I knew the two of you were seeing each other again. One of my friends saw you together at the bar in her building. I asked her about it," he confessed.

I nodded, vaguely remembering her mentioning the confrontation. "I don't know if that was the trigger. I think we both realized us being together was just not going to happen. Your dad would never accept me—never."

"I only told her I knew because I didn't want her making a mistake and getting caught by dad. I don't know what he'll do if he finds out."

I shrugged a shoulder. "No worries. There's nothing to find out. It's over."

"Jack, I know you better than that. Besides, I don't like seeing her so melancholy."

I mulled over whether or not to tell him about seeing her the other night. If we were going to be friends again, I wanted to be honest. I didn't need to give him all the details, but I wanted him to know I wasn't going to disappear from her life altogether.

"I stopped by her place the other night," I said, waiting for his reaction.

His glass was halfway to his mouth. "You did?"

"I was worried about her after you stopped by my office."

He relaxed and took a drink. "And?"

"And I agree, something is off, but she wouldn't tell me what it was. She said she was under a lot of stress with her new job and the move," I explained.

"Bullshit."

I chuckled and took a long drink. "I agree."

"She's tougher than that. The new company is moving along without any problems. She's kicking ass. My dad is thrilled with her progress. There's no reason for her to be stressed." He nearly growled.

I held up my hands. "I'm only telling you what she told me. I didn't believe her and tried to press her for more information, but she isn't talking to me. Things are a little strained between us."

"I'm sorry about that. You said you had a date the other night?" he asked.

"I did."

He grinned. "I take it things didn't go so well."

"Elijah, I'm not going to lie. I'm in love with your sister. I know we can't be together, and I accept it. I'm doing my best to move on. It doesn't mean I'm looking forward to the moving on, but I want to do what's best for her. She deserves to be happy. I'll take a step back and let her move on. That's what I'm trying to do. I'm hoping to date and that she'll date, and eventually, all this will go away."

He leaned forward, and I got the sense he was very serious. "But what if that isn't the right thing to do? What if she's brokenhearted because of your decision to move on?"

I shrugged a shoulder and shook my head. "We've been trying to make it work for years. It isn't going to. We're moving on," I said firmly, even though I didn't truly believe it.

"All right, all right. I'll let it go. How's everything else been going?" he asked, effectively switching subjects.

I smiled, happy to put the Natasha thing to rest. I wanted to be friends with Elijah and that meant not dwelling on the past and what had driven us apart. We talked a bit more about our jobs and what we hoped to do down the road.

"Any chance your dad is going to retire soon?" I teased.

He groaned. "I don't think so. He doesn't trust me to run the company. I don't think he'll ever willingly retire."

"Sorry to hear that."

"I can't say I'm surprised. He's been telling me for most of my life I wasn't good enough to fill his shoes."

I shook my head, hating to see the guy struggle for the acceptance from his father. I didn't think he'd ever get it. Wayne Levy had some very high standards. I had to wonder if his jaded view of life was partially my father's fault. For that, I was very sorry. The Levy children didn't deserve to pay for what my father did. Hell, Wayne was intent on punishing the entire world for what my father had done. It was a little ridiculous and I would love the chance to tell the man to get over it.

"I think I'm going to have to call it a night," I said around midnight.

"Me too. When did we get old?"

"Somewhere around five years ago," I joked.

"It was good to catch up. I hope we can do this again," he said.

"I'd like that. Give me a call. You know my number," I told him.

We stood and shook hands before I left the bar. It was good to have that bridge mended. I'd really missed having him in my life. Although things had been a little strained between us, because I'd had to lie to him for so long, I was looking forward to a renewed friendship.

CHAPTER 60

NATASHA

I stared in the mirror, remembering what Jack had told me Elijah had said about me looking sick. I didn't want my parents to be of the same opinion and grill me about being sick. If they thought I was under the weather, they would insist I go to a doctor. That would not end well.

Instead, I decided to be crafty and cover it all up. I carefully swept the blusher over my cheekbones, feeling a little silly for putting on so much makeup just to go to dinner at the family mansion, but it had to be done. I wasn't in the mood to answer a bunch of questions about my health.

Elijah was going to be there, and I didn't want him thinking I was truly sick. He had a tendency to be a little overprotective, which I didn't really mind. It was nice to know I had someone looking out for me. I could admit I had been a little paler than usual. That tended to happen when the first hours of the morning were spent vomiting and the hours after were spent nibbling on saltines. I hoped the blush and the new foundation I had put on disguised my sickly appearance. I added a pale-pink lipstick and called it good. I didn't want to go overboard, then they'd suspect something was up.

I was damned if I did and damned if I didn't. I grabbed my jacket and headed down to the ground floor where the car I had ordered would be waiting. I was dreading the dinner only because I knew I had a secret to hide and wasn't sure if I could keep it much longer. I had barely stepped off the elevator when my phone started to ring.

"Hey," I answered when I saw it was Ashley.

"Are you on your way?" she asked.

I groaned. "I am. I put on a ton of makeup."

"Good. You'll do fine. Just try and act normal," she advised.

I laughed. "You've met my family."

"No one can tell. It isn't like you have a big baby bump. Just be cool and it will be fine. Although, you will have to tell them eventually."

"I know, I know, I just don't want it to be today."

"Good luck and try to have fun."

I was strolling toward the front entrance and stopped. "Come with me," I blurted out.

She burst into laughter. "I'm not going with you to a family dinner."

"Come on. You're like a part of the family. You know my parents always invite you. Come on, don't leave me alone," I begged.

"I'm not leaving you alone. You're going to be okay. Eat dinner, chat, and then go home."

"Fine," I mumbled, hanging up the phone and heading outside, the cool evening air blowing my hair and sending a chill down my spine.

When the car pulled in front of the house, I looked up at the huge double doors and felt a sense of foreboding. I took a deep breath and got out of the car, then walked up to the door and glanced back at the car that was moving to park farther down the driveway. I could still escape. I thought about jumping back in and ordering the driver to get the hell out of there.

"No, you can't," I whispered moving up the walk and knocking on the door.

It felt a little strange to knock and I knew I didn't have to, but I didn't live there. I was a guest. One of the housekeepers answered the door, looking a little confused but gesturing for me to go inside.

"Everyone is in the formal living room," she told me.

"Thank you," I said and made my way down the hall.

I could hear the silent buzz of conversation and smell my father's cigar. That wouldn't be good for the baby was my first thought. My second thought was the smell was making me feel nauseated. I could do this. I had to pretend everything was normal.

"Hi, everyone," I said in greeting, walking in with what I hoped was a bright smile on my face.

"There you are," my father grumbled, and I could tell he was in a bad mood right away.

I should have stayed home. I shouldn't have bothered getting out of the car. When my dad got in one of his moods, it was never good. I looked up to see Elijah giving me a subtle shake of my head, telling me to tread carefully. We both knew our father well enough to know his moods could be volatile.

Elijah held up a glass of red wine. "Here, you'll need this."

I walked to where he was and grabbed a bottle of water. "No, thank you."

He raised an eyebrow. "Really?"

I smiled. "I had a little too much to drink last night. I'll stick with water."

He nodded. "I understand completely."

I forced a giggle. "Did you go out last night?"

"I did. I had a few drinks but I'm not as young as I used to be," he said on a sigh.

I tried to smile and appear normal. "No, you're not."

He studied my face. "You look better, healthier. Is everything okay now?"

"It was never not okay. You should have talked to me if you thought I was sick," I told him.

"I did. You told me you were fine, but it was clear you weren't. I'm glad to see you looking more like your old self," he said in a hushed tone.

I took a drink of water. "Thanks."

"Let's go on in to dinner. We don't want to eat it cold," my mother announced.

I was happy to leave the small intimate room where all there was to do was talk. At least at dinner I could pretend to eat and have a distraction. I trailed behind as we moved down the hall, still considering my escape options. We took our seats and were served salad almost immediately. It was always a well-choreographed dance when my mother had a dinner served. It was generally at least five courses. I knew I had to pace myself to make it look like I was eating more than I was. I listened silently as the three of them chatted about nothing in particular. I did my best to smile and nod when appropriate without actually saying a word. I was lost in my own thoughts, pushing the lettuce and vegetables around the plate, silently counting down the minutes until I could make my escape home.

"What's been going on with you lately?" my dad asked in a gruff voice.

I looked up from my plate to find him staring at me. "What?" I asked with confusion.

"You're not saying a word. You have something more important to be doing?" he growled.

I shook my head. "No, Dad. I was listening to you guys talk," I reasoned.

His lip curled in disgust. "We didn't invite you to dinner to have you sit there and mope. You know I don't like moping at the table."

I took a deep breath, setting my fork down on the plate. "I'm not moping."

"Something's not right with you. Everyone has noticed. What is it? Have you changed your mind? I knew this would happen," he muttered under his breath.

"What are you talking about? What would happen? I haven't changed my mind about anything!"

"You haven't been to any of the weekly meetings. I hear you're skipping work and you're behind schedule. I knew you weren't ready to have your own company. Look at your brother. He's years older than you and he isn't ready," he accused.

I felt Elijah stiffen beside me and immediately felt guilty for bringing him into my father's wrath that was currently directed at me.

I blinked several times. "I'm not skipping work."

"You've not been showing up to the corporate meetings," he shot back.

I shrugged a shoulder. "I didn't think I needed to."

"Bullshit." He slapped his hand on the table, the silverware clinking as it bounced.

"Wayne." My mom hissed.

"Dad, relax. She's starting a new company," Elijah said defending me.

"You keep out of it. You wanted this, Natasha. You begged me to let you have this company," he lectured.

My mouth fell open. "I didn't beg you. I wanted to do it on my own. You're the one who insisted I open the company as an offset of Levy Industries. I could have done it on my own," I insisted, hurt and angry at the same time.

He rolled his eyes. "You couldn't have done it on your own. I was trying to be nice. You need to pull your weight, or I will take it all away."

I shook my head. "You can't take it away. It's mine."

"You don't want it."

"Dad, it's mine. I do want it. I'm doing the best I can," I said, fighting back a sob.

He took a drink, staring at me with such malice I could practically feel it. "You've been neglecting your responsibilities. Look at you, you've barely said two words since you've been here."

"Dad, she's not feeling well. I think you need to lighten up," Elijah said again.

His fury that had been directed at me turned to Elijah. "I don't need your two cents. You sit there and shut up. This is my business. You have no room to talk. You've been skating by for years."

He shook his head. "That isn't fair."

"Shut-up and save your whining for work," he snapped.

I couldn't believe he was acting so callous and mean. I had seen him angry before, but I couldn't remember him being so dismissive. He was looking at Elijah and me as if he hated us.

His angry gaze turned back to me. I actually flinched. "Well?" he boomed.

"Well what?" I asked, feeling a little exhausted.

"What's wrong with you?" he asked exasperated.

I stared back at him. I could lie and tell him nothing was wrong. I was so tired of hiding. I was being stretched thin and keeping my secret was killing me slowly. He was going to find out eventually. What was the difference if I told him now or in a few months or in a year when I showed up with a baby on my hip.

I looked at Elijah, who was clearly very interested in what I had to say. My mom was pretending to sip her wine, but judging by how fast it was disappearing, I could tell she was guzzling it in a very unlady-like fashion.

"I'm pregnant," I said the words, feeling them crossing my lips, but barely hearing them.

Elijah leaned closer to me. "What'd you say?" he whispered.

My father's glare intensified. "I don't think I heard you correctly." My father's cold, steely voice hit me like a glass of ice water being dumped over my head.

I took a deep breath. In for a penny, in for a pound. "I'm pregnant."

"Holy shit." Elijah gasped from beside me.

My mother stared at me, her glass hovering above the table as she held it, then she turned her gaze slowly to my father. He scowled at me as if I had just announced I had murdered someone while being high on heroine.

No one spoke. Hell, I don't think anyone breathed for several long seconds. At first, I was beginning to think I hadn't actually said it. Maybe it was one of those weird daydreams where I only thought I had said it, but really, I hadn't.

"Who's the father?" my dad asked, his voice dead cold.

There went my theory that it had all been a daydream. I opened my mouth and snapped it shut. Shit was about to hit the proverbial fan. I really wished I could have a glass of wine, or a bottle was more like it.

CHAPTER 61

JACK

"**A**re you headed out?" Grayson asked when I stopped by his office to drop off the report.

"Yes, I'm meeting Mason at the gym."

Grayson chuckled. "Do you think he's going to be sticking around?"

I shrugged. "I have no idea. Seems like it. He's changed a lot in the last year, don't you think?"

"Maybe, but how long will it last?" he asked.

"That's anybody's guess, but it makes Mom happy to have him in town. She likes it when we're all close," I replied.

"True. Keep him happy so he'll stay around," Grayson ordered.

I burst into laughter. "Maybe we could go get a couple tats together. I could grow my hair out and buy a motorcycle."

He shrugged a shoulder. "Whatever works."

"Thanks. I'll take one for the team."

He laughed. "I would, but I don't think Hannah would be okay with me hanging out in those biker bars."

"It's cool. I don't mind. I like hanging out with him," I said honestly.

I did like hanging out with Mason. I had been pleasantly surprised to find Mason and I had a lot more in common than I expected.

"Have fun," he said when I turned to leave.

I glanced back, unable to resist the easy opening to make fun of him. "You might want to think about hitting the gym with us one of these days."

He looked stunned and offended at the same time. "What? Really?" he asked, looking down at his chest and belly.

I howled in laughter and walked away. A little old-fashioned joking among brothers was good for the soul.

I walked into the gym, expecting to find Mason hitting on the woman running the smoothie bar or maybe in the locker room with another woman. One never really knew when it came to him. He was impulsive and didn't seem to have one particular type. He loved all women equally. I was surprised to see him on one of the weight machines, already working on his legs.

"Damn, you're an overachiever," I said, walking toward him.

"I didn't know if you'd show up and I wasn't going to waste time," he replied with a grunt as he lifted the stack of weights with his heavily muscled thighs.

"I told you I was coming."

He smirked. "Shocking."

"Whatever. Not all of us have the luxury of being a gym rat."

"Hey, you have just as much money as I do. You can be a gym rat. No, scratch that, you'd never make it."

"Are you done?" I asked with exaggerated irritability.

"Get dressed, I'll be here." He grunted again.

I nodded and headed for the locker room to change into my shorts and tank. I needed a grueling workout. I was starting over on my self-imposed Natasha banishment. Hitting the gym was one way to work out the frustration. I made it back out to the gym floor and took my turn on the weight machine. I lifted a little less than Mason. Few men lifted as much as he did.

"What's with you and Natasha?" he asked working his triceps and making me look really bad.

"There is nothing with us. I ended it."

"What happened with Elijah? I didn't get the call to come and bail you out or take you to the emergency room, so I assumed things went well or the little weasel stood you up."

I smirked. "It went fine. We're going to be friends again or at least try not to kill each other."

He guffawed, switching to do his other arm. "I guess that's progress. I still think you should hit him at least once."

"It could still happen," I replied. "We talked a little. It was good to catch up with him. I don't really blame him for what happened. He was only doing what his father ordered. If it wouldn't have been him, it would have been the goons. I fucked up. I should have been more careful," I said, long ago coming to terms with what had happened.

"He doesn't want to kill you for banging his sister?"

I scowled at him. "I'm not banging his sister. It was never like that. It doesn't matter now because it's over."

Mason stood in front of me, looking me dead in the eye. "Bullshit."

"What?" I asked, shrugging a shoulder.

"I can tell you're lying. It isn't over. I can tell by the way you talk about her that it isn't over. You get that look in your eyes."

I wrinkled my nose. "What look?"

"It's a look. You want her."

"Of course, I want her. I'm not denying that."

"When's the last time you saw her?" he asked directly.

I sucked in a deep breath. "Elijah wanted to talk to me about Nat. He was concerned about her, which made me concerned about her."

He grinned. "Thought so. You were so concerned for her, you had to see her for yourself."

I hung my head down, not looking at him. I felt like a kid getting busted with his hand in the cookie jar. "I stopped by her place last week to check on her. I stayed a while," I said, not telling him anything, but knowing he'd know what happened.

Mason was grinning. "I knew it. Does big brother know?"

"He knows I went by. I didn't give him details."

"You don't think he suspects anything?"

371

I shrugged. "I don't know. I don't think I care. If he suspects anything, he didn't say it. He almost seemed to be telling me to try and get back together with her."

He whistled low. "You're walking on thin ice. If Elijah finds out you lied to him, he's going to be pissed. It's one thing to stop by, it's another thing to do what I'm guessing you did."

"I didn't lie to him. I did go to her place to check on her. That was my only intention. I am worried about her, just like he is. He told me he thought maybe he was wrong about the situation."

"Wrong about what situation?" Mason asked.

"Wrong as in he shouldn't have butted his nose in and worked so hard to split us up. I think he sees how upset Nat is and realizes what we had wasn't just a fling. It was serious," I snapped.

"I think you need to be careful. Those Levys are no joke. I'd hate to see what happens when they find out you didn't listen after the first warning," Mason warned.

"I'm not worried about Elijah or Wayne. I know something isn't right with her. Even if we can't be together, I still care about her. I won't let them intimidate me or keep me away from her if she needs me."

He shook his head. "You're asking me if it's okay for you to go see her, aren't you? You want me to tell you it's okay."

I wrinkled my nose. "I'm not asking you shit. I don't need your permission."

Deep down, I did want someone to tell me it was okay. I wanted someone, just one person to be supportive of my relationship with Natasha. As much as I said it didn't matter, there was a little part of me that wanted someone to be happy for us, to say we should be together.

He chuckled and moved to grab a heavier weight. "Listen, can I give you my honest opinion?"

"Ha! Like you really need to ask me. You're going to tell me anyway."

"You're right. I am, and I think you should listen," he started, and I knew I was in for his usual brutal honesty.

"Hit me."

"I think you went about ending it all wrong. You're still into her and she's still into you. That whole wanting what you can't have thing is still pulling you two together," he reasoned.

I shrugged with a nod. "I get that."

"Cold turkey is tough on anyone. It isn't for the faint of heart and I think it is a method best applied to things like drinking and smoking, not love. Love isn't something you can just turn off or quit."

"We tried to ease apart, and it didn't work. The only other thing was to just cut things off completely. You don't understand how it is with us. I can't have her a little bit. Whenever we're together, it's like a magnetic force. I can't keep my hands off her," I confessed, feeling a little ridiculous.

"Jack, you've always gone after what you want. Granted, you're rarely ever denied anything you want, but this thing with Natasha, I think it's making you a little crazy. You want her, and you can't have her."

It wasn't a big surprise. I had already figured that out. Natasha knew it as well. The idea of wanting what we couldn't have was exciting, but we had gone beyond that. We loved each other. We weren't simply rebelling.

"Thanks for that insight," I mumbled.

We finished working out, not talking any more about Natasha or the forbidden relationship. I agreed to get a smoothie with him after our workout. It was then he brought up the Nat situation again.

"You love her?"

I nodded. "I do. I really do."

"Then why in the hell are you holding back?" he asked bluntly.

"It isn't that easy. You don't think I've already tried? I'm holding back because I have no intention of ruining her life and making her miserable."

"Didn't you just tell me she is miserable?" he shot back.

"Yes, but she'll get over this. She would never get over her father disowning her and that is exactly what will happen if she is with me. I'm not going to do that to her."

He sucked on his frozen smoothie, reminding me of a little kid. "I don't know. The Jack I knew went after what he wanted. This isn't like you."

It wasn't like me to give up or walk away from something I wanted, but I truly felt I was doing it for her. I wanted her to be happy. I finished my smoothie, grabbed my clothes from the locker room, and headed for my car. I got inside but didn't start it. I sat there staring at the wheel before grabbing my phone.

"Hi," I said when Nat answered the phone.

"Hi," she said, and I could tell something was wrong.

"Nat, what's wrong, sweetie?" I said, switching to a soft voice.

"Nothing. I'm fine," she said, and I could tell she was anything but fine.

"Are you at home?" I asked her.

I heard what sounded like a hiccup. "Yes, I am. Why? What's up?" she asked, trying to sound lighthearted.

"I'm coming over," I told her.

"No!"

"Nat, we need to talk," I insisted.

I heard her muffle the phone. "Jack, now isn't really a good time. Can we talk later?"

I thought about it for a second. "No. I want to see you now."

"Jack, please, can we do this later? I'm really not up for company," she said, exhaustion in her voice.

A thought occurred. I cleared my throat. "Do you have someone there?" I asked, almost afraid to hear the answer.

"No, no, it's nothing like that. I just want to be alone," she whispered.

That's when I made up my mind. "I'm coming over. Don't try and lock me out. I have cash and your security guards like me," I said, ending the call and starting my car.

She was going to tell me what was going on with her. I was worried about her. If she was truly miserable because I had ended things, then I was going to tell her we would fight her dad. The way I saw it, she was going to be miserable in either situation, but at least if we were together, I could try and make her happy. And selfishly, I would be happy as well.

I pulled onto the street, anxious to see her. Wayne Levy could kiss my ass.

CHAPTER 62

NATASHA

I hung up the phone and dashed into my bedroom. I was a mess. My eyes were probably red and swollen. Not probably. I knew damn well they were. My life was a mess. My big idea to tell my dad about my pregnancy had gone worse than I expected.

I looked at myself in the mirror and winced. "Not good," I muttered, rubbing my hands down my cheeks before reaching for the powder on my vanity.

I quickly brushed some powder over my red nose and realized that wasn't enough. I grabbed the concealer and dabbed it under my eyes before gently rubbing it in, minimizing the dark circles but not concealing them.

I brushed my hair before pulling it into a ponytail, then yanking it back out. With my hair pulled back, it made the dark circles and red eyes look more pronounced. Then it was a look at my outfit and I groaned again. There was nothing to do about my appearance I realized. He was going to see me at my worst.

When I heard the door buzz, I knew my time was up. I was going to have to face him. I hit the button, letting him come up without having to pay the guards. I opened the door and waited for him to step off the elevator.

The moment he looked at me, his face fell, and he rushed toward me, cupping one of my cheeks in his palm and looking into my eyes. "Nat, what's wrong?"

I shook my head. I didn't want to tell him. "Nothing. Just a bad day," I said, trying to play it off.

He grabbed my hand and walked with me to the couch, ordering me to sit.

"Please tell me what is going on here and don't say nothing. I know you well enough to know when something is wrong. You haven't been yourself for over a month now. Is it me? Us? Is this because I said we had to end things?"

I smiled, not wanting to tell him that he hit the nail on the head. "No, I know that was the right thing to do. I've been saying it for years and you were just the one to make it happen."

"Nat, come on. Did something happen since then? That night you went to my house, I knew something was wrong. I should have made you talk to me then. Please, tell me. I won't take no for an answer this time," he said, and I knew he was serious.

I took a deep breath. "My dad found out about us."

"He already knew about us."

"No, I mean, when I got back from California. He knows we were seeing each other."

He nodded. "Well, that was then. It's over. We aren't together. He should be happy. He won."

I visibly flinched at his words. It hurt a little to hear him say them so callously. I had to come clean. I had already pissed off my entire family, I may as well get it all out in the open. The sooner it was out, the sooner I could start picking up the pieces and moving on. Delaying the inevitable was only going to prolong the pain and suffering.

"Jack, there's more," I said hesitantly.

"What is it, sweetie?" he asked gently.

I looked into his eyes and dreaded what I had to say. Ashley's words echoed through my mind. I owed him the chance to make his own decision about his involvement. I didn't need him in my life.

Ashley would be there for me. She was a strong woman and would be there for me when things got tough.

"I'm pregnant," I said the words that had nearly destroyed my life just a short couple days ago.

It was like waving a loaded weapon around. The words had the power to destroy and ruin relationships. I had been treated as if I were dead.

"You're what?" Jack asked, his hand still holding mine, his gaze steady and unblinking.

"I'm pregnant," I repeated.

"You're pregnant," he said as if the words were a foreign language.

I was growing tired of the shocked expressions. "Yes, Jack, pregnant. I'm pregnant. With a baby."

He nodded before he started to shake his head. "Wow."

"Yes, wow."

"That's what has been wrong with you?" he asked as if it was all coming together in his mind.

I sighed. "Yes, which by the way, is still rude."

"I'm sorry. You look pale. Are you well?" he asked, still appearing dumbfounded.

"Yes, I'm well enough. I'm not dying. I'm pregnant," I said, really getting irritated.

He was staring at me, then his eyes dropped to my belly. "You're pregnant," he said it again.

I decided to sit back and wait until the shock had subsided. Hopefully once it all sank in, we could have an actual adult conversation.

"Oh, I forgot to add, my dad knows."

"Your dad knows?" he asked leaning back on the couch as well, our shoulders bumping against each other.

"Oh yeah. He knows and as you can imagine, he didn't take the news well."

Jack sat forward and turned to look back at me. "What did he do? Are you okay? Does he know it's mine?"

I smiled. I liked that he didn't ask if he was the father. I wasn't sure how I would have handled that question. I would have understood if he did ask, but I was glad he didn't.

"I'm fine. He is mad, furious really."

"But he knows it's mine?" he asked.

"He does now," I confessed, wincing at the memory of his response.

It had been an ugly, explosive, nasty rant that my father had erupted in once he figured out who the father of my child was. There was no one who could have stopped the horrible things my father spewed at me. The only thing that ended the tirade was me walking out the front door.

"Nat, what did he do? Did he hurt you?" he asked, his hands moving over my arms and then my face, searching for injuries.

"He didn't hurt me."

"I'm so sorry you had to do that. I should have been there."

I burst into laughter. "Absolutely not. That would have made things a lot worse."

He was shaking his head, anger making the vein at his neck bulge and throb. "What did he do?" He hissed.

I took a deep breath. "Let me get us something to drink. I'm feeling rather dehydrated."

I stood up and walked to the refrigerator, grabbing a couple ginger ales and carrying them back to the couch. Jack was sitting on the edge, his face buried in his hands. I knew I had just dropped a huge bombshell on him. I felt a little guilty for not telling him sooner. I should have.

"Thanks," he said, taking the bottle.

I sat back down on the couch, not quite as close, but near. "He has disowned me."

"I'm so sorry, Nat. I know this is going to sound really stupid, but how did this happen?"

I grinned, so happy to have everything out in the open. "Well, I would imagine it happened that first time after I got back."

"But why now? I don't understand. We've been having sex for years. I've never worn protection. I thought you said it was handled.

I'm sorry. I would have taken precautions. I should have taken precautions," he said.

I grimaced. "I was. It was the move. I got distracted and I didn't always take my pill. I'm sorry. It was irresponsible on my part."

"No, don't blame yourself. I can't believe this," he said, his shock still evident in his voice.

"I should have told you earlier. I'm sorry I didn't. I was still trying to come to terms with it," I explained.

"It's okay, really. What did your father say?" he asked again.

"I told him I was pregnant. He asked who the father was, and I thought about lying, but then figured once you found out, it would be pointless to try and hide it. Plus, I really didn't want to hide it. To hide it would mean I was ashamed. I'm not ashamed," I explained.

He nodded and reached for my hand again. "Good. Okay, but what did he do? I can tell you've been crying. It's pretty obvious things didn't go well."

"It was a family dinner. My mom and Elijah were both there. My dad was laying into me about slacking off at work and said I was just kind of screwing up, and I just lost it. I blurted out I was pregnant. Then things got a little crazy. Basically, it ended with him forbidding me from ever darkening his door again. He doesn't want to speak to me ever again."

Jack's jaw clenched. "Bullshit. He has no right to treat you like that. You're a grown woman."

"I've never seen him so angry. He broke some of my mother's crystal. Elijah tried to calm him down, but it was no use. I'm not even really sure what my mom thinks. She was too busy freaking out over the broken crystal," I said, shaking my head.

"He's mad. He'll settle down," he said, trying to reassure me.

I shook my head. Jack didn't understand the situation. I cleared my throat. "Jack, I've never seen my dad so furious. I'm worried he is going to come after you."

His face twisted in anger. "He wouldn't dare and if he does, that's fine with me. I've got a few things I'd like to say to him."

"You can't!" I gasped.

"I can. I'm tired of him treating you like you're a two-year-old. You're a grown woman. You're having my child and I will not be ashamed. I'm sorry he said things that clearly hurt you. That isn't okay. I want him to stay away from me and if he can't treat you with respect, he doesn't need to be around you either."

I scoffed. "That'll be easy enough, considering he isn't speaking to me, and says he will never speak to me again. He made all kinds of threats about taking my company. He can't, I know he can't, but he is going to try and make things rough. Please don't make it worse for me," I begged.

"Nat, I'm telling you, I will not back down to him. Not anymore. I won't do anything that makes things worse for you, but I won't stand by and watch him hurt you," he said firmly.

I smiled, appreciating how nice he was being and how well he was taking the news. He was a remarkable man. I had known that for a long time but seeing him and watching him get so angry about the way my father had treated me was sweet. It made me feel warm and fuzzy inside. I knew he would be protective.

"Jack, please be careful. I don't know what my father might do. He was really angry, and I know he feels I betrayed him. To him, I just committed a horrible crime."

"It isn't a crime. It's my baby."

I took a drink from the bottle of ale and felt myself relax a little. I was glad he had insisted on coming over. I wanted to believe the worst was over. Somewhere in the back of my mind, I knew it was more likely the worst was still to come. I had only seen the first wave of my father's anger. If I knew my dad, he was already plotting and planning his revenge. He would go after Jack. It wasn't a matter of if, but when.

I just prayed Jack was truly ready for it.

CHAPTER 63

JACK

I felt as if I needed to be pinched to make sure I wasn't caught up in one of those dreams that felt super real but was nothing more than a dream. Nat looked scared, truly terrified, and it made no sense to me. She was worried her father was going to do something to me. I didn't give a shit about Wayne Levy in that moment. I was still trying to wrap my head around the idea Nat was pregnant. With my baby. It had to be my baby. I knew her well enough to know that—didn't I?

"I'm not worried about your dad, so please don't worry about it either," I assured her.

She gave me a small smile. "You say that, but we both know how my dad can get."

I shook my head. "I don't care. It's you I'm concerned about."

She leaned back, looking up at me with worry all over her face. "Are you mad?"

"Am I mad *at* or about what?" I asked, my brain felt as if it were a gooey puddle of mud and moved incredibly slow and sluggish.

"About the baby, me being pregnant?" she asked in a small voice.

"What? How could I be mad?"

She shrugged a dainty shoulder, her eyes still full of such pain and regret I wanted to make it all go away. "Because I didn't tell you?" she whispered.

"Nat, I'm not angry. I mean, I'm guessing you haven't known all that long and honestly, you can't be all that far into this thing. I wish you would have told me earlier, only so I could have tried to help you in some way. I knew something was off, but I didn't know what. I don't know what I could have done to help, but I would do anything to take some of the burden," I told her, meaning every word.

"I'm sorry. I wanted to tell you, but then you said we should stop seeing each other."

"Because I didn't know. I said that because I wanted to make things better for you," I explained.

She smiled. "That's another reason I didn't tell you."

"Because I wanted to make it better?" I asked with confusion, my head still lagging in the conversation.

She pulled away from me completely and rubbed her hands down her face. "Yes. Jack, you're the kind of man who takes everything on. You would have given up everything to be there for me. I didn't want to trap you. I didn't want you to feel trapped. I'm perfectly capable of handling this situation."

I shook my head. "I don't feel trapped."

"Jack, we're over. You said it. I said it. We're through," she said, reminding me. Her words stinging a little.

I had said that. She had insisted on it. That was before I knew there was a child involved. I understood what she was saying. We couldn't be together just for the child's sake. Why not?

"Natasha, whatever is happening with us and the part where we can't be together, it doesn't change how I feel about you. You know I love you. I care so much about you it is all I think about most days," I told her, reaching out and cupping her cheek in my hand.

She smiled again. "I care about you as well. I do, but I can't keep doing this back and forth."

"I know. You shouldn't have to. I hate seeing you so stressed out and sad."

She looked away, staring out the windows. "I'll be okay. It was just a lot to deal with at once. This is my problem to deal with, and I will."

I bristled at her word choice. "I don't think it's a problem at all."

"Not the baby, my family situation. We can't be together because my family is horrible." She pouted.

"Nat, it's up to you, but I think you really need to think about what's best for you now," I said, trying to broach the subject as gently as possible.

"What do you mean?"

"I mean maybe it's time you worried about your own happiness and quit worrying about what everyone else thinks. This is your life."

She smirked. "It seems like I've made a real mess of things."

"No, you haven't. You've done nothing wrong."

"I tried to spare my family the horrors of me falling in love with the wrong man. I was willing to let you go and what we had just to make my family happy. I thought with time, things would get better. In the back of my mind, I kept thinking maybe one day my dad would suddenly say he didn't hate you and that if I wanted to be with you, I had his blessing. I should have known it would never happen like that. I know my father and when he sets his mind to something, that's all there is. There's no changing it," she said, the strain and sadness in her voice made me hate her father more than I already did.

"Natasha, for once, let's not worry about anyone else and what they feel about us being together. We've put our lives on hold for almost five years because we were trying to make everyone else happy. You love me, and I love you. That's all that matters."

She giggled softly. "We've said that before, too, and look how that turned out."

"I survived," I said, knowing she was referring to the beat down over a year ago.

I would do it all over again. I would take a much harder beating if it meant I could be with her and raise our child together. This had all gone on long enough.

"I knew you would say all this," she said on a sigh.

"That's because you know me well and I know you. I know you want me," I said with a sexy grin.

She laughed. The sound was refreshing after seeing her so sad and in such pain. "That has never been our problem."

"Our bodies can't be wrong. Our bodies and souls know we're supposed to be together. There's no other explanation for the way we feel when we're in the same room. It's an attraction that goes beyond anything a person can explain. There is a connection between us that will never go away, and I don't want it to," I told her, basically pouring my heart out and feeling very nervous about doing so.

She released another long sigh. "I wish it were that easy."

"It can be."

"Jack," she said my name in weak protest.

I shook my head. "Natasha, this is right. We're right. The child growing inside of you is right. I don't want to fight your family anymore. I just want to be happy. I want you to be happy. I want to be happy with you."

"You make it sound so easy. You know it isn't. Look at what we've been through. We keep trying and we always end up right back in this place where one of us is pushing the other away."

"Are you pushing me away?" I asked, suddenly realizing I may have had everything all wrong.

She didn't immediately answer me. "I don't know," she finally said in a small voice.

I was stunned. Hurt and furious at the same time. She was really going to try and push me out of her life while she was carrying my child. All because her daddy didn't like me.

I stood up, needing to put some space between us. I walked to the windows, taking deep breaths to tamp down my anger before turning to look at her.

"You didn't want to trap me?"

She shook her head. "No, I didn't."

"What you're really saying is *you* didn't want to be trapped." I hissed, anger burning a hole in my gut.

"No! I'm not saying that at all. The baby, it was unexpected. We had already decided to go our separate ways. You yourself said you understood why it was better that way. You can't go back on that now," she said, standing, but not moving toward me.

I shook my head, running a hand through my hair. "I said that because I finally understood what you had been saying all those years. I didn't realize there was a child involved!"

"Exactly. You said what you felt, which is exactly why I didn't tell you about the baby. You wouldn't have told me how you were really feeling. You would have tried to go along as if everything was okay, when inside you were feeling anything but happy. You said we could never be happy together. Maybe you were right," she said, shrugging.

I wanted to scream at the ceiling. I should have let her go first that night. I should have kept my mouth shut. Why, after five fucking years, did I choose that moment to agree with her? I wished I could go back, rewind, and redo.

"Natasha, that isn't fair. You've been pulling me along for years. I finally understood what you were trying to say. You know it isn't what I wanted," I said.

"But, isn't it right? We will never have a normal life with our families showing up for family dinners or holiday gatherings," she insisted.

I shook my head. "I thought that, too, but who cares? Who cares if they're happy? They had their lives. This one is ours. This is our life, our happiness. I'm not going to live for someone else. You're what makes me happy," I said with renewed vigor to make things work between us.

"You make me happy, but Jack—"

I held up a hand. "Don't say it. He's already kicked you out of his life. What've you got to lose?"

I moved toward her. I could see her processing my words and realizing I was right. She'd already crossed the bridge, burned it, and blew the damn thing up. There was no turning back, no taking back what had already happened and the hurtful things that had been said. I wasn't the kind of man to hold a grudge and I would be willing to open my door to the Levy family in the future, but it would be on my terms. I was tired of dancing around the man.

"But what if—"

I shook my head again, reaching out to cup her cheek, stepping closer to her, and letting her feel me—all of me. "They don't matter."

She sighed and leaned her cheek into my hand. "I want to say we can. I want to throw caution to the wind, but there's a part of me that's scared."

"I'm throwing caution to the wind. I want you and you want me. I'm not worried about anyone else except for us," I said, dropping my hands to her hips, pulling her lower body flush against mine.

I heard her gasp, her lips parting, and I took advantage, pressing my mouth over hers, pushing my tongue inside, and holding her in place when she tried to shove away.

"We shouldn't," she said, turning her head to the side, exposing her lovely neck.

"Why? Why shouldn't we do this?"

"Because, it complicates things," she said on a soft moan as my tongue ran a trail from her ear to her collarbone.

"Natasha, do you want me?" I asked in a husky tone.

She groaned again as I sucked her flesh between my lips.

"That's never the problem." She gasped.

"Then there is nothing stopping us. You want me. I can feel it. I can taste it. I can smell it," I whispered, moving my lips back to her ear.

"This is so bad, so wrong," she said, her arms finally going around my waist, pulling me even closer against her.

"It isn't bad. It's absolutely fucking perfect. Just like you, Nat. You're perfect. I want to show you how perfect you are," I told her and then lavished her neck with my mouth, as my hands held her hips against mine while my erection bloomed between us.

CHAPTER 64

NATASHA

He was too much for me to deny. Every little neuron in my brain was telling me he was all I needed. His hard length between us was making me quickly forget all about everything else. The way his mouth moved over my neck excited me. I gasped as he nibbled at my flesh, moving over my collarbone, tugging my shirt away. I held onto his hips as if I needed grounding.

He reached down, dragging my shirt slowly up my body until I leaned back, my arms in the air as he pulled it off.

"You're beautiful." He breathed, his knuckles brushing over my skin before beginning to love me with his mouth all over again. I couldn't move. I didn't want to move. His hot mouth left a trail of fire behind as he dropped to his knees in front of me, sliding my pants down a little at a time, his tongue making a ring around my belly button. I stepped out of the pants and stood before him in my panties. He gazed up at me with such sweet tenderness in his eyes that I wanted to drop to my knees in front of him and hold him close.

"Jack," I said his name, wanting him naked.

He kissed my belly again before standing and taking off his clothes in no real hurry at all. Every button heightened the anticipation. I could feel my desperation growing with each passing second. The heat between my legs caused me to squirm a little. I reached out, touching the patch of hair on his chest before trailing a finger down his flat stomach.

He stood in front of me, his black briefs stretched in the front with the outline of his hardness. I smiled reaching down to cup him before stepping close, wanting the skin-to-skin contact that always brought me such joy. My breasts rubbed against the crinkly hairs on his chest, setting off a fresh wave of goose bumps spreading over my skin and taking my breath away.

"Let's go to your room," he said, reaching his hands out to cup my cheeks before kissing me.

I turned, leading the way toward the double doors at the end of the hall. I didn't bother turning on the light as I strolled across the plush white carpet. His hands reached out and grabbed my hips, stopping me from getting in bed.

I turned to look at him, an eyebrow raised. His sexy smile told me he wasn't quite ready for bed, which was fine by me. I knew whatever he chose to do to my body was going to leave me quivering with desire. His mouth lowered to mine, kissing me deeply and stirring up the embers of the fire he'd started in the living room.

I groaned, my head leaning back as his mouth moved to my breasts. He suckled, pinching with his teeth before moving his hand between my legs, sliding under the fabric of my panties. I was already wet and hungry for him. His index finger parted my folds before gently probing inside. I stiffened as his finger pushed in, his mouth still working my breasts, and his other hand moved to cup my ass, squeezing hard. There were so many warring sensations happening at once as I felt that familiar, spinning sensation, and I knew I was close to losing control.

"Let it go. I've got you," he whispered, his mouth moving to my other breast as he continued to slide his long finger in and out, toying with my clit before pushing back inside.

I groaned, a long, low sound bubbling up from my belly as the orgasm started a slow burn through my body. The sensations of pure ecstasy spread throughout my body, leaving me gasping and arching as he took me higher and higher.

"There you go," he said, coming back up to stand in front of me, walking me backward until my legs hit the bed.

I could always depend on him to give my body exactly what it needed, even when I didn't know what it was. He stripped off his underwear before moving to slide mine down my legs. I stayed standing, giving him full control. Somewhere in the back of my mind I laughed at the idea of me giving him the control. He had all the control. He always did. He could dominate me in the bedroom. I didn't mind. In fact, it was exactly what I wanted. I didn't want to be the bossy woman running a company. I wanted to be the woman dominated by the sexiest man alive.

"I want you to ride me," he whispered, looking me straight in the eyes.

I nodded. "Okay."

He got onto the bed, propping himself up high on my pillows, his hard dick jutting forward as he held my eyes in the faint light streaming through the windows. I thought about closing the blinds, but quickly changed my mind. I liked watching him as he came, watching him as he made me orgasm.

My eyes roamed his body as I stood beside the bed. He made no move, daring me to look to my heart's content. When he reached down to wrap his hand around himself, I bit my bottom lip. He glanced down at himself and slowly stroked up and down before looking back at me.

"I'm waiting," he said in a raspy voice.

I crawled onto the bed, my knees sinking into the mattress on either side of him as I positioned myself over him. His hand was still wrapped around himself, holding his shaft as I tried to lower my body onto his. His knuckles brushed against my thigh as I pushed down. With his hand in the way, I could only get the first couple inches inside.

"Jack." I moaned, rotating my hips around him.

"What do you want, Nat?" He grunted as I pushed harder, his hand not budging.

"More."

"I didn't hear you," he rasped, his free hand moving to cup my breast.

"More, I need more!" I demanded, pushing down with more force.

His hand dropped from my breast, moving to squeeze my ass hard. "Say it again. Say it like you mean it!"

"More! More, God, I need more!" I screamed, using the full weight of my body to slam down on him, his hand pushed away by the force as he slid deep inside me.

My body exploded around him, bucking and arching as the orgasm tore through me with no warning at all. I heard myself crying out, jolting forward over him as everything turned a bright white.

"Fuck me." He growled, his hands moving to my hips and pulling me forward before pushing me back.

I whimpered as his dick scraped inside me, triggering another wild sensation of exploding nerve endings still raw from the orgasm. I moved, doing my best to please him. He was desperate, pushing and pulling my body over his, grunting and gasping as I took him deeper each time.

"Goddamn, you're so wet." He breathed.

I tried to agree. I couldn't speak. My body was completely in tuned to his. I was chasing another orgasm and this time, I was taking him with me. I could feel it in the way he was holding my hips, he was close. He was on the verge of losing control.

"Harder," I ordered, not sure if I was talking to myself or him.

"Go!" he shouted.

I felt like a jackrabbit, bouncing up and down, sliding back and forth in a frenzied race to an invisible finish line. I was determined to get there. I wouldn't stop until I reached the end. My breathing was coming fast and hard. I grabbed onto his shoulders, needing to brace myself as I let myself lose all control.

"Keep going! Don't stop," he roared.

There was a fierceness in his voice that kept me going. I could feel our bodies coiling together, knowing there was a violent orgasm at the finish line, I kept moving.

"Jack!" I screamed, feeling the first lightning bolt of ecstasy shoot through me.

"Don't. Fucking. Stop," he said through gritted teeth.

I didn't stop—I exploded. My body felt as if it shattered over him. I stiffened, not able to move as every muscle clenched. His loud roar felt as if it were coming from a thousand miles away. My body was paralyzed by the orgasm. He stiffened and rocketed his hips upward as he took his own release. Both of us gasping as our bodies joined on some higher plane.

I collapsed against his chest, my mouth opened as I struggled to grab air. His arms were around me, hugging me to his naked chest. I could feel his heart pounding under mine, beating hard and fast. I shuddered once and then again.

"You're cold," he murmured, moving to push the blankets down before somehow managing to pull them over our bodies, mine still draped over his.

"Wow," I whispered, turning my head to press my lips against his neck.

He chuckled, the sound vibrating against my chest. "That's one word for it."

"We have the most amazing sex," I said on a sigh.

"That we do," he agreed, rubbing my back.

"I should get off you," I mumbled, making no move to actually do it. I was hugging his warmth. I could see myself falling asleep exactly as I was. He was so comfortable and warm. His large body providing the safety and security I was craving after the situation with my father.

He laughed again. "I kind of like you clinging to my body, especially when you're naked."

I kissed his neck again, before finding the strength to dismount and cuddle next to him. "Stay?" I said the single word that meant so much.

"I will," he replied, before sliding down the bed and getting comfortable.

I rolled to my back, staring up at the ceiling and trying to think about what to say. I had told him about the baby, but we really hadn't gotten much further than that. I still didn't know where things stood. I needed to know how involved he was going to be. How much of this was I going to be doing on my own?

"Jack, what are we going to do? What does this mean for us?" I asked in a soft voice.

He reached down and splayed his hand over my belly. "We don't need to worry about that right this minute."

"What are we?" I asked, not satisfied with his answer.

He didn't answer for several minutes. His silence spoke volumes. I began to think he wasn't going to answer at all, which got me to thinking all kinds of horrible things. Maybe he wasn't the man I thought he was. Maybe the idea of having a baby with me was the final straw that broke the camel's back and he would truly leave me. I had been so worried about him wanting to be with me out of obligation, I hadn't even considered the other option.

"Stop," he whispered.

"Stop what?" I asked. I hadn't moved a muscle.

"I can hear you thinking the worst. I don't know what we are. We can figure things out together. Right now, sleep. It's late and we both need our rest," he ordered, his hand still over my belly as if he were protecting our unborn baby.

I closed my eyes, trying to calm my fears of doing it all alone. I knew he would be there for the child, but in what capacity I didn't know. My heart clenched at the thought of him sticking to his earlier decision and us staying apart. I should have told him I wanted to be with him. I should have told him he was right, and I didn't want to keep trying to please my father. There was a lot of "should haves" between us.

CHAPTER 65

JACK

Yesterday had been a bit of a blur. I had been in a weird fog, fumbling my way through the day, not entirely sure what I had done or said. I hoped I hadn't made any huge business decisions yesterday. If I did, I couldn't be responsible for how they turned out. I hadn't been thinking rationally. Today wasn't all that much better.

I couldn't talk to Grayson about what was going on. It felt too weird. I definitely couldn't talk to Elijah. I wasn't sure where our friendship stood after he found out I knocked up his little sister. I had a feeling things were going to be right back to where they were before we kissed and made up. He was probably already plotting the many ways he wanted to kick my ass.

That left Mason. I wasn't even going to let myself start thinking about how my younger brother, the one I had barely spoken to in the last ten years, had suddenly become my closest confidant. I was grateful he was around. He'd been a huge help to me and I owed him. I was hoping I could count on him one more time to help me figure out what to do next.

I drove to the address he had given me and the farther I got away from downtown, the more concerned I grew. Mason was a billionaire.

Why in the hell was he living in Brooklyn? Not even the up-and-coming part of Brooklyn.

I parked out front, already assuming my car would be stripped by the time I returned. I patted the silver Porsche on the hood, saying my goodbyes before ringing the buzzer on the what looked like an old warehouse.

Mason appeared, pulling open the door, slightly out of breath. "Sorry, I was upstairs, and the elevator isn't working yet."

I raised an eyebrow. "You live here?"

He shrugged. "I don't know yet."

I walked inside the huge, open space and was surprised it wasn't all that bad on the inside. He had a massive living room set up on the left with a gourmet kitchen directly ahead. I almost wanted to step back outside and make sure I was really in the right building. The warehouse looked more like one of the multimillion-dollar townhomes I expected to see downtown.

"This is nice," I said in total shock.

He grinned. "I know. It's a diamond in the rough."

"That's one way to put it."

"Come in, have a seat, and I'll grab us a couple beers. You sounded like you had something big to tell me. I'm waiting to hear you're quitting the company and going on that cruise with Mom."

I shook my head. "Not quite that big," I said, taking off my suit jacket and making my way to the huge leather couch, offset by the biggest TV I had ever seen before. It was more like a movie theater screen.

Mason returned with a couple bottles of craft beer, popped the tops, and handed one to me before sitting in a matching leather chair. "Hit me," he said, taking a long drink.

I took my own satisfying drink before looking him straight in the eye. "Nat's pregnant."

His dark bushy brows shot up. "Holy fuck!" he shouted.

I shrugged. "Pretty much."

"Holy shit!" he repeated.

"You're not really helping," I said dryly.

395

He shook his head, running his hand through his shaggy hair. "What the hell? You? You knocked her up? You're always the responsible one."

"I didn't knock her up," I protested.

"Uh, I think that is exactly what you did. Wait—it's yours, right?" he asked.

I rolled my eyes. "Yes, it's mine."

"Okay, well, shit," he said before bursting into laughter.

In the back of my mind I was already thinking I was going to have to tell him to clean up his language once my child was born.

"She told her family and has been essentially disowned," I told him.

He grimaced, sucking air through his teeth. "That's rough."

"It is."

"So, what's going on? Obviously, something has you hot and bothered."

I smirked, shaking my head. "That's one way to put it."

"You want the baby, right?"

"Of course!"

He shrugged. "Then, what's the problem?"

"She is worried about the future and because I broke things off. She doesn't want me to feel trapped or to be with her just because of the baby," I explained.

"What do you want?"

"I want her. I've always wanted her. The only reason I broke things off was because she kept saying it. I realized we could never really have that happiness we were looking for with her dad hanging over us," I told him.

He took a long drink. "I think you have to do what you want. What she wants. Don't think of it as being trapped. Maybe you can start over, date and see if things can be good for you."

"Date? I think we're past that," I quipped.

He shook his head. "No, you two have been sneaking around, not really giving yourselves the chance to go out and do things together. That's another part of being in a relationship. It has to go beyond the bedroom or this shit isn't going to work."

He had a point. We had never gone shopping together or went to a concert together or things that took us out of her place or mine. I wanted to take her to dinner or grab a coffee together like a normal couple. I wanted to talk about nothing and not have to worry about someone seeing us and revealing our secret.

"You're probably right," I admitted.

"Probably? I am. I may not be a relationship expert, but even I know you need to get to know each other beyond the bed. Just because things are great between the sheets doesn't mean she's going to be someone you can really spend a lot of time with and not want to strangle her."

I laughed. "We do know each other pretty well. When you're locked up with someone with nothing to do but talk, you get to know that person. I know we'll get along just fine. I want to be with her and I know she wants to be with me. It's her damn dad!" I hissed, feeling that familiar anger bubbling up again.

"It's fucked up, no doubt about it, but you can't let that influence you and what you do. This is about you and her and that little baby you made," he said, the hint of a smile tugging at the corner of his lips.

"Do you think it's selfish of me to encourage her to let me back in her life?" I asked, needing to hear another opinion. I already knew what I wanted, but I needed someone else to say it was okay.

"I don't think it's selfish at all. I think you've been an idiot for letting that asshole dictate your life this long," he said bluntly.

I grinned. "Gee, Mason, tell me how you really feel."

"I'm serious. I don't know how you've put up with the guy this long."

I shrugged a shoulder. "I don't know. I guess because I wanted her."

He got up, walked to the kitchen, and returned a few seconds later with two more beers. "Man, Mom is going to flip," he said in a low voice.

I groaned. "Damn, do I have to tell her? She's going to be pissed."

He chuckled. "She isn't going to be pissed. She's going to be thrilled. You know she wants an entire soccer team. If you don't start

397

putting out some grandkids, she's going to start coming to me, and we all know *that* is not going to happen."

"It could happen as much as you screw around," I shot back.

He shook his head, drinking his beer. "Nope. Not me. I know better."

"I have to tell Mom," I muttered, the realization weighing on me.

"Yes, you do. She's going to be happy, once she's done being pissed at you."

I grimaced, thinking of the lecture I was going to get when I had to confess what I had done. I knew she wouldn't hold it against me too long.

"Man, she is not going to be happy knowing she shares a grandbaby with the Levys. How weird is that going to be?" I said, still trying to get my head around everything.

"Do you think there will be big birthday parties and shit like that?" Mason asked.

I rubbed my face with my hand. "This is exactly why I tried to break things off."

"A baby. You're going to be a daddy. I'm not sure what to say. I mean, I knew it was coming, but to think of you actually with a baby, man, that's kind of weird," he said, his voice revealing a lot of what I was feeling as well.

"I know. A baby. Holy shit. Have you been to Grayson's? Have you seen how much shit he has in his place?" I said, shaking my head.

My head was spinning. Talking to Mason made it all so real. A baby. I was going to be a daddy. I didn't know how things were going to work out with Natasha, but the baby was still going to be in my life.

"I don't know if I can picture you pushing a stroller or even carrying a baby," he said, bursting into laughter.

"Shut up. It isn't funny."

He shrugged a shoulder. "It is a little funny."

"I should probably get going. My car is probably already stolen or stripped," I grumbled.

"It's not that bad."

I raised an eyebrow. "I think it is. Why do you live here?" I asked, standing and looking around the place again.

"I like it. I don't like living in those luxurious places you guys live in. That's not my style. It's too stuffy," he complained.

"They're safer. I don't have to worry about my car getting stolen five minutes after I've been inside," I said dryly.

"No one has ever touched my bike or my car," he replied.

"Look at you. You look like you eat puppies for dinner. Nobody is going to mess with you."

He grinned and winked. "Exactly why I live here. Can you see me in one of your fancy penthouses?" He grimaced and shuddered as if he were terrified.

"Well, don't expect me to visit you out here too often. This place is frightening."

"When are you telling Mom?" he said, quickly changing the subject.

"I don't know."

He put a hand on my shoulder. "You better do it before she finds out through the grapevine."

"You think Levy is going to brag about his daughter being impregnated by a Bancroft? I think this is something he is going to keep on the downlow for as long as possible," I said.

He shrugged a shoulder. "Unless he goes to Mom and blames her."

"He wouldn't dare. James or anyone of us could be there and any one of us would kick his ass if he showed up at Mom's," I asserted.

He nodded in agreement. "I'd kick his ass for the bullshit he pulled last year."

"Exactly. He isn't going to tell her. He isn't going to tell anyone. I will tell her. Keep your mouth shut until then. No one else knows. Nat isn't ready to tell anyone, and I will respect that."

"Fine, your secret is safe with me, but how safe is it with the Levy family?"

I left, knowing he was right. I couldn't put off telling my mom too much longer. She would be hurt if she found out from anyone besides me. That was going to be an awkward conversation.

CHAPTER 66

NATASHA

With my secret out, I didn't really care who knew I was shopping for baby gear. It was too exciting not to go to the stores in person and shop. I wanted to touch and see all the things. For the first time since I'd found out I was pregnant, I was a little excited about the idea of having a little one in my life. I didn't care whether it was a boy or a girl. I couldn't wait to meet my baby and snuggle with him or her. Ashley had jumped at the chance to go shopping. I cut out of work early. Whoever was spying on me for my dad could run and tell him I left early. I didn't care. He didn't think much of me at the moment anyway.

"I love this one!" Ashley exclaimed from behind me.

I turned to see her lovingly running her hand over the smooth cherry wood crib that had caught her attention. I reached out as well, the shiny surface begging to be touched. It was gorgeous.

"It is very pretty. I think I like the warmer wood tone. I was thinking white, but I don't know, this is really nice," I said, picturing my baby's nursery in my mind.

"I like white, but this wood, I love it. It looks so ... so, I don't know, sturdy?" she offered with a giggle.

I nodded. "I think white is nice, but you're right. I like the wood tone. I could offset the dark with lots of pastels. Do you think I should order this one?" I asked, hesitant to actually make the first purchase.

She shrugged a shoulder. "You're going to have to make the first purchase at some point. We can look around some more."

I was a little sad I couldn't ask my mom to help me design the nursery. I had always imagined her being involved. I did love her decorating style and knew she could create a beautiful space that would be comforting and pretty to look at. That wasn't going to happen. My baby was stuck with me and my inexperienced eye for design.

"I really like this one," I said with more finality in my voice.

"Look at all the furniture that matches it," she exclaimed, picking up a brochure next to the crib.

"Jack knows," I blurted out.

She stopped, her hand midway to touch a matching changing table, and turned to look at me. "Jack knows?"

I slowly nodded, watching her facial expression. "Yes. I told him."

"Oh my God! When did that happen?"

"Monday."

"And you're just now telling me?" she shrieked, earning looks from some of the other shoppers.

I shrugged. "I haven't seen you and it felt like something I should tell you in person."

"Uh, I have a phone. What did he say?"

My sheepish smile revealed more than I had hoped. "He had a lot to say."

"You had sex with him?" she whisper-shouted.

I looked around the store. "Yes, sheesh, you don't have to announce it."

She slapped a hand to her forehead. "Oh, Nat. You will never learn."

"Probably not, but I don't regret it."

She grinned. "Does that mean the two of you are together again?"

"I don't know. We didn't really talk about it. I mean, he said he was tired of trying to make everyone else happy, but we never actually said we were together, together. I don't even know what that looks like with us. We've always been together, but it's never been official. It's hard to even picture that relationship with him," I explained, still trying to figure it out for myself.

"Your dad is going to blow a gasket, but I agree with Jack. You are happy with him and he loves you. There is no reason the two of you can't be together. You'll figure it out," she stated matter-of-factly.

I smirked. "My dad already banished me from the house and doesn't want to see or talk to me, I don't know how much madder he can get. I guess there's really nothing stopping us from being together."

"True, but maybe it's meant to be. Maybe this is how things are supposed to work out. You and Jack, I think the two of you are going to make excellent parents," she said with a warm smile.

"I hope so," I mumbled. "I really don't want him to be with me because he feels obligated. It feels very forced."

"I don't think that's the case at all. He is still attracted to you, and I don't think he stopped loving you overnight. You had sex, right? Obviously, that wasn't obligation."

I sighed, thinking back to our night together. It had been romantic and sweet, and it definitely didn't feel like he was forcing himself to be nice to me. I was the one who'd tried to tell him no.

"I guess we'll see how things go," I said, a little nervous he wouldn't call me again. It had been a few days.

"Are you sure you shouldn't be looking at all this stuff with him?"

I laughed. "I seriously doubt this is what he would consider fun."

"I don't know. I think Jack seems like a hands-on guy. I know I've only met him a few times, but he doesn't seem like the kind of man who wants to take a back seat in anything."

I nodded in agreement. "I agree, but there's nothing to say we're going to live together after the baby is born. I need a crib. He can pick out the crib he wants. I want to get as much done now so I don't have to worry about anything when it comes time to have the baby. I don't want to be one of those moms who freaks out in the hospital because I don't have this or that. Things are going to be stressful enough as they are."

"I'm all for preparing. I have the list the saleslady gave us. We can start checking things off. Your place is certainly big enough to store the amount of crap you need for this little bundle of joy," she murmured.

When I had first seen the list, I had been a little overwhelmed, but the saleswoman assured me it looked far more intimidating than it actually was. I was already imagining the deliveries that were going to be arriving over the next several months.

"I want to get some of the big stuff now," I said, making up my mind.

"Do you want to shop around?"

I shook my head. "I don't have a lot of time and I'm sure it's all the same. I mean, a crib is a crib, right?"

A woman who had been standing nearby made a sound that said that was not the case at all.

"Apparently not," Ashley whispered.

I burst into laughter. "Well, if this one doesn't work, I can always buy another one."

We both laughed before heading to the front counter to get assistance on how we needed to go about picking what we wanted. The saleswoman was all too happy to come along with us and use her little tablet to add things to my list.

Once we were finished buying the furniture, we drifted through some other baby stores, picking up little things here and there.

"I cannot wait to find out the sex. I want to buy cute little shoes and pretty dresses and overalls and just everything!" Ashley squealed, picking up a frilly pink dress that looked like it could fit a doll.

I was getting more excited with every store we visited. Things weren't great, but I had a feeling the baby would change everything.

"Want to grab some dinner?" I asked, feeling famished after a hard two-hour shopping spree.

"Of course," she replied.

We headed for one of our favorite restaurants, ordering our meals.

It was strange to drink water instead of wine. I knew it was one of the many things I was going to have to get used to.

"Thank you for today. It was fun," I told her.

"Anytime. Really. Anytime you want to go baby shopping, I'm your girl. That is an absolute blast. I might just have to have me one of those little things so I can shop," she said giddily.

"It is exciting, but I really wish I could have the support of my family. I can't believe I've been banished. I don't think I've quite wrapped my head around the idea."

She shrugged a shoulder. "Your dad will come around. You're his princess after all. Just give him some time."

I grimaced shaking my head. "I don't think that's going to happen. I've never seen him that mad. I was afraid he was going to have a stroke or a heart attack."

"I'm sure it was a shock. Don't let yourself get too worked up about it," she lectured.

I shook my head. "You don't understand. He was throwing glass, breaking things, and he was horribly violent. It was a little scary. Elijah tried to calm him down, but he was beyond worked up. It was terrible," I said, thinking back to the scene.

I had known he'd be upset, but his response had shocked me. I could have never prepared for such a violent outburst. Some part of me thought he would be happy to be a grandpa, but clearly that was not the case.

"I'm sorry it was so bad. I'm sure things will get better."

"I don't know. Look what he did to Jack the last time he was angry. I'm afraid things are going to get really bad. What happens if they run into each other at some event or just walking down the street?" I asked in a voice full of fear.

Ashley smiled. "When does your dad ever walk down the street?"

"Stop. You know what I mean. He is liable to attack Jack."

She giggled. "I don't think Jack is going to come out on the losing end of that matchup. He's younger, in a lot better shape, and I think he would fight to the death for you."

I smiled thinking about how loyal Jack was. He was a good man. I only wished my father could see it. Unfortunately, all my dad could see was Jack's last name. I didn't think he'd ever really had a conversation with Jack. He was biased for no reason at all.

"I wish things were different. I want to enjoy all of this. I want to be able to talk to my mom about the pregnancy and have my dad be happy for me. This is not how I pictured my life going," I muttered.

"You have to stay strong. I'm here. Jack isn't going anywhere. Your dad will come around. You might not have a real close relationship again, but I think once he realizes the baby is his grandchild, he'll have to accept him or her," she assured me.

I tried to smile. I wanted to believe that, but there was a part of me that doubted that could ever happen. Everything I had been trying to prevent from happening, had. My dad was disgusted by me and wanted nothing to do with me. My mother would be forbidden from talking to me or being in my life. Elijah—he was a wild card. I wasn't sure how he felt.

He'd been the one to try and stick up for me that night and Jack said the two of them had worked things out, but that was before he knew I was pregnant. I loved my brother dearly and wanted him to be a part of my life, but my father was a powerful man. He was manipulative, and he could threaten to take everything from Elijah if he did not act like the good little soldier and avoid me like the plague.

CHAPTER 67

JACK

I felt a little goofy as I stared at the pale-green Onesie with the words "Daddy's Pride and Joy" across the front, placing it back on my desk. It had been a spur-of-the-moment purchase. I'd been out grabbing a coffee and happened to walk by a specialty shop that had a bunch of baby stuff in the window. Before I knew what I was doing, I was inside the store buying the cute little garment, which I later learned was a Onesie. I already felt like I was a little smarter in the baby department. I had spent some time browsing the store, marveling over the tiny clothes and the soft blankets. I couldn't believe I was going to have my own child. The woman in the store made it a point to look at my finger, checking for a wedding ring. I politely declined her offer to grab a drink some time and left the store with my little blue bag.

I had made up my mind while I stood there in that store, touching the soft cotton baby clothes. I was going to go over to Nat's place and talk to her about the next step. I had been so overwhelmed when she told me about the baby, I had let my emotions and feelings for her lead the way. I had left before we had a chance to talk about what we were going to do next. I wanted her to understand I wanted her. I wanted to be with her. I wanted to be a part of my child's life. I just needed to convince her we could be happy, even if her father hated me.

I wasn't ready to propose marriage. I had a feeling that would only scare her in the opposite direction. She would definitely think it was a pity proposal to a shotgun wedding. I needed to ease her into the idea of us being together. *Baby steps.* I smiled at the irony. I was going to convince her it was time to move forward with our relationship. I was ready.

I put the Onesie back in the bag and shut down my computer, anxious to see Natasha. I had been working out what I would say all afternoon. The first step was to let her know how excited I was for the baby. Worshipping her body was not the way to do that. I needed to actually say the words and convince her. I needed to let her know she wasn't an obligation.

I heard a knock on the door. It wasn't my secretary, that was for sure. The knock was rough and demanding. I stood up, instinctively knowing a confrontation was coming. The second the door pushed open I could smell the cigar and knew immediately who my visitor was.

"What do you want?" I snapped, already knowing damn well what Wayne Levy wanted.

"You little bastard." He hissed, pushing my door open wide before turning to slam it shut.

I put my shoulders back, ready to go toe-to-toe with the man who'd been making my life hell for the last five years.

"You need to leave," I said in a calm voice.

He shook his head, stepping closer to me. "I'm not going anywhere until I've said my piece."

I shrugged, a smirk on my face. "I don't give a shit what you have to say."

"You should, you selfish little shit. What gives you the right? Who do you think you are?" He hissed.

"Jack Bancroft, and it's not a pleasure to finally meet you."

He sneered, looking me up and down with pure, unadulterated disgust. It was a little unnerving. I finally had a good understanding about why Nat was so terrified of him. The man had a way of making you feel small and worthless with one of his looks.

"You are a disgusting, horrible piece of shit and are no better than your father. What kind of man goes around knocking up women?" He hissed.

I stepped closer. "I didn't knock her up. We're having a child."

The man seemed as if he would blow a fuse. "No!" he screamed. He stalked to the built-in bookshelves along one wall and grabbed one of the glass awards I had won years ago.

It hit the ground and shattered in a thousand pieces. He picked up another one, slamming it to the ground again. I watched him throw an epic tantrum and made no move to stop him.

He stopped, turning to look at me, his hands moving to his hips as he glared at me with so much hatred it radiated off him in waves.

"Are you done?" I asked.

"No! Stay away from my little girl!"

I shook my head. "That's not going to happen. She's having my child."

"No! She'll move in with us. My family will help her. I'll support her financially and her mother will help with the baby. You'll have no contact with her!"

"That's not going to happen."

His face twisted into an ugly snarl. "I will not allow my daughter to be saddled with you and your horrible family. You don't need to call her ever again."

I laughed. "I'm going to call her. It's my baby. I'm tired of listening to you. Your opinion doesn't matter. I've sat back long enough and let you call the shots. That's over. You don't run my life."

"I run hers and that means you stay the hell away!" he shouted.

"You don't like me because of something my father did. How stupid is that? I thought you were some smart guy. You're clearly not. You're so stuck in the past you can't see how good the future is. You're a sad, miserable man, and I'm so glad I'm not you. I'm so glad my mother moved on with my father. You would have made her miserable," I said in a low voice.

"You bastard! How dare you! You don't know shit about any of that!"

I shrugged a shoulder. "Considering how pissed off you are right now, I guess I know a lot more than you want me to. Admit it, you're the jilted lover and you can't stand to see me or my brothers because we are reminders of the woman you loved who walked out on you. You envied my father. Did you covet his wife? Is that your problem? How does your wife feel about you still holding a candle for another woman?"

He shook his head. "You selfish, spoiled little shit. You don't know anything. I don't want your mother. I was better off once she left."

"Be careful." I growled. "You can talk all the shit you want about me, but you disrespect my mother and I swear to God, I will put you down right where you stand."

I stared him dead in the eye. I would not tolerate him saying anything bad about my mother. It was bad enough he was disrespecting Natasha.

"Stay away from her."

"I won't."

"She's my daughter! I'm telling you to stay away!"

"Not this time. I'm not backing down. You've been controlling things for too long. It's my turn. Our turn. You don't get to say who I spend my life with. We've been trying to make you happy for too long. No more," I said in a steely voice.

I'd had enough of Wayne Levy. He wasn't going to intimidate or manipulate me in any way.

"She doesn't want you. The only reason she was with you was to defy me. It was immature. It's time to grow up now. She's coming home," he said, stomping his foot.

I chuckled. "That's mature. Why would she go home? She's a grown woman who has a good head on her shoulders. She isn't alone in this. You seem to be missing the point—it's my baby and I will be there," I asserted once again.

"I will not allow you in my house!"

I shrugged a shoulder. "I have no intention of being in your house.

Natasha can choose where she lives, but I will see my child and I will be a part of his or her life. And, God willing, Nat will be as well."

"Who do you think you are? You think you're good enough for my little girl? You're nothing but a slimy snake, just like your father. She deserves better than you. You had no right to touch her!" he seethed.

I could see his face turning tomato red and actually pitied the man. He had so much hatred for my father that he was letting it dictate his own life. He was willing to throw away his daughter because of how he felt about my father. It was sad.

I shook my head, looking at him with the pity I felt. "Mr. Levy, I think it's time for you to go. This conversation is getting us nowhere but closer to you having a heart attack. Despite what you think of me and your daughter, I wouldn't do that to her. Go."

"I'm not leaving you until you tell me you'll stay away from her!"

"That isn't going to happen. You don't get to tell me who I can and can't see. Face it, she wants me, I want her, and she's pregnant with our child. No matter how much you hate me or my father, those are the facts. Get on board or don't, I really don't give a shit at this point," I said, tired of the game with the man.

"You don't get to tell me that."

"I already did. You have a grandchild coming. Either you choose to be a part of that baby's life or you choose to walk away. You won't get to see your grandchild if you can't figure out how to be decent toward Nat or me. I won't have you poisoning my child with your misguided hate and animosity. Hate me all you want. I don't care. That's your burden to carry, but you won't see my child and you won't get the chance to spew your hate to carry on another generation," I told him and stepped closer to him, speaking in a calm voice.

"Are you threatening me? Are you actually trying to tell me I won't see my daughter's child?" he said, growling.

"It's not a threat."

"It certainly sounds like one!"

"You can take it however you want. I'm telling you Natasha and I will be raising this baby. To be honest, I hope you decide to figure out how to accept me in your life. Nat loves you. Nat has been tearing herself apart these past few years trying to figure out how to keep you happy. No more. It ends now. Get on board or get out."

His mouth dropped open. I could see the anger rolling off him, but I held my ground. He was not going to bully me another minute of my life.

"You don't know who you're talking to."

"I know exactly who I'm talking to and it's time you figured that out as well. I'm not a pushover. I'm not a man who is going to step back and let you trample all over the woman I love. She is going to need you through all this. She wants you and her family in her life as she goes through something exciting. You choose whether you're a part of her life or not."

I watched him, the anger still burning bright in his eyes as he glared at me. "I hate you."

I smiled and shrugged a shoulder. "So be it. I don't care. Figure it out. Now, you need to leave. Do I call security and have you dragged out, or are you going to be a man and walk out of here?" I asked.

He glared at me and for a brief second, I was sure he was going to hit me. I would take it. I wouldn't hurt Natasha's father, but it would certainly seal his fate in my life.

CHAPTER 68

NATASHA

I had just wrapped up my meeting with my assistant, going over the day's business and giving her a tentative schedule for next week when my cell phone rang. I saw it was Jack's number and quickly answered it. He never called me.

"Jack?" I answered in a low voice as my assistant walked out the door of my office.

"Hey," he said in a breezy voice I could tell was completely faked.

"What's wrong?" I asked, knowing immediately there was something wrong.

"I wanted to give you a heads-up. Your dad stopped by here," he started, and I felt my stomach drop.

I leaned my head back in my chair, putting a hand over my eyes. "And what happened? Is it bad? Are you in jail?" I asked sitting forward and realizing I could be his one phone call.

He chuckled softly, the sound warming the chills that had spread over my body. "I'm not in jail, but I think he's a little pissed. I would feel better if you stayed the night at my place."

"What?" I gasped, dread washing over me like a heavy blanket.

"I'm sorry, baby. I am. He came into my office, like a bull in a china

412

shop. He trashed the place pretty good before security dragged him out."

"Oh no." I breathed out, images of him breaking my mother's crystal came flashing back.

He cleared his throat. "I'm sorry. I know you love your father, but he went too far."

"No, it's fine. I understand. I'm the one who's sorry. I don't know what his problem is," I said, moaning.

"Say you'll come over. I'll make dinner."

I glanced up at the ceiling, wondering when my life became such a mess and then remembered the exact moment things went to hell. It was the first time I kissed Jack and realized I was crazy for him. I knew then things would never be easy, but I didn't think they would ever get this bad.

"I'll be there. I need to finish up a few things here first," I said on a sigh.

"I'll be waiting. Be careful," he said before hanging up.

I ended the call and looked around my office. I wasn't worried my father would ever be physical with me, but I prayed he didn't come storming in and trashing the place. I had just gotten the walls up—literally. I didn't need him busting holes and creating a scene. It wouldn't be good for him or myself.

My head wasn't in it. I realized I was never going to get any work done, so I called it a day. I was too worried about my father storming in. I packed up my things. I didn't think my father would go to my place, but there was a chance he would be waiting. I quickly debated what to do before deciding to stop at one of the department stores that was on my way to Jack's apartment. I did a little speed shopping before giving the driver Jack's address. It was a little strange to be planning a sleepover, but I was looking forward to spending some time with him.

"Hi," he said, after I knocked on the door, pulling me in and giving me a kiss on the cheek.

"Hi," I said, a little embarrassed to be dragging a large bag from the department store with me.

He looked at the bag, then me. "Decide to do a little shopping first?" he asked with that sexy grin that always melted my heart.

"I didn't want to go to my place first. This seemed easier," I said, shrugging a shoulder.

"You're probably right. Come in. Dinner will be ready in about thirty minutes," he said, taking the bag from my hand.

I loved when he wore a vest. There was something so old-fashioned and inherently sexy about seeing a man with a vest, his shirt sleeves rolled up, and his ass perfectly accentuated in a pair of slim-fitting slacks. I wasn't sure if it was the pregnancy hormones or him in general, but I was so attracted to him, I had to fight the urge to pounce on him. I watched as he put my bag next to the couch before heading back into his kitchen.

"What are you making?" I asked out of curiosity.

I could smell lots of herbs and lemon. The smell was making me hungrier than I realized I was.

"It's baked chicken with a lemon sauce and rice pilaf. I'm not going to lie and pretend I made it from scratch." He laughed.

"It smells delicious."

"I have some club soda in the fridge or milk," he said, his voice unsure.

I smiled, knowing he was navigating new territory with the no alcohol thing. "Have a beer or wine, don't let me stop you. I will have a club soda," I said, moving to open the refrigerator.

I smiled, looking at the different types of milk in the fridge and knew he had picked those up with me in mind. It was sweet and endearing, and I appreciated the gesture.

"I'm good with a club soda," he said easily.

I walked to him and couldn't resist putting my arms around his waist, resting my head against his back. He covered my hands with his as we stood in silence. It felt so good to have him against me. His presence brought a sense of comfort I could never find anywhere else. It was him and his easy way, solid and strong, and completely unmoving in his love for me—most of the time.

"So, tell me what happened?" I asked, moving away and sitting on one of the barstools.

He smirked, shaking his head before he told me about my father's epic temper tantrum. I was horrified and mortified at the same time.

"I am so, so sorry," I said, feeling absolutely horrible over what he'd been exposed to.

"Don't be. It was time your father and I finally talked. I've sat back long enough. I need him to know I am going to be in your life for a good long while and he can either deal with it or choose to walk away. I know you love him and I really hope he comes around, but I can't let him treat you like that. It kills me to see you hurt by him."

I knew he was right and I wasn't going to argue with him anymore. "I know."

He looked a little surprised but said nothing more. He dished up two plates before coming to sit beside me at the kitchen island. We ate our dinner, talking about work and everything besides the baby. I began to wonder if he was going to pretend it didn't happen. Maybe he was in denial.

"Let's go sit down. You look exhausted," he said, taking my hand and leading me into the living room. He sat, ordering me to sit at the opposite end with my legs over his lap. He took off my heels and began to gently massage my feet, nearly lulling me to sleep.

"That feels so good." I sighed, completely relaxed and comfortable on his couch.

He grinned. "Sit tight for a second," he said, carefully moving my legs before jumping up and heading down the hall.

I looked around his place, mentally placing baby furniture. His place was probably a little smaller than mine and definitely not child friendly with all the glass shelving. I had already begun to think about what I would need to change in my own home to make it a fun, comfortable place for my child.

He returned a minute later, carrying a pale-blue bag. He lifted my legs before sitting down again. "Here," he said, handing me the bag.

"What's this?"

"Look," he said, a nervous smile on his face.

I opened the bag and pulled out a soft cotton Onesie. I read the words on the little outfit and felt tears spring to my eyes. "This is adorable."

"I want to be the proud daddy. I want us to do this together," he said, his hand resting on my knee.

"Really? Even after all the crap my dad just pulled?"

"Even more now. I know what I said a month ago, but that was me giving up. I don't want to give up. It isn't just the two of us we have to think about. It's our child. I want that baby more than anything in this world and I intend to be a part of his or her life. I'm asking you to let me be a part of yours. I want to do this together," he said, his hazel eyes staring into mine.

I could see how serious he was and felt my heart skip a beat. "Okay," I whispered.

He grinned. "Damn straight okay. We are going to do this. This is going to change our lives forever—for the better."

"I'm thrilled to be doing this with you. I can't wait to meet our baby."

"Me either. I'm going to take care of you. I want you to relax. Don't worry about anything else but being healthy for you and our child," he said, moving back to rub my feet.

"I'm trying. I'm type A, which means relaxing is a little difficult, but I am going to do everything I can to be healthy," I said, feeling a renewed strength blossom inside me.

He laughed. "That's okay. That's why I'm here. I can tell you when to slow down. I can help you."

"Thank you."

He shook his head. "No way, don't thank me for doing what a man should do. You're doing the hard part. I'm here to try and lighten the burden as much as I can. That means I'm going to be feeding you and taking care of you in every way I can."

I giggled. "I'm not an invalid. I can feed myself."

"You know what I mean. I'm going to make sure you have good meals every night when you get home from work. You're not going to have to lift a finger."

I nodded in agreement. He didn't mention where that home would be. I wasn't too worried. We'd figure out the logistics later. I was mentally and physically exhausted. Being with him in his quiet apartment, my belly full and my body completely relaxed was making me very sleepy. I closed my eyes, wanting to rest them for just a minute.

The next thing I knew, he was gently touching my shoulder, pulling me forward.

"What are you doing?" I asked, slightly dazed.

"I'm taking you to bed. You're beat," he said in a soft voice, helping me to my feet.

I followed him into the room and let him undress me before he picked out one of his T-shirts and pulled it over my head. I crawled between the sheets, the cool fabric chilling my skin. I wasn't cold for long. He nestled in behind me, his arm going around my waist as he gathered me against his warm, hard body, curling his around mine in the sweetest gesture.

"You feel good against me," I murmured, feeling the first stirrings of an arousal.

I wiggled my butt against him, teasing him just a little. His hand moved to my hip, stopping my wiggling before anchoring me against him once again.

"Shh, sleep," he ordered.

I sighed, knowing he was right. I needed rest. I could certainly get used to falling asleep in his protective hold every night. My eyes drifted closed once again, relishing in the feel of him holding me close, his breath swishing over the top of my head as he rested against me. Things were going to be okay, I realized as I finally fell asleep.

CHAPTER 69

JACK

I climbed out of the pool located in the basement of my building. It was a perk I couldn't pass up when I had been shopping for an apartment so many years ago. It was quiet first thing on a Sunday morning, which I liked to take advantage of. Most people didn't think about swimming in the cooler weather, but I did. I loved the smell of the chlorine and the humid air in the pool room. I grabbed my towel and quickly toweled off. I slid my feet into my sandals and headed for the elevator to shower and get ready for my lunch date with Natasha.

Last night, she insisted she go home. I didn't want to pressure her by trying to move too fast, too soon, so I reluctantly agreed. I wasn't worried her father would actually hurt her, but his words could be just as damaging in my opinion. She promised to call if he showed up. She also promised to go home, put her feet up, and worry about nothing. I smiled when she told me her plans were a date with Netflix and a bowl of ice cream. I had gone to bed with the conjured-up image of her sitting on the couch, wrapped up in a warm blanket.

I jumped in the shower, finding myself singing a song I wasn't even sure what the title was. I was happy, like really, truly happy. I saw a bright future for Natasha and me. Things were going to be okay. I still needed to tell my mom about the baby, but that could wait. I needed to figure out exactly what Nat and I were doing before I told my mom, knowing her first question would be about us getting married. My mom was old-fashioned, and she would expect me to do the right thing—even if it was the twenty-first century and that was not something anyone really believed in these days.

Nat and I were going to grab lunch and then do a little shopping for the baby. I couldn't believe how excited I was to do something so girlie, but I was. I had thought about calling Grayson and asking for recommendations, but I wasn't quite ready to tell him either. For now, this was mine and Natasha's thing. Well, ours and the handful of people who knew.

I had some time before I could claim it was the lunch hour and decided to do a little internet browsing. I was halfway through reading a paragraph about the first trimester of pregnancy when I heard a knock on my door. *Nat.* She couldn't wait to see me, either, and had decided to come early.

I rushed to the door, anxious to see her. "Elijah?" I said, staring at the man standing on the other side of my door.

"I wanted to talk," he said, pushing inside my apartment.

I groaned, knowing it was probably not going to be a conversation I enjoyed. It seemed it rarely was when it came to the Levy men. His abruptness was telling. If that wasn't enough, his disheveled appearance also said he was not in a great mood.

"Have a seat," I said, gesturing to the couch where he was already moving to sit down.

I sat across from him, happy to see the conversation was not going to be on our feet, with our fists raised. That was a good sign, but I wasn't ready to let my guard down. I'd learned my lesson the hard way.

"She probably told you I know about the baby," he blurted out when I looked at him, waiting for him to say his piece.

I nodded. "She did."

"And she told you my dad blew up?"

"She did."

"And the part about her being banished and all that?" he asked.

I nodded. "Yep. Plus, he stopped by my office on Friday to let me know what a piece of shit I was," I told him.

He winced. "Sorry about that. He can get a little out of control."

"A little?" I scoffed.

He grimaced. "I'm sorry. I wish there was something else I could say. I've never been able to calm him down. I'm afraid all I do is make things worse."

"You're sorry?" I asked, taken off guard by the apology.

I was expecting a long lecture and maybe a few punches to the nose. I knew he had to be pissed I got his little sister pregnant. It was guy code. I had violated the rules in a big way. Elijah was the epitome of a protective big brother. In my defense, I would have married her a long time ago if he and his dad hadn't stood in my way for so damn long. They were partially to blame for her current marital status. If they would have left us alone and let us be happy together, she wouldn't be unwed and pregnant.

"I'm sorry for the way my father acted. It wasn't cool. I tried to stop him, but when he gets like that, there is no toning him down. It's taken me a long time to see him for what he truly is. I've always made excuses. I've always tried to explain away his temper and I can't," he said, disgust in his voice.

"Thank you for trying. What brings you by, Elijah? Is this a friendly visit or are you here to tell me to back off, leave her alone, and the Levy family will circle the wagons, keeping me away from my child? I've already told your father, and I will tell you, I'm not going to stay away. I'm not going to let your family raise my child without me being a part of his or her life," I stated, not wanting to get swayed into a false sense of security.

He shook his head. "I would never do that. I believe a father should be in his child's life. I'm glad you're being a standup guy and not taking the easy way out. I wanted to come by and let you know I'm not angry with you and to say congratulations," he said with a grin.

I smiled, relaxing at his easy manner. "Thank you. I really appreciate that. It means a lot to have you in my corner."

"I'm there—for you and Natasha. I'm here for you and will do whatever I can to help."

I grinned, feeling the same happiness I had felt earlier. "You're going to be an uncle."

"I am. I knew it would happen someday, I just didn't think it would be so soon."

"She's not exactly a kid," I reminded him.

He laughed. "I know, but now I have to acknowledge I'm old enough to have a sister having a baby."

I burst into laughter, slapping my thigh. "I hate to tell you, but you've been old enough for a long time."

He shook his head. "I feel like it was only yesterday we were pranking our high school teachers. When did life pass us by?"

"When we weren't looking," I replied, feeling the same way.

"I really hope my dad relaxes. I want you and Nat to be happy and no matter what my dad says or does, I want to be a part of the baby's life," he said, looking me straight in the eye.

I held up my hands. "I have no objection to that. Nat is going to need her family around her. I'm sorry it has come to this, but I'm not sorry to have finally forced your father's hand. I had all but given up I could ever have a life with her."

"It has been a long time coming. I will admit, I wasn't thrilled about you hooking up with my little sister, but I can see it is more than that. You two were meant to be together. I'm sorry it took me so long to come around. I just wanted the best for Natasha and unfortunately, I know you a little too well," he said, his grin telling me it was a joke.

"I get it. If I were in your shoes, I'd probably feel the same way. I've changed. I haven't been the guy from college in a very long time. I have been completely faithful to your sister and I always will be," I told him, meaning every damn word.

He nodded. "I know. I know that, I really do, and I'm happy she ended up with you, even if it took me a long time to get to that point."

"Thanks, I appreciate it. I should have talked to you about dating her way back in the beginning, but I wasn't sure where it was going."

He took a deep breath. "I hope all of this blows over. I really want us to be a family again. I hate the thought of being torn apart and I know it is my dad's fault, but I want it to get better."

I smiled and shrugged a shoulder. "I hope it will. I know we'll never be the big happy family, but I do hope things can be cordial."

"Stranger things have happened," he replied.

"Indeed. So, what are you up to today?" I asked.

He let out a long sigh. "Nothing. I was supposed to go golfing with my dad, but he doesn't want to see me. He was nice enough to have his assistant call me this morning to let me know."

"Is he mad at you because of Natasha?" I asked.

"Yes. I tried to talk to him the other day. Tried to make him see reason. He hates me."

"No!" I said, quickly coming to his defense.

He shrugged. "He does. He always has. I've never been good enough. Nat was always his princess but now with all this, well, he doesn't like either one of us. We're disappointments, he says."

I closed my eyes, trying to think of the right words. No matter how bad Elijah talked about his father, I knew he loved him. It wasn't the first time I had heard that same speech. Wayne had been a hard-ass for as long as I had known Elijah. The guy could literally hang the moon and Wayne would bitch it was crooked or not high enough.

"Go out to lunch with Nat and me," I blurted out.

He smirked. "No."

"Come on. She'll be happy to see you. It'll be like old times, the three of us can hang out and have fun for the day," I assured him.

"I don't want to crash your plans. I'm sure you two have a lot to discuss," he said hesitantly.

"Nope. I want you there. We have a lot to discuss and plenty of time to do it. Today is just lunch. She'll be thrilled to see you. I know this week has been hell on her. Having you in her corner is going to go a long way to making her feel better," I told him.

He shrugged. "Okay. Thanks, but seriously, if I'm a third wheel, please tell me."

"You're not a third wheel. At this point, you are her only living relative. She needs you," I told him, completely serious.

"You're right. I tried to call her all week, but she wasn't taking my calls. I'm sure she thinks I'm doing his bidding. I don't blame her for dodging me."

"I'll grab my wallet and we can go," I said, standing.

He stood, reached out, and hugged me. I was a little stiff at first. The hug was a surprise. I managed to give him a quick hug back before walking away. I was glad to have him back.

"Let's go, Uncle Elijah," I said with a grin.

He laughed. "That is so weird. It's going to take me a while to get used to that."

I guffawed in response. "Try getting used to being called 'Daddy.'"

CHAPTER 70

NATASHA

Having him beside me holding my hand meant a lot. It meant everything. The last few weeks had been fabulous. He'd been doting on me and taking care of me. No matter how happy I was with him, I couldn't quite forget about the situation with my dad. I missed my parents. In the past, I'd gone months without seeing them, but this was different. They were in the same city and yet, I couldn't see them. There weren't any texts between us and certainly no Sunday dinners.

As much as my mother grated on my nerves and my dad was over-bearing and drove me crazy, I missed them. I missed them hounding me and asking me questions about what I was doing and how my life was. I never thought I would miss it, but I did.

"Relax," Jack whispered, leaning over and squeezing my hand.

I kissed him, quick and fast on the lips. "I am. Thank you for being with me."

"Stop," he said, his hazel eyes inches from my face.

"Sorry," I muttered, squeezing my eyes closed.

"I'm telling you one last time. You don't have to thank me for doing something that I should be doing. It *is* my baby too."

"I know, I know, it's just, I don't know. It feels like I have to say thank you," I said, feeling foolish.

"Everything is okay. The baby is fine, and everything will be great. You're healthy. I'm healthy. Our families are healthy," he assured me.

I nodded. "I know, it's just, it's so stressful. I keep thinking about all these things that could go wrong. I keep thinking about the tests and what do we do if we get bad news?"

"Don't think like that. You have to be positive. There's nothing to worry about. If something comes up, we'll deal with it together. Relax and just assume everything is okay," he said, squeezing my knee.

He turned and sat back in his chair. We'd only been waiting for ten minutes, but it felt like forever. The fact my bladder was full wasn't helping matters. I really had to pee, and I really wanted to see my baby. The ultrasound had only been given because I practically begged. The doctor had assured me there was no real reason to do an ultrasound so early in the pregnancy in a healthy woman, but I insisted.

"Natasha Levy. " I heard my name and practically shot out of my chair.

Jack was right beside me. "Let's go," he gushed out.

I laughed, realizing he was just as anxious as I was despite his calm demeanor. We followed the nurse through a door, hot on her heels. I was up on the table, my shirt pulled up, my pants lowered past my belly, and I could barely breathe.

Jack leaned down and kissed me. "Relax. Breathe," he whispered.

I inhaled through my nose. "Okay."

The tech returned a second later and started the ultrasound. Several times Jack had to remind me to breathe.

"Would you like to hear the heartbeat?" the tech asked.

My eyes nearly popped out of my head. "Yes!" Jack and I both said at the same time.

The tech turned a few buttons and then the sound of a heartbeat thumping, in what sounded like a bowl of water, filled the room. I watched the screen, looking at the numbers registering the baby's heartbeat. It sounded steady and strong, thumping away as the little bubble on the screen bounced in time to the beat.

"That's our baby?" Jack gasped, grabbing my hand and holding on tight.

The tech smiled. "It sure is. Steady and strong."

"Is the heart beating too fast?" Jack asked. "I mean, one hundred and forty beats seems really fast."

The tech smiled and shook her head. "Nope. It's perfect. Babies have speedy little heartbeats."

"Oh, okay. Good," Jack said, relief in his voice.

"That's our baby," I said, tears filling my eyes, making my heart feel so big in my chest it almost hurt.

I felt so much love for the unborn little peanut I saw on the screen and for the man who helped make it. I closed my eyes, feeling the moment with every fiber in my being. We had created a life together. I could have never imagined how amazing it would be to know I had a little piece of Jack growing inside me. It was making my head spin as I thought about being forever bound to Jack in this one way.

"I'll print out a couple pictures. Sit tight and I'll be right back," she said, leaving us in the room.

I stared at the image still on the screen. "Can you believe that?" I asked on a breath.

"I can't. I mean, I can, but wow," Jack said, his voice mimicking the same awe I felt.

"Are you okay with all this?" I asked.

Everything felt different. Knowing I was pregnant was one thing, but actually hearing the baby's heartbeat and seeing the new life growing inside was completely different. It made it all so real. I was stupefied by how overwhelming it felt.

"I'm so okay. I can't believe how okay I am. I mean, I knew I wanted a family, and I'm ecstatic it's with you, but wow. Absolutely wow. You're my baby mama," he said, bursting into laughter before leaning down to kiss me.

We were both so involved with each other, neither of us heard the tech reenter the room.

"You guys are adorable. I'm a little jealous," the tech said, flipping on the light.

"Thank you," I muttered, pulling my shirt down.

"You two are going to make excellent parents," she said in a way that made it sound like she knew it for a fact.

"Why do you say that? I mean, why will we make excellent parents?" Jack asked, clearly intrigued.

She smiled. "I can see the way you two look at each other. There is a lot of love there. I can see how much you both love that child."

She was right. We did love the child.

"Thank you," I muttered, not knowing what else to say.

She was fiddling with her machine. "Dang it. I will be right back, guys. You're going to want a picture, trust me."

She rushed out of the room again, leaving Jack and I alone with her words.

"I love you," Jack said, wrapping his arm around me as I lay on the gurney.

There was no stopping the tears. "I love you."

He kissed me. It was a sweet kiss that held a great deal of promise. I reached up and held his head, wanting him more than I wanted air. Everything felt so right. My dad and all that drama didn't matter. All that mattered was Jack, me, and our life together.

"You ready to get out of here?" he whispered close to my ear.

"I am."

I wiped off my belly and sat up on the edge. The tech came back in, holding a cardboard picture frame. "Here you go," she said, handing it to me.

I opened it and stared at the black-and-white photo that revealed almost nothing. I wanted to say I could see the baby, but all I could see was the little blob and the word saying it was the baby. I was going to have to take the tech's word for it.

"Thank you."

"You two take care and I hope to be the lucky one to do the next ultrasound. You two are great. Good luck," she said and waved as we all walked out of the small room.

Jack took the cardboard frame from me and studied the picture as

427

we headed out of the clinic. Once we were back in his car, he sat behind the wheel of the car, staring at the picture.

"Are you okay?" I asked him, a little worried he was having a bit of a breakdown now that it was all very real.

He glanced up and I could see what almost looked like disappointment in his eyes. He lowered his gaze back to the picture and traced his finger over the front of the frame.

"Nat, I'm sorry," he murmured, and I felt my blood turn to ice. I could hear the ocean swimming in my ears as my world tilted.

"Sorry?" I squeaked, clearing my throat and trying to find my voice.

He started shaking his head, still staring at the picture before meeting my eyes. In that moment, that little world I had traveled to while lying on that bed in the ultrasound room imploded in my brain. I had been a fool to think we could have that happily ever after I had very briefly imagined.

He continued to shake his head. "I don't see it. I don't see a baby. Am I the worst father ever?" he asked, horror laced his voice and was written all over his face.

"What?" I asked, absolutely lost as to the direction of the conversation.

"I don't see a baby. It says baby, but I don't see a baby! Do you?"

I leaned my head back on the seat, the relief washing over me. "Not really. It's not that far along yet. He looks exactly like he should —a peanut."

"A peanut?"

I started laughing, almost uncontrollably. "Doesn't it look like a peanut?"

He studied the picture a little longer. "It's a peanut. We have a baby peanut."

The absurdity of it was hysterical. I couldn't stop laughing. He joined in. Together, we laughed away all the stress and the bubble of uncertainty, which hung around us.

"Let's get lunch," he said, starting the car.

"Don't you have to go to work?" I asked.

He shook his head. "Nope. I took the day off. What about you?"

I thought about the meeting I had scheduled and decided to reschedule. "Let me text my assistant."

I sent the text, thrilled to be spending the day with my baby daddy. It was a little weird to think of Jack as a daddy, but he was—or he would be. Jack, my sexy, hunk of a man was going to be a daddy. That made him even sexier in my mind.

"All good?" he asked.

"It is. Let's eat and then I'm yours for the rest of the day if you want."

The heated look he gave me sent chills spreading out over my body. "I want," he said in a husky voice.

We sat down to lunch, both of us still riding the high of getting to hear our child's heartbeat for the first time. I knew I still had months to go, but I couldn't wait to meet our baby. I couldn't wait to see what we created, who he or she would resemble.

"How are you doing?" I asked him.

His brows shot up as his cheeks blew out. "It's a lot. Every time I think I have my head wrapped around it, something like that happens. I feel like I need to go back to middle school health class and review the whole baby-making process. I am mind blown. Like, I've seen my niece and I've seen babies, but to think how it all begins. To think we did that. We created a little life, and it absolutely blows my fucking mind." He hissed.

I found myself smiling. I loved hearing him talk about the miracle of life. It was endearing and absolutely contradicted everything I thought I knew about him. I loved that I was the only person who knew him like this.

"I love you," I said, leaning my elbows on the table and smiling as I looked into his eyes.

He reached out and pushed a strand of hair to the side. "I love you."

Everything was good. I knew that. I could feel it. Everything was going to work out.

CHAPTER 71

JACK

I pulled into the driveway of my mother's house and shut off my car. I made no move to get out. I sat there, pondering how I would tell my mother about Nat. I couldn't put it off any longer. Nat would be showing soon and if my mother found out any other way about Natasha's pregnancy, I had no doubt in my mind she would kill me. I had to come clean.

I could see Grayson's car and Mason's motorcycle already parked ahead. Mom was throwing a family dinner of sorts. It was the first time in a very long time that all my brothers were in town. We had all adjusted our schedules to make time for Mom.

With my nerves a little frazzled, I climbed out of the car, stopping to look at it as I moved past. My little two-seater Porsche was not exactly baby friendly. I was going to need to do some car shopping I mused, adding it to the many things that needed to happen over the next six months.

The moment I walked through the door, I could smell Mom's cooking and hear the low rumble of deep voices. They were in the den, as expected. I headed in their direction, trying to decide if I wanted to tell my mother now or after dinner. I didn't want to ruin dinner, but I wasn't sure if I would be able to get her alone.

"I see I'm the last to show," I said, strolling into the den.

"As always," Grayson quipped.

I walked to the side bar and poured myself a small glass of scotch. "Is Mom in the kitchen?"

"Yep. She's making meatloaf," Mason said, rubbing his stomach.

The carnivore of the family could put away a lot of meatloaf. If I knew my mother, she was making enough food to feed an army. I looked around the room and realized the six of us were a small army.

"All right, I need to talk to her for a few minutes. Stay out," I ordered.

Mason caught my eye and grinned. "Good luck."

Grayson looked at me, then him. "What's going on?"

"Nothing." I growled, giving Mason a look and ordering him to keep his mouth shut.

I walked out of the den, sipping the scotch for a little liquid courage before heading into the kitchen. I stopped and watched my mom for a few seconds as she whipped up a big pot of mashed potatoes. She looked up and saw me, gesturing for me to enter her domain.

"There you are. I was wondering if you were going to show," she said with a smile.

"Of course I would be here. I wouldn't miss meatloaf for the world."

She laughed before returning to her meal prep.

"Mom, I need to talk to you," I said.

She stopped what she was doing and put her hands on the counter, looking at me. "You're in love with Natasha Levy," she said, smiling as she said the words.

My mouth dropped open and I blinked several times. "What?"

"You're in love with the Levy girl."

"How did you know?" I asked, wondering which of my brothers had been running his mouth.

"Oh, Jack. I've known for quite some time. I was waiting to see if you gave into that cranky old man."

431

"Gave in?" I asked, my train of thought completely thrown off with her revelation.

"Yes. I know Wayne has been horrible to you. I know he hates the idea of you being with his daughter and while I can't say I'm thrilled to have our families associating with one another, I would never deny your happiness. I figure this must be the real thing if you've been sticking it out this long, especially after he nearly had you beat to a pulp," she said, her lips pursed and her eyes flashing with anger.

My eyes widened again. "You knew about that?"

She shook her head with disgust. "Yes. That man likes to brag. His bragging is going to get him in serious trouble one of these days. I never said anything about it. You seemed to have not been injured too badly, but let me tell you, it took everything I had not to go over there and give that man a piece of my mind."

I laughed at the thought of my petite mother giving Wayne one of the lectures I had been on the receiving end many times throughout my life. I had a feeling she would have torn into him and he wouldn't have fared well.

"Thanks, Mom. I guess I don't give you enough credit."

She shrugged. "You're not supposed to. So, was that it or did you have something else you needed to tell me?"

I looked down at the glass in my hands and then back into her eyes. "Yes, there is more."

She nodded. "Okay, hit me."

I laughed before I reached into my jacket pocket, pulling out the photocopy of the ultrasound picture. Nat had the original on her refrigerator door. I handed it to my mom, who took it, and then she stared at it with a big smile.

"We're pregnant," I said the words that I had a feeling she already knew.

She was staring at the picture. Her finger reached out to touch it before she looked up at me, tears in her eyes. "Oh, Jack. I'm so happy for you."

"You are?"

"Yes! This is amazing. You're going to be an amazing father."

"You're okay that I'm having a baby with Natasha Levy?" I asked, wanting to make sure she realized who the mother of my child was.

She came around the counter and grabbed both forearms, forcing me to look down at her. "I know you are a smart man. You know what to do here. I trust your judgement. If you like this woman, that's good enough for me. No, I don't care for her parents, but I know she isn't them."

I shook my head. "No, she definitely isn't. She's different. She's kind, loving, beautiful and so smart."

Her eyes were glistening as I spoke. "And you love her."

I sighed. "I do. I love her. I have loved her for a very long time. I tried to stop. I knew it was wrong, but it wouldn't go away."

My mom slapped at my arm. "It isn't wrong. Just because that crotchety old fart thinks it's wrong, doesn't make it wrong."

"Thank you. Thank you for not rejecting me or my child."

"I would never! I don't subscribe to Wayne Levy's ridiculous beliefs that our children should pay for things we did a long time ago. That's his burden to carry. It takes more energy to hate and so much passion to hold a grudge, it zaps the life right out of a person. That man will never see it. He clearly loves being miserable. It is one of the many reasons I couldn't be with him. I couldn't live my life being mad at people and hating this person for something they did years ago. It was always like that with him. We'd go to parties and he'd point out all the people in the room who had wronged him. He ordered me to stay away from them."

"Really?" I asked, not all that surprised to learn it wasn't just our family he hated.

"Really. It was exhausting. I couldn't keep all the grudges straight. I found myself being more and more isolated the longer I was with him. It's one of the reasons I left. I wanted to live. I wanted to enjoy life and you can't be happy when you hold onto that much anger," she said, shaking her head.

I nodded, agreeing with everything she said. "I'd like to bring Natasha by to meet you one of these days, if that's okay?"

Her smile was bright and friendly. "You better bring her by. I need to get to know the mother of my grandchild."

"Grandchild?" Grayson said, coming into the kitchen. "You already know Hannah."

My mom was still beaming as she went back to work on the potatoes. "Not Hannah, Natasha."

Grayson turned to look at me. "No shit?"

"Grayson Bancroft! Not in my kitchen! You take that talk back to the den where it belongs," mom scolded.

I burst into laughter before heading out of the kitchen, Grayson hot on my heels. "Is it true? Nat's pregnant?"

I nodded. "It is."

Grayson smiled. "Congratulations! Our kids are going to get to grow up together."

I winced. "I hope so. Things are still a little strained between the families. Nat's been all but disowned. Her dad is pressuring her to move back to the mansion and have nothing to do with me. So far, she isn't going to do that, but I'm worried he will wear her down."

Grayson shook his head. "Not if you're a good boy. It's probably time you put a ring on her finger."

"I don't think she's ready for that."

"She's having your baby. I think that's a pretty serious commitment."

"Slow down. One thing at a time," I said as we walked back into the den.

Mason gave me a look. I nodded, letting him know I told her. He smiled in return. I finished my drink with my brothers before mom called us into the dining room. We all took our seats, but before we could dig in, she stood up at her position at the head of the table.

"Boys, I want to make a toast," she said, holding up her glass of wine.

We all looked at one another before picking up our own glasses and waiting for what she had to say.

"First, I want to thank you all for being here tonight. I know you are all so busy, but these little moments are very special to me."

We all assured her we would try harder, before taking a drink and toasting her.

"And, I would like to welcome a couple new people into our family," she said, turning to look at me.

I felt a little put on the spot but considering half the people at the table already knew my secret, it wasn't that big of a deal.

"New members?" James asked, looking around the room as if he had missed someone.

"Jack and Natasha are going to have a baby!"

There was a moment of stunned silence as all my brothers looked at me.

"Told you she'd be cool with it," Mason said with a grin.

"Levy? Seriously? You got her pregnant?" James asked with a combination of horror and shock on his face.

I gave him a look that told him to watch his tongue. "Yes, I did, and she will be a part of our family."

"We will all welcome her and the baby with open arms," my mother affirmed.

There was some shrugging, jesting, and then a raucous round of cheers as we celebrated the news. I answered questions and took plenty of advice from Grayson as we enjoyed our dinner together. It felt good to have my secret out in the open. I had been carrying around the secret relationship and fear of disappointing my mother for so long. As I dined and had a good time with my family, my thoughts kept going back to Natasha. She was probably home alone right then. She didn't have the support of her family. I couldn't have imagined going through this stage of my life without my mom and brothers behind me.

My heart went out to Nat, but I knew my mother would welcome her with open arms. She would do all she could to be both sets of grandparents for our child. I knew it wouldn't be the same, but I wanted Nat to know she wasn't alone. She had my entire family behind her, ready to help and support her. Things would never be easy, but we'd get through.

CHAPTER 72

NATASHA

My nerves were an absolute wreck. I had thought about what I was going to do all day. I hadn't told Jack my plans. If I had, he would have tried to stop me or insisted on going with me. This was something I had to do by myself. I wasn't a quitter. I wasn't the type of person who took anything lying down without putting up some kind of fight.

I was willing to fight for my family. I knew how precious life was and how quickly things could change. I wouldn't let my father evict me from the family without putting up a fight. He was a stubborn man and rarely saw reason, but I had to try—one last time. If he refused to budge, that was okay, I told myself. I would know I had tried, and if he died before we ever made up, I would have the comfort of knowing it was his grudge that destroyed our relationship.

"Thank you," I told the driver before stepping out of the car in front of my parents' mansion.

It had been a month. I hoped that was enough time for my father to have adequately cooled off. I knew my mom was out for the evening. That meant it was just my dad and me. I wasn't worried he would hurt me, but I couldn't deny there was a hint of fear he would lose his temper again. If he did, I would leave.

I walked down the hall, my heeled boots clacking against the marble as I moved with purpose. I nodded to one of the housekeepers and kept moving toward my father's study. I could already smell the scent of cigar smoke and hear the muted mumblings of the television. I knew it would be on a news channel. He'd probably be reading the newspaper or reading a book.

I paused at the doorway and took a deep breath before gently knocking on the doorframe. He looked up, his eyes meeting mine before dropping back to the paper in his hand ... without saying a word.

"Dad, I want to talk," I said, walking in to the study and taking the chair across from him.

At first, he didn't acknowledge me. He kept the paper up before sighing loudly and crunching it onto his lap. He stared at me and I was thankful to see anger, but not that ugly disappointment and disgust I had seen the night I told him about the baby. That was progress.

"I don't know what else there is to say," he said.

I took a deep breath. "There's a lot to say. You said a lot, but you've never really given me the chance to say anything."

He opened his mouth to argue, but I put up my hand, quieting him.

"Fine. What? Are you here to tell me what a horrible man I am? Your brother already did that. I don't need to get parenting advice from the two of you."

I shrugged a shoulder. "I'm not here to tell you that. I am here to tell you it's time you stopped hating the man I love because of something that happened a long time ago. Something he had no part of. I'm not even sure he knows what happened that made you hate him so much. Your anger is misplaced."

He shook his head, that familiar stubbornness rearing its ugly head. "He's a Bancroft. That's a big enough sin in and of itself."

"For the longest time, I believed that. I let you make me believe my being with him was some horrible sin. I let you hold me back from finding true love and happiness because you imposed your own biasness and anger on me. I love Jack. I've loved him for a very long time. I

437

know you can't understand that, but it's the truth. No matter how much you try to tell me it's wrong, I now know it isn't."

He rolled his eyes. "There, you got that off your chest, do you feel better?"

I sighed, disappointed he was going to hold onto the anger. "No, Dad, I don't feel better. I'm sorry you're disappointed in me. I tried to be your dutiful daughter. I tried not to love him. I left for two years and had no contact with him. I kept telling myself what I was feeling was wrong. You don't know the hell I put him through trying to please you. It wasn't fair to him, but no matter how awful I was to him, he was always there, ready to take me back because he loved me."

He scoffed. "Of course, he'll take you back. You're a wealthy, beautiful woman. He's a red-blooded man."

I wrinkled my nose. "You make everything so ugly. Jack doesn't care about my money, Dad. If you remember, he has plenty of his own. He takes me back every time because he loves me. He's put his life on hold for five years, being faithful to me, while I tried to gather the courage to tell you it was him I wanted. He's been waiting for five, long years and that is something truly special."

I could see his expression softening just a fraction. "You don't know that he was faithful. Your brother was out with him all the time."

I smiled. "Yes, he was, and Elijah will tell you the same thing—Jack has always been waiting for me."

"Elijah has known about everything all this time?" He hissed.

"No, he hasn't. He only found out when you made it an issue. You destroyed that relationship as well. Jack is Elijah's only real friend. Don't you see how your hate is like a poison? You've polluted our lives with your venom. You are keeping us from being happy. You have to get over it, Dad. You have to let us choose who we want to be with and who we love," I said, pleading with him to be reasonable.

He picked up the paper and snapped it open, effectively ending our conversation. I sat in the chair, clutching my purse. Somewhere in the back of my mind, I had this little hope he would apologize for being such an asshole and welcome me back into his life with open arms. I should have known that was nothing more than a dream. My father was not the kind of man who ever forgave or accepted.

I reached into my purse and pulled out the copy of the ultrasound picture. I stood up, pushed his newspaper down and handed it to him.

"What's this?" he spat, taking the picture and looking at it with disdain.

"That's your grandchild. He or she is healthy and due to arrive in about six months. You are the only grandpa that baby will have. You have the opportunity to be a great grandpa. You can choose to love this baby and fill your life with joy, or continue to wallow in this self-imposed misery," I said before heading toward the door.

"Nat, wait," he called out.

I stopped, blinking back the tears that were threatening to spill over, and turned to face him. "Yes?"

"Sit down. Let's talk."

It wasn't exactly a loving invitation, but it was a step in the right direction. I walked back to the chair and sat down. He was holding the picture and staring at it.

"You're not a disappointment," he stated.

Again, I almost burst into laughter at the dry tone. My father would never win any awards for being sentimental.

"Thank you, that actually makes me feel better. I don't try and irritate you or upset you. I need you to understand this is my life and I am not you. I don't have that need to hate anyone."

He nodded. "I hope it stays like that for you. I hope you never get screwed over and have to hate anyone. It is why I am the way I am. I wanted to protect you from all the people out there who would try and hurt you."

I smiled. "Thank you. I know you've always looked out for me and I know you love me. I appreciate that. You've been a good father to me and I want you to be a good grandfather to my child."

"I will love your child," he said, but I could hear the reservation in his voice and knew there was a very big "but" in that sentence.

"But?" I asked.

He shook his head. "I don't know about that family, though."

"Dad, Jack is a good man. I wish you could see that."

He was silent for several minutes and I could see him warring within. "He might be, but his father, well, his father and his mother, they really did a number on me. It tore me up when Kathy left me. When I found out she had left me for him, it nearly did me in. It crushed me. I was so angry and promised to get revenge on him. I wanted to make them both pay for what they had done."

"It was a long time ago. You found Mom. Sometimes fate has a funny way of doing things. We have to go through hard, ugly stuff before we can get to the good stuff."

He chuckled softly. "You're the kid, I'm the father. I'm supposed to be giving you words of wisdom."

I smiled and shrugged a shoulder. "You've given me plenty of wisdom, but this is something I know a little more about. It's taken me a long time to get to where I am today. I wasn't sure I could ever be happy, but I am. I am happy with Jack and I'm very excited for our future. I want you to be a part of that future."

"Nat, there is a lot of water under that bridge," he replied.

"Dad, I love you. I do, but it's time I started thinking about what makes me happy. I tried to do what I knew you wanted, but it wasn't working for me. I was miserable, sad, and lonely. I'm going to be with Jack. I don't know for how long, but I do know he and I are committed to raising this baby," I told him.

"I love you. I've only always wanted what was best for you. I want you to be happy."

"Good, then you'll put aside your feelings about Jack's father and accept him," I said firmly.

He sucked in a deep breath before leaning forward to look me in the eyes. "I promise I will try to accept Jack. I will try my hardest to forget about all the crap his family has put me through."

I shook my head. "Not his family—his father."

"And his mother."

"Dad, let it go. You have to let it go. You are the one keeping this thing alive."

He ran his hand over his face. "I said I'll try."

I stood up, he rose as well. "Try isn't going to cut it. You can't do your best. You have to accept him. It is that simple."

He made a growling noise before reaching out and pulling me into his arms for a big bear hug. I wrapped my arms around him, hugging him tight. It felt good to have him back in my life. I hoped it was for good. I knew there was sure to be some rocky roads ahead, but I would take each bump as it came.

"I'm glad you came by," he said from above my head.

I could hear the emotion in his voice and damn near burst into tears again. I was going to be cried out by the time the baby was born. I felt like all I did was cry anymore.

We said our goodbyes, with the promise I would check in with him soon, and to come by for dinner some time during the week. When I walked out of the house, I could feel my life changing for the better with every passing minute. Things were good, and I prayed they stayed that way.

CHAPTER 73

JACK

I left work and chose to walk the few blocks to the corner bar where I would be meeting Elijah. I hadn't driven that morning, anticipating the bar meetup. I wasn't sure how the conversation was going to go and wanted to make sure I could drink heavily if it didn't go well. I sat at the bar, waiting for a table to open up, and ordered a beer.

My eyes roamed around the bar, using the mirror to watch people behind me. It was Friday night and the bar served as a place to meet up before heading out to dinner or a club. I watched as men and women came in and out, all of them celebrating the end of the work-week. I thought about my life a year ago. I was one of those people. Now, everything was different. I wasn't looking forward to a night out on the town. I was looking forward to going home and seeing the woman I loved.

I had to meet Elijah to get some business settled. I kept telling myself it was the right thing to do. I was nervous as hell.

"A table just opened up," the bartender said, pointing to a table that was being bussed.

"Thanks, man. Will you send over two more beers?"

He nodded. "Will do."

Elijah showed up a few minutes after the beers had been delivered. He grinned, sitting down in the chair on the other side of the table. "Now that's what I call service," he said, taking a long drink from the bottle.

"I aim to please."

"I was surprised to get your call," he said.

I shrugged a shoulder. "I wanted to catch up. It's been a bit. I didn't want you to think I was ghosting you."

He laughed. "I figured you and Nat would be doing baby stuff."

"Not always."

"What's up? Anything new and exciting?" he asked.

"I told my mom about the baby," I told him.

He winced. "And? I know it couldn't have been as bad as my dad, but how'd she take it?"

I smiled thinking about her reaction. "She's thrilled."

"Good. I'm happy for you. Does the rest of the family know?"

"Yep. Everyone is all good with it. I'm going to take Nat to dinner at my mom's next week. My mom insists."

Elijah nodded. "Good, Nat could use all the family she can get."

I raised an eyebrow. "Really? I thought things were better."

The look on his face told me that wasn't the case. "Yes and no. My dad is trying, but it isn't like he's going to jump up and welcome you with open arms."

"I expected as much, which is why I asked you to meet me," I said, figuring now was as good a time as any.

"Oh?"

I reached into my pocket and pulled out the little black box I'd been carrying around all week. I opened it to show him the ring.

"I thought you were into my sister. I may have given you the wrong impression about how friendly I wanted to be," he joked.

I rolled my eyes. "Ha. Ha. It's for Nat."

"I figured that. That's one hell of a rock in there."

"She deserves the best," I replied.

He nodded. I could tell by the look on his face he wasn't thrilled by the ring. "She does deserve the best."

"I wanted to ask for your blessing," I mumbled.

"My blessing?"

I nodded. "I know I didn't go about things the right way in the beginning. I want to change that. I want to show you I've changed and I'm serious about your sister."

"You want me to give you my blessing to ask my sister to marry you?" he repeated, and I knew he was stalling.

I had thought he would be cool with it. I thought he was okay with Nat and me being together, but judging by his reaction, he wasn't okay with any of it. He wasn't happy about it in the slightest. I immediately went on the defensive, reverting back to my old way of thinking.

"I love her. I thought I made that clear. I want to spend the rest of my life with her. I want our child to be born into a loving family," I said, fighting to keep my anger in check.

"Jack, I know you love her, but is this really the right thing to do?"

I was floored by his ridiculous question. "She's pregnant. We love each other. How is proposing marriage not the right thing to do?"

He shrugged a shoulder. "Maybe you're rushing things."

"Rushing things!" I nearly shouted.

"Yes, you just got back together," he pointed out.

I shook my head. "I don't know what you and your father can't seem to understand. Nat and I didn't just get back together. We've been together five years. Granted, we couldn't truly be together because you father would have lost his shit. Oh, wait, he did that already and guess what, we're still in love. We've been together, but none of you could see it."

"Relax, I'm not saying I don't want you to marry her. I'm only saying that giving it some time would be a good idea," he said in a low voice.

I shook my head, pissed and surprised. "I've waited long enough. I thought you understood I loved her. I thought you understood how much I wanted to be with her, and I know she wants to be with me. Are you seriously going to deny her her happiness again?"

Elijah ran a hand through his hair. "I don't want to deny anyone anything. I'm saying I'm hesitant to give my blessing. My dad would kill me if he knew I gave you the green light."

"I don't care."

"Yes, you do, which is why you're asking me. You're putting me in a shitty position."

I took a deep breath, trying to get my anger in check. "I'm asking you because it is your opinion I value. I already know what your father will say. I'm no longer interested in trying to please him. That's a game I can't win and I'm not going to waste my breath trying."

"You're right, which is why I'm asking you to hold off."

I looked at the ring and then back at him. "No."

"What?"

"You heard me, no. No, I won't wait. I won't keep waiting for something I know will never come. This is about Nat and me and our happiness. I'm sorry you think you have to hold back your blessing because your father won't give it. I'm doing this," I said firmly.

He looked at me before turning to raise his beer, catching the eye of the waitress and holding up two fingers. I was so glad I didn't drive. I had anticipated the meeting with Elijah wouldn't go great. I was going to need a lot more than a couple beers to swallow this pill, I mused.

"Jack, I've always admired you for doing what you thought was right. You've never been afraid to speak up when you didn't like something. You always stood up for me and I appreciate that, but in this case, I'm not sure it's right."

I shrugged a shoulder, no longer giving a shit about what he thought was right. "That's too bad."

"You're really going to go through with this?"

"Yep," I said, putting the beer to my mouth and downing the last half of the bottle.

He was quiet as the waitress delivered our beers and took the empties. "Do you think it's what Nat wants?" he asked, obviously trying a new tactic.

"I think she does, but I guess I'll know for sure when I ask her," I replied sarcastically.

He smirked. "I guess so."

"Elijah, I thought you understood. Maybe I was wrong. Nat and I have loved each other a long time. I know we've gone back and forth, and our relationship is anything but traditional, but ultimately, I think it is what we both want. That night you busted into my place, it was going to be our last night together. We had agreed to try and cool things between us. We were going to try and make your dad happy, date other people, and see how things went. If, in a year, we still felt the way we did, we were going to get married."

"What? You were?"

I nodded. "Yes. It was my idea, but Nat agreed to it. We've been talking about marriage and being together for a while. Things changed when she got back from California because she was worried your father would strip her of that company. Our feelings for each other never stopped, despite the time, distance, and the efforts of your family to tear us apart."

"Okay."

"Okay, what? You're going to beat me up now?"

He laughed. "No. Okay. Ask her."

"Really? I mean, I'm going to anyway, but you're okay with it?"

He nodded. "You two know what you feel. I don't. I'm pretty much the last person that can give marriage advice. I can't even give relationship advice."

I laughed along with him. "Thanks. I appreciate it. I know things are a little weird, but this is something I have to do for her and for myself. I want a family."

"I get it."

We drank our beers, watching the people around us. "I'm asking her tomorrow," I told him, feeling like I needed to give him fair warning.

"Good. I know she's going to be happy."

"I wonder if she's going to want a big wedding," I mused aloud.

"Do I get to be your best man?" he said with a grin.

"If she wants a wedding, you're the best man. I really want to be married before the baby's born, but if I know Nat, she is not going to want to wear a wedding gown with a baby belly," I grumbled.

Elijah was chuckling and shaking his head. "I can just see the look on my father's face."

"Yeah, maybe we should wait until after the baby."

"You do whatever is right for you guys. Don't worry about what I think or what my dad thinks. You're right about being happy. You've inspired me."

"I have?"

"Yep, I'm going to start taking the dating thing seriously. I want to find a good woman and settle down. I've been waiting until my career was on more solid ground, but I'm tired of waiting for something that may never happen."

"Carpe diem," I said holding up my beer bottle.

He laughed and clinked his bottle against mine. "Wish me luck. I'm going to need it."

"You'll find someone. I bet Nat would love to hook you up with someone. What about her friend Ashley? I see her checking you out all the time."

Elijah blushed a little. It was something I had never seen before. "I don't know if that's a good idea."

"You've already slept with her?" I asked.

He grinned. "Maybe once. It was a really long time ago."

"But you like her?"

"I do, but she's always been Nat's friend."

We both laughed at the absurdity of that statement. "And I've always been your friend. I think you should give her a call. What could it hurt? Natasha would probably be happy to set the two of you up. Girls aren't like guys. They don't have all those weird rules about dating siblings."

Elijah nodded. "I'm going to do it. I'm going to get her number and ask her out."

CHAPTER 74

NATASHA

Jack had called a little bit ago and asked me to go to dinner with him. He wanted me to dress nice for a special night. I looked in the full-length mirror and nearly threw my shoe at my reflection. I had gone to bed last night, normal as could be and then when I woke up this morning, I had a pooch. The baby bump showed up overnight. I had thought it would be a gradual thing. My pants and skirts had been a little snug, but I could still button them and zip them up.

Not today. Today nothing fit right. On top of everything, the store where I had ordered a bunch of stuff from called to inform me they were going out of business. My card would be refunded, but I had to start my shopping all over again.

My nerves were shot after a long, horrible week at work and this clothing situation was not helping matters. I stomped back into my closet and yanked off the dress I reserved for those days I was feeling bloated.

"Please zip," I whispered, tugging at the zipper.

I took a deep breath, sucking in my belly as best I could. The zipper finally slid up. The dress was on. I turned to get a side view and groaned. I had a bump. I shouldn't be embarrassed by it, but I was a little. No one knew about the pregnancy and no one knew about Jack. I was a little ashamed to be stepping out, showing off the bump with no boyfriend in sight.

"Who cares what anyone thinks," I mumbled.

I cared. A little. Jack had said we were going public with our relationship, which I was excited for, but I could already hear the rumors. I quickly put on a little makeup, leaving my hair down, before sliding into my pumps that felt too tight on my feet.

I looked down at me feet. They looked normal, but the shoes felt tight. "This can't be happening." I moaned.

I walked out of my room, grabbing my purse and stomping out the door. I had three messages on my phone letting me know the car I had ordered was waiting. I apologized to the driver for my lateness before giving him Jack's address. I wasn't sure why we didn't meet at the restaurant but didn't say anything.

As I rode the elevator up to his floor, I thought about asking him if we could cancel the reservation and order in. I didn't feel like peopling. I wanted to kick back with my feet up and put on a pair of comfortable sweats. I was happy to eat at his place. I was already figuring out how to bribe him with sex to get him to agree to stay in.

I stepped off the elevator and headed for his door. I knocked once, doing my best to snap out of the crappy mood I had fallen into. He had sounded excited about the night and I wouldn't ruin it for him.

The moment he opened the door, my crappy mood was no longer an issue.

"Hi," he greeted, stepping out of the way and pulling me into his apartment. He was wearing a simple polo shirt and slacks, his hair hanging loose just the way I liked it. It always reminded me of that fresh-out-of-bed look that I loved so much.

I gasped at the sight of the candles burning throughout the place. There wasn't a single light on, but the apartment was well lit. All the light was provided by the hundreds of candles in various shapes and sizes burning on every surface.

"Jack?" I said, questioning what was happening. I looked down to see red rose petals in a line on the floor.

"Follow me," he said, taking my purse and then setting it on the entry table before leading me into the dining room where the table was already set. There were rose petals scattered around the table and on the floor. I couldn't imagine how many rose petals there were but guessed it to be in the thousands.

There were silver dome lids covering each place setting. "Are we staying in?" I asked.

He turned to look at me, stepping toward me and kissing me. It was a sensual kiss that tickled all my senses. The combination of the scent from the candles and his cologne was making me dizzy. His hands moved over me as he continued to kiss me.

In that instant, I needed him. I had to have him. I was no longer hungry for food. I heard the zipper on the back of my dress and intensified the kiss. I wanted him badly.

Cool air hit my exposed back as he pushed the dress down my arms, sliding over my hips and pooling at my feet. I kicked off my heels and wriggled the dress out of the way as my hands worked at the button on his slacks.

"Off, I need them off." I panted.

He was as hot and turned on as I was. He shoved my hands out of the way and stepped out of his pants before pulling his polo shirt over his head, his hands moving to my waist and jerking me close. I ground my pelvis against him, wanting to feel his hardness. His hands moved to my thong, pushing it down for me to shimmy out of, leaving me with only my bra on, which he quickly removed with a quick flick of his hands.

"Here," he said, moving to the opposite end of the long, formal dining table.

"Here?" I gasped.

"Yes." He growled, his mouth slamming over mine as he lifted me to sit on the table.

I didn't argue. I opened my legs and pulled him close, kissing him as my arms wrapped around his neck. I reached between us, wrapping my hand around his heavy cock and squeezing. His fingers went between my legs, spreading me open before pushing two fingers inside me.

I gasped, shocked to feel my body ready for him with very little effort. "Oh God." I moaned, wanting him badly.

"I'm sorry," he whispered.

"Sorry?"

"I have to have you," he grumbled, removing his fingers and replacing them with his hard cock.

"Take me." I groaned, leaning back on my elbows, watching him slide inside my body.

I closed my eyes when the sensation of him filling me became too much. He moved inside, stretching me as he pulled out and slid back in. I opened my eyes to find him staring down at the place where our bodies were joined. The candlelight cast a soft orange glow over the room. I moaned as he slid in to the hilt.

"You're so beautiful, Natasha. I can't get enough of you. I want you day and night. I want to be with you all the time." He grunted, pushing in and pulling out.

I nodded, unable to speak as I watched the motion. It was erotic, hot, and bordered on the verge of nasty as he fucked me on the dining room table, our dinner at the opposite end. It was a testament to how much we wanted each other. Nothing else mattered but getting our fill of each other. Dinner could wait. The world could wait. All that mattered was him inside me.

His hand reached between us, his finger doing a slow leisurely circle over my hard, swollen nub, sending shock waves of pleasure through my body.

"Jack!" I screamed his name as he applied hard pressure and begin circling.

My body came apart, milking him as he continued his slow in and out slide. "Yes, baby, there you go, give it all to me."

When my body began to relax, he stepped back, pulling out of me before gently lifting me from the table. He turned me, placing my hands on the smooth warm surface where my body had just been splayed out. He moved behind me, his arm anchoring around my waist as he pulled me back and against him.

"I love you," I whispered, turning my head to look at him.

He leaned forward and kissed me before using his hand to guide himself inside me. I moaned low in my throat, bending forward a little more as he pushed inside me. One hand held my hip while the other went to my shoulder, gently pulling me back against him as he thrust once, then twice before finally getting the depth he was seeking.

His hand released my hip, slapping my ass softly at first and then hard enough to sting. I cried out, the pain releasing intense pleasure through my body as he continued to work inside me. I was gasping, begging for more.

"More?" He growled.

"More!"

His hand reached up, twisting my hair around it before gently tugging backward. A fresh wave of pure ecstasy washed over me.

"Do you like that? Your body is gushing over me." He growled.

"More. I want more," I said, my voice guttural.

"More?"

"Yes!"

He tugged my hair a little harder. I arched my back only to be rewarded with a stinging slap against my bare skin. I screamed as my body released an orgasm so powerful I would have collapsed had the table not been under me. I was arching and begging for more, crying out each time he slapped his hand against my ass.

"Goddamn!" he cried out.

I moaned, backing against him, pushing him deeper inside.

"Fuck!" he roared as he exploded deep inside my body.

His body jerked and spasmed, his arms wrapping around me as he held me close against him. I rested my forehead on the table as we both floated down from that high up place he had taken us again with his skilled lovemaking.

"That was so much better than dinner out," I said on a sigh.

He chuckled, stepping away from me and moving to grab our clothes. I managed to stand up straight, looking down at the dress.

"If you don't mind, I'd rather put on sweats," I said, looking at the dress with loathing.

"I don't mind at all. I want you to be comfortable."

"Good, I'll be right back," I said, grabbing my panties and walking naked down the hall to his room. I was so glad I had left a few things at his place. I couldn't wait to get comfortable.

When I returned to the dining room, he had his pants on, but no shirt. I could look at his beautiful chest all day.

"Have a seat. I'll be right back," he said and headed down the hall.

He returned a second later wearing sweats and a T-shirt as well. I smiled, loving that we could be that comfortable around each other.

"You didn't have to change for me. I was just having a hell of a time finding anything to wear tonight," I told him with disgust in my voice.

"I want to wear sweats. I don't wear sweats often enough. Have a seat," he said, pulling out one chair for me.

"Thank you. It looks amazing in here. I'm impressed."

"Thank you. I wanted tonight to be special."

I grinned and waggled my eyebrows. "Well, it certainly started off on a good note."

He laughed. "Sorry, I hadn't meant for that to happen. I saw you in the candlelight and it was all too much. I had to have you."

"Trust me, I didn't mind. Although, is it weird we just did that on the table?"

He shrugged a shoulder. "I don't know. We've done it in your kitchen. Besides, we're not actually eating on that end."

I could feel my face turning red. "True."

"Now, sit tight and I'll grab the cider," he said, walking out of the dining room and leaving me alone.

I wanted to peek under the dome but was a good girl and resisted.

CHAPTER 75

JACK

All day long, I had been nervous and a little terrified of what I was going to do, but now that she was in my apartment, the nerves were gone. I knew what I wanted to say and was ready to do it. I grabbed the bottle of sparkling cider from the fridge and carried it back to the dining room.

She was sitting in the chair, her hair slightly mussed from our impromptu lovemaking and her cheeks slightly flushed. She was the most beautiful woman in the entire world and I was about to ask her to be my wife. I stopped and took a mental snapshot. I wanted to remember this moment for the rest of my life.

"Champagne?" she asked.

"Sparkling cider."

"I see. Are we celebrating?"

I sat down in my chair. "I hope we will be. Are you hungry?"

She giggled softly. "I am. I'm absolutely dying to know what's under this dome."

"I ordered in from that Italian place you like."

She quickly lifted her lid and squealed with delight. "This is perfect. Thank you so much for reading my mind and ordering in. I was so not up for a night out."

"Nat, you should have told me."

"I didn't want to disappoint you. You sounded so excited I figured I could get through one dinner."

I leaned over and grabbed her hand. "Thank you for making that sacrifice, but in the future, if you're not feeling up to going out, please tell me. I can eat anywhere."

"I will."

We both dug into the meal. Our earlier exertions had left us both with a hearty appetite.

"What's with all the candles and the roses?" she asked.

I smiled. "I wanted to do something special and romantic."

"This is very romantic. It is so perfect in every way."

"I'm glad you said that," I said, feeling a hint of nerves rise up again.

"Why?" she asked, suddenly looking apprehensive herself.

"I wanted to talk to you about something," I started.

She put her fork down and took a drink from the water glass. "Oh."

I could see the fear and dread in her eyes. "It's nothing bad," I assured her.

"What's going on? Did my father come and see you?"

"No. I did see Elijah yesterday, though."

"You did?" she asked, her voice high and strained.

I nodded. I needed to get it out, but I was suddenly hesitant. It was the mention of Elijah. I thought about his warning and advice to take it slow. Maybe she felt the same way. I could be rushing this and potentially ruining our relationship by trying to move too fast.

"I did. We went out for a couple drinks. I wanted to check in with him and make sure things were okay between us," I explained.

She smiled and relaxed a bit. "Good. I'm so glad you two are friends. I don't expect things to be like they were, but I hope they can be better."

"They will be. Nat, I did all this because I wanted to talk to you about something important," I started again.

"Okay, I'm listening."

I reached into my pocket and palmed the box in my hand before sliding out of my chair and dropping to one knee beside her. Her eyes widened, big as saucers as she turned her body to face me.

"Natasha, you make me so happy I can't explain it. You truly do complete me. You are my other half. I'm miserable when I'm without you and I never want to be without you again. I don't like this world when we're not together. I want you to be with me forever and always."

Tears were streaming down her cheeks as I opened the box and presented her with the ring.

She looked down at it, her hand covering her mouth. "Jack," she whispered my name.

"Natasha, will you marry me?" I asked.

She sobbed, nodding but saying nothing.

"I think I actually have to hear the word," I gently teased.

"Yes! Yes, I will marry you!" she shouted.

I got up on both knees and moved closer to her. She leaned down, cupped my face in her hands, and kissed me deeply.

We both stood, holding each other, kissing and then embracing each other again. I was still gripping the box with the ring in it in my hand. I had a feeling I was doing this all wrong. We had sex, then dinner, then the proposal, and she didn't even have the ring on.

I stepped away, removing the ring, before setting the box on the table. "You're going to make me a very happy man," I said, sliding the ring over her slender finger.

"You've already made me a very happy woman."

We left our dinner on the table and moved to the living room. We sat on the couch, me holding her close as she stared at the ring on her finger.

"We're going to do this. We're going to make it work. I know your dad isn't thrilled with the idea, but I think he'll come around. We love each other too much to let anything stand in our way. I'm so excited to take this next step with you."

She leaned her face up and kissed me. "I am too. This baby is going to be spoiled rotten. We're going to give him or her the best, most loving home any child could have."

"Damn straight we are."

"You know, when I first found out I was pregnant, all I could think about was how much my life was ruined. I kept thinking everything was going to change for the worst. I can't believe I ever thought that. Everything is so good now. It is a blessing. I'm so grateful I forgot to take the pill. I wasn't trying to get pregnant, but I'm glad I did," she said.

I laughed. "I am too. I didn't even know I wanted a baby until it happened. I wouldn't have it any other way."

"We were meant to be together."

"Yes, we were. Sit tight. I'm going to grab the cider, so we can toast this moment," I said, heading back to the dining room to grab the glasses.

I filled each glass before sitting beside her once again.

"Thank you, Jack. Thank you for being so patient with me and not giving up on us. I'm a handful. I know that. I'm a little neurotic and it will probably get worse before it gets better," she said with a laugh.

"Thank you for marrying me. Thank you for being in my life. I love you. Every day I love you a little more. This is to our future and may it be bright and filled with lots of love and laughter."

We toasted and drank the cider before settling back in to the couch.

"I can't wait to tell Ashley," she whispered.

"Uh, speaking of Ashley," I said, figuring I better let her know I had encouraged her brother to hook up with her best friend.

"What about her?"

"Elijah likes her."

She burst into laughter, the sound ringing around the room. "Are you serious?"

"I am. I kind of told him to go for it," I said, grimacing and waiting for her to rage at me.

"Wow. Really? I'm surprised."

"I'm sorry. I should have asked you if you were okay with it, but he mentioned it and I told him he should go for it. I've seen the way they look at each other and never understood why they didn't go out before," I said.

"Because Elijah has always been a player."

"True, but I think he's ready to settle down. I don't think, I know. He told me as much."

"Good. I'm happy for him and I'm totally fine with him and her dating. I know she's had a crush on him forever," she said, confirming what I suspected.

"You're so beautiful," I told her again.

She sighed. "I feel a little guilty for ruining your big surprise with my outfit."

"Don't feel guilty. I want you to be comfortable and I don't care what you're wearing. Quite frankly, I'd prefer it if you wore nothing at all," I said, leaning down to nuzzle her ear.

"Good. I have a feeling this will be my regular attire for the next several months. I feel like this baby erupted in my belly overnight," she complained.

I reached down to put my hand on her stomach, noticing the slight bump and smiling. That was my baby she was growing in there.

"About the bump, do you want to wait to get married until after you have the baby?" I asked her.

She let out a long sigh. "I don't know. I want it both ways."

"You can have anything you want," I promised her.

"Really? What does that mean?" she asked, turning to look at me.

I kissed the tip of her nose. "We could have a quick and simple wedding now and then plan a big one after the baby is born if you want. I would love to see you in a beautiful gown. I want our families to be there and I want the entire world to know I was lucky enough to get Natasha Levy to marry me."

She seemed to think about it for a few seconds and then nodded. "I think that's a great idea. I know my mom will be thrilled to plan a big wedding. I don't want to take that away from her. That way she will have plenty of time to plan as well. I'll have Ashley be my maid of honor and we can have Grayson's daughter be our flower girl," she said excitedly.

I laughed softly, happy to hear she was already planning the wedding of her dreams. She deserved it all. "Then it's settled. We can get married in a small ceremony or just you, me, and a judge."

"The sooner the better," she whispered.

"I agree. Can we dance? I feel like dancing," I said, reaching for the remote and turning on the sound system.

I stood, helping her up, and began a slow dance together. I loved holding her in my arms. I cherished every minute with her. It wasn't long before the atmosphere in the room shifted. I could feel the change in her breathing and knew she felt it too. We were both ready for another round. I used my finger to tilt her chin up and covered her mouth with mine. Our bodies melded together as we moved around the living room, swaying together.

"I love you," I whispered.

"I love you."

I kissed her again. "I want you. I need you again."

She giggled softly. "I think we better do this as often as we can while we can. It won't be long before I'm too big to do anything."

I kissed the side of her neck. "We'll find a way. Where there's a will there's a way and trust me, with you, I'm always going to want you."

She laughed again. "We'll see about that."

I wrapped my arms around her, pulling her hips against mine as I ground my erection into her. Together, we moved around the apartment, blowing out the candles as we prepared to spend the rest of the night together loving on each other.

By the time we made it to my room, we were both naked and panting. I had a feeling it would always be like that between us. She would always turn me on. I would be the old man in a wheelchair chasing after his younger, hotter wife.

The End

Other books by Ali Parker

Baited

Second Chance Romances
Jaded
Jaded Christmas

Justified
Justified Christmas

Judged
Judge Christmas

Alpha Billionaire Series
His Demands, Book 1
His Needs, Book 2
His Forever, Book 3

Bad Money Series
Blood Money
Dirty Money
Hard Money
Cash Money

Forbidden Fruit Series
Forgotten Bodyguard

Bright Lights Billionaire
Stage Left
Center Stage
Understudy
Improv
Final Call

Pro-U Series
Breakaway
Offside
Rebound
Homerun
Freeststyle

The Rules
Making the Rules
Bending the Rules
Breaking the Rules

My Creative Billionaire

Money Can't Buy Love

My Father's Best Friend

The Lost MC Series
Ryder
Axel
Jax
Sabian
Derek

The Dawson Brothers Series
Always on my Mind
Wild as the Wind
Mine Would Be You
Don't Close Your Eyes

ABOUT THE AUTHOR

Ali Parker is a full-time contemporary and new adult romance writer with more than a hundred and twenty books behind her. She loves coffee, watching a great movie and hanging out with her hubs. By hanging out, she means making out. Hanging out is for those little creepy elves at Christmas. No tight green stockings for her.

She's an entrepreneur at heart and loves coming up with more ideas than any one person should be allowed to access. She lives in Texas with her hubs and three kiddos and looks forward to traveling the world in a few years. Writing under eleven pen names keeps her busy and allows her to explore all genres and types of writing.

Made in the USA
Columbia, SC
09 July 2025

60544444R00281